As All Our Fires Burn

A Novel

Hildred Billings
BARACHOU PRESS

As All Our Fires Burn

Copyright: Hilded Billings
Published: 8th December 2018
Publisher: Barachou Press

This is a work of fiction. Any and all similarities to any characters, settings, or situations are purely coincidental.

All rights reserved. No part of this publication may be reproduced, stored in retrieval system, copied in any form or by any means, electronic, mechanical, photocopying, recording or otherwise transmitted without written permission from the publisher. You must not circulate this book in any format.

Chapter 1

SAYURI

The lights and sounds of Roppongi normally drove Sayuri crazy. Unfortunately, she couldn't recall how she had stumbled upon the long avenues piercing through the Roppongi Hills and TV Asahi buildings. Nor did she know how she always walked beneath the imposing elevation of the Metropolitan Expressway #3, a large, loud toll-road that straddled Roppongi Odori and supported behemoth trucks traveling between warehouses and intended destinations.

Sayuri couldn't remember anything before that morning. The few times she returned to her senses, she realized that she had strayed much too far from home. She was supposed to be in the sleepy Tokyo suburb of Fujimi, a good hour away by train.

Instead, she was in one of Japan's most internationally infamous neighborhoods. On one side: the well-to-do socialites, the executives, the celebrities, and the politicians' families that called affluent Roppongi home. On the other? The seedy underbelly that heralded a nightlife to only rival Shinjuku's. Sayuri had heard more than one story from her school's foreign teachers that told of male expats having every *yen* systematically stolen off their persons.

Where was she now? Did she care?

The occasional man in a suit bumped into her. Women with Hermès scarves and Prada purses scoffed when Sayuri refused to move out of their ways. If she walked much farther, she would find the Azabu police station. A crew of sharply dressed policemen held a small conference outside of their building. One of their vehicles had broken down, and the chief on duty made it his responsibility to go over protocol with every available officer on the night shift.

It reminded Sayuri of the faculty meetings at her place of work. The principal at was infamous for making his teachers stay longer than other faculty in Fujimi City.

Summer vacation was now. Sayuri's excuse for staying sane and present was gone.

One year. It had been one year since the unthinkable happened.

She saw ghosts everywhere. Signs that she was never meant to forget the only person who had ever mattered. Calls to her maternal memory that begged her to come closer and find what she had lost in a senseless accident.

As All Our Fires Burn

At the intersection of Roppongi Odori and another main thoroughfare was a large LCD screen playing the same five ads over and over again. A drink meant to rehydrate the body during the humid summer months. A child-friendly snack advertised by grown men and women. Programs by both TV Asahi and nearby TV Tokyo that dueled for the same coveted prime time viewership. And a classic TV children's show that had been rebooted for a new generation.

"Welcome to Azabu-Juuban! The home of a Tokyo legend!" So happened that another Azabu police car drove by at that moment, lights flashing. It turned toward the supposed seedy underbelly, a reminder that there were few in-real-life heroes who could transform and save Tokyo from itself.

Her son had loved that show. Every time they passed a capsule toy machine featuring the heroes of love and justice, he begged his mother to buy him a chance for his favorite.

It was on that faraway night he finally got the one he wanted. The toy rolled between his small hands in the backseat of Sayuri's car as she attempted to navigate the rainy summer night.

Now, her phone burned hot in her hand. Every time she looked at the screen, however, she didn't see any new notifications. Not even responses to the million messages she left her ex throughout the day. *"Today's the day. The first anniversary. I'm going to Inokashira Park and the petting zoo like we did that day. I wish you could go with me."*

Except Sayuri wouldn't drive home that night. She was too drunk on grief s to get behind the wheel of a car.

Fuck driving. Only people with death wishes drove.

"Ma'am?" One of the police officers stood beside her. "*Daijyoubu desu ka?* Do you need assistance?"

She blinked away the evening haze, although her eyes could barely focus on the man writing in his notepad. "I'm fine," she said, meek. "Looking for the subway station."

"It's right over there, ma'am." The police officer pointed across Roppongi Odori. "See? Do you need an escort?"

The crosswalk light changed at that moment. "No, thank you." Sayuri stepped off the sidewalk and into the flow of pedestrian traffic. Cars carrying diplomats and trucks carrying dollar store goods waited on the edge of the crosswalk for the light to change again.

Sayuri stopped halfway across the boulevard. Other people surged around her as if she were nothing but a speedbump.

She could stand there forever, she supposed. Eventually the light would change, and it would be over.

Except when the light changed, she was honked at until the police officer zoomed forward and hustled her out of the crosswalk and to the other side of the street.

He insisted on passing her off to a subway station attendant who looked as if he would rather eat nails than deal with someone like her. When both attendant and officer asked where she lived, Sayuri muttered something about transferring at Ikebukuro. The attendant in turn muttered the possible connections she could make using the Hibiya subway line.

She barely glanced at him as she pulled out her pass and stepped through the Hibiya ticket gates.

As All Our Fires Burn

Her thoughts oscillated between what to make for dinner and the horrors of one year ago. Passengers crowded onto the train, forcing her into the corner seat and staring into the crotch of a businessman who insisted on standing in front of her with his newspaper. The seat next to her was occupied with a young mother and her bouncing toddler who carried a stuffed Totoro.

Bile surged into Sayuri's throat.

One year ago. It was only one year ago. He would be four now. We would be...

She attempted to text her ex one last time. *"I'm sorry to bother you with this. I'm having a hard time today."*

The fact her ex-girlfriend never responded was only the cherry on the shit sundae. A miracle. That's what she needed. One strong miracle to bless her with a mulligan on her life.

Instead, she fled the crowded subway train in some nowhere Tokyo neighborhood on some train line she never remembered for the rest of the night. Because her memory no longer belonged to her.

The last thing she remembered, before she completely dissociated from reality, was the image of a young female station attendant directing foot traffic to the two platform exits. She raised her gloved hand into the air and brought it back down to give the engineer the all-clear for departure.

The train powered through the dark tunnel. Sayuri didn't own her body after that.

Chapter 2

MIWA

Miwa pressed her gloved finger on the schedule posted to the corkboard. Her touch flattened the paper, making it easier to read.

Yup. Her schedule was still a mess.

This was what she got for being the only woman on staff, not including the custodians who were more often than not contracted. Sighing, Miwa opened her pocket scheduler and jotted down the closing shifts she was subjected to for the next two weeks. Beside her, a coworker named Kohei made a *che!* sound in the depths of his throat.

"You and me, Ban-*san*. We're taking on the platform all night next week."

"At least I get to be on the platform." That's what Miwa told herself. Not that it really made her feel better. What good was it to work so hard to get this meager position? Because she should be grateful for it? Because she was a woman? If anything, working until last train was more dangerous than doing the midday shift. More than one drunk passenger made a pass on her after he was yanked out for being a perverted *chikan*.

Kohei laughed. "That's the spirit. *Jya, ikou ka?*"

They still had ten minutes until the start of their shift, but there was much to do before they were formally on the clock. Miwa spent half that time in front of the office mirror making sure her uniform was crisp and clean. Her long hair was pulled back into a tight bun that made her scalp and neck sore most nights. (Yet what could she do, other than cut it?) Her shoes were buffed and shined. The white gloves that so many tourists whispered about were as impeccable as her freshly-brushed teeth. Every time Miwa considered her appearance in the mirror, she was taken back to her childhood, when she stared at station attendants with awe.

Twenty years later, she was finally living her dream job. Yet it was far from glamorous. When she wasn't dealing with unruly passengers, lost tourists, or people who didn't know a bar of soap from their own asshole, she was subjected to the systematic sexism that placed the onus of being the best and going above and beyond every single male coworker entirely on her shoulders.

It had taken Miwa twice as long to achieve her position as it had Kohei, and he was mediocre compared to her. Competent, but mediocre. There was a reason he had the closing shift at their quiet neighborhood station. Miwa, on the other hand, could only dream of working her way up to mid-shift, or, gods bless her, *morning shift*. That's where the real action was!

"*Youshi*," she muttered, pumping herself up for a long night of watching trains come and go out of the subway station. "*Densha taimu wa ima da ze!*"

She did a little fist pump to further brainwash herself into thinking it was the most badass job in the world. Kohei laughed behind her, mimicking her erratic movements. The coworker who manned the ticket booth shook his head in disbelief.

The evening shift was understaffed. Only four employees were on hand at any moment. Granted, it was a one-line station with trains spaced 15 minutes apart and little foot traffic that late at night, but it was in Tokyo, and anything was liable to happen. Not only to their station, but the entire line, or perhaps their neighborhood of Amaya-koen. Miwa always thought it fitting that she might die in a neighborhood called *Gate of Heaven*. The Shinto shrine only half a kilometer away attracted parishioners and tourists during the day, but hardly a soul at night. The only passengers boarding and getting off at Amaya-jinja-guchi Station were locals, and most of them were elderly.

One employee in the kiosk. One in the back answering phones and doing the bulk of the paperwork. Two on the platform, representing both directions.

Some women may have found it quaint. Miwa wanted to scream.

Instead of shouting into the subway's abyss, however, she took her position at the bottom of the stairs to Exit 1 and swung her arms to get the blood flowing. Within two minutes, she received the first signal of a train coming in, right on time.

For five hours she performed the same tasks over and over again. She watched passengers deboard the train and pointed to the exit nearest her. Once the platform was cleared, she blew her whistle and signaled the train driver that it was safe to leave. When the tracks were empty, she kept her eye on the passengers waiting for the next train. 99% of them sat or stood with their earbuds in and eyes glued to their phones. Only a few spared her a second glance, most of them probably wondering if she was really a woman.

A train came. Miwa snapped out of her thoughts and raised her arm, whistle between her teeth and breath blowing through metal and plastic. The five passengers on the platform lined up behind yellow lines while the automatic announcer implored them to do anything *but* cross it.

Only two passengers deboarded: a weary businessman on his way home, and a young woman Miwa had never seen before.

Miwa didn't know the names of most of the regulars, but she recognized a few faces. The businessman usually came in late, either apologizing to his wife on the phone for having to work so late or stinking of beer. Sometimes he nodded to Miwa on his way up Exit 1. Most of the time, however, he ignored her.

The woman was a complete unknown. Based on the way she wavered on her feet with glassy eyes and a slightly rictus mouth, Miwa had no idea what to make of her.

While the young female passenger stared at the vending machine on the platform, Miwa waved the train down the tracks. The driver waved back at her as he pulled out of the station. Just one of hundreds of well-oiled transportation machines around their corner of Tokyo.

Kohei radioed her. "You seeing this woman here?"

Miwa pretended to stare at the giant rectangular ads hanging on the station wall, when in reality she kept one careful eye on the woman. "*Hai.* I see her."

"Keep an eye on her, would you? She's acting strange on your end. Radio me if you need assistance."

Miwa turned in time to catch the woman disappearing behind a pillar.

Station attendants were trained for anything. People sick on trains. Perverts getting kicked off and handed over to security. Children running loose and getting dangerous with the tracks. Natural disasters. Emotional ones, like the woman tripping over her own feet.

She was either on drugs or, worse, suicidal.

Miwa never had a jumper on her watch. There was one three weeks ago during the afternoon, only two hours before her shift started, and the mess was so big she spent most of her hours writing late notices for employees and students who couldn't get to their destinations in time because the tunnels were closed. But she had missed the inciting incident and the subsequent investigation by the police.

Jumpers were the #1 thing to look out for in her line of work, above assaulters and terrorists. Jumpers were not only gruesome, but they bogged down the workings of the delicate train system, and nothing upset customers like someone's suicide inconveniencing a whole city.

This woman didn't really *jump,* though. Instead, she stood at the edge of the platform, wobbling back and forth as if she were about to tumble down into the tracks at any moment.

Miwa had to act fast. If she could do it without alerting Kohei, even better.

"Ma'am?" She put one careful hand on the woman's arm. "Are you okay? Do you need assistance?"

The woman stared at Miwa as if she spoke a different language. Maybe she wasn't Japanese. Korean? Chinese? Filipino? American tourist?

"Maybe you should…"

Dead weight collapsed against Miwa as the woman went down toward the tracks and attempted to take the station attendant with her.

Chapter 3

MIWA

Oh, man. Oh, shit.

"Shimatta," Miwa hissed, propping Sayuri's ragdoll-like body up on a bench. The train attendant glanced up to make sure Kohei didn't see the mischief taking place on the platform. Luckily, he was too busy speaking into his headset. It was probably the nightshift overseer relaying a delay. Only a matter of time before Kohei came over to tell Miwa.

The woman wasn't injured, but that was damn close. The next train may have been over ten minutes away, but Miwa would have had to call it in, hit the emergency button, get Kohei to help her pull the young woman out of the tracks, and then wait around for the authorities and medical personnel to take care of her. Meanwhile, people trying to get home before 1

As All Our Fires Burn

AM were fucked, and they would take it out on the train line, which would trickle down to the humble station attendants.

"*Daijyoubu desu ka?*" Miwa lightly patted the woman's face, whose chin rested against her chest. Faint puffs of breath shot out of her nostrils. "*Ogyakusama? Daijyoubu desu ka?* Do you need medical help?"

The woman muttered something incoherent. Miwa was so close to calling it in that she had her hand on her headset.

"Hey. What's happening here?" Kohei appeared behind the bench. "Is she okay?"

"I think so. She must be drunk."

Kohei sniffed. "I don't smell any alcohol."

"Maybe she's sick."

"Better call it in. Make sure she doesn't get near the tracks."

Miwa sighed. "You got things taken care of here?"

"Get her up the escalator and to the office. Oda-*san* will take it from there. You should be back in five minutes before the next train comes."

Miwa slung the woman's arm around her shoulders and helped her stand up. A harried sound gurgled up her throat. She was alive, at least. "Let's go, ma'am. You let me know if you're going to fall, okay?"

The passenger didn't respond.

Shinnosuke Oda was on duty at the ticket gates. He took one look at the mess coming up the escalator and motioned for the overseer in the back to come forward. They had already conferred among themselves by the time Miwa approached the gates with her half-fainted passenger.

"Tanaka-*san* radioed us about the situation." Shinnosuke came out of the ticket booth to help Miwa bring the woman into the back room. "We'll look after her and figure things out from here. Try to figure out if she has family or at least where she's going, I guess."

Miwa bowed in appreciation. "I must get back to the platform."

"Ah, yes, the 00:35 is due at any moment. You better go back up Tanaka-*san*."

Miwa would do that. She would finish the last half hour of her shift and find out what the hell happened to the passenger.

After the final train of the night left the station and nobody was left on the platform, Miwa and Kohei headed up the defunct escalators. Shinnosuke was doing his end-of-shift paperwork in the ticket booth. The gates were shut and the overhead tickers dark for the night. All it took was one switch of Kohei's hand, and the connection to half the lights in the station went off. The only bright lights left were in the stairwells to the street and in the back office.

"*Otsukaresama deshita!*" Four voices echoed at once in the little office. Overseer Wataru Endo went back to his phone call, speaking in a hushed but reverent tone. Either he spoke to his higher ups… or someone from a hospital.

Indeed, the young woman from the platform lay across the loveseat crammed into the corner of the office. It was usually reserved for these unfortunate occasions, although the little kids, pregnant women, and heat exhaustion victims who most often occupied the "sick sofa" in the office were conscious and at least able to answer simple questions like, "Who are you?" and "Who can we call for you?"

"Ban-*san*," Shinnosuke said as soon as Miwa approached her locker. "We need you to please try to find this woman's identification."

"Right away." Miwa, sore and sleepy from her shift, bent down next to the sofa and gingerly searched the woman's coat and skirt pockets. She didn't have a purse.

She didn't have any kind of identification. It must have been in her bag, wherever it was.

She did, however, have her phone in her jacket pocket. A dark pink Softbank flip-phone that flashed because of a missed call. A Sailor Moon charm clanked against the plastic case when Miwa stood up, phone in her hand.

Endo hung up with a mighty sigh. "Find anything over there, Ban-*san*?"

"Only her phone. She must have lost her purse."

"*Youshi*, Tanaka-*san*." Kohei perked up at his name. "Please do one last sweep of the platform for this woman's purse."

"*Hai*." Miwa recognized a flicker of annoyance in her coworker's eyes. He also wanted to get home, not look for more missing items.

"I spoke with the nearby hospital," Endo said. "They'll send a bus over if we can't get a hold of her family, but they can't do much without an ID. The police will have to be notified as well."

"What a bother," Shinnosuke muttered. "At the end of the shift, too."

Miwa held up the phone. She couldn't get past the lock screen, but that number flashed every time she hit the power button. "We could try calling this number. Maybe it's a family member looking for her."

"I'll leave it to you, Ban-*san*." Endo gestured to the office phone. "I'm going to look into something else."

Miwa didn't have any choice but to sit down at the overseer's desk and pick up the phone. She punched in the number she had almost already memorized. All the while she kept one eye on the woman slowly tossing and turning on the sofa, as if asleep.

The phone rang three times before a groggy voice picked up.

"*Moshi moshi?* Is that you, Sayu?"

Sayu? Miwa briefly looked away from the woman. "I'm so sorry to bother you this late at night, ma'am," she began, "but this is Miwa Ban from the Amaya-jinja-guchi Station calling because we have a passed out passenger under our care, and we're trying to find her family."

The other woman was silent for a few seconds. "Are you kidding me? *Che.* Passed out! Is she drunk?"

"Are you related to the owner of this phone, ma'am?"

"Not anymore, I'm not." The other woman said that much too quickly. She followed it up with, "I'm sorry. I guess I'm the closest thing to next of kin she has now. Where are you, again?"

"Amaya-jinja-guchi Station."

"*Ara!* Is that in Tokyo? You really must be kidding!"

As All Our Fires Burn

It took a few more minutes to convince the woman to do something about Sayuri Kawashima. She was reluctant to get too involved, and based on the answers she fed Miwa, all one could conclude was that she was an ex-relative of some kind.

Miwa shook her head when she hung up. By then, her boss was back and looking for answers.

"That was some distant relative of hers," was all Miwa could say. "She gave me some identification to forward."

"Let's call them and get this taken care of, then."

Within half an hour, an ambulance arrived to drive Ms. Kawashima to the nearest hospital. The two EMTs loaded the woman onto a stretcher and expertly wheeled her up the stairs and onto the street, where the ambulance waited.

"*Jya*, let's all go home, shall we?"

The incident had been recorded. Miwa only needed to change into her street clothes and head up to her bike chained behind the station. Her coworkers bade her goodnight as they either walked home or hopped into their cars.

But Miwa wasn't in a hurry to get on her bike and start the twenty-minute ride home. Her mind was on the mysterious woman who had no identity and no diagnosis until a random woman was called.

She was going to jump… Even if the woman had not been entirely of sound-mind – and what jumper was, really – she was still going to *jump* and end her life.

Miwa sat on her bike, bag jammed into the basket, and shed a few sympathy tears before proceeding home – and continuing to think about that woman for the rest of the week.

Chapter 4

SAYURI

For the first two days, the only one to visit Sayuri in the hospital was her ex. Emiko stepped in long enough to make sure the hospital was adequate before asking a couple of questions and excusing herself from Sayuri's life once more. The nurses on duty were concerned that their patient had no family.

Indeed, she didn't.

Emiko was in no hurry to take responsibility for Sayuri's actions. Let alone her medical bills or helping her get home. Ever since they broke up, Emiko had taken up residence in Saitama City, and the distance between there and Fujimi was too much for the full-time transit mechanic to deal with.

Remember when we were the most respectable lesbian couple? That's what Sayuri thought when her ex hurried out of the hospital room, never to be seen again that day. *I was the schoolteacher, and you worked for Japan Railway.* The only way their jobs could be better was if one of them went into civil service.

They had it all, didn't they? Good jobs, a good home, and the best little boy either of them could ask for. When they decided to have a child after two years together, Sayuri was the one who volunteered her body. And her heart. And her *soul*.

The last time she spent any time in the hospital was when her son was born. After that… the only time she came into these hallowed halls was for her son…

"*We're so sorry, Kawashima*-san…" That's what she expected to hear every time a nurse came into her room. "*We did everything we could for Yuma*-kun."

No, they hadn't. If they really had, wouldn't he be alive right now?

"Doctor says it's almost time for you to go home, *ne?*" A nurse fluffed Sayuri's pillow as she continued to stare out the window. "Do you know who will come to pick you up?"

She said nothing. Because she had no idea. If not Emiko, then who? One of her coworkers from school? Could she trust Ishihara-*sensei* or Aramaki-*sensei?* Nobody knew she was in the hospital. One of the small favors of it being summer vacation – she didn't have to call into work and request time off.

Her parents were alive. Neither of them would give a crap if she lived or died. Not after she chose her sexuality over them.

God. What good was that now? Ever since the accident, and ever since Emiko split from her, nothing had been the same. Sayuri wasn't sure she would ever feel a sliver of sexual attraction to someone again. She didn't care. She was in her thirties, anyway. Maybe it was for the best. *Let this Christmas Cake go stale.* Like one of those wraiths from the children's tales.

"Kawashima-*san?*" Another nurse appeared at the door. "You have a visitor. She says she's a friend."

Sayuri tilted her head. Her tangled, greasy hair coiled around the metal barriers keeping her from falling out of the hospital bed. Warm. The metal was warm, and she didn't know why. *Must be one of the teachers from work. Who told them?* Ah, her work would be on her file, wouldn't it? The hospital must have informed her employer.

"Her name is Ban-*san.* Do you want me to send her in?"

Ban? Sayuri didn't know anyone named Ban. Then again, who was she to turn away a kind face when she was in this sunny prison? "*Hai,*" Sayuri softly consented. "Go ahead."

Five seconds later, a face appeared in the doorway.

Sayuri didn't recognize the name, nor did she recognize the woman sheepishly showing herself into the room. She was on the shorter side, although her leather jacket and heavy backpack weighing her down certainly did not help her posture. She looked like the kind of student Sayuri had to reprimand in the classroom. *"Sit up straight! Do you want your back to grow like that? Your mother isn't raising an auntie."*

"Good afternoon," the woman, with a deeper voice than Sayuri anticipated, said. She pushed her long hair out of her face. "I mean... *Hajimemashite.*" The unknown guest bowed. "I'm Miwa Ban. You probably don't remember me, but..."

As All Our Fires Burn

Miwa Ban... now things started to sound familiar, but Sayuri couldn't remember from where. "Do I know you?"

The woman jerked backward, her backpack threatening to fall down her shoulders if she didn't spin it around and place it on the floor next to her feet. Honestly, her posture didn't improve much. "I was the one who helped you at the train station the other night. You probably don't recognize me without my uniform on." She pulled a rubber band off her wrist and yanked her hair away from her face. "Or without my hair like this."

Sayuri cocked her head. Did she know someone named Miwa Ban who looked like this? Everything was familiar, yet Sayuri didn't recognize a damn thing. "You must be the one who called the ambulance for me."

"It was more like my boss who did that but, yeah, I was there. I, um..." Miwa looked around the room before continuing, "I was the one who pulled you away from the tracks."

Sayuri's eyes widened. "The tracks? *Ara,* I had no idea it was that serious!"

"You must have been really out of it to not remember. You almost fell into the tracks."

"Goodness!" Sayuri didn't have an official diagnosis. The doctors at the hospital claimed she was having fainting spells resulting from dehydration, which may have been true. She didn't know. She didn't remember anything after arriving in Tokyo. "Thank you so much for helping me that night. I don't know how to repay you."

Miwa held up her hands. "I'm not looking for repayment. I only wanted to make sure you're okay. Honestly, my employer doesn't even know I'm here. I'm not sure I should be."

"Your employer?"

"Yes. You really don't remember me, huh?"

Sayuri slowly shook her head.

"I'm a platform attendant at Amaya-jinja-guchi Station. That's where you collapsed."

Sayuri had never heard of that station before. It sounded suburban and so far away from where she should ever be. What *had* happened the other night? Was she really that out of it? "You're a woman."

Miwa was taken aback at that statement. "Yes. I am. Suppose that's still unusual."

"Oh, sorry. Didn't mean it that way." Yes, she did. What really were the odds? "Thank you again, Ban-*san*." Sayuri bowed where she sat up in her bed. "I may have really been in trouble if it weren't for you."

Before Miwa could insist that she hadn't really done anything, the nurse stepped in, clipboard in hand.

"*Shitsureishimasu,* Kawashima-*san!*" The nurse nodded to Miwa before going to Sayuri's side. "Afraid I really must write down your discharge arrangements right now. Our systems are about to go down for routine maintenance, and we must log who will come to pick you up tomorrow."

"Ah, well…"

Silence swept through the tiny hospital room. Sayuri gazed out the open window, wondering if she could convince Emiko to come pick her up and take her back to Fujimi. *To my little apartment full of sad memories.* If Sayuri really begged, Emiko would do it. What other choice did she have?

"*Ano...*" Miwa interrupted. The nurse turned her head. "If there isn't anyone handy, I can help her get home. I have tomorrow off."

Sayuri was quick to decline. "Oh, no! I couldn't let you do that. I live way out in Fujimi."

She expected Miwa to have no idea what she was talking about. "Fujimi? It's outside of my employee pass, but I know how to get there no problem. Tobu-Tojo Line, right?"

Sayuri nodded. "Please don't think you have to do it, Ban-*san*. I couldn't possibly put you out like…"

"It's fine. What time do you have to be out of here?"

The nurse answered in Sayuri's stead. "By noon, if it's all right. We'll have her ready to go and fill you in on any medications she needs to take."

Sayuri had no idea what was happening. Who was this woman? Why was she doing this? Did she have some kind of ulterior motive? Did she want money? A favor? She had already done enough by saving Sayuri's life! What kind of moral debt was Sayuri racking up right now?

"It's settled, then. See you tomorrow, Kawashima-*san*. I have to get going now."

The nurse also left the room. Fifteen minutes later, a small bouquet of flowers was delivered to Sayuri's room. She didn't ask about who they came from. She knew, and she was more confused than ever.

Chapter 5

MIWA

What the fuck am I doing? Miwa parked her bike in the garage in front of the main hospital entrance. *This isn't my responsibility. I don't even know who this woman is.* She removed her helmet and tucked it behind the seat.

Maybe someone else has come to pick her up and nobody told me. Nope. There she was. Sayuri sat in a wheelchair, her sweater over her lap and her face glum. While her fingers were glued to her cell phone screen, the rest of her looked like she would rather shrivel up like a withered prune.

Well, Miwa had foolishly signed up for this, so she might as well get it over with. Fujimi wasn't that far away, really. It made more sense to ride back to her place first, since her train pass started at her local station, but Sayuri should be well enough to ride tandem, right?

As All Our Fires Burn

"*Ohayou gozaimasu,*" Miwa greeted both Sayuri and the nurse approaching her from behind. "I'm sorry if I'm late."

"You're right on time." The nurse bowed her head in greeting before rechecking something on Sayuri's wheelchair. "Kawashima-*san* is ready to go home as soon as you're able."

"I'm so sorry for putting you through this. Again."

"It's no problem. Really." Miwa looked on in mild trepidation as Sayuri attempted to stand from her chair. Legs wobbled and eyes rolled back. For a moment, Miwa feared that Sayuri would fall back into the chair. "*Ano...* are you okay?"

The nurse presented Miwa with a page from the discharge papers. "Kawashima-*san* is still a bit woozy from her momentary illness. The doctors are sure that she'll have her full strength back within a few days, but until then, please be careful whenever she walks or stands for long periods of time."

"*Sou ka...*" Miwa glanced over the heavy medical terms and the brief doctor's note that said, "*Isn't a danger to herself or others.*" Nothing inspired confidence like that. "It should be okay."

Sayuri finally had her land legs again, but the look she offered did not make Miwa feel better. The poor woman was probably embarrassed out of her mind. She didn't have anyone to help her get home from Tokyo, and the hospital wouldn't let her go on her own. No family was one thing, but she didn't have any close friends, either? Hard to believe. *No it's not.* Miwa kept her sigh to herself. She would know firsthand about having few friends or family to lend a hand.

Maybe that's why she was quick to volunteer. She knew what it was like to live in that limbo.

"My vehicle is this way." Miwa offered her hand to Sayuri, but it was declined. "If we leave now, we can beat the lunch hour traffic."

Sayuri glanced back at the nurse, who politely waved them off from the curb. Before the invalid had the chance to run back into the hospital, the nurse had wheeled the chair around and directed it back into the building. Time for someone else to use it.

"Thank you for doing this," Sayuri mumbled on the way into the garage. "I hate putting a stranger out like this. You really didn't have to."

Miwa had anticipated this scenario unfolding, but she was still embarrassed to hear it. "It really isn't a problem. I have the day off today and no other plans."

"Were you really the person who helped me at the train station?"

"Yes. Like I said, you probably don't recognize me because I'm not in my uniform." Miwa always looked so cool and collected in her attendant's uniform. In real life, however, she was a mess in baggy sweatshirts and worn-out jeans. It was a miracle if her hair didn't become a huge greasy mess in either a ponytail or flying free in the wind. "Even my own mother didn't recognize me the first time I sent her a picture of me in my uniform."

Sayuri almost continued into a different section of the parking garage. When she realized Miwa had gone in another direction, she hurried to backtrack and almost tripped over her feet.

As All Our Fires Burn

"Are you here on behalf of the station?" She didn't mention that they had entered the bike garage. Rows upon rows of bicycles and street motorbikes lined up in a colorful array of seats and handlebars.

"No. They honestly don't know that I did this." Miwa stopped behind her bike and pulled out her key for the lock. "I'd actually appreciate it if you didn't bring it up to my employer. They might get weird about it." Only a little bit. The most they were authorized to do was send a get well card to the hospital, and every employee had to sign it. "This is it, by the way."

Sayuri stared at the humble bicycle. "I see."

"We can walk toward the train station. I don't live too far from it. Here." Miwa offered Sayuri the handlebars. "Use this to hang onto. It's okay. Let me know if you're feeling too dizzy to continue."

"Thank you."

They must've looked the sight walking down the sunlit street. Sayuri, in her flowy skirt and blouse – the same ones she had been wearing when admitted to the hospital – walked with a banged up bike that was clearly too short for her to effectively ride. Miwa followed alongside her, a backpack covered in anime and video game keychains jingling with every step. Miwa was the only one who knew where they were going and had to direct Sayuri, who led the bike as if she had never ridden one before and had no idea how to touch it.

It was certainly one way to make their way through the back streets toward Miwa's apartment.

"Were you also the one who sent me those flowers, Ban-san?"

Miwa slowly nodded. "Your room looked really drab. I thought it could use some sprucing up with colors. The lady at the florist next to the gift shop said it was a perfect get well bouquet." She didn't mention she bought it premade, alongside a dozen other "perfect" get well bouquets. "I hope I didn't overstep my bounds."

"Suppose I'm merely confused as to why you're being so kind to me." Sayuri laughed. "Not that I don't appreciate it, but it's difficult for me to understand. We never met before the other night, and I barely remember it."

"Seemed like the thing to do."

In truth, Miwa had no idea why she did it either. She shouldn't have even visited Sayuri in the hospital, but how could she restrain herself when she kept thinking about those narrow eyes that looked like they had seen a world beyond her own soul? Some people were simply memorable. When Miwa woke up yesterday morning, her first thought was of Sayuri and her predicament. Intuition. She supposed she could call it that.

"Thank you again."

"There's really no need to thank me," Miwa said. "Now, you say you live in Fujimi?"

"*Hai.* If you could show me the direction to Ikebukuro, I can get home fine on my own. I have money for tickets."

Miwa nodded again. "As soon as we drop my bike off at my apartment, I can take you to the station in my neighborhood. It goes straight to Ikebukuro. Easy connection."

As All Our Fires Burn

"Thank you... I mean..." Blushing, Sayuri almost released the handlebars in her weakened grip. "Oh, is there any news about my missing bag?"

"I haven't been back to work since that night, but I can check for you tomorrow."

"I really don't know where I left it. I feel so stupid about that night." Sayuri left it there.

"Are you going to be okay?" Miwa wanted to pry more, of course, but didn't. "We were all worried about you at the station."

Sayuri's cheeks were even redder. "*Hazukashii.*"

"*Gomen.* I don't mean to embarrass you."

"Suppose it can't be helped. I was having a bad day."

Bad day? What kind of bad day made a woman nearly collapse into the train tracks? Sure, Sayuri hadn't looked her best, but that could've easily been explained by any number of conditions. Miwa had never assumed that Sayuri had done something to herself.

That's not true. I worried she was trying to commit suicide.

Miwa stopped in front of a side street. "This way. My apartment, that is."

Sayuri directed the bike down the narrow street. During the day, Miwa's neighborhood looked more boring and devoid of amenities than usual. That's how a single woman paid for an apartment in Tokyo. The only way Miwa really got by was having a nice employee pass for train fare, but it didn't go everywhere. Only where her company went, and it wasn't the biggest one in Tokyo. *If I worked for JR, I could really go anywhere...* Yet she didn't work for JR, so she better pinch her *yen* and hope her bank account stood against the inevitable rent increases.

They never encountered another soul walking up to Miwa's old apartment building. Most of the people living on that tiny street either worked during the day or all night. Those who were at home were fast asleep in their futons and praying that the sunlight didn't disturb them. *That's how I feel most days.* Sometimes Miwa didn't get to sleep until five in the morning. She was lucky to be up by noon.

If you didn't play so many stupid video games... Miwa took over control of her bike so she could lock it by her front door. "If it's okay," she began, "I'll grab another jacket from inside. Should only take a moment."

"All right."

Miwa opened her half-rusted door and immediately encountered a frequent problem: a mild earthquake had knocked over her laundry basket and spilled her dirty clothes across the *genkan*. This was a nuisance when Miwa was the only one walking through her door. With a guest following close behind?

Mortifying! Those were her panties on the cement floor!

"*Shimatta!*" Miwa barreled forward and hurried to toss her clothes back into the basket. "Sorry! This happens all the time!" Thin walls, a shoddy foundation, and a rickety shelf meant the next Big One would probably collapse the place. Miwa had a theory that the Great Tohoku Earthquake had fucked up the building's foundation. They were as good as dead next time.

"Is everything okay?"

My pride is shot. At least Sayuri was a woman. Maybe she wouldn't be offended to see Miwa's sports bras and cotton underwear tossed back into their basket. *Does this make us even?* "*Daijyoubu yo.* Just annoying. Sorry!"

Sayuri glanced around the cramped entryway before inching across the threshold. "*Shitsurei shimasu,*" she muttered.

Miwa placed the tub of clothes back on top of the shelf. "I can't remember what I came in here for now."

"Something about a jacket?"

"Oh. Right. In here."

Miwa scrambled for an appropriate jacket to wear to the nearby train station. Sayuri was left to stand in the efficiency kitchen, where a dirty bowl with half-eaten ramen remained. *Crap! I'm such a slob!* Sayuri was the one fresh from the hospital, but she looked like a composed housewife compared to Miwa the total mess. Oh, well. Too late to clean it up and save face now. Sayuri had already made her judgments, hadn't she?

"Your place is cute, Ban-*san.*"

"Oh, uh… thanks." Was she nuts? The place looked like some kind of shut-in lived there. Half-eaten food, crumbs on the floor, panties falling out of baskets… shit! What was Miwa thinking, leaving her video game posters up on the walls? That was more embarrassing than the mini train models taking over her humble coffee table. *Try plugging your PS4 controller in next time!* The poor thing had been left to rot in the middle of the floor when Miwa went to bed the night before. "I'm sorry it's such a mess. I don't have a lot of room."

"My place is small as well." Sayuri stared at one of the posters. "We make do with the space we're given."

"I guess so." Miwa snapped a jacket off its hook. "*Ikimashou ka?*"

The station was only a few minutes away by foot. Sayuri walked without the need for aid, although Miwa always lurked nearby to offer a hand if desired.

"*Ano...*" Miwa stood by the ticket machines outside. It was a one-line station that boasted a humbler ridership than the station she worked at a few kilometers away. The only people lurking inside were a couple of students, an elderly woman, and the station master on duty. He didn't look twice at Miwa. Likewise, she didn't know him. "If you go this way, you'll end up in Ikebukuro. It's a relatively short trip, although you have to wait for a local train to come by."

Sayuri smiled. "Thank you for everything, Ban-*san*." She bowed at the waist, a move that conjured the attention of the station master in his booth. "I insist on acquiring your mailing address so I can send you my thanks in the post."

Miwa knew better than to fight it. She coughed up her address on a business card and handed it over. When Sayuri waved herself through the ticket gates, Miwa could only think, *I have a feeling this is going to be a thing.*

The day was still young. She could either go back home and play video games, or... well, she couldn't afford anything else. Video games on her day off would have to be it.

Chapter 6

SAYURI

Somebody crashed into the door between the hallway and the teachers' room. Sayuri jerked up from her desk. Until that moment, only she and one other teacher had been in the whole building. That was supposed to be the boon of getting work done during summer vacation – no distractions!

"*Sensei!*" A boy in shorts and a red Anpanman T-shirt slid the door open. "Kawashima-*sensei!*"

His companion, another boy with gangly legs sprouting from his shorts and a black shirt that made him sweat like a sports star, smacked him on the arm and angrily bade him to have more manners in the presence of their teachers.

But Shota Shimazaki was not known for his polite manners. He had been an excitable boy since his first day of first year, and now that he was a third year student with nothing to hide, he often bothered his home room teacher no matter what time of year. *How did he know I was here today?* Sayuri had come on a lark. After spending a whole day at home, cooped up in her air conditioned apartment of sour memories, she decided to spare herself the heartache and get some work done. The school may not be air conditioned, but an oscillating fan kept Sayuri's skin dry and her brain focused on her autumn lesson plans.

Until Shota barged in, anyway.

"Shota-*kun?*" Sayuri turned her folder over and placed her pen on the edge of her desk. "What are you doing here? Shouldn't you be out playing?" The only explanation was that Shota's mother, the nosy Mariko Shimazaki who lived two buildings away from Sayuri, had seen her walking toward the school with her work bag slung over her shoulder.

"*Shitsurei shimasuuuuu!*" Shota waited until he was by his teacher's side to excuse his arrival. His friend stood behind him and briefly nodded to both Sayuri and the teacher sitting on the other end of the large room. "You'll be proud of me, Kawashima-*sensei*. I've been doing my homework every day."

"He's lying," the other boy, whose name continued to escape Sayuri since he was not one of her students, said. "He was up the whole night doing the math."

Shota blushed and *tsked,* habits he probably picked up from his grandfather. That man always sat on the corner of Sayuri's street, playing *go* with the other elders of the neighborhood. The man wasn't a nuisance, per se, but he was as loud and boisterous as his grandson.

As All Our Fires Burn

"*Sensei* knows that math is not my thing. I'm an *eigo boi*."

Sayuri sighed. It was rare for children to barge in like this during vacations, but as long as the gates were open and staff wandered the halls, children were free to come and go. Part of the "open door" policy fostered between teachers and students. Yet when a teacher grew accustomed to some peace and quiet during the August season, it was a bit much to deal with the likes of Shota. *I know your mother, kid.* A little too well. More than once Mariko helped with Yuma when he was a tiny baby. Sayuri was inclined to listen to her advice since the woman had raised a boy of her own. Her advice about how to avoid the "garden hose" was invaluable.

Now when their paths crossed... Mariko politely said hello and gave Sayuri that look of *I'm so glad I'm not you right now.*

Sayuri gritted her teeth while reminding herself that Shota had nothing to do with her problems. "Okay, *eigo boi,* let's see those workbooks I'm sure you brought me."

"*Youshi.*" Shota slammed his bookbag on the floor and unearthed a small stack of thin workbooks. Math, earth science, English, *kanji,* and composition spilled out like Niagara Falls. Shota dug through them until he found his English workbook. His friend was left to clean up the rest of the mess. "*Hai, onegaishi-ma-suuuu, sensei!*"

Boys were so damn rowdy. Sayuri snatched the English workbook and opened her top drawer, where she kept a pocket dictionary and the national study guide for third year English.

"Have you been practicing your English at home, Shota-*kun?*" She clicked her red pen and started checking his answers.

It was a nuisance, but at least it would be one less thing to check at the end of vacation. "Remember, I know your mother. I'll know if you're lying."

"*Eburii dei, sensei!*" His vocabulary was correct, but his accent left much to be desired. "I've been doing the summer program at the English school. *Itzu fun!*"

To be fair, Shota's English marks were one of the highest in his class, but he also had a habit of stretching the truth when it suited him. Such was life with nine-year-old boys.

"Good. Let's see your daily journaling."

Sayuri had assigned each of her students a journal to complete during vacation. The same shit she had to do when she was a kid, and she knew how it worked: the kids waited until the last week of vacation to sit down and write their daily journals, making up whatever pleased them or sounded the easiest to write. The point wasn't to be truthful, anyway. The point was to show that they could construct sentences using the letters and words they had learned over the past few months.

At the end of summer, Sayuri would have a whole stack of books to go through, and each one of them would say things like, *"Today I went to the zoo. It was fun. I saw elephants and polar bears."* For every child who could knock out their daily journal in one minute, there was another who took an hour to spit out one sentence. Oh, well, as long as they got them done...

When the boys left at the end of the hour, Sayuri exhaled a sigh of relief and endured the chuckling of her coworker, Ishihara-*sensei*. The homeroom teacher of 5-C had nothing on Kawashima-*sensei* and her 3-A class.

As All Our Fires Burn

"At least you have students who care enough to see you in the summer!" he called from across the room. "All of my fifth year students have forgotten my name already!"

Sayuri cleaned up her desk and grabbed her sweater. "He's very *genki, ne?*"

"I'd kill to be that energetic again. Alas."

Sayuri had never been an energetic person. Even when she was Shota's age, she was a shy girl who preferred working in the school garden to playing dodgeball or soccer. "Me too, perhaps." She picked up her bag and bade farewell to her lone coworker. Shota's interruption had killed her momentum. Besides, she had an important errand to run.

I must get a thank you gift for Ban-san. Miwa had been at the forefront of Sayuri's mind ever since she came home two days ago. That woman would probably be fine with never hearing from Sayuri again, but someone had been brought up with proper manners that dictated she was to find an adequate gift to express her gratitude.

She just didn't know what.

What was she supposed to get the woman who had saved her life? Who had helped her out of the hospital when no one else would? Traditional Japanese sweets wouldn't cut it. Flowers were cheap, even when they weren't. Sayuri knew nothing about Miwa's likes or dislikes. Nothing about her aside from the fact she worked for a train company and liked locomotives, based on the few things around her apartment. There had been a lot of gaming items, too, but Sayuri knew little about video games.

Gift certificates were impersonal. Jewelry was too presumptive. Perhaps the sweets and a trip for two to an *onsen?* Did other people like that sort of stuff?

Sayuri wandered down the shopping park between the school and her apartment building. Aunties and entrepreneurial thirty-somethings sold the usual wares: shoes, clothes, stationery, dishes, and toys. None of it was personal. Not even the handmade items lining shelves and hanging from racks on the edge of the street.

I used to bring Yuma to this toy shop to find something new to play with. Emiko used to take him to the sweet shop to spoil him with cavities. *I wanted to have another child. I wanted a little boy and a little girl to bring through this park for the rest of my life.*

Sayuri snapped out of her thoughts and encountered the perfect gift for Miwa right in front of her. Too bad she had yet to realize that she much preferred thinking about Miwa than any of the people she had lost in the past year.

It was a start, though.

Chapter 7

MIWA

Miwa reached for more Pocari Sweat only to discover she had drunk both bottles. She was in the middle of an intense boss battle and *now* chose to run out? She waited until it was her move in the turn-based RPG and bolted outside, where the hot August air threatened to choke her and wring the last of the moisture out of her body. Good thing she only had to make a quick trip to the vending machine on the corner of the street to get two more bottles of Pocari Sweat. Before the game could yell at her for taking too long to make a move, she was back in her dark apartment and sitting in front of the oscillating fan. She couldn't afford to run the air conditioner.

She would rather run her PS4 and the HD TV she saved up for months to buy. *Best. Purchase. Ever!* Her sweaty fingers slipped across the controller buttons as she selected the moves to take out this obnoxious boss.

This was how a woman best spent her days off. After another hot and stressful week at work, the only thing Miwa cared to do was sit in her beanbag chair and smash buttons. It had become a ritual of sorts. On her last day of work, she would stop by the convenience store in her neighborhood and stock up on drinks and instant food. Maybe she'd splurge and hit up the local McDonald's, KFC, or Yoshinoya for dinner that night. Anything that made it easier to bring her dinner back and mindlessly eat it while immersing herself in a video game's world.

"Aw, c'mon." She pointed an accusatory finger as the boss used a cheap move that wiped out half her party. "You're cheating!" So what if she was replaying this game on Hard mode? Was the boss supposed to have *that* many moves at his disposal? Especially the cheap ones!

At least when she lived by herself, nobody was around to call her an *otaku*. Because that's what they called her back in her hometown. What kind of average-looking girl was into *video games?* That was for geeks. Nerds. The ill-spoken of *otaku* who shut themselves up in their rooms to play nothing but video games and watch idol videos. The only time they socialized was with their families, who shoved food beneath their doors and chastised them on their way out of the house to go to another idol show.

Miwa saw nothing appealing about that life. Video games were her primary hobby, nothing more. A hobby she spent a

As All Our Fires Burn

lot of money on, but wasn't that true for most people and their hobbies? One of her friends was obsessed with K-pop boy bands and spent all her money on CDs, trading cards, DVDs, and tickets to their Japanese shows. She even took herself to Seoul as a birthday present! Another friend was an artist who dumped her paychecks into art supplies and spent her evenings and weekends dreaming up fantastical landscapes. Why were those hobbies considered less geeky than Miwa preordering the next Final Fantasy game?

Because this is a "guy" thing. Miwa guzzled her third bottle of Pocari Sweat and continued to pride herself on her all-female party taking down the demonic boss. Well, the main character she was forced to play wasn't female, but she role-played the guy as a very butchy woman in her head. It worked for her, because what guy would call himself *Miwappo Bansho?*

She almost spat out her drink. Miwappo Bansho. Who knew that terrible nickname the kids in elementary school gave her would one day become her PlayStation handle?

The doorbell rang.

Miwa wasn't sure she heard that right at first. She wasn't expecting any deliveries. The NHK collectors and Jehovah Witness recruiters had already been by the day before. Who the hell would come to call on *her* on such a precious day off as this?

After a few seconds, the doorbell rang again.

"*Chotto matte kudasai!*" she called, pausing her game and sending her apartment into silence. Miwa leaped up on unsteady feet and stumbled toward the front door in her cluttered, cramped hallway, past the ancient washing machine and the two-burner stove in her tiny kitchen. She leaned over from the edge of the *genkan* so she wouldn't have to take off her house slippers before opening the door.

She should have looked through the peephole. She really, really should have!

"*Konnichiwa.*" Sayuri Kawashima, dressed in an airy pink sundress and carrying a large straw tote bag, nodded her head in greeting.

Miwa fell into her *genkan,* her house slippers sliding across the dirty concrete and creating one of the most stellar moral quandaries to ever befall a Japanese woman in her own home.

Normally, she would pretend that hadn't happened and continue to use her slippers around the house. Maybe brush off the soles first, but who cared if her mother wasn't around to freak out at her?

But Sayuri was here. She had seen what Miwa did.

"*Ara...*" Sayuri lost her smile. "*Daijyoubu desu ka?*"

No. Now I have to buy new slippers. Miwa slowly slid out of her slippers and piled them next to the washing machine. Her only choice was to stand on the edge of the *genkan* barefoot. Or she could hop into her sneakers, she supposed. Damnit. She should do that, huh?

"I'm okay." Miwa stuffed her bare feet into her sneakers, the backs pressed beneath her heels. "You surprised me, is all."

"My apologies." Sayuri continued to stand in the hot sunlight, sweat glistening on her forehead and pink fingers gripping the strap of her tote bag. "Please excuse me for coming unannounced. I happened to be in the neighborhood, and…" She stopped herself, continuing to smile in self-admonishment. "*Usou deshita.* I came here from Fujimi because I wanted to apologize for all the trouble I put you through."

"Trouble? It wasn't trouble at all." Miwa opened her door all the way. She had forgotten how much cooler it was in her apartment than outside. Apparently, closing her blinds and running the fans really *did* help. "You don't have to apologize."

"I really would like to, though. My foolishness and inability to properly take care of myself led to that situation. One that you certainly did not sign up for, Ban-*san.*" Sayuri lowered her eyes. "I know you were only doing your job at the train station, but there was no reason for you to have to pick me up from the hospital. I feel like such a blundering…"

"Please, stop." Miwa looked up into Sayuri's pinkening face. "And please come in before you burn in the sunlight, Kawashima-*san.*"

"I couldn't impose."

"Please. You came all this way." Couldn't impose, Miwa's ass. The woman admitted to coming all the way from Fujimi *just* to see Miwa. If Miwa didn't invite her in, she might as well cop to being the rudest woman her mother could've raised. First stomping her house slippers into the *genkan*… then refusing to let such an honored guest into her home… Miwa may not get along well with her mother, but she wouldn't let that weigh upon the woman's soul.

Miwa stepped out of the way. Sayuri bowed her head in acknowledgment before slowly entering Miwa's humble abode.

There was no extra pair of slippers for Sayuri. They both walked barefoot down the cramped hallway and into Miwa's...

God. Damnit. *Into Miwa's messy-ass apartment!*

By herself, it was perfectly presentable. With a guest in her shadow, however, Miwa wanted to offer herself as a sacrifice to the gods of cleanliness and retribution.

Not only did the remnants of her mid-binge remain, but Miwa hadn't cleaned a damn thing up in the past week. Her trash was stuffed with ramen bowls, chip bags, and empty pep bottles that should have been sorted into the recycling. The floor was covered in more containers and pieces of her train set that had fallen apart to make room for her video games. Her futon was left out and in complete disarray... and could it smell any mustier in there? Even if it weren't summer, Miwa could bet that her apartment smelled like bad BO.

God. More evidence that she didn't have a social life. Especially one that followed her home. *Maybe I am an* otaku. Worse. Maybe she was a *hikikomori* after all!

"Please pardon the mess." She couldn't bear to look Sayuri in the eye. "It's definitely messier than the last time you were here." So was Miwa. She stood in a sweaty T-shirt and a pair of pajama shorts. Her perfect summer weekend-at-home clothing.

Kill me. Could this be any more embarrassing? Here Sayuri was, in her effortlessly pretty sundress and with her perfect hair... and Miwa couldn't look slovenlier if she tried. She was only missing a couple mustard stains on her oversized T-shirt.

"Your apartment is very homey, Ban-*san*." How dare Sayuri sound so cheerful? "I can tell that you live here."

As All Our Fires Burn

"You... can?" She knew it. She was disgusting. Not even her shiny train station uniform could hide the fact she was a disgusting pig. *Of course I am. I must be the most feminine* otaku *to hit the streets! Look at me! Playing video games and working at a train station!* Miwa almost stepped on a stray piece from her model train set. The poor thing always came apart when she parked her ass in her apartment for her weekend.

"Of course! I don't know much about you yet, Ban-*san,* but I would guess this was your apartment from the few interactions we've had."

"You... *would?*"

"I can really feel your love for trains in here."

Miwa tilted her head in absolute amazement.

"There's your uniform hanging there." Sayuri pointed into the opened closet. "Your train set down here. A JR poster over there. A *Scenes From Kagayama Stations* photobook... and... ah! Your video game! It takes place in the subway, huh?"

Miwa swung her head toward her TV screen. She had paused on a scene in a subway, overtaken by demons from another world.

"I'm sorry for interrupting you on your day off," Sayuri said, "but I had said I wanted to properly thank you for what you did for me, and I could only do that in person. Mailing something would not have been enough."

"N... no?"

Sayuri reached into her bag and pulled out a box professionally wrapped at a gift shop. *Oh my God. She got me something, didn't she?* Miwa looked around as if the gift were intended for someone else. "I wanted to get you something that you would appreciate, Ban-*san*." Sayuri handed over the gift with a bow of her head. "Please accept this gift as a mediocre response to you saving my life!"

Miwa was forced to take the box and hold it close to her chest. It wasn't that heavy. Nor was it that big. It could have been anything, from a small pack of sweets to a diamond necklace. *What would I do with something like that?*

"Thank you so much for your thoughtfulness." Nope. Miwa still sounded like a dumb rube trying to speak in *keigo*… let alone in her current outfit. "I really can't accept this…"

"You haven't even opened it yet."

She wanted her to open it right now? In front of her? Damn! She was nuts!

"Of course." Miwa's fingers hesitated to pull back the delicate wrapping. Sayuri continued to grin in anticipation. Maybe it wasn't something generic after all. "You really shouldn't have."

"I insist."

The wrapping peeled back. Miwa could hardly believe her eyes.

It was an expansion to her train set. Specifically, the *Saitama Prefecture Fun Adventures* pack, featuring the old wooden clock tower in Kawagoe and the gates to the Mitsumine Shrine. Miwa looked up in shock.

"If there was one thing that I noticed the most about you, Ban-*san*," Sayuri sheepishly said, "it's that you really love trains."

As All Our Fires Burn

Miwa felt awful about stepping on half her train set, currently crammed against the tatami mats beneath them. "Thank you so much. Nobody's ever gotten me something like this before." Not since she was a child. Her parents stopped entertaining her fascination with trains after elementary school. That was a male pursuit, after all. Anything Miwa wanted after that time in her life she had to buy for herself.

"You must really love trains to work so hard to become a station attendant."

"Yeah. I really loved them as a kid." Miwa gently lowered the box to the one empty corner on her table. "I guess my two favorite things are trains and video games. I have a few simulation games... but you get kinda spoiled after working in a train station."

Sayuri turned toward the TV. "What kind of game is this?" Her tone implied she knew what she was about to say was false. "A simulation game?"

Miwa laughed. "No, it's a RPG. Turn-based."

"I'm afraid I'm not too familiar with video games."

I sound like such a nerd! "It means you take turns in a fight. The enemy attacks you, then you have your turn to decide what you want to do and attack. It's very strategy based as opposed to reflex based. Real time games include a free-for-all in attacks." Miwa didn't care as much for those. Too much anxiety. "Turn-based is Japanese style."

"Very fair and pragmatic. What is this game called?"

Neeeeerrrrrd! "It's Demon Death Squad 5. You play high school students who go around collecting demon souls and using them in battles. This one takes place in Tokyo, so it really focuses on the train system." Miwa laughed. "I was a fan before they did this, though. I've played all the games in the franchise, but this is the latest one. It came out last year and I'm on my third playthrough... ah, never mind me."

"Sounds interesting. My son..." Sayuri stopped.

"You have a son?" Of course. She must have been married. Someone as pretty and polite as her... *but why didn't her husband pick her up from the hospital?*

Sayuri continued as if she hadn't interrupted herself. "My son really loves video games, but I think this one would be too old for him."

"Yeah, it has the highest rating. They talk about some heavy stuff in it." The demons were the easiest part to digest. The first dungeon was about a perverted high school teacher abusing his students, for fuck's sake. "Oh! By the way..." Miwa turned to her guest. "Could I interest you in some tea? I think I have some around here."

"Oh! Sorry, but I really must be going. I have an errand to run before heading home."

"Of course. Thank you for coming by and for the present."

Miwa showed Sayuri out with a few more parting words and phrases of gratitude. How strange. She had dreaded bringing Sayuri into her home, and now she almost didn't want her to leave. Why couldn't she stay for tea?

Why was Miwa comfortable enough to invite her to stay?

When Sayuri was gone, Miwa returned to her beanbag and picked up her game controller. She was halfway through another RPG battle when she decided to turn off the game and instead open her present. Perhaps she would spend the evening with takeout and her train set. A much more peaceful time than yelling at the video game for making cheap shots because it was Hard mode.

Chapter 8

SAYURI

"Thanks for letting me have this." Emiko sat at Sayuri's table, fingering one of their son's old baby blankets that still had a bit of his dried-up spittle in the corner. Sayuri forced herself to drink more iced tea so she wouldn't gag at the depressing thought that she would no longer have this precious piece of her son's existence. "Seems weird to want a blanket so much, but feeling it in my hands makes me think that he's not so far away from us."

Sayuri wiped something away from her eye.

"*Gomen,*" Emiko apologized. "I know it's harder for you."

"You were his mother, too." Sayuri was the one who carried him, birthed him, and nursed him until he was old enough to feed himself, but Emiko had done her share of midnight feedings, changing diapers, and swinging their son around the living room while they pretended he was the fastest airplane in the world. Yuma always laughed so hard that Sayuri worried her son would throw up.

He only did once. On that blanket. No matter how many times Sayuri treated and washed it, that one little patch never came out. She had almost thrown it out back then. Now? She was losing it anyway.

This is the right thing to do. She still had most of his clothing and toys. All Emiko really had to remind her of their son's existence were a few photos and a lock of his hair. Sayuri had a lock as well. Wasn't it smart of them to do that when he was still alive? Back then, Sayuri thought it would be a nice reminder of her son's babyhood. One day, he would be a grown man with a life of his own, and his old, silly mother would want to relive those days of holding her baby in her arms and being in complete awe that her humble body made such a thing.

"So how's Hina?" Sayuri dropped honorifics from the name. She had no idea how to refer to the woman her ex now lived with.

Emiko folded up the blanket in her lap. "She's doing fine. She's at work right now."

"At the factory, right?"

"Yes. She managed to get transferred to the day shift so we could have more time together."

Sayuri bristled. She remembered a time in their relationship when Emiko worked the night shift for the railroad company.

Trains that came into terminus with concerning issues were sent straight her way, and her job had been to get them back in running order before the lines started back up again. The day she was transferred to day shift was a gift from God.

"Sorry I wasn't able to pick you up from the hospital the other day," Emiko said. "We both had to work."

Sayuri shrugged, as if she hadn't spent most of her hospital stay paranoid that nobody would be there to pick her up. "It's fine. A friend managed to do it at the last minute." She wasn't sure if Miwa was a friend, but how else was Sayuri supposed to explain it? *The woman who saved my life at the train station came to pick me up.* Sayuri had done her due diligence in properly thanking Miwa for doing her job, but had it been enough? Was Sayuri doomed to forever be a nuisance to the other women around her?

She felt like that in her relationship with Emiko, too. It must have been true, if the woman Sayuri once loved so much was able to leave her for another woman so easily.

I don't hold it against her. The death of our son ruined everything. Emiko had claimed it was too hard to be in this apartment, where there son had spent his whole life, but when Sayuri suggested they move to get away from the pain, Emiko had instead suggested that only *she* leave. Three months later, she was in the arms of factory-worker Hina Nakajima, a regular at the Shinjuku Ni-chome bar Emiko visited on Saturday nights. Sayuri never had the temperament for the bars. She preferred the ladies' club she used to attend, before having a baby and the subsequent grief of his loss made her stop going.

"A friend, huh?" Emiko forced a flirtatious smile. "Didn't know you were seeing someone."

"I'm not." That came out a little too forceful. "I mean, she's just a friend. It's not like... us. I mean, what we used to be. I mean..."

"It's fine." Emiko stood, blanket in her hands and drink half-finished. "I gotta get going. I promised Hina-*chan* I would take her out for dinner when she got off work."

"*Sou desu ka...*" Sayuri remembered when one of her greatest pleasures was cooking dinner for her family. Her mother may have been disappointed in her daughter's choices for love, but one thing she couldn't fault Sayuri for was her homemaking skill. Sayuri had half a mind now to send her ex-partner off with a few handmade rice balls. *They were your favorite. You always said I used* umeboshi *the best.*

Sayuri hated how much she still pined after that old life as she followed Emiko to the door. Shoes slipped onto feet. Farewells were exchanged. Sayuri watched her boy's baby blanket leave her life. Another piece of him gone. Gone with a larger piece of Sayuri's life, still dressed in the same denim jacket and worn-out T-shirts Emiko always wore.

The postman almost bumped into them.

"*Sumimasen!*" he said, carefully avoiding Emiko. The man in the Japan Post uniform only had eyes for Sayuri, whose name was emblazoned across the top of a small package in his hands. "Kawashima-*san?*"

Sayuri was too distracted to have seen Emiko go around the corner. "H... *hai.*"

The postman nodded as he handed over the package and offered a slip for Sayuri to sign. Once he had his pen back, he hopped onto his scooter and jetted down the street to the neighbor's house.

Sayuri ducked back into her apartment with her package. As soon as the door was shut and the air conditioning enveloped her once more, Sayuri sat down at the kitchen table and studied the label.

"*To Sayuri Kawashima-sama. From Miwa Ban.*"

Sayuri's eyes widened.

The contents of the package only made her widen her eyes more. When she saw the chocolates' label, her heart stopped. When she realized it was a mixture of chocolates from around Japan, her mouth salivated – and her heart leaped up her throat.

A full box of gourmet chocolates. What in the world was this for? Had Miwa thought she owed Sayuri something for the model train set? That was a thank you gift for saving her life and taking her home from the hospital! This made them totally uneven again!

It didn't help that chocolates were the universal language of flirtation. Or maybe that was Sayuri's life experiences making her think Miwa was somehow flirting with her.

No... there's no way she's like that. There's no way she likes me... Sayuri downed the last of her iced tea to get that lump down.

There was no note. Of course there was no note. Miwa had done this to torture her, hadn't she?

Sayuri helped herself to one of the chocolates and hoped she wasn't losing her mind. Again.

Chapter 9

MIWA

"If you hear this sound," the demonstrator from the alarm company hit a button on his remote that initiated a series of terrifying, squealing noises that echoed ten-fold in the subway, "then that means a fire has ignited one station over."

"Yes, and please begin evacuation procedures immediately!" Overseer Endo called over the deafening alarm. Miwa was the only one with her hands clasped over her ears – it was a wonder she understood her supervisor at all. "As we went over earlier, the first step is to calmly and orderly…"

Miwa hated these late-night training sessions with so much passion that she could almost taste the disdain in the back of her throat. Not only was it "that time" of the year again, but the rail company had installed a brand new natural disaster alarm system in every station within Tokyo's Special Wards. There were two training sessions at Amaya-jinja-guchi: the closing shift trained right after the last passenger was escorted out of the station, and the opening shift came in bright and early one hour later. The mid-shifters had their choice of closing or opening. Only a few opted to join Miwa's shift after they finished work.

"Who knows how many seconds *maximum* can pass before flames reach our station?"

Miwa's arm shot up in the air. When Endo pointed to her, she answered, "Twenty seconds is the maximum allotted time for evacuation."

"Exactly. And during morning rush hour, we can have as many as two-hundred people on this platform at any given moment. Let's go over what to do if you're standing by Exit 2 and the alarm goes off..."

I should be having my shower right now. Miwa had work again the next day. What would she do if she only got four hours of sleep because they had to do two hours of training? Okay, so it wasn't two hours, but it sure felt like it! It was a miracle she wasn't wobbling where she stood and yawning her head off!

Kohei yawned, though. Exactly once, which he politely turned his head to do. Endo caught him, anyway. The flames coming from the overseer's eyes were hot enough to set off the newly installed alarms.

"I'm *so* glad to know that these alarms work," Kohei muttered when they were finally dismissed. He and Miwa hung back as the small congregation of station representatives ambled up the steps of Exit 2. "They were barely loud enough to keep me awake for my drive home."

"We're going to be so dead tomorrow," Miwa said with a sigh. "This whole thing is a catch-22, *ne?* If we don't install the alarms and do the training, we'll absolutely have some horrible emergency one day. Yet if we do it, we all suffer."

Endo stopped halfway up the steps and swung his head toward them. "You weren't working this job when 3/11 happened. Trust me when I say you're glad we did this."

Kohei shrugged. "He's got me. Started this job in 2012."

"2014 for me." Miwa didn't want to imagine what it was like working even in Amaya-jinja-guchi when the Tohoku Earthquake hit. There had been plenty of earthquakes on the platform during Miwa's tenure, but none of them had been strong enough to knock someone in to the tracks or – God forbid – bring the station down on top of them. There had been a crack in one of the pillars after 3/11. Fixed shortly after Miwa started working there, but other attendants called it "God's Wrath and Grace" because of what it represented. The only one at the station who had been working that day was Endo, who hadn't yet become overseer.

From the way he reacted to his subordinates, Miwa wasn't keen to ask him for some harrowing tales of that day. *Bad enough I was in the middle of class.* Miwa had never gripped the leg of a desk so hard before. Her entire classroom was nothing but tears and frantic calls home.

Every generation had that "Where were you?" event that shook people to their cores. That generation's was The Great

Tohoku Earthquake of 3/11. Nothing sobered a *nomihodai* like bringing that happy nugget up.

Speaking of drinking parties... God, Miwa could really go for one right now!

Too bad everyone looked like they would rather curl up on the couch and sleep the rest of the week away than discuss a drinking party. Miwa grabbed her personal items from her locker and quickly changed into her street clothes. That bike ride home would be extra rough thanks to her heavy eyes.

Somehow, she survived. No fires. No earthquakes. No meteorites striking the Earth before her. She grazed a parked car on her street because she chose that moment to unleash a mighty yawn, but the owner would never notice. Maybe.

Mail had been jammed into her box. Miwa thought about ignoring it until later that morning, but the red envelope poking out of her box made her stop halfway through her door and groan. Red envelopes were important, right? Probably the water company ready to chew her out for a late payment. Again.

It wasn't the water company. It also wasn't her mother, harassing her because she hadn't been heard from since the last time Mrs. Ban attempted to set her daughter up with a male date.

It was a letter. From Sayuri.

You stupid dumbass. What did you think was going to happen when you mailed her chocolates? It had been a spur of the moment decision when she found a buy-one-get-one deal at the local supermarket. One was for her, of course, since she deserved some good chocolate lately. The other... well, it had sounded like a good idea at the time, when she mailed the box to Sayuri as a thank you gift for *her* thank you gift.

Except it had been too intimate, hadn't it? Women didn't send other women they barely knew *chocolates*. That was a remnant from Miwa's embarrassing past as a hopeless romantic. To her, sending a woman chocolates was natural. It meant you liked them.

"*What are you, gay?*" echoed the memories of high school.

Miwa had always kept her sexuality at a respectful distance, and it wasn't merely a "respect" she paid to society. For the longest time, she had no word for what she felt around other girls and never around the boys her mother always pushed her toward. Words like "lesbian" did not exist in her neighborhood. Lots of girls didn't like boys. It had been natural, right? Even her own mother told her, "*What woman really likes doing those things with men past a certain age?*" For the longest time, Miwa had resigned herself to having sex with boyfriends and her future husband for his sake. It wasn't until one of her high school friends shotgunned Miwa some cigarette smoke while they stood by the river that she realized kissing girls was *awesome*.

It had been all downhill from there.

Miwa collapsed on her futon while the first rays of dawn appeared beyond her window. She was covered in sweat, but decided to wait until she woke up later to shower. It would be a miracle if she ever changed her clothes.

She was too depressed to move.

Damn, this came out of nowhere. She tried to tell herself it was the fatigue from arriving home so late that made her feel this way, but she knew the truth. For a scant few days, she had allowed her heart to flutter because a pretty woman from Fujimi City had a death wish and chose to end it all on Miwa's watch.

Depression was contagious. Sayuri was patient zero.

I have the worst taste in women. Whenever Miwa condescended to entertain her sexuality for a few weeks, she dated and bedded some of the strangest women. At first, she blamed naivete. There were no dating guides for lesbians – hell, they barely had them for straight women. How was college-aged Miwa supposed to know that a woman with three tattoos, blue hair, and a tongue piercing was nothing but trouble? All that mattered was what she could do with a tongue ring!

Once in a while she went to the bars. That was the primary way of meeting other women for sex and romance, although the internet made it easier to chat with people from the comforts of her own home. *At least at the bars you know they're not messing around with you.* Miwa had been burned more than once by supposed online dates. They were all ghosts when it came time to meet.

Besides, she wasn't likely to meet the kind of woman she preferred at a *bar*. When the stars finally aligned, she would be blessed with the kind of sweet angel she thought only existed in books and movies. A woman who was as beautiful on the outside as she was on the inside. Good with kids and maybe not opposed to having some, however that worked with two women and no men involved. Okay with Miwa having a full time job and zero housekeeping skills. *I want to come home and hear* "Okaeri nasai!" *sung with the prettiest voice.* She wanted giggly kisses and tender touches while they watched TV during dinner. She wanted a gaming partner, or at least a woman who enjoyed watching Miwa play. *Why don't I ask for a billion* yen *while I'm at it?* Because she didn't want the impossible already... the woman she had been looking for was someone like Sayuri.

Too bad Sayuri was probably the straightest woman in the world. She had a kid, for fuck's sake! *God... she has a kid.* A kid that almost lost his mom one dark night.

Maybe Miwa simply set herself up for constant failure. If she crushed on straight women, then she had a reason to stay single.

I wish I wasn't single...

Those were the kinds of thoughts that lulled Miwa to sleep while the world awakened beyond her window. In those crystal clear mornings, she could hear a JR train speeding through the neighborhood with morning commuters in its cars. It was often drowned out as the day wore on, but if anything could finally convince Miwa to go to sleep... it was a train clacking against the tracks.

What woman would want to be with me? I'm a train and video game nerd. Hard enough finding women who liked other women. Finding one who could understand her more masculine interests... that *weren't* "macho?" Miwa needed to head to her neighborhood shrine on her next day off. She had a few prayers to say.

If she insisted on having an angel... well, she would need to make her pleas to the gods. Only then did she have a chance in hell of having the wedding of her faraway dreams. Kimono, white dresses, little Christian chapels… the works. Every time Miwa flipped through wedding magazines, she was convinced she had a little sliver of paradise.

Yet her reality called. As soon as she caught a few winks and took a shower that *might* make her more presentable to the public. Let alone the woman of the dreams she soon had.

Chapter 10

SAYURI

Obon was once an excuse for Sayuri to stay home or go on vacation – anything but attend to her daily life as society dictated. After the death of her son, however, it took on a new meaning that often left her bereft.

Her first *obon* with her son's spirit had been too raw. Yuma was only a few weeks dead when she lit candles, left out food, and said a few desperate prayers in a beseech for him to come visit her when the veil between the living world and the afterlife became thinner than a strand of hair. She had sworn that she felt her son's spirit with her during those tumultuous times. Emiko had been there, too, crying alongside the mother of her child and begging every god listening in Heaven to bring back their little boy.

Now Sayuri was alone. She was also devoid of tears as she opened the shrine to her son's spirit, tucked away in the corner of her living room.

She had erected it in the corner that once housed his basket of toys and picture books. They were still there, carefully arranged within the shrine or stored beneath the sturdy mahogany panels. His favorite snacks, which ranged from the customary mandarin oranges usually bequeathed to the dead to the soft candies most little boys loved, were replaced every week during the rest of the year. During *obon,* however, Sayuri replaced them every day. She didn't want her son's ghost getting bored with stale candy.

Honestly, Sayuri was impressed with herself. Not once since the start of *obon* had she cried. A few tears here and there... some sniffles that celebrated the fact she still had a mother's soul. But nothing that embarrassed her. It was as if the first anniversary of her son's death had purged her heart and soul of the most traumatic stages of grief.

She accepted the fact her son was dead. She didn't like it. It broke her heart. Made her worry that she may never have children again. Yet she had already suffered the worst grief a human could. Parents grew old and died. Siblings got into accidents. Romantic partners suffered from illnesses. Children? They were always younger than their mothers. The most unnatural sensation in the universe was outliving one's child.

Yet Sayuri had survived. The more distance between the present and the first anniversary of Yuma's death, the more she realized that she had also almost died that night.

As All Our Fires Burn

A habit I need to break. The police told Sayuri that if her car had been one foot forward, she could have been in serious trouble. Either way, Yuma was dead. The fact she survived with only a few scratches and two bruised ribs was something she had to accept as well.

Perhaps it wasn't an evil trick by the universe. Maybe it was fate. Sayuri was still needed for something else.

Not that she was in the market to discover *what* anytime soon. For now, her goal was to make it through one day at a time. Her life was still full of children. Other people's, but...

She knelt on a pillow before the shrine and bowed her head. Both hands grasped her thighs, but she wasn't prepared to pray or make a wish to the universe. Instead, she blinked away the strange images before her mind and reminded herself to light the candles before she forgot one of the most important parts of *obon*. If her son was to come get his candy, he needed to be shown the way.

Sayuri lit a match and brought both candles to a flame. She clapped twice before bowing her head.

All around the country were families and solitary individuals following similar rituals, begging their lost loved ones to come back for a few nights of the year. "*Why is* obon *in the summer?*" Sayuri had asked her mother as a child. "*Why do we have to light a bunch of candles when it's already so hot?*" Her mother hadn't known the real answer, of course. She had simply said, "*I guess it's because everyone used to go outside at night. You know, back before they had air conditioning to stay comfortable in their houses. If everyone is outside, then the ghosts can get them.*"

The older she got, the more Sayuri thought that it didn't make much sense, but her mother had never been good at providing the answers Sayuri sought. *"Why is the sky blue?" "Why do we always eat curry on Tuesday nights?" "Why doesn't Matsuda-sensei like me?" "Why do girls have to bleed every month?" "Why don't you want me to be happy, even if it's with another woman?" "Why did my son have to die?"*

Sayuri last saw her mother a few month's after Yuma's death. It had been shortly after Emiko moved out and moved on with someone else. Mrs. Kawashima had dared to suggest that Sayuri had been given a fresh start on the road to righteousness.

While Sayuri had appreciated her mother's presence during the toughest weeks of her life, she knew that her mother wouldn't be much help once it was time to move on.

As if summoned from the ether, the image of Miwa in her uniform appeared in Sayuri's mind.

What?

It certainly hadn't been there a moment ago. It also wasn't very appropriate, considering what Sayuri was doing! *I don't recall inviting you into my thoughts, Ms. Ban.* Yet Miwa wasn't up to any mischief in Sayuri's mind.

She was extending her gloved hand, asking Sayuri if she was all right.

No. I'm not alright, Miwa-san. I'm lost. Station attendants weren't only for minding the place and making sure nobody did anything funny. They gave out directions. Directions Sayuri sorely needed.

As All Our Fires Burn

I'm going to lose my life if I keep going down this path, Miwa-san. A year ago, Sayuri would have been fine with that. What did she care, as long as she was with her son again? Now, with the fog of grief lifted and her brain ready to accept the fact that it was time to move on, even if her heart always lagged a little behind... she needed guidance from an outside source. Her mother was the last person to call for advice. Emiko was a living remnant of a painful past, and had made it clear that she and Sayuri no longer had anything in common. Coworkers were for talking about the kids at school and where to go for vacation. Neighbors like Mariko Shimazaki lived in bubbles where everything followed a certain path, and if someone went off it – let alone the *schoolteacher* – then it was grounds for dismissal. Sayuri would be signing her termination papers if she told Mariko anything about her personal life. It had been difficult enough convincing everyone involved with the elementary school that Emiko was "just" an old friend helping out with the kid in exchange for a cheap place to live.

Sayuri had decided to avoid love. Finding Emiko and falling in love with her – let alone deep enough to have a child together – was a once in a lifetime thing. Sayuri never pursued relationships, anyway. She was terrified of the gay bars in Shinjuku, and going online was too dangerous with her job. What if somebody recognized her?

No... she couldn't be... would she? Sayuri didn't want to believe that Miwa was more like her than what appeared on the surface. It was easier to believe that she was another, regular woman who would judge Sayuri like everyone else did.

So why did Sayuri continue to torture herself with these images in her head? Especially at such an inappropriate time!

She sent me chocolates... That had been what really set Sayuri's imagination in motion. Receiving that small box of gourmet chocolates was like being sent a bouquet of a dozen red roses. On top of that, what business did Miwa have helping a stranger out of the hospital? It couldn't have been pressure from her job. She made it sound like nobody knew she was there.

So why? *Why?* Other than to torture poor Sayuri?

Yet wouldn't it be wonderful to have something like romance again? With a woman as pretty and unique as Miwa? It would also be an interesting coincidence to date another woman who had a job in the railway industry. Emiko had been a formidable mechanic, but Miwa was an *attendant!* The only thing more impressive was being the conductor! Attendant was one of those careers kids like Yuma dreamed of achieving. To be a woman in such a male dominated field... how could Sayuri not be impressed with Miwa? Even if her apartment was old, cramped, messy, and smelled a little too much of take-out garbage melting in the summer heat...

Nobody was perfect.

What would it be like to be Miwa's friend? Was she even interested in Sayuri's friendship? Of course not. Sayuri was the crazy lady who almost killed herself while on Miwa's watch. Who would want to be friends with that?

Let alone something more?

Yet no matter how many times Sayuri attempted to redirect her brain to more appropriate pastures, it continued to return to a woman named Miwa Ban. The petite height that somehow commanded enough presence to be seen on a station platform. The hair that would be fun to play with, whether it was in a tight bun for work or hanging loose around her shoulders when she was off the clock. The intriguing face that was both youthful and serious enough to gain respect at her job. The fact that she could go from prim and proper station attendant, in her white gloves, brisk uniform, and hard countenance to a gamer girl who sustained herself on cups of noodles and iced tea from the convenience store. Sayuri was intrigued by both sides. Being intrigued led to other inappropriate fantasies. The first of their kind since suffering too much trauma a year ago.

There were few things that could penetrate those wandering thoughts. Smoke was one of them.

Sayuri's eyes snapped open the moment she smelled it. While she had been daydreaming about a woman she barely knew, one of the candles had tipped over and started a small fire on the burgundy cloth draped over the top of the shrine.

"*Shimatta!*" Sayuri grabbed the vase holding a few flowers and dumped the dirty water on top of the small flickering flames before they could grow bolder. Within five seconds a fire had raged to life and been snuffed out again. Only now a large, smoldering patch was left behind on the cloth. At least it hadn't touched any other part of the shrine. Although Sayuri dreaded to see the damage to the wood.

Adrenaline fueled her to clean up the mess as best as she could, all while berating herself for falling to temptations while she was supposed to be venerating her dead son's soul.

"I'm so sorry," she said to the photograph of her son upon the shrine, untouched by the flames. "I don't know what came over me."

Reckless fantasies. That's what had happened to her.

She had discovered the punishment for such wishful thinking. Whether she was punished for thinking those thoughts about Miwa in particular, or for thinking them about *anyone,* she had no idea. All Sayuri knew was that consequences always came for her whenever she thought she had found something worth living for. Those consequences usually burned the last of her dreams.

Chapter 11

MIWA

Miwa's hopes for a drinking party came to fruition Friday night, when Shinnosuke Oda and shift overseer Wataru Endo approached her and Kohei at the end of their shift. "My in-laws are visiting," the overseer brusquely explained. "I'd rather drink and raise our camaraderie than have my mother-in-law ask why she doesn't have a grandson yet."

Nobody mentioned that he had three perfectly healthy daughters, the oldest of which often came by the station to study the physics of trains for her middle school's science club. Endo never said a praising word about the teenager who looked like a young, female version of himself, but he always spared her a beaming glance whenever he could take his eyes off the goings-on of Amaya-jinja-guchi Station.

The eldest Endo daughter would not be accompanying the closing shift to the nearest izakaya, however. Nor would she be up late enough to witness her father stumbling home, drunk off his ass while his father-in-law likewise ambled home drunk enough to piss in the bushes outside the house.

But that was a tale Miwa would hear through Shinnosuke on Monday. For now, she was a mixture of excited to blow off some steam and dreading her role in the festivities.

Technically, she was still the freshest recruit among them, although she had worked with this small crew for over three years. That alone was enough to make her the temporary slave at the drinking party, doomed to pour every round of drinks and offer her superiors their selection of appetizers while keeping the scraps for herself. Compounded with being a woman… well, she had to hand it to her coworkers for never sexually harassing her. At the same time, however, she was far from "one of the boys." Once the first pitcher of beer came to their table in the smokiest corner of the cramped restaurant, everyone looked to Miwa for the honors.

Yeah. Honors.

"That's our diligent *kouhai*." To his credit, Shinnosuke focused on her employment in the company. At the end of the day, Miwa was no office lady. Nor was she receptionist, not that she saw much difference between them and the recognizable OLs filling the ladies' only trains in the morning. "Look at her finesse! Nobody pours a glass like our Ban."

"Dunno about that," Endo said, scratching his late-night stubble. "You used to be a lot faster back in the day."

As All Our Fires Burn

Kohei laughed. Ever since Miwa began working at Amaya-jinja-guchi, he had thanked his luckiest of stars that his tenure as the youngest on the staff had come to a quick end. Meanwhile, Miwa was still waiting three years later.

"It's my honor to look after my *senpai*." Miwa hoped the growl underlying her words couldn't be heard. Luckily for her, the izakaya was so busy with laughter, drinking, and smoking that it was almost impossible to hear Kohei right next to her. Yet hearing her phone blow up with a message from an old college friend was no problem! Of course it had to happen while she was pouring Station Master Endo's glass. Her hand jerked enough to spill some beer foam onto his share of the wasabi-laced edamame. "Ah…"

"What was that about finesse, again?" Endo asked Shinnosuke.

"Jeez, Ban," Kohei said with a chuckle. "We all think he's a tyrant at times, but do you gotta go and make his hands sticky?"

Endo laughed. That was all the rest of them needed to know that the mood of the evening was nothing but fine.

Beer was beer, so unlike the appetizers that came out one after another, the bottoms of the pitchers weren't as bad as the worst pieces of gyoza or clumps of seasoned rice. Alcohol also did an admirable job of loosening up bodies and tongues. Endo put himself up on the chopping block when he was so tipsy that his chopsticks constantly dropped the finest gyoza on the top of the stack. Eventually, it landed on the floor, where nobody could enjoy it.

"Well, shit," Endo said. "Why couldn't it be my own mother at home? She could feed it to me, instead!"

Miwa was the first one to guffaw in disbelief. When her superior laughed back into her face, Kohei and Shinnosuke gradually joined in, although neither seemed to get the sex-based joke.

"That's the nice thing to unite us all," Shinnosuke said, mouth half-full of pot stickers. "We've all got mothers that would probably show up to stuff food in our faces. Or maybe my mom has a little too much Kansai blood in her. They constantly feed everyone down there!"

"How do you think I got this big?" Kohei gestured to his robust figure, which cut fine in his station uniform but looked more its age when he wore jeans and a sweatshirt like that night. "I was my mother's only child. She wouldn't stop stuffing food in my mouth."

"You played baseball in high school and college, right?" Shinnosuke asked. "You'd make a nice and hefty catcher."

"The way she fed me, you'd think I was training for sumo!"

More laughter erupted around the table. When everyone turned to Miwa, she assumed they wanted their drinks topped off. Yet when she picked up the half-empty pitcher of beer, her boss asked, "Your mother a good cook, Ban?"

She hesitated before easing the nozzle into Kohei's glass beside her. "She was decent."

"Decent? Was?"

She shrugged before putting the pitcher back down onto the table. "I don't talk to her much anymore. I doubt she'd be in a hurry to feed me right now." Unlike her coworkers, Miwa didn't reminisce about the food of her youth. She hadn't been lying when she said her mother was a decent cook. Perfectly edible. Nobody she was in a hurry to emulate.

"*Sou ka...*" Shinnosuke sucked breath through the gap of his two front teeth. "You're an enigma, Ban-*san*."

Brows raised while she sipped her beer. "Excuse me?"

Endo slapped his hand on his subordinate's shoulder with a grin that subtracted ten years off his visage. "I think what our friend means is that you're the kind of woman that gets people talking. Even if you're really a regular gal, *sou?*"

All eyes were on her. Miwa stiffened, hand clasped around her glass of beer and vision darting between the expectant faces of her curious coworkers. Endo was sure of himself, but Shinnosuke nervously chuckled, and Kohei looked like he had no idea where he lived. Miwa couldn't decide if this was a trap of some kind.

She didn't trust people when they pried into her business. It usually didn't end well.

"People talk about you," Endo explained. "Some of the regular commuters have asked me about you." He smacked his lips as if that were the most ridiculous thing. "Usually the aunties and uncles who hang out at the shrine. Don't worry, most of the comments are good!"

Most, huh... Miwa tried not to think about it.

"*What kind of woman wants this job?*' most of them ask, not that it's any of their business." Endo downed the last of his beer and held out his glass for Miwa to refill. The pitcher was drained. Kohei summoned the waitress to order another. She was only more than happy to load them up with more beer. "Though I gotta admit, when my own manager informed me that a woman was being transferred to my humble little station, I was rather shocked. I had never worked with a woman since I started this job almost twenty years ago."

Miwa rubbed the back of her ear. A nervous tic her mother used to hound her to quit. *Not as much as she hounded me to quit other things, though...* "I'm aware of the stares I get."

"Why *did* you go into this business?" Kohei asked with a slight slur of his words. "Think you told me once, but I can't remember for the life of me."

She refrained from rolling her eyes. "Why did *you* get into it? Because trains are cool."

"But it's a..."

"You think little girls don't get as enamored with trains as boys do?" Endo said. "*Che.* You're an idiot."

"Next she'll be saying she played baseball, too," Kohei muttered.

"Actually, I was in the anime club in high school."

A chorus of her coworkers shouting "*Otaku!*" commenced in time for the waitress to return with a fresh pitcher of beer. Miwa let it slide. Not the first time she heard that word hurled in her direction.

"What's your favorite anime?" Shinnosuke asked, his face sizing up how old she was and what the big hits of her childhood may have been. "Sailor Moon?"

"Dragonball, actually."

Everyone fell backward while shouting, "Dragonball?"

"You're one tough woman, Ban," Kohei said in disbelief. "You sure you weren't meant to be a boy?"

"Now I know what the old aunties mean when they ask how you're gonna attract a husband wearing the uniform." Endo laughed as if that were the funniest contribution. "Think they don't realize that you're really a man underneath there. Anime club… Dragonball… don't you like video games, too?"

Miwa showed them her ire by pouring herself the first serving from the pitcher. "I dabble with the PlayStation," she said through clenched teeth. "Can we pick on someone else now? I hear Oda-*san* has…"

"I gotta watch out for my daughter," Endo said. "She really likes trains too. Says she wants to be an engineer one day! The kind that builds trains, not drives them. Maybe I better make sure she's not watching anime or asking for video games. Otherwise, her mother will get on my ass for allowing us to raise an unmarriable daughter."

The men laughed. Between the alcohol and the free-for-all in Miwa's direction, she was liable to slam her chin upon her hand and pretend that none of them existed. Not that she could get away without offending anyone, least of all her supervisor who could request her transfer to a worse post. Amaya-jinja-guchi wasn't exactly the *big time* in their company. A demotion would send her way out into the 'burbs. The commute alone would be brutal.

"You got a boyfriend, Ban-*san*?" Kohei asked. Big words for a man constantly having girlfriend trouble. Didn't he know she would fling it right back in his face? "Does he know he's dating a boy?"

Her silence spoke volumes. Yet she couldn't bring herself to play along with this game any longer. *I only wanted to go drinking... jeez...*

"Uh oh," Shinnosuke said. "She ain't got a boyfriend."

"Sheesh, Ban!" Endo shook his head. "You can't be such a weirdo and *not* have a boyfriend! You've gotta balance yourself out! No wonder your mother isn't feeding you. She's gotta think you're a lost cause."

Everyone exploded into laughter again. Even Kohei, who had been swallowing one of the last edamame when he heard the funniest thing of the night. The man was choking beside Miwa, but she could barely bring herself to smack him on the back and offer him more beer. She only did it so she wouldn't get into more trouble.

The conversation quickly turned to Kohei's foibles, and their coworkers spared no expense tearing him apart with laughter on their lips. Yet unlike Miwa, he laughed along and fed them more fodder for making him feel like the biggest loser in the izakaya. *This is supposed to be normal.* Miwa looked around the restaurant, full of businessmen in suits, construction workers in jumpsuits, and groups of old friends splitting the costs of their dinner into equal parts. This was how camaraderie was built in a society that asked everyone to be on their best behavior and exude only the politest of manners to each other, let alone to their superiors. Alcohol, tobacco, and fried food was the perfect excuse to lower their walls and get to know one another without the threat of offense. These people were the closest things to real life friends Miwa had.

How sad was that?

"Tanaka can't keep a girlfriend," Shinnosuke snorted when Kohei finished laughing about how he offended his last girlfriend by never putting the toilet seat down, "and Ban can't get a boyfriend. Future generations are useless!"

"Maybe they should date each other, huh?" Endo said.

Kohei blushed. Miwa drank more.

By the time they split the check and stumbled out of the izakaya, Miwa was too drunk to ride her bike home. What was usually a half hour ride through the dark, residential streets of Tokyo was now a little over an hour of walking and greeting the dawn when she finally pulled her tipsy ass to her apartment door. She had almost abandoned her bike at multiple intersections while stewing over how her own coworkers treated her interests and lack of a boyfriend.

The worst thing? It wasn't surprising. At all.

The only good thing to come out of it was the desire to change her situation. With drunk bravado filling her intoxicated veins, Miwa slumped down at her coffee table and plugged her dying phone into the wall. Only then did she have the power to do something so unbelievably stupid that sober-Miwa would travel back in time to kick her dumb ass.

She looked up Sayuri's phone number. Because the more her coworkers goaded her single life and called her a boy, the more inclined she was to stick it to them by pursuing the first woman to romantically cross her path in years.

Romantic! That's it! That's what we have! Not too difficult to discover Sayuri Kawashima's phone number once Miwa logged into her company's staff portal and reviewed the most recent forms she had filled out. Between the mother who temporarily lost her child and request for bathroom repairs, there was the incident report about a woman passing out on the platform.

Miwa switched to her SMS window and attempted to sound sober. It didn't work.

"*Heeey. This is Miwa. Remember me? The woman from the station? We should meet up sometime soon. Have some tea or something.*" Yeah, tea sounded fancy! "*Assuming you're not too busy, of course. I know you live all the way out in Saitama, so how about we meet in the middle, in Ikebukuro? You live on Tobu-Tojo, right?*"

She hit send before she lost the nerve. Two minutes later, Miwa collapsed into her futon without bothering to change her clothes. When she woke up a few hours later, she was mortified to realize what she had done.

She was even more mortified to have received a reply.

"*Very kind of you to invite me out, Miwa-san…*" Miwa didn't have the courage to read beyond the preview. She had some throwing up to do, first.

Chapter 12

SAYURI

Although Sayuri had plenty of occasions to dress up in her outing best, that Sunday was the first time in a long while that she did so with the flutter of nervousness in her stomach. She pulled out a skirt she bought at a department store sale two years ago – back when she was celebrating losing the last of her baby weight when her son entered the terrible twos. It was elegant in length and texture, and the white flowers with vines crawling ever-so-lightly up to the waist reminded her of her grandmother's trellis in a garden of wisterias and gardenias. *I haven't worn this since I had lunch with my college friends.* Seven months ago, when she was still raw with grief. She had put on her best face and pretended that everything was fine. She hadn't lost a child. Her partner wasn't about to leave her for another woman. Everyone at work didn't look at her with extreme pity and ask if she might like to teach the older children again.

On that warm Sunday, she decided to pair it with a plain white blouse that covered most of her torso but allowed the breeze to tickle her skin. She brushed her hair a hundred times – making sure to count each stroke – before clipping a few strands behind each ear. The one thing she could commend about her appearance were her high cheekbones, and they were best shown off with her hair pulled back.

I'm acting like this lunch will mean anything... She stared at the top of her vanity, a cup of coffee turning cold within hand's reach. *She was clearly drunk when she asked me out for...* Out? Asked her *out?* What, was Sayuri nuts? There was no way this was a date.

Although she would certainly like it to be.

Stop setting yourself up for disappointment. Miwa wasn't gay. Even if she was, how could she be interested in someone like Sayuri, who was more than a humble mess? *The way we met alone...* Then again, Miwa was the one who showed up to the hospital to take that mess home. She invited Sayuri into her apartment for a few minutes. She texted her at four in the morning, asking her out... for lunch.

Lunch in Ikebukuro. It was the exact situation that either screamed "old friends meeting again" or "new couple attempting to impress each other."

No, no, no! Sayuri shook her head in admonishment to her reflection. *She asked to have lunch in Ikebukuro as a courtesy to me...*

As All Our Fires Burn

Sayuri lived way out in Saitama, the suburbs of Tokyo. The fathers of her students often worked in the city and commuted more than an hour. The mothers joked that they were lucky to see their husbands for more than two hours a day. Meanwhile, Miwa was a city woman who had her own apartment in the heart of all the action! She could have easily asked Sayuri to come to *her,* and nobody would have thought anything of it. Of course people met in Tokyo! Ikebukuro Station was a straight shot on the Tobu-Tojo Line from Fujimi Station. She could even take the express and be there in less than half an hour!

Sayuri groaned. Why was she doing this to herself?

Because I'm desperate. There. She put it out there. She was agreeing to go out with a drunk station attendant while wearing her best clothing because she was *desperate.* Sayuri lost her best friend when Emiko left. Since then, she had been too depressed to make new friends, let alone start dating again. Who was she to turn down a friend who showed up in her face? Miwa was doing all the work! Showing up! Inviting her out! Sayuri would be daft to turn her down.

She picked up her phone. A little voice in the back of her head said that there would be a message from Miwa, canceling their lunch. No such message was on her phone, however. The only notification was from the city government, informing residents that certain streets in a few neighborhoods would be inaccessible while repairs were conducted.

Good thing Sayuri was taking the train.

She inhaled a deep breath for courage before grabbing her purse and heading out the door. Her brain was so single-focused that she almost forgot to backtrack and turn off her air conditioner.

"*Ara, atsui desu ne,* Kawashima-*sensei?*" Mariko was the only other in the street, her watering can a wilting sight in her hands. She wore her hair back in a ponytail – the first time Sayuri had ever seen such a thing on the neighbor. Not that she could blame her. The heat immediately beat upon Sayuri's clothed body, making her want to retreat back and blast the air conditioner. Bad enough she would soon be returning to a classroom that had no such thing. Yet Mariko wore a long-sleeved blouse and a yellow Anpanman apron over her clothes. Typical for a mother who had a son with an affinity for bread-loving heroes. Shota was nowhere to be seen, however. Probably either cooped up in the cool house playing video games, or at a friend's house doing the same thing.

I remember when I used to wonder what games my son would like… Being a schoolteacher meant Sayuri had insider knowledge on all the most recent, trendy video games. Mario had been the coolest thing when she was a child. Then Pokémon swept through the '90s. These days, she saw all sorts of characters, including the classic plumbers and pocket monsters. Sayuri had never played a Final Fantasy game, but she knew the plots to each one thanks to her students and the other teachers who filled her in so she wouldn't look like a loser in her classes.

"*Deshou?*" Sayuri already pulled her handkerchief from her purse and dabbed her face. "You're such a good homemaker, Shimazaki-*san*," she continued with a smile. "Still outside in the hot sun, tending to your garden!"

As All Our Fires Burn

"Someone has to do it. Won't be my husband or my son." Mariko nodded to her neighbor. "Where are you off to on such a hot day?"

"Heading to the train station. I'm meeting someone in Ikebukuro."

"*Ho!* Should be a lot of fun!" Mariko acquired a mischievous grin that made Sayuri more than a little nervous. "Not going on a date, are you, Kawashima-*sensei*? You know what they say about dating during *obon*."

No, she couldn't say she did. Nor was she quick to deny that she was off on a date.

Mariko continued without any prompting. "They say you might end up with a ghost!"

"I know for a fact that this person is not a ghost," Sayuri said.

"So it *is* a date?"

The corners of Sayuri's mouth twitched. Of course, that could have been from the sweat beading down her face. "You didn't hear it from me, Shimazaki-*san*."

She took her leave before Mariko could pry any more. Bad enough she might blab to someone at the school about Sayuri dating again. If people found out it was a woman? Easy enough to brush Miwa off as nothing but a friend. Probably was what she only was, anyway. Assuming she really had been drunk early Saturday morning and that wasn't her true nature…

Sayuri realized what she was doing as soon as she stood on the train platform. The prerecorded voice announced that the express train taking her to Ikebukuro was about to arrive. Yet the live voice, straight from the mouth of an attendant, sounded nothing like the men Sayuri was used to hearing whenever she hopped a train somewhere.

It was a woman. When she turned around a few seconds later, she saw another one in uniform directing passengers to please wait behind the yellow line. Otherwise, they might fall into the tracks, and they wouldn't be any better than Sayuri Kawashima, the woman who got dates by bringing whole train lines to a stop.

***

Ikebukuro Station was a level of hell that Sayuri tried to avoid.

Technically, Shinjuku Station was bigger and busier than Ikebukuro. Trivia games the world over loved to ask, "*What is the busiest train station in the world?*" and a lucky few would know that it was the legendary Shinjuku. Yet few outside of Japan had even heard of Ikebukuro, where manners and decorum went to die.

Oh, Sayuri was used to navigating the throngs of people during peak times at a train station. She did it all the time in Fujimi, sometimes when all she wanted to do was pass *through* the station or, heaven forbid, go around it. There were tips a girl picked up when she grew up in a culture that prided itself for its robust transportation system. She had even taught her son a few manners as soon as he was old enough to walk and talk.

As All Our Fires Burn

"*Bumping into people is unavoidable.*" She said that while Yuma cried against the wall. A woman with a large suitcase had bowled him over, and instead of stopping to say sorry, she had continued to hurl down the hallway as if getting to her destination was more important than ensuring the safety of a small child. "*All you can do is say you're sorry.*"

How to navigate trains and their stations were but few of the lessons she had begun to rehearse when her son met his untimely end. "*Don't be afraid to bump into people, but don't do it on purpose. That's rude.*" "*Do not stop in the middle of the crowd. Keep the flow going. You can always turn around later.*" "*Don't look at your phone and walk at the same time. Maybe you can do that on a sidewalk, but never in a busy train station!*" She had yet to give her son access to any LCD screens, however. That was something she and Emiko argued about toward the end, because Emiko's parenting style was to let her phone or a tablet babysit the kid for a few minutes while she caught up on chores or sleep. "*Ask the station attendant for advice if you need to. Giving directions is one of their many jobs.*" So was saving unfortunate lives.

She wished she listened to her own advice now!

Sometimes, Sayuri swore that Ikebukuro was a bigger mess than Shinjuku. While the station layout was fairly straightforward and processed not as *nearly* many people, the halls were narrower and the crowds more determined to transfer lines *now*. Sayuri couldn't remember which of the many exits she wanted. All she knew was that the moment she stepped off the train at its terminus, she was doomed to follow the crowds wherever they willed.

She was shoulder-to-shoulder with businessmen, tourists, students, and fashionable women such as herself. More than one bag bumped into her arm. The thunderous sound of thousands of feet tramping upon the floor almost deafened her. Body odor, perfume, and fried foods filled the air. People called out to one another, attempting to touch while a herd of stallions passed between them. Blood burst in Sayuri's mouth when someone shoved into her and she accidentally bit her tongue. With one hand pressed against her cheek, she weaved between the thinning crowd dispersing at the west exit. Freedom came when she hit daylight and held herself against a wall. Only then could she assess the damage to her tongue and determine if someone had stolen her purse.

She groaned when she looked at her GPS and realized she wanted the *east* exit.

There was no waiting for departing passengers to leave the station and taking the precious few minutes to run through without trouble. Not when there were a dozen lines coming in and out of the station, and each one staggered with the others, ensuring no rest for the weary traveler.

"*Gomen...*" she texted Miwa. "*I'm running behind. I'm at Ikebukuro Station, but I went out the wrong exit. Please give me a few more minutes.*"

She didn't wait for a reply. Not when she had to reorient herself and try yet again to get to her destination.

This time, Sayuri did not allow the other passengers to bully her. She kept one eye on the yellow signs directing her to the proper exit and another on everyone around her, as if every old woman with a cane and businessman with a briefcase were her mortal enemies, prepared to lop off her leg or give her a concussion. She stayed far away from ticket gates to avoid the biggest of the surges in the crowd, but it didn't save her from the shoppers filing out of department stores and the little shops that dotted the walls. One shopper didn't watch where she stepped and almost knocked into Sayuri. The only reason they avoided contact was because she expertly dodged the woman. Perhaps her purse grazed her, but... who cared at that point?

The things I'm doing for a date!

She had to think of it that way now. It was what inspired her to get her ass out the east exit in one piece! Once she accomplished that, she could find anything, anywhere.

Or so she thought, until she encountered crosswalks that sprouted off in a million different directions. At least she had the freedom to pull out her phone and bring up her GPS again.

The café Miwa suggested was as the top of a building a few minutes away. Sayuri followed her GPS as she traveled down the busy streets of Ikebukuro, avoiding shop employees hawking the latest wares and tourists stepping back to take yet more pictures of the same old thing. *Tokyo in a nutshell.* Sayuri didn't envy people who lived in the middle of the city. She would take her mediocre neighborhoods any time after this!

By the time she reached the café terrace in the deceptively quiet ninth floor of an otherwise nondescript office building, Sayuri was so sweaty that she searched for a restroom before daring to show her face to Miwa.

Too bad someone had already made it there before her.

A hand shot up into the air from the corner of the room. Miwa had commandeered a table between two walls of windows, and the only thing stopping a server from showing Sayuri to her own table was a cry of, "*Hey!*"

She certainly is genki… That was a thought Sayuri usually reserved for children. Particularly, boys who had too much energy and took it out on each other and whatever adult happened to be in their way of raucous rampage.

Miwa wasn't on a rampage, however. Sayuri was more than familiar with how girls expressed their excitement. That tone and the look in her youthful visage had nothing to do with screaming out superhero words and everything to do with girlish frivolity.

Sayuri sighed in relief. She told herself the hard part was over. A woman that happy to see her wouldn't care about the sweat on Sayuri's brow or the wrinkles in her blouse. If anything, Miwa looked amazed that Sayuri had shown up at all.

Why should she keep Miwa waiting?

Chapter 13

SAYURI

"I've never been here before," Miwa said. "I think I might have underdressed."

Sayuri was taken aback to hear that, only because Miwa looked so *fashionable*. A far cry from the frumpy clothes bedecking Sayuri's uncomfortable body. The air conditioning inside the café wasn't affecting her quickly enough. Didn't help that she had yet to steal away to the bathroom and rinse off. "I like your outfit," she said in a near whisper.

Miwa went from slightly embarrassed to grinning like one of Sayuri's schoolgirls within a second. It made her outfit stand out even more: a pair of slim, black leggings and a green and black plaid shirt-dress that showed off her tomboyish style while still asserting her feminine side. Her hair was pulled back into a low ponytail that kept the sweat off the back of her neck. A silver cross hung from her neck, but Sayuri somehow doubted that Miwa was religious. *Although I wonder if she carries an* omamuri *in her wallet...* Sayuri carried two. One for ensuring the passing of a soul of a loved one to the other side, and one for good driving. Clearly, she needed it.

"It's because you're so used to being dressed up for work," Sayuri then said. "You have such a nice uniform and look so kempt. I mean, you look more than kempt right now!" She was beet red by the time the server brought a glass of water. "Sorry. I'm flustered from getting here."

"I should be the one apologizing," Miwa said. "It's because I chose this place that you're so flustered."

"No, no!" Sayuri realized that this was heading nowhere quite quickly. They would spend the next ten minutes taking on the blame for this situation instead of having any meaningful conversation if one of them didn't do something to stop it. *I think I might be the older one... so I should do it.* "I'm simply not as familiar with navigating train stations as you are, Miwa-*san*."

"I think you forget that I work at a nowhere-station. The only heavy traffic we get is on New Year's when the shrine bursts at the seams. Well..." Miwa glanced upward in thought. "Guess *obon* makes it kinda popular right now, too."

"You don't get *obon* off?"

"No. Train lines have to keep running, you know." Miwa shrugged. "I also work Golden Week and New Year's. Easy enough for me to take on the responsibility when I have no family."

As All Our Fires Burn

"*Sou ka...*" Made enough sense. Still, Sayuri couldn't help but pity the people who worked on holidays. While she appreciated them for taking care of her when she went shopping or traveled somewhere on those days, how could she help but pity them? She came from a world where she got one whole month off a year. *Well, not technically. I still have to go into the office sometimes.* She still wasn't finished with her lesson plans for fall term, and a fat stack of summer homework books would soon be on her desk to grade. Sayuri had been avoiding going outside in the heat, because the teacher's room at school wasn't always air conditioned. "Still, *taihen, desu ne?* It can't be easy dealing with so many people every day."

"You get used to it. Didn't you say you were a schoolteacher? I'd think that's crazier!"

"Ah, yes. This year I teach the third year students at my elementary school, but I've taught many grades over the years." Sayuri had almost forgotten what it was like to teach the older kids. Usually, her youthful demeanor and hyper-feminine style got her pigeonholed to younger students who were looking for a mother figure at school. *I didn't mind it until...* Thinking about her son so much couldn't be helped.

"*Sugoi.* I could never be a teacher. Kids don't like me."

"Whaaat?" Sayuri laughed. "But you must look so cool to so many kids where you work!"

"You might be surprised how many hide behind their mothers. Even the older ones."

"I find that hard to believe." Sayuri opened the menu and perused the cakes and teas offered. *They have cheesecake here?*

Wow. "Then again, I know children pretty well. Maybe they're shy because you look *so* cool."

Miwa's chuckle borderlined disbelief. "How long have you been teaching?"

"Oh, almost ten years? Started right out of college, although I took a year off when I..." she swallowed, before remembering she had already mentioned her son in front of Miho before. "My district was kind enough to give me a year's maternity leave when I had my son."

Miwa looked as if she were trapped between surprise and awe – in case Sayuri was not aware that a woman could be both. "Ten... years?" That was the first thing out of her mouth. The second was asking for a fresh iced coffee from the waitress, while Sayuri asked for a matcha latte and a slice of the cheesecake. Both were a bit too expensive for her tastes, but how often did she get to have lunch with a friend anymore? "Wow," Miwa whispered, once they were alone again. "I didn't realize you were older than me."

"May I ask how old you are, Miwa-*san?*"

That sheepish tinge to Miwa's cheeks brought out the green in her plaid shirt. "Twenty-seven," she muttered.

"Ah, you aren't so old!" Wait, that wasn't what she was worried about. "Or so young, for that matter..."

"Still, a bit younger than you."

"I'm only thirty-two."

"You look much younger."

"Do I?" Sayuri attempted to take the compliment, but she found it more than a little difficult to believe that she looked younger than Miwa, the woman with such a casually youthful energy and a style that went well with someone taking the day off from hard work. "I always thought I dressed like a housewife." She left out the *well-to-do* part swimming in her head. That's what her old college friends told her when they had lunch last time, but Sayuri figured her demeanor had something to do with it.

"And I dress like a college student. What a pair we make, Sayuri-*san*."

After a pause, they both laughed.

"I'm sure you like to dress this way because your job has you in such a pristine uniform all day," Sayuri mused. She also thanked the waitress for bringing the latte and slice of cheesecake that had her name on it.

"Yeah, it gets a bit stuffy, especially down there in the trenches. The air conditioner doesn't always work way down there. Can't tell you how many times I wished I could rip that uniform off my body and scream in relief that I was finally free. Then I remember how hard I worked to get into that uniform. I still remember the day I was handed my first one."

"How long has it been?" Only fair to ask since Sayuri had already divulged she'd been teaching for a decade.

"A little over three years. I'm still a baby in my company, let alone my station."

"Ah... I suppose ten years isn't very long in your industry. In teaching, I've already seen so many young teachers come and go. You either make it a long time, or you quit after two years." Sayuri shrugged. "A lot of people have grand ideas about being a teacher, but it's a lot harder than you might anticipate, especially if the kids don't take to you."

"Your students must love you."

Sayuri snorted into her latte. The foam blew over the edge of her cup and settled into a napkin on the table. It took her so long to notice it that by the time she did, Miwa had already handed her another napkin. "*Gomen,*" she apologized. "I don't know if my students really like me, but they respect me enough. I'm good with kids."

Miwa stared at Sayuri's hand as she mopped up her spilled foam. What was she looking for? More mess? Age spots? A wedding ring? *Now, don't get carried away…* Sayuri was the kind of homemaker who would get lost in fantasies of weddings, honeymoons, and little wooden houses tucked into quiet neighborhoods out in the 'burbs. She didn't need to put that pressure on Miwa after only one… no, this wasn't a date. She had to keep reminding herself of that. *She doesn't even know I'm gay. I probably shouldn't share that so readily.* Yet when she looked at Miwa, dressed in her tomboyish clothes and exuding a calm energy that reminded Sayuri so much of Emiko… ah, that was it, wasn't it? Sayuri easily associated this woman with an ex-girlfriend who was comfortable in her sexuality. Sayuri was attracted to that kind of person. She may not have pursued men, but she certainly enjoyed the company of a woman who was a bit tougher and more masculine than herself. They didn't have to be full-butch like many of Emiko's friends from the bars… but not giving a single fuck about what society thought of their lack of makeup was a huge bonus.

As All Our Fires Burn

"May I ask where your son is today?"

Sayuri nearly dropped her cup. Instead, she dropped her dirty napkin on top of her untouched slice of cheesecake.

What should she do? Tell Miwa the truth? Label herself as a bereaved mother, and then reveal that the night they met had been the one-year anniversary of the accident? Yeah, right. Sayuri didn't want to bring down the mood. She didn't want those unfortunate labels attached to her person so shortly after meeting Miwa. Besides, it was her own fault for bringing up Yuma before. She already had her chance to tell the truth. What was wrong with putting it off for now?

"He's at home," Sayuri squeaked. Partially the truth. A part of his ashes were on his shrine that she almost burned down the other night. Right next to one of his stuffed rabbits and a toy train he chewed on whenever Sayuri turned her back for more than two seconds. He had done it from the time he was a baby until his third birthday. "He is being take care of." She let Miwa assume what that meant.

"So it's like a day off from all children today, huh?"

Sayuri half-heartedly chuckled. "Guess you could say that."

"Wow. I'm honored." Miwa sipped her new iced coffee. "So, watched any good dramas, lately?"

Sayuri was grateful for the change in subject. She was even more grateful that Miwa had seemingly forgotten the origins of this relationship and what it meant for two such different people to be having lunch in downtown Ikebukuro. Yet as long as Sayuri could forget the burst of heartache she suffered every time she was reminded of her son, she could go along with any conversation, even if it were about subjects she didn't know much about.

Like video games.

"I don't play them for myself," Sayuri admitted, "but many of my students do. Which do you recommend for someone who doesn't know much about them?"

Miwa's eyes widened over the rim of her iced coffee. "Guess it depends what kind of games you like to play."

Sayuri tilted her head in thought. "Hmm. Nothing violent. Or causes too much anxiety. At the end of a long day dealing with kids, I want something very relaxing. Maybe has a good story? Although a story isn't necessary."

"You sound like you would enjoy dating simulators," Miwa said, although a bit of disappointment laced her voice. "They are story and text based, although a lot of the ones these days have slick animation. You don't have to worry about hand-eye-coordination or battle strategy. They're as relaxing as getting your way from the beginning, or they have some that require raising stats to date certain people or progress your relationships. There are fantasy types, office situations, high school life... the world is your oyster, heh."

"Sounds nice, actually." Sayuri chuckled. "I haven't dated in forever!"

That garnered her another tilt of the head. "Oh, because you've been married for so long?"

"Huh? Married?" Damnit! Sayuri had forgotten another core component of motherhood! There was usually a husband in the picture! *Does that mean she really was looking for a wedding ring earlier?* She and Emiko had never exchanged rings, even after having a child together, because they didn't want to raise suspicions about the true nature of their relationship. "*Chi... Chigau.*" This she should not lie about. Not if she held out any hope about the true nature of *this* relationship. "I am not married."

"Oh."

"The other parent of my child and I are no longer together. Actually, I had him by in-vitro, right after they relaxed the rule about unmarried couples having babies like that." It was either that or have a baby the old-fashioned way, and while Sayuri was desperate to be a mother, the thought of finding a man to impregnate her was less than… desirable. *Not to mention Emiko's jealousy.* Like Sayuri wouldn't have been jealous had it been the other way around!

Miwa propped her head up on her hand, her face smooshing to rounder proportions. "Don't think I've ever known someone who went that route before."

"It's a lot more common than most people realize." Especially for lesbians looking to become mothers. "I would do it again, too." She still had a few eggs frozen in a clinic somewhere. Although the raw brutality of losing her only child still weighed heavily upon her, one of the only things keeping her going through both that and breaking up with Emiko was the knowledge that she could try again on her own one day. She would have to corral one of her male friends to pose as her boyfriend again, since Japan did not condone treatments for same-sex couples *or* single women, but if she could do it once, she could do it again. Being a woman on a mission to become a mother meant she was willing to skirt both local and national laws. *It's either that or go to another country to do it, and that's even more expensive...*

"Everything about pregnancy and childbirth sounds too scary for me," Miwa confessed. "Guess that makes me sound like a selfish wimp."

"As someone who has done both pregnancy and childbirth before, I commend you for knowing you don't want to do it." Sayuri was the first to admit that it wasn't all sunshine and rainbows, although she argued with her own mother about whether the implantation was worse than the actual birth. *She was already so pissed at me for having a child out of wedlock.* Yet the moment Yuma was born, Grandma was all smiles and offers to babysit. It was amazing what a baby could do to salve old wounds between one homophobic woman and her only daughter. *Now it's back to like we've never known each other.*

"Never really thought about having kids before. Sounds like the kind of thing that happens to other women."

Sayuri wasn't sure how to take that. Didn't help she kept holding onto some hope that Miwa might be gay. Most lesbians didn't think motherhood was ever in their cards. Not when there were so many laws preventing unmarried women from conceiving unless they wanted to take their chances with a man they may or may not know in a love hotel. *I had a friend who did that...* A former teacher who dated and slept around with men with the sole hope of getting pregnant, although everyone in her life told her she would regret bringing a bastard into the world. *I never thought of my son as a bastard...* Legally, he was, and that was all people cared about. Sayuri saw it all the time at work. How many kids had an asterisk next to their file to designate them as bastard-born. Enough for her to understand the repercussions of what she did.

It had still been worth it.

"Do you have a picture of your son?" Miwa asked.

What a rhetorical question! Of course a mother had pictures of her son!

Sayuri brought up the photos on her phone and spent the next ten minutes gushing about a boy she almost forgot was gone. Miwa was patient enough to listen to the stories behind the photos while Sayuri relived the better moments of her life.

"Who's that?"

Sayuri pulled her phone back and realized it was a picture of Yuma being held by his other mother. While Emiko wasn't often mistaken for a man, there was no denying that she was a woman of certain character. Assuming Miwa recognized that character, anyway.

"An old friend." Sayuri shut off her phone. "Sorry. I forgot that picture was in there."

Miwa's eyes buzzed a mile a minute with thoughts Sayuri couldn't read. "How's the cheesecake?"

"Great."

When Sayuri reflected upon this lunch later, she realized that there were many opportunities for things to feel disparate. They were two different kinds of women who had met because of an unfortunate accident on one of the worst days of Sayuri's life. The only reason they knew each other this well was because of Miwa's unsolicited kindness. Yet when Sayuri began to dwell on their circumstances, she realized that Miwa clearly *wanted* to be with her. This was the woman who had gone beyond her job to ensure Sayuri made it home safely. She sent her chocolates, for fuck's sake. Now? They were having lunch in Ikebukuro, after some liquid courage had inspired Miwa to ask Sayuri out.

There she went thinking this was a date again... when would she learn? That was how a woman was set up for disappointment!

"Can I ask you something?" Sayuri bowed her head in acknowledgment that it was a strange way to open a statement. "When you messaged me about meeting you today..."

Miwa's reddened cheeks were all Sayuri needed to know that her suspicions were correct. Someone had been a little inebriated the other night. *I wonder if her cheeks were this red when she messaged me...* Red from a touch of alcohol. The kind that made women like Miwa bold enough to say hello.

"Yeah?" Miwa squeaked.

Sayuri attempted to not chuckle and embarrass her new friend. "I like how casual you were." That was a bit of an understatement. A woman with no interest in Miwa – friendly, romantic, or otherwise – would have cut the cord on that relationship immediately had they received what Sayuri awakened to Saturday morning. It was the kind of language that could have found them *both* fired from their jobs! "I hope that we can have a casual friendship like that going forward." They already called each other by first names. They were practically married.

"Friendship…" Miwa almost looked disappointed to mutter that, her eyes focused on the fake flower arrangement in the middle of their table. "Yeah."

"I admit, I don't have many friends." Another understatement. Sayuri lived with the persistent knowledge that she had lost most of her friends when she lost her son and broke up with Emiko. All the friends had gone with her. Nobody wanted to hang out with the depressed, grieving mother. *Emiko lost a son as well, but I absolutely took it the hardest.* One of the reasons they broke up was because Emiko couldn't tolerate a house of sadness. She was the kind of woman that used playing around as a balm for her spiritual wounds. She also moved on quickly. Moved on from the loss of a child. Moved on from Sayuri, as if she were yesterday's news. Moved on from whatever job was no longer convenient to her. Sayuri had once liked that about her. It allowed her to be the emotional one while Emiko was her rock.

Now Sayuri had to be both.

"Might be nice to have some friends again."

Miwa looked back up at her new friend. Whatever that little smile really meant, it was accompanied with, "Yes, it really would be nice to have friends again. I don't have many, either."

"So who were you drinking with Friday night, huh?"

"My coworkers."

"Ah…" That was something Sayuri had missed out on in the working world. While most other groups of coworkers went out drinking regularly, it wasn't as common with schoolteachers. Some might grab a beer together when it was convenient, but the school board made it clear that packs of drunken schoolteachers would not make a good impression on the parents of the children they taught. Miwa and her coworkers saw many of the same people every day, but they didn't have the kind of personal and intimate relationships with their riders that schoolteachers did with their students' parents. Too bad. Sayuri did love getting tipsy once in a while. "From the station, yes?"

"There are only four of us on the night shift. Everyone but me has been there for years. Soon it will be *years* for me, but the guys have a huge head start over me. I'm the *kouhai*."

"We have a new ALT coming to my school this week." Sayuri grinned. "It's nice that we usually have a fresh meat *kouhai* every year. I mean, we get a few Japanese ones, too, but the *gaikokujin* teachers are fun to mess with."

"I bet they're the ones most disappointed that you all don't go out drinking every weekend."

"You see a lot of drunk foreigners on your shift?"

"Sometimes. Tourists, especially. My station isn't so popular for foreigners to live at, let alone go drinking at, so it's mostly a few stumbling businessmen late on Friday nights."

Sayuri giggled to imagine one lone businessman coming on last train and needing assistance getting up the stairs.

They formally exchanged numbers and calling cards before they paid for their meals. Miwa admitted she had somewhere else she had to be by the evening, and Sayuri desired to get home before nightfall so she could get a jump on sleep before school started up again. "I'll look into that video game suggestion," Sayuri said, as they parted ways outside of the café. "I need a new hobby to occupy my evenings, especially as the days won't be so long now."

"Typhoons are coming soon, anyway." Miwa sighed. "We have to train for them at work, in case something happens at the station."

"Like what?"

"Oh, power outages, stranded passengers, floods…" A shrug implied that Miwa had seen it all before. "Seems like we're always training, though. It means I have to stay extra late and get home around dawn."

"Does that mean I get some fun text messages to wake up to?"

Miwa sighed. "Now there's pressure to be witty at four in the morning? You're kidding."

"I didn't say witty."

"You seem like the kind of woman who appreciates witty."

"Well, maybe…"

Chuckling, Miwa slapped a blue baseball cap on her head and waved to her new friend. "Thanks for meeting me today, Sayuri-*san*. Let's do it again soon."

Sayuri hoped Miwa couldn't hear the grin reverberating on her face.

Chapter 14

MIWA

The signal came through right on time, like it did for most of Miwa's shift. *Like clockwork, the whole system ticks along.* She raised her hand, both to motion for passengers to stay the hell behind the yellow line and to give the engineer of the oncoming train the OK to pull up to the station.

There was never any time to catch a proper glimpse of the engineer, not when Miwa worked the entrance of the platform. Kohei sometimes radioed her from the other end to say, "*Takeshita*-san *still has a black eye from that baseball game, huh?*" or "*Wonder what Kawakami*-san *would look like with blond hair. You think the company would let him? I should suggest it.*" Miwa barely knew who these engineers were. They were mere names in her log book and occasionally showed up to the corporate shindigs they were obligated to go to a few times a year. Speeches. Hobnobbing. *Networking.* The shit Miwa was supposed to be good at if she wanted to advance in the company.

Most days she did well enough keeping Overseer Endo happy.

A blast of cool air hit Miwa's face as the train flew past her. Blurs of silver metal and the colors of the line rumbling through parts of Tokyo Miwa rarely visited flashed before her. The indiscernible faces of passengers heading home or to late dinner dates gradually became more focused as the train pulled to a stop. The automated message announcing where the train was alerted sleepy passengers to grab their belongings and rush out to one of two exits. Few came Miwa's way.

She held up her hand and waited to hear Kohei's whistle at the other end of the platform. As soon as the sound echoed down her way, Miwa likewise blew her own whistle and lowered her hand. The train doors closed. Soon, it was off again, the cycle to repeat in ten minutes.

"Excuse me."

The English words almost made Miwa jump out of her skin. Not because nobody talked to her, but because she wasn't used to hearing such clear and concise English in her station. Her brain dithered between *Customer!* and *Foreigner!* The dutiful employee inside of her responded to all customers. The woman who couldn't speak a lick of English wanted to run far, *far* away.

One always won out over the other. Especially if Miwa liked the idea of keeping her job.

"*Hai.*" She turned to the tall, white foreigner with sandy blond hair and a T-shirt that spread across his muscular torso. *Jesus! A man like him is in my station!* She only saw tall, stocky, blond foreigners on TV. The foreigners that usually came her way were the ones who barely got second glances. This guy here probably turned heads wherever he went.

He was so impressive that Miwa almost overlooked the short, brunette woman beside him. She sure as hell couldn't place their strange accents. They weren't American, and it didn't help that the man soon switched to slapdash Japanese.

"We want to get to Ikebukuro." The woman with him nodded in agreement. "Which way should we go?"

Miwa was so entranced by their looks that she almost didn't understand what the man said. "Ikebukuro Station?" she repeated.

"Yes. Should we go this way?" The man pointed to where the last train had gone. "Or that way?"

"You have to transfer. Neither goes to Ikebukuro."

Unfortunately, it didn't look like they had understood her.

"Go this way," she said in simple Japanese. "Change train here." She pointed to a map of the line, indicating the exact stop they wanted to transfer to the Fukutoshin Subway Line, which would take them directly to Ikebukuro Station.

"Thank you so much!" The man waved his huge hand over Miwa's face. Her eyes widened, and it was only then that Kohei ambled over with a grin on his countenance. "Let's go, hon!"

"New friends of yours?" Kohei asked. "Don't get many Australians around here."

As All Our Fires Burn

"Is that what they are?" Miwa muttered. "They scared me half to death sneaking up on me like that."

"Too bad nobody here speaks English. Could come in handy sometimes."

"I'm not entirely convinced that was English." Miwa had a hard enough time understanding standard American and Canadian English. The Brits were their own breed of indecipherable, but at least Miwa was used to hearing the accent once in a while. Australians, though... Miwa's mind wandered as she contemplated whether she had ever met a New Zealander before. South African? Definitely not.

"Still, I'm seeing more foreigners around here recently. Might not be a bad idea to take some English lessons again. Bet it could mean a promotion."

That got Miwa's attention. Dangerous, since the next train was due in a few minutes, and both she and Kohei needed to get to their positions. "Promotion? You've heard something?"

"Talkin' places like in Shinjuku and Shibuya."

"Wow..." Those were the *big time* compared to their tiny station in a sleepy neighborhood. Would definitely come with a raise, and that was *before* the hazard pay that came from working in high-traffic stations like those near Shinjuku's core. Miwa wouldn't be doing too bad for herself if she could get promoted to one of those stations before her first five years in the company were completed. Then she could concentrate on possibly making station master somewhere. Right now, her best hope was Shinnosuke getting transferred and beating Kohei out for *that* position.

Learning English would certainly open a few doors. Too bad it had always been one of Miwa's worst subjects in school. Her Japanese marks hadn't been much better. *My mother used to say it was a miracle I could speak by the time I went to school.* Some things had not been a priority when she was a small child.

"Ah!" Kohei jumped right into his English practice. "Look alive, Ban! *Tee mai-nissu saa-tee!*" She supposed that meant they had thirty seconds before they endangered the whole platform.

Luckily for Miwa, no other passengers threatened to scare her to death for the rest of her shift. Unluckily for her, however, her thoughts were consumed with the prospect of taking the initiative and boosting her career to the next level. Even if Kohei were talking out of his ass, it still wasn't a terrible idea to learn the kind of English that behooved people in a train station. The signs may have been mostly bilingual, but that didn't help passengers who had more nuanced questions.

Too bad she couldn't afford expensive tutoring. Too bad most adult classes were in the evening, when she had her shifts. All the good it did her.

It wasn't until her dinner break that she had an epiphany. When she passed Shinnosuke on the stairs, his ivory white gloves preparing to take over her position so she could break, Miwa realized that she already knew someone who might be able to help her with her English.

"*Hello,* sensei," she texted to Sayuri, while eating her cup of noodles in the staff room. "*Don't suppose you're good at English, huh? Because I could really brush up on my* eigo *if you have a little time to meet.*"

She should offer to compensate Sayuri while she was at it, but Miwa couldn't afford anything more than 'insulting.' Besides, the point wasn't that Sayuri might do it for free. The *point* was finding excuses to hang out! Assuming she hadn't completely misread the chemistry between her and…

"My English is acceptable." That reply came much sooner than Miwa anticipated. *"But don't expect me to teach you how to debate politics with Americans."*

"I think I would get fired from my job if I tried that."

"This is for your job? Too much pressure!"

"I deal with a lot of foreigners, okay?"

"Maybe I should hook you up with the ALT at my school."

"Thought you said you hadn't met him yet?"

"Details, details…"

Miwa couldn't believe that her half-baked plan worked. By the end of her shift, they had hashed out plans to meet again before Sayuri went back to work full time. After that, she claimed, it would be more difficult to meet regularly. Even the weekends might be too busy for the prettiest schoolteacher in the Kanto region.

Not that Miwa would let it get her down. It was tentative plans like the ones she made with Sayuri that gave her a reason to work with a smile on her lips.

Those smiles gave her coworkers a reason to chide her every time they had a moment to themselves. *"You think Ban*-san *is seeing someone?"* Overseer Endo was heard asking Shinnosuke. *"We gave her all that crap about being single, and it might not be true?"* She wasn't shocked that his mind went there first.

Naturally, Miwa was in no hurry to say she was *dating* anyone. She would never tell her coworkers that she longed for the arms of a gentle woman, but she was also in no hurry to give them the satisfaction of teasing her because she was a giddy girl falling in love. It would be too easy.

"Earth to Ban!" Kohei nearly shouted into her ear. She slammed her locker shut, her street clothes absorbing the sweat that came with her sudden rush of adrenaline. "You still spacing out? Damn. I hope whatever you're thinking about is good, because it has to be worth the dumb face you're making."

He said this right in front of their boss, yet Overseer Endo merely laughed.

"Thinking about learning English..." Miwa muttered.

As according to plan, her coworkers were too confused to continue to tease her.

Chapter 15

SAYURI

An electrical storm waged in the clouds on one side of the city. Sayuri maintained a safe distance as she walked down the sidewalk and kept one eye on the flashes of lightning streaking from one gray cloud to another. Pedestrians like her hurried inside. One man went to open his umbrella, muttering that it would rain at any moment, but his wife implored him to keep it shut. "Better wet than electrocuted!" she chided.

Sayuri was one of the few people in her neighborhood who wasn't perturbed by the August electrical storms. She had been fascinated by them as a child, and more than once her mother had torn her away from her fixation before it invited certain doom. Often, Sayuri was relegated to humid windowsills to behold the lightning dances that lit up the whole dreary sky for hours on end. While others saw gloom hovering above them, Sayuri saw the potential for something beautiful.

Still, as an adult, she knew better than to stand around and wait for the lightning to come to her. She hustled down the sidewalk and ducked into the local used goods store before the storm came any closer.

The place was packed for that time of day in the middle of the week. *More people staying away from the lightning. Not a bad idea.* Sayuri, however, had come there on a mission. She bypassed the aisles of books and clothing, where browsers went to pass the time, and headed straight to a section she had never lingered in before. *Electronics.*

There were the usual suspects, such as young and middle-aged men who gaped at the archaic consoles of yesteryear while reminiscing about their youth. Then there were the little kids screaming for the newest Pokémon game. Occasionally, a girl dressed like Miwa, in her jeans, baseball cap, and ostentatious necklace, asked a clerk to hand her something from the glass case. They were the kind of people who knew exactly what they wanted and only needed interference when it was time to pull out their wallets.

Sayuri knew nothing about video games. She had done some brief research online, in between putting together her lesson plans and grading the first slew of summer break homework to come her way, but it was useless. As soon as she stood before the used video game consoles, let alone the bins full of old games, she was more confused than the time she caught her son counting to ten in Spanish.

As All Our Fires Burn

Boy, this was a mistake. Sayuri pulled out her phone to text Miwa before realizing she was probably already at work. *I'm on my own, and I don't know what it is I want.* She wanted assistance. The kind that could tell her, "*Get this system. Then get these games. Here, why don't I install it all for you?*" It didn't help that some of the systems were *numbered!* The higher the number, the more recent it was, right? Or did those numbers mean something else? How much power they took? How many discs they played at once? What was the difference between a Nintendo Wii and a Nintendo Wii U? Was one an expansion of the other? If so, why did it cost so much more?

Sayuri had a headache. No wonder a young man who came up to her and asked if she needed help.

You have no idea, kid. Sayuri sighed to admit it. Yet what should she say? How embarrassing would it look for a thirty-something woman who dressed like someone's stylish housewife to ask for video game help? Let alone for what *she* had in mind?

"*Yes, hello, I would like to fill the romantic void in my life by purchasing relaxing yet 'stimulating' dating simulators, please. The gayer, the better. Oh, no, not that kind of gay, please. I prefer the ones with two grown women going at it, if you have any. You do? Wonderful. Box it up and put it in a bow for me.*" She'd rather die.

"I'm looking for a gaming console and some games to go with it," she blurted. "For… my husband."

The young man tilted his head. "We have quite the selection of older models and a few more recent ones, depending on what he likes."

My husband? I've completely lost my mind. Sayuri had no idea where she was doing. What wife bought her husband *dating simulators?* What kind of husband did she have, anyway? Damnit. No matter what she said, she looked a bit silly. Now she had no choice but to keep the story going. "My friend recommended a PlayStation, but I'm confused by how many there are."

"The PlayStation 4 is the latest one, but it's the most expensive. We have quite a few threes that were traded in."

Sayuri was taken on a confusing journey that made as little sense in the end as it did in the beginning. Yet she admitted that the more she looked over the systems, compared the specs and prices, and perused a few of the games that each console supported, she became more excited about her future life as a gamer. Didn't help that she narrowed down which console she wanted based on what she told the employee next.

"My husband really likes the kind of games where you can date people."

She was losing him. The poor young man was so confused, yet too professional to lose a sale to a woman willing to spend a few thousand *yen* on a used console and some old video games. More money in the store's pockets, and less stock on the shelves taking up precious room!

"This system in particular has quite a few classic dating simulators that are very reduced in price," he said. "We actually have bundles of them for sale at 1,000 *yen* each. You don't know for sure what you're getting, but we guarantee that all games work and each are unique in the bundle."

As All Our Fires Burn

"Really? That would be wonderful. Because I have no idea what to get… him."

Sayuri walked out of the store with a bag heavy enough to make her skip the supermarket on her way home. Besides, she was too excited to set up her system – assuming she didn't make a huge mess of it – and waste the rest of the gray day doing the kind of thing some of her students daydreamed about while she lectured them on English, math, and Japanese. She could heat up some instant curry and throw in some rice from the cooker to call it good for dinner.

Two hours later, she had both the first game booted up, and a warm plate of curry and rice on her coffee table. Usually, Sayuri was the kind of woman to be proud of herself for making a stellar supper to enjoy while watching her favorite TV shows. Now, however, she eschewed the culinary arts for something a bit more provincial.

There were ten games in her bundle, and the first three she tried out were a little too basic for her tastes. One took place in a high school, which was a bit creepy. The other was at a junior college, but was about a young man on the hunt for as much sex as possible. *I'm not that desperate… yet.* The third game got weird when a seemingly normal office lady stumbled into a bar full of people in animal suits, and the game all but insisted that Sayuri watch animations of these people making out with one another. *No, thank you. I don't want to sleep with my pets.*

She put in the fourth one while eating the last of her instant dinner. Almost immediately, the sultry voice of a woman shook the speakers on Sayuri's TV.

"*Loneliness in this city is at an all time high. Humans are social creatures. Why is it we avoid those who would love us? Do we think it will make us better, stronger people? It's time to embrace the world of love once more.*"

Sayuri had no idea what was going on, but she was intrigued.

The game began like the others, imploring her to create a basic character – female, in this case – and go about the town after getting off work in an office building. Every decision she made brought the clock forward fifteen minutes, limiting the other choices she could make over the span of one night.

"Is it game over if I don't sleep with someone, huh?" Sayuri blew air out of her cheeks. "Typical. Sounds like college." Dating in college? Hell. Also the last time she went to the gay bars as a single gal. (Never again.)

The thing that kept her glued to this particular game wasn't just the time mechanic. It was that she could flirt with both men *and* women, which meant Sayuri naturally chose the women working behind counters, sitting at bars, and shopping for groceries. Her first few attempts to talk to anyone went down in flames as she repeatedly picked the wrong answers. The closest she got to a date was reminiscent of her time with Miwa. "*Would like to get some coffee?*" a young OL, still in her office uniform, asked Sayuri's character in a donut shop. "*There's a place around here…*"

Sayuri fucked it up by accidentally hitting the wrong button.

"*Too bad.*" The animation depicted the woman tossing her hair and getting out of her chair. "*You have a really nice butt.*"

As All Our Fires Burn

"*Uso!*" Sayuri said to her TV. "I have a really flat butt!"

She started it over one more time. Every instance she restarted, she reiterated by making completely different decisions. Instead of going to the train station, she went to a convenience store. Or she went for a walk down an alley. Or she sat in a café and ordered coffee. Most of these decisions led her to male characters – especially the one in the alley, which she found quite distasteful – so she backtracked to places she knew led her to female characters looking for companionship. Eventually, she ended up back in a bar where, usually, a male diner offered to whisk her away to the Caribbean for a weekend. Instead of politely turning him down, Sayuri told him to go fuck himself before she called the cops.

She didn't understand how this could end well for her. Yet when the man skedaddled out of the bar and Sayuri's character ordered another drink, she was approached by a woman with a demeanor who reminded her a little too much of someone else.

"*Don't you hate it when men think they can get into your pants like that?*" The plaid-wearing woman with silky hair sat down next to Sayuri. "*What a Neanderthal. He was probably going to take you to a love hotel and kill you.*"

Sayuri looked at the listed options for her response. She had no idea which one to choose.

"*Do you usually distrust men so much?*" That one was definitely a gamble, but Sayuri was quickly learning that sometimes the best responses were the most unlikely ones.

"*It's not that I distrust men,*" the woman with the sultry voice from the intro said, "*Women are so much more… satisfying.*"

Well. This was clearly the right woman to talk to.

Not that Sayuri had any idea what to say. Even if she were suave in real life, in a game where answers could lead to *any* crazy outcome? She was more lost than her students attempting English worksheets. Her gut instinct told her to say, *"I agree,"* but that was too boring. A woman like this one wanted someone who was "satisfying," after all.

"Men can't give me what I want, it's true." Sayuri selected that with her eyes closed.

At first, she worried the disc was scratched, because nothing happened. Then, as if the dating sim gods only wanted to fuck with her, a cut scene began. Nothing scandalous, unfortunately. Only the woman offering Sayuri's character a coy smile and a simple, *"I like you."*

Had she done it? Had Sayuri successfully seduced this woman?

No!

She needed coffee and a snack before tackling this scenario. Even then, she scared the woman off with her answers more than once, forcing Sayuri to start over again. She wrote down the answers that advanced the scene while thinking that the person who created the dating sim must have been a genius. The ability to start a conversation over again as if a faux pas had not occurred? Brilliant. How could Sayuri sign up for this in real life?

It might come in handy with Miwa.

She couldn't help but keep thinking of the woman with so many sides to her identity, and Sayuri had yet to completely chip away everything there was to Ms. Miwa Ban. *I wonder what the kanji for her name is.* Sayuri screwed up selecting a dialogue option she had encountered five times already because her brain was running through the possible character combinations for Miwa's name. *Does she have any brothers or sisters? She acts like she has a lot of brothers...* The woman in the dating sim finally divulged her name: Satin. Sayuri repeated it, struggling to remember what it meant. She couldn't help but hit the dialogue option asking Satin if that was her real name.

"*Of course not,*" Satin said, as Sayuri wondered what it would be like for Miwa to have a name as slick yet delicate as *satin*. "*My real name is boring and common. I chose the name Satin because it represents something important to me.*"

Sayuri puffed out her cheeks and looked at the clock. She should've been getting ready for bed. She was due at the school by nine in the morning to meet the new foreign English teacher.

Instead, she kept playing.

"*What fabric do you associated with me, Satin?*"

"*You look like virgin cloth.*"

Sayuri sat back from her screen. What? Did she act like a virgin or something?

"*Don't be so offended,*" Satin continued. "*I only mean that you look untouched by certain pleasures.*"

Wow. This was getting serious.

"*What pleasures are those, Satin?*"

"*Why, the most delicious kind of all. Do you want to know?*"

"*Only if you're willing to share.*"

"Oh, honey... I think you'll find that I'm always willing to share those unbridled pleasures with the right woman."

Sayuri hesitated before asking if she was the right woman.

After a few missteps that required her to keep going back to save points, Sayuri was finally invited to Satin's "Love Den." Quite the convenient name for a shag pad in a video game. Sayuri fell into a fit of giggles once she realized the game had gone into "love mode," which meant she couldn't screw up the experience for anyone but herself. Because, no matter what she picked, Satin was getting erotic, complete with graphic animations as provided by a very attentive game studio. Yet there were still options to pick, and they determined the kind of experience Sayuri had with the NPC who was more than willing to give *or* take.

Sayuri wasn't much of a giver. At least not a first date.

"What do you have in mind for me, Ms. Satin?"

"Take off your clothes and put your hands in those handcuffs, sweetie. We're just getting started."

Two seconds later, Sayuri realized that no matter what options she picked, Satin was the BDSM NPC of the game.

"Ara!" She dropped her controller in disbelief. It clattered to the carpet, her face so hot that she instinctively turned up the air conditioner. Thunder rumbled outside her apartment window. It did nothing to drown out the embarrassment in Sayuri's burning body.

Virgin cloth was right!

She left the screen on the image of Satin half undressed, bare back turned to the TV. Her animated hair fell in long, black locks down her shoulder as she mimicked taking off her clothes for the player-character. The sultry eyes looking right into the camera had Sayuri getting up and pacing before her coffee table.

Honestly, the fact she was about to see something *erotic* was enough to embarrass her. Throwing in BDSM elements was almost too risqué. Yet the big fat cherry on the top of this awful sundae was the fact Sayuri had really been thinking about Miwa the whole time.

Miwa… BDSM… no way. Sayuri couldn't handle it. That was the kind of shit sending her soul straight to hell, where it belonged!

Miwa-san couldn't possibly be into stuff like that, right? What if she was? What if the only way Sayuri had a chance with her was if she became the submissive little "virgin cloth" a woman like Satin – er, Miwa – desired? *What am I talking about? There's no way she's into that! It's a miracle if she's even into girls!* Sayuri swallowed the lump forming in her throat. No. This had gone too far. Not only was it a terrible thing to think of Miwa in such ways, the recommendation to play a dating sim was only because Sayuri was so boring. This wasn't anything like the games Miwa played! She was into those RPGs and action-story games. While Sayuri sat here being the lamest loner in the world, Miwa was kicking bad-guy ass and saving worlds.

So. Lame. I'M SO LAME.

Emiko was somewhere laughing at her ex-girlfriend right now. She always said that Sayuri's imagination ran away from her, whether it was in the bedroom or out on the streets. Every faraway look Sayuri acquired was either some sexual fantasy or nightmare that a bandit was about to rob her in the alleyway.

Sayuri turned around and realized that her curtains were still open. Although she lived several stories up... what if somebody saw what was on her screen right now? What would the neighbors think!

She hurried to shutter the windows and isolate herself in a dark world. She turned off most of her lights and looked at her phone screen. Although Miwa was in the middle of her shift, Sayuri still found a message from her there.

"So? Did you buy a game?"

It must have been sent on her dinner break. Even so, Sayuri shuddered to think of Miwa suddenly appearing in the apartment and seeing what transpired on an otherwise innocuous TV screen. *"What's this? Why are you with the one who kinda looks like me? I mean, if I ever wore something like* that! *What kind of name is Satin, anyway? Kinda looks like Satan. You know who Satan is? The guy you're gonna see when you die."*

Sayuri wanted to die. From embarrassment. From dread. Shame. Terror.

Her mind wouldn't stop jumping between the shame she felt for herself and the crippling arousal she felt when she thought of Miwa.

She's in her uniform right now...

Sayuri inhaled a deep breath and picked up the controller. Soon, she would take the coldest shower possible. Or, maybe, the hottest bath she could stand. Either way, she danced with extremes that prevented her from getting proper sleep that night. She was too inundated with sensations that made her do something she hadn't bothered to entertain in weeks. Not since she first realized it might be time to do something with her life again.

Too bad she had run out of batteries.

Chapter 16

MIWA

Years had gone by since Miwa last had a friend (of any variation) who tried to talk to her, let alone see her on an almost weekly basis. Other friends had come and gone since high school and college. Unfortunately, most of those friendships were built on half-truths that Miwa couldn't be bothered to uphold for more than a few months. *Like pretending to be straight...* It had been one thing to be labeled a queer in college, when she could avoid students outside of class and pretend they didn't exist while the lectures commenced. It was quite another to have a respectable job with a large company and worry that she would get in trouble because she admitted to kissing girls on the weekends.

(If only she kissed that many girls... on the weekends or not.)

She became convinced that this relationship with Sayuri, which only became more comfortable as the next three weeks went by, was a dream about to bottom out as soon as Miwa awakened in the sweaty discomfort of her futon.

It didn't help that Sayuri remained the unachievable fantasy for a woman who lusted for the kind of touches that made a girl sigh.

No matter what Miwa wore, she always felt like a childish fool next to the stylish Sayuri, who was never without her patterned skirts and blouses that highlighted her womanly figure. When she didn't wear her hair down around her shoulders, it was tucked neatly into a low-hanging bun. The nape of her neck always eluded Miwa's sight, but there were other – more private – places on Sayuri's body she was more inclined to think about than that. *I wonder what she thinks of my wardrobe...* Miwa experimented with more tomboyish looks and business casual wear that hopefully made her look more mature. Sayuri was in her *thirties,* after all. She didn't want to be with someone who looked like she had to roll into a junior college class by the end of the day. Even if the sneakers, denim, and baseball caps got the most compliments after a few meetups of experimentation. *I probably look like her kid sister to other people...* Didn't help that half of their meetings included Sayuri brushing Miwa up on her latent English skills. The first time she pulled out an elementary school workbook, Miwa wondered what the hell was happening. Then she remembered how she suavely suggested her new friend tutor her in English. Well, she got it now! Complete with cartoon characters and popular songs from ten years ago to aid her journey in nostalgic learning.

Wonder how you say, "I really want to kiss you," in English. Half the time Miwa couldn't concentrate on lessons or conversations because she was too preoccupied with the pair of lips speaking in her direction. *Does she know she has gorgeous lips?* Miwa became obsessed with an older song that spoke of *"Amai Kuchibiru,"* or the sweet lips that the singer couldn't help but taste every time he had the chance. If Sayuri tasted anything like she smelled, then she was a sophisticated symphony of flowers and honey, the two smells dominating her small selection of perfume every time she met with Miwa.

What did Miwa smell like? Sweat and fried convenience store food. God, she really had to stop eating like an old single man.

Sayuri had taken her advice to purchase an old gaming system and a stack of dating simulation games. Miwa coyly asked for Sayuri's handle so they could be friends on the network. Sayuri didn't seem to know what the hell her friend was talking about, even after the connection online was made and Miwa could now see the achievements as Sayuri completed them. *She's playing* that *awful game?* Miwa often thought, regardless of what Sayuri burned through. *She must really like men then... there are so many male choices in that game.* She thought that until the night she logged in and saw a new alert from Sayuri's profile. *"ACHIEVEMENT UNLOCKED: Satin's Sheets."*

As All Our Fires Burn

Miwa stared at the screen. No. No way. Sayuri had *not* played through a hardcore BDSM *lesbian* scene! That was the definition of too good to be true! Maybe not the BDSM part. Maybe. Miwa could be into it. For the right woman. Still, she would not let this bit of information color her opinion of Sayuri, including what it might mean for her sexual interests.

They often met in Ikebukuro, since Miwa could use her train pass to get there for free while still being on Sayuri's train line. The trek on their days off was worth it when it meant a few hours of coffee, laughter, and getting to know one another beyond the crazy way they met earlier that summer. The only thing that kept Miwa on edge was wondering about her new friend's son. The boy was what, four? Shouldn't he be with his mother more? It wasn't that Miwa thought Sayuri a neglectful mother. As likely she had someone to look after him so she could occasionally go out by herself. Besides, Miwa often reasoned, it must be stressful to drag a kid to Tokyo for a few hours. Better for him to stay home with grandma.

Still, wasn't it strange that she had yet to meet the kid? Wasn't it weird that Sayuri didn't really talk about him? When she did, it was with an animation that reminded Miwa of the child in question. Miwa had once asked why Sayuri decided to become a teacher. *"Because I love children, I guess,"* she had answered. If that were true, then didn't she love her son the most of all? Sayuri talked about her students more than the little boy named Yuma.

Yet nothing troubled Miwa more than the thought that there might be a Mr. Kawashima, although Sayuri had assured her that she was single. Like Miwa had made sure to mention that she was single, too.

The fall term had started for schools across Japan, meaning Miwa saw her new friend even less than before. Yet they stayed in communication over text, sometimes spending whole evenings shooting one another messages about their days. Sayuri would mention that a small gang of students had attempted an uprising in her class, insisting that Kawashima-*sensei* was a tyrant intent on making their lives miserable. *"My mom says it's training for being an adult!!"* one child reportedly said. *"I say we never become adults!"* The moment Sayuri started calling him "Peter Pan" because of his views was the moment he stepped down out of embarrassment.

Miwa, meanwhile, revealed the mundane side that was working in a train station. *"Not many people really think about it,"* she texted in the morning, when she struggled to sleep. Sayuri would later wake up to one giant paragraph about Amaya-jinja-guchi Station. *"But there is a lot of paperwork that goes on even in the smallest stations. We have reports to fill out, announcements to read and respond to corporate about, and a huuuge litany of daily bullcrap that is always the same until one day it isn't. Infuriating!"* That may have happened that evening, when Miwa did the final run-through of the station before calling it a night. A light had gone out behind one of the billboards passengers saw when they waited on the platform. Maintenance would be summoned in the wee hours of the morning, before trains began to run. Now, why did that require three different forms for her to fill out before she could get the hell out and ride her bike home in the pre-typhoon rain?

As All Our Fires Burn

They both lamented the trouble a typhoon brought to the region. The subway line was held up due to flooding during the peak day of the storm, and the businessmen and women who still had to go to work were later than it was worth for any of them to suffer. Miwa was in charge of writing the notification slips for passengers to hand to their employers when they were inevitably late to work. A whole stack of them were available for such occasions, but some required personalization, and they *all* had to be stamped with the official seals of both the company and the station. Her hand hurt more than when she spent half her nights fighting hardcore boss bottles on her PlayStation 4.

"It was so awful," Sayuri said over the phone on the rare Sunday they didn't meet. "The power blew out, but they refused to cancel classes. We were burning kerosene lamps because the administration didn't want to bother the parents and make them pick up their kids!"

"Maybe I simply grew up in a sensitive area," Miwa said, referring to her boring hometown in Chiba Prefecture, "but half our classes would be canceled in September. The typhoons were always wiping out our power. Even my mom prepared for it by phoning the power company and demanding that our bill be deducted 100 *yen* for every minute we were out of power." That was but a mere example of what Mrs. Ban had been capable of when she was pissed the hell off. Which was frequently.

"The typhoons here mean I stay inside and go insane," Sayuri said. "I'd rather visit you in the city."

Hildred Billings

Miwa almost grabbed a Q-Tip to clean out her ears. Sayuri hadn't seriously said that, had she?

Yet they scheduled a home visit for the following weekend, during one of the last major heatwaves of the year. The forecast warned that such heat after a typhoon usually meant another big storm was on the way. Nobody paid it any mind, however, since there was work to do, children to raise, and dinners to cook. The whole country was built to withstand most of the natural disasters the world threw at it. Shit like what to do during a huge typhoon was for the authorities to figure out.

Miwa was barely an authority at her job. Only when passengers needed someone to explain why they were late…

She went into a cleaning frenzy on Saturday, determined to turn her humble abode into a perfectly clean specimen of what a single woman's lifestyle was like in the heart of Tokyo. *She's been in here before… she knows how gross it can be.* At least the terrible summer smell from the kitchen drain was gone! The winter stench was right behind it, but hopefully Sayuri wouldn't be around for that.

What was an inept hostess to do once she was finished cleaning and replacing every linen with something fresh? Miwa took down some of her more embarrassing video game posters she only put up for something to look at, and replaced them with tasteful calendars given away for free at work. Her boss had asked her what the hell she planned to do with the abandoned stack of calendars, now that the year was half over. "*I collage now,*" Miwa had said. "*I can cut up the images to make pretty things.*"

As All Our Fires Burn

Endo told her she got weirder by the month, but it was rather entertaining.

Miwa was prepared for everything, including the scorching weather that threatened to burn the city in an unholy blaze of summer's last attempt. The days were so much shorter now, but Miwa continued to sweat in her uniform as if she spent the minutes between trains running up and down the platform.

Yet she was not prepared for her air conditioner refusing to turn on.

"*Ara!*" She hit the side of her unit, convinced that was the best way to get it working again. She wanted the apartment nice and cool by the time Sayuri arrived, so her guest wouldn't have to drown in a puddle of her own sweat before the first iced tea was served. Then again, it might be a nice excuse to go to the nearest family restaurant instead. *Where does that put me if my unit isn't working at all, huh?* Miwa contacted her landlord, who told her he could take it a look at it early Monday morning – he was currently out of town.

He had to be kidding her!

"Hello?" Sayuri's voice filtered into the apartment while Miwa scrambled to put on cool yet covering clothes. "Miwa-*san?* Are you home? Your door is unlocked!"

Yes, yes it had been unlocked, because Miwa ran in and out, attempting to figure out what was wrong with her air conditioning unit and whether the neighbors were having the same problem. Yet Miwa was caught with her metaphorical pants down as she turned to her guest, a sheen of sweat covering her face.

"It's hopeless." Miwa meant that both toward herself and to the woman occupying the *genkan*. "The air conditioner is broken."

Sayuri hurried to close the door behind her, before more hot air could come in. Miwa closed the blinds on her window and cranked up every oscillating fan in her possession. The ice in the tea was melted before her guest could drink the first sip.

"*Gomen.*" Miwa collapsed onto the futon couch in front of her TV. Sayuri sat on the edge of the other end, her short skirt pressing her sweaty legs together. *Fuck me for noticing that. Ugh.* "I'm a terrible hostess. I didn't know it was broken until I tried turning it on this morning…"

"I'm used to this kind of heat in such small spaces, Miwa-san." Sayuri dabbed her forehead with a handkerchief from her cross-body bag. "I'm a schoolteacher, remember? We still don't have air conditioners in our classrooms." She glanced around the small living area. Did she notice what had changed since the last time she was in there? "Although there is one great advantage to suffering these conditions in somebody's home as opposed to my place of work."

Miwa added more ice to the tea. Was it really melting *that* quickly? "Huh?"

She turned around to witness Sayuri removing her sweater. A ruby-red silk tank top was beneath it.

Miwa had never seen so much of her friend's skin before. While Sayuri continued to stare at one of the train company's calendars, she absentmindedly fiddled with the cuffs of her sweater and flexed the tops of her toned arms.

As All Our Fires Burn

That was rude. How dare a woman entice another like that? *She has no idea how hot she is, does she?* Oh, sure, Sayuri was quite aware of the sweat trickling down her skin and her rising need for something cool to drink. Except she had no idea how *beautiful* she was. The kind of beautiful that was a tractor beam to a woman with a tray of iced teas, already half-melted.

"Are you... comfortable?" The tray shook in Miwa's hands. Was she sweating because of how hot the air was? Or because of how hot *Sayuri* was? *Oh, my God. Her skin is so pale. She's as white as the lilies she's named after. Please, God, kill me now. I can't help myself. I'm going to scare her away if you don't do something right now...* She didn't know to which God she beseeched assistance, because they were all bastards for letting her debase herself like this. "I could try finding another fan if..."

Sayuri turned her head. One of the oscillating fans pointing in her direction blew a lock of hair in front of her face. She pulled all of her hair back into a simple ponytail that draped over the back of the futon couch. *OH MY GOD, I AM NOT OKAY.* Miwa maintained a poised demeanor as she offered her guest the iced tea. Inside, however, she screamed.

Maybe the stereotypes about lesbians being wanton sex fiends who were a terror to all pretty yet unsuspecting women were true. The demons that made it so currently gripped the back of Miwa's arms and made the corners of her mouth twitch. Nothing was as unfair as a horny woman forced into the closet around her friend.

"I think I'll be fine, thank you." Sayuri accepted the iced tea with a smile. "I'm excited to see you play."

"You can't really expect me to... you wanna watch *that?*" Miwa laughed. Sayuri had suggested that they spend the day playing video games – mostly Sayuri watching *Miwa* play video games, because someone claimed to be utterly useless – but Miwa insisted that would be too boring to make a trip all the way out to Tokyo. Yet when they were both on Miwa's futon, attempting to avoid the heat pressing down upon them like a blanket of hot moisture, Sayuri suggested once more that Miwa pick up the gaming controller and show her this RPG she loved so much.

"I've always been curious about these types of games," Sayuri said. "But I'm afraid I'll be so bad at them that it's hopeless for me to purchase."

"There are really easy modes on most games these days." Miwa picked up her PS4 controller, currently at full charge. "They're basically story modes. They let you casually enjoy the story while using a modicum of strategy. You're really not supposed to overthink it."

"I promise you that I will. Why don't you show me?"

All right, if that's what Sayuri really wanted to do on their day together...

Miwa had always figured that if she couldn't have a girlfriend who was a gamer like her, then having a girlfriend who liked to watch was more than the second best thing to possess. Sayuri proved to be that type of woman when she became engrossed in Miwa's favorite game of the year, asking a million questions about the storyline, the characters, and the mechanics of catching demons and turning them into fighting machines. The story was far too complicated to explain in any detail that day, but Sayuri received enough entertainment from watching her friend play through a dungeon on one of the hardest levels.

"That's not fair!" she shouted when the dungeon boss knocked three of Miwa's party members out in one blow. Luckily, she had enough SP for the healer of the group to revive everyone – although it probably meant sacrificing her in the next round. "How can he be allowed to do a cheap shot like that?"

"Because it's hard mode. It's supposed to be... hard."

"That's fun?"

"This is my third time playing the game the whole way through," Miwa explained. Nevertheless, she had a fresh bottle of Pocari Sweat ready to go. She needed the electrolytes to get her through this battle without the air conditioner to keep her content. "I need a challenge."

"That's not a challenge! That's mutiny!"

"Mutiny?"

"Mutiny of your own gaming machine against you!"

Miwa turned to Sayuri, who was red in the face. Or maybe that was her silk tank top reflecting in her skin. *Either way, I appreciate the passion.* Sometimes, Miwa forgot that she wasn't the only one who got heated playing – and watching – these games. No wonder she had no problem putting down her controller while half her party begged to have their status ailments lifted. "You gotta branch out beyond the dating sims. Play something that gets you red in the face like you are now."

"Eh?" Sayuri slapped her hands into her lap. She had long pulled her bare legs up beneath her, and Miwa couldn't say she hated the view. "How do you know I'm playing those?"

"We're friends on the network. I can see everything you're playing... and your achievements."

"My... achievements..."

Miwa chuckled as the realization settled in over Sayuri. "You can see mine, too, so it's not like I'm up to anything nefarious."

"You can see my achievements..."

"Uh huh." Miwa turned back toward her TV. "You're dating some really interesting people in those games." She returned to the boss battle she was probably doomed to lose.

Sayuri remained as stiff as a forgotten log on the other side of the futon. "I like to play through all of the options," she said, as if she were a robot reciting lines. "And you really can't anticipate what's going to happen, sometimes. You think you're going out with one person, and you end up with another..."

Is that how you ended up with a female character who graphically ties you up and takes you for a wild ride with her tongue? Like Miwa hadn't played that game before. Hell, the disc was in one of the blanket cases beneath her TV. If there was a dating sim with lesbian sex in it, she probably owned it. A girl got lonely.

Maybe Sayuri got lonely, too.

"I try not to discriminate, you know? It's a game, right?"

Whatever she told herself. Especially since the evidence pointed to her going out of her way to date the female characters in games.

As All Our Fires Burn

Do I really have a chance? Is my gaydar actually that good? Miwa didn't want to believe it, in case it meant her emotional downfall.

Besides, what was more important? Having Sayuri as a potential lover? Or as a dear friend, whose loyalty was unwavering? Did she want to risk it?

"Ah... *muri.*" She conceded defeat in her boss battle when she realized she was out of items that would keep her alive. Meanwhile, she had barely made a dent in the boss. Not only was he one of the harder ones in the game, but Miwa had been a little distracted by her gorgeous friend sweating only a few feet away. "It's hopeless. He's gonna kill me."

"You can't give up. You've made it this far."

"So? Some days you can't win."

"Do you really wanna have to start all over again, though?"

The concerned look on Sayuri's face implied she really believed Miwa would have to start over again. *Oh... that's kind of adorable.* "I have save points, you know." Miwa had to bite back laughter that would do nothing but embarrass her friend. "I saved right before this battle. I can go back to that save and start over again with all of my items and health points."

Sayuri sighed in relief.

"Did you think this battle would really make or break my game?"

"I mean... I don't know much about this stuff."

"Yet you were so distracting the whole time?" Now, Miwa could not hold back the grin overtaking her visage. "You're adorable, Sayuri-*san.*"

Her friend took that compliment with a renewed blush to her cheeks, but she didn't say anything. Perhaps Miwa was the one embarrassing them now.

She allowed the boss to kill her without putting up much more of a fight. As soon as the Game Over screen appeared, Miwa leaned back in her couch and sighed. The controller sank between her legs. "I only have one controller, but I could put something a little more newbie friendly in and you could give it a spin."

"Huh? No. I couldn't possibly…"

Miwa got up and switched out the disks. She glanced over her shoulder while she was bent over in her cotton shorts, and caught Sayuri staring at her. *Is she checking out my ass?* Miwa stood back up and motioned to the game's logo. "This one's easy. You basically run errands for townspeople. Here." She handed Sayuri the controller. "You'll like it. The next step up from dating simulations."

Sayuri slowly accepted her fate. "If you say so."

Unfortunately, she was not as acclimated to this controller as the one she had in her own home. Miwa had to constantly lean over and press buttons for the frustrated woman who stewed in some faraway misery her hostess could not penetrate. *Is she angry at the game? Or at me?* Difficult to tell when Sayuri cursed out some old lady in the game because she didn't specify that she wanted *brown* rice instead of white rice from the grocer's. It was the first time Miwa had heard Sayuri curse.

"*Mou!*" Sayuri slapped the controller down into her lap. "I don't get this at *all*. Why do they make this so difficult?"

As All Our Fires Burn

Miwa had to refrain from laughing at her friend's misfortune. Nothing about this game was difficult, which was why she chose it for Sayuri to play. The next best thing was a puzzle game, but she had a feeling Sayuri would throw the controller out the window when she didn't win within five seconds.

Suddenly, the appeal of Satin and her wondrous BDSM sins made sense. *Think I was approaching it from the wrong angle, though.* Now, if Miwa could refrain from shuddering, she'd be in business to flirt some more with the woman next to her.

"Maybe you don't have the patience for video games," Miwa said.

Sayuri blew air out from her cheeks. "Kinda weird. I have patience for people, and they're some of the *worst* when it comes to challenging your patience! But give me an electronic, or a game, or *something,* and I have absolutely no patience whatsoever."

"Games have no feelings. You're allowed to blow up at them. Unlike people."

"Guess that's true." Sayuri handed the controller back to Miwa. "Perhaps you're patient with both."

"Maybe. I have to be patient with dumb passengers, but I don't interact with most of them every day. Not like you. You're surrounded by *kids*. And you deal with their parents."

"What if I told you that one of my most memorable students lives a few houses down from my apartment building? I know his mother fairly well. In fact, she sees me off when I come into town to see you."

There was another shudder, but this one wasn't in the name of desire. "*Kimoi,*" Miwa spat.

"*Deshou?* When you put it that way..."

"I don't live anywhere near my coworkers. Or my passengers, probably." Miwa paid a bit for it during her commute, but what else was she to do when her own trains stopped running when her shift ended? That was the whole point! Except she refused to live closer to the station. Overseer Endo and his family had a house only half a kilometer down the street. The man walked home every night. Miwa couldn't risk her boss seeing her out and about. What if they bumped into each other at a family restaurant? She would die!

"Very lucky. Sometimes I think about moving, but my apartment is too convenient to everything I need, including work. Comes in handy, like with a typhoon headed our way. I don't have to worry about getting home in case school is canceled halfway through the day."

Miwa hopped up and grabbed the empty glasses of iced tea. Both clattered into her sink as she already missed the cool caress of the fans running in her living area. *Or do I miss something else?* That something else was most definitely Sayuri's presence. Didn't keep Miwa cool at all, but she wasn't opposed to a little extra sweat if it came from the woman of her current dreams.

"Would you like something else to drink?" Miwa was already fishing ice water from her small fridge. Well, the ice anyway. She hoped the water coming out of her faucet wasn't terribly warm, but at least it was clean.

As All Our Fires Burn

"Water's fine." Sayuri glanced between the paused video game on Miwa's TV screen and her hostess. "What shall we do now?"

Know what I would like to do right now… May or may not have included getting Sayuri out of more of those clothes. Were they hot enough to suggest taking a shower? *Damn. I'm forward as fuck when I'm hot.* Sure. Blame the heat. While Miwa was at it, she might as well kiss the woman stewing on the couch.

"Since my AC is on the fritz, we could go to one of the restaurants or cafes around here. I mean, they ain't fancy, but at least they're cheap and have cool air, I'm assuming." Miwa truly assumed a lot. How was she to know that this wasn't a neighborhood-wide issue? For all she knew, the Jonathan's restaurant was as sweaty as her apartment. Or the Saizeiriya inundated with too many people escaping the heat and putting the place at over capacity.

Maybe it was better for them to stay there…

"*Douzo.*" Miwa handed her guest a fresh glass of iced water. "Sorry I don't have much else to do." She sat down next to Sayuri. "As you can see, I spend most of my time playing video games when I'm at home. I don't even have a lot of books."

"You build model trainsets, too."

"Not a lot of room for those, unfortunately." Miwa looked around her cramped apartment. "This is real Tokyo living right here." She barely had room for a TV on the wall and a futon in the corner. She could open the fridge door from her tiny two-person futon, the biggest piece of furniture in her apartment. Cleaning up the place had been like trying to stick a camel through the eye of the needle. She honestly might as well have tried swimming to San Francisco. Would've been as wet, that was for sure!

"My apartment in Fujimi isn't much bigger."

"Do you at least have a separate bedroom from the rest of your house?"

"Yes, I do."

"So it's way better!"

Sayuri giggled. Even with the room hotter than hell, Miwa was convinced that she had never felt more content than when she sat next to this giggling woman.

The magnetic pull Sayuri carried with her everywhere she went was enough to keep Miwa following her. She could start suggesting that they meet in Fujimi to make things easier for her, and Miwa would happily go like a lovesick puppy. *What I would give to have her even pat me on the head like I was a puppy...* Sounded like a dream come true to Miwa. She could quit her job and become Sayuri's full-time bitch. Live in her one-bedroom apartment in Saitama. Wait for her to come home from the elementary school and go for a brisk walk. Eat treats and sit in her lap for the rest of a dog's natural life. Play with her little boy and become his best friend through childhood. Belly rubs. Snuggling in bed. Playing fetch...

"Miwa-*san? Daijyoubu ka?*"

Miwa snapped out of her daydream. "H... *hai. Gomen,*" she apologized. "I'm sorry. The heat is getting to me."

"Me too." Sayuri tucked her hair behind her ears. *Oh, has it fallen out of its ponytail?* Miwa hadn't noticed. She was too busy dreaming of the day when she might get to kiss this woman on the lips. Or anywhere, really. "We really should go somewhere else. I don't want us getting sick because it's too hot."

Her words dissipated in the humid air. The TV turned itself off. Energy saving, or had the power blitzed out? *I don't care. She's too beautiful for me to care.* As long as the sun shone outside, Miwa was content to gaze upon Sayuri's effortless beauty and pretend that they were more than awkward friends.

"I'm okay here. Really."

Miwa couldn't understand why. Surely, her company wasn't great enough to warrant such praise, was it?

"So…" Sayuri began.

"So…" Miwa echoed.

That magnet continued to pull Miwa toward the woman sitting next to her. Then what? Touch her? Dare to offend? Miwa didn't even dare to snuggle up against Sayuri. It was too hot to come up with an excuse for that. *The only excuse I have is that I really want to touch her.* A good enough reason for Miwa, but Sayuri probably wasn't interested.

Probably…

"*Ano…*" Sayuri said again, as if she had forgotten that the word was already uttered in the past minute. "There's something I should tell you, Miwa-*san*. About me."

"Huh?"

"Well… I…"

They stared at one another through glazed-over eyes. The ice water remained untouched, and Miwa could only confess that her mouth was too dry to say a single word. *She wants to tell me something. Is it some terrible secret? Or are we on the verge of something wonderful?*

Years later, when she was a middle-aged woman wondering how her life had gotten to where it was that day, she would look back on this moment and realize… she had no idea. *One moment we're sitting here, avoiding eye contact and pretending that everything is normal. The next?*

The next moment changed everything. Kissing each other could only have that effect.

Chapter 17

SAYURI

She didn't know who kissed who first. All she knew was that she hadn't been pushed away.

Excitement fluttered in her stomach, and adrenaline pulsed through her veins. *Who said this was allowed? What God granted us the right to kiss one another and enjoy it?* Had Sayuri read all the signs correctly? Was it possible that she had been correct in assuming that Miwa might be into girls? *I don't know why I think that. A hunch?* A big enough hunch for her to take a chance and kiss the woman who had saved her life and invited her into this humble home?

Or had Miwa kissed her first?

There was no use debating it. Fact of the matter was, Miwa's lips were on Sayuri's, and they were going down like two heathens who knew a little too much about what bonfire they approached.

She's a really good kisser! That's all Sayuri could think as she naturally fell back against the futon. Yet she was no submissive maiden who let the other woman do all the work. Sayuri had been as eager as Miwa to get this make-out session started, and she was unafraid to grab the back of another woman's head and pull her down like they were going to hell together.

The whole reason Sayuri insisted on staying in Miwa's smoldering apartment was so they had an excuse to be together like this. Why would she want to go to a café when she specifically came here to spend time in Miwa's apartment? The AC not working was a convenient excuse to take off the sweater and reveal the skin she didn't often show to the world. For Miwa, though, she'd show off anything!

All right, so maybe Sayuri didn't hold out all hope that the end game would be them making love in the sweaty box that was Miwa's apartment. She did, however, hope that they would spend half their day tentatively exploring what it might mean to be a romantic couple. Going from zero to sixty on the ero-scale, however, was neither unwelcomed nor verboten!

Yes, yes, touch me there. Sayuri suffocated between Miwa's body and the futon that held in the heat of both of their undressing forms. Yet she couldn't care. Not when her heart fluttered in anticipation, and her body wondered if this would be the first time she made love to someone since Emiko left.

Miwa reached her hand beneath Sayuri's tank top. There was no holding back the gasp of desire now bursting from

Sayuri's body. How was she supposed to swallow the groan easing through her throat? Or pull back the leg desperate to wrap around Miwa's? The only reason she didn't snake her own hand beneath Miwa's T-shirt was because she was too frozen in happiness to think about it. Given a few more minutes, however, and Sayuri would show her friend how nice it was to make love together.

Not like Miwa didn't advertise her intentions when her tongue shot into Sayuri's mouth and pinned her against the futon. The only way Sayuri and her curling toes were getting out of there was if Miwa released her.

That wasn't going to happen, right? So why did it, only a few moments later?

"Ah…" Sayuri held her fingers to her lips while her legs collapsed against the futon. Miwa had pulled away, braced against the arms of her couch and slapping her elbow against her knee. A terrible grunt reverberated through her body.

The worst part? Sayuri still wanted her, even in her personal turmoil.

"*Kuso,*" Miwa cursed, hand grabbing a chunk of her greasy, sweaty hair. Sayuri's wasn't much better. It had collected a majority of the sweat easing down the back of her neck, and it would take a long shower to wash it well enough for work in the morning. "The fuck am I doing?"

Sayuri cleared her throat. "I…" she began, voice cracking, "I don't mind. I, um…" What should she say? That she liked it? That she was gay? That she was game to get back at it and show Miwa what she could do with her tongue? *All three?*

Of course, what Sayuri *really* wanted to say was some semblance of *Fuck me, damnit!*

"I shouldn't be doing this." Miwa hid her face behind both of her hands.

Oh, no. So it was like that?

"Don't feel bad about it." Sayuri shot forward, refraining from touching her friend, yet adamant that they only stay mere inches away from one another. "Lots of women like other women. It's the twenty-first century. It's not like I'm…"

Miwa cut her off. "You've got a kid. For all I know, you've got someone else in your life."

"How many times do I have to tell you that I'm single?" Sayuri knew people found it hard to believe that a woman could be single *and* have a kid, but women did it every day! All over the world! "Because I am."

"You've got a kid."

Sayuri didn't appreciate the stab to her heart. Not when that heart was beating with renewed vigor for the first time in months. "So? Am I not allowed to be alone with somebody?"

"It doesn't feel right."

Was she making up excuses for herself? Probably. Yet Sayuri couldn't help but think she had contributed to this ruined mood by lying through omission. "Don't worry about my son." Sayuri turned away, something tightening in her chest and preventing her from properly breathing. *Don't do it. Don't say it. Don't make it real again.* "He's dead."

She had done it. Reminded herself of the one thing she always tried to forget.

As All Our Fires Burn

"Eh?" Miwa's breath filtered through the air, that one sound the only thing Sayuri heard for many seconds.

Sayuri's shoulders slumped until her forehead almost touched her knees. "I *had* a son. He died. A year ago." Was that enough to placate Miwa's worries? Because the tears were now threatening to come back. It wasn't supposed to happen. Sayuri was supposed to be... happy. In love. Indulging in some physical affection that hadn't touched her person in so, so long. "So he's not waiting for me. Nobody's waiting for me back home. I have no partner, no son, no family." Here came the pity party. The smallest party in the world.

"I'm sorry," Miwa whispered. "I had no idea."

"Yeah, well... it happens." Sayuri sniffed the one sob coming for her like a train down the tracks. "The night we met was the one-year anniversary of his death. I thought maybe it was fate that I met you, because..." No. Now wasn't the time to drop a G or a L word. No Bs or Ts, either, not that they were ever words she used to describe herself. *The G and L are hard enough as it is.* Sayuri had other words as well. Words like *Mother, Teacher, Lover.* On days like today, she threw in *Mourner* as well.

"I'm really sorry." Panic rose in Miwa's voice. "I didn't mean to... I thought that..."

"It's not like I told you that little detail." Sayuri shook her head, sweaty hair falling into her lap. "I never meant to tell you I had a son at all, because I knew I wouldn't be able to say more than that. I try not to think about it."

"Meanwhile, you're in my home, and we..."

Sayuri peeled her skin off the futon and stood up, sweater in her hand. Even if Miwa took back the interruption, Sayuri had been thrown into the kind of mental spiral that was not conducive to fooling around. The mood had been ruined. She might as well go home, where she could look her son's picture in the eye and apologize for not being honest about him with anyone. "It's all right. Please don't beat yourself up about it." She searched for her purse until discovering it had been pushed beneath the futon. Probably by her own foot as it flailed for purchase while she made out with her biggest crush since Emiko walked into her life. "I was the one who wasn't completely honest."

She spared Miwa one last look before showing herself out of the apartment. *I thought I would see remorse on her countenance. Yet all I see is shame.* That had not been Miwa's first time kissing a woman, Sayuri was sure, but that didn't mean Miwa accompanied it with anything but shame and embarrassment.

They said nothing else before Sayuri slipped on her sandals and walked to the nearest train station. As she ascended the steps, sweater still hanging from her hand instead of conservatively covering her bare skin, she thought back to the woman who had pulled her back from the tracks on the second to worst night of Sayuri's life. Gloved hands. A crisp yet well-worn uniform. Hair pulled to the nape of the neck and showcasing the fragile youth still apparent in one woman's face.

Hard to believe it was the same woman she had kissed. And the woman she now left behind.

Chapter 18

"Quiet, please!" Sayuri raised her hands, as if a simple movement like that would do anything to calm down her classroom of excited third graders. *"Shizuka ni shite!"*

It didn't help that they had a new addition to their classroom that fine September morning. While the winds outside gradually picked up in time for the oncoming typhoon, the third graders at Sayuri's school bounced up and down like large chunks of hail at the prospect of a brand-new foreigner in their midst.

It *also* didn't help that Dean-*sensei* was over six feet tall and a former goalie for his university's football club. (He made sure that they all knew it was *football,* not soccer, like the Americans insisted on calling it. He also insisted that no, he was not American, thank you very much. Did his Australian accent not give him away?) While foreigners were a common enough site in Fujimi City, rarely did these kids get to be so up close to one who could tear them apart with one roar. Sayuri also had to deal with her female coworkers swooning over the married man like he was the prized catch on display at the local fish market. Most of the younger teachers were still unmarried, but the older, *married* ones still giggled like they were studying abroad and had their choice of nice young men ready to bed them without wedding them. Dean-*sensei* was also a notorious flirt. The worst part? His wife went along with it! Was that really how they did things in Australia?

Maybe I don't get it. Sayuri was too broken in the heterosexuality department to understand the appeal of a man like Dean. Thankfully, she somewhat understood it from the point of view of a nine-year-old.

"Dean-*sensei* wants to introduce himself!" Sayuri shouted over the rabble. Usually, she didn't have this much difficulty getting her students to calm down the ruckus. She didn't know what they had been up to over their summer break, but each one came back more riled up than dogs that had been cooped-up in their houses for a whole week. *They drool and bark enough, too...* Sayuri sighed before turning to the man six inches taller than her – a feat, since she was taller than the average Japanese woman. "I'm so sorry," she said in Japanese. Another reason the teachers went crazy for Mr. Dean Wagner was because he spoke semi-fluent Japanese. Not that the students were supposed to know that. "You have to forgive them. They're eight."

As All Our Fires Burn

His Western-sized smile remained on his face as he surveyed the chaos reigning in the classroom. The boys drummed on their desks and shouted "*GAIJIN-DA!*" while the girls giggled. Their whispers were inaudible on Sayuri's side of the classroom, but she was pretty sure they were wondering how to get blond hair like his.

"Hey guys!" Dean's voice bellowed in the room, silencing all but the two rowdiest boys. Even then, Shota had to get in the last word by loudly announcing to the class that Dean-*sensei* was "taller than King Kong." "Thank you, yes, for that astute observation." Dean wasn't allowed to speak Japanese in front of the students, who were tricked into assuming that he was a walking, talking, English-only robot. He knew that nobody in the room, including Sayuri, understood what he said. *The only reason I understand that much is because I watch too many Hollywood movies.* "Astute observation" was said in many of her favorite detective shows. "Let's meet each other, huh?"

Sayuri was grateful that he got everyone's attention in one burst of his voice. She bade her students to please pay attention while Dean-*sensei* introduced himself in English. She was supposed to translate for the class. Good thing they had gone over in the teacher's room what he would say, because Sayuri stopped listening after "*I love ramen.*"

"Are there any questions for Dean-*sensei*?" Sayuri asked the class.

Half a dozen hands shot into the air. If she didn't pick on Shota, who was falling over his desk in the front-center where she could keep an eye on him, then he'd surely interrupt whatever student she *did* pick. Unfortunately, Sayuri was fairly aware of what he would ask.

"Is it true that Americans have the biggest poops in the world?"

He beamed in pride as the whole class laughed uproariously. *God give me strength.* Most children were obsessed with poop for some awful reason, but Sayuri had to hand it to her class of third graders for taking it to another level. These were the same kids who wanted to call their Culture Day café "Le Unko," in honor of their favorite bathroom topic. Sayuri also received a stack of summer break journals dotted in smiling poop stickers and personal sketches of characters like Mario and Minions straining themselves a little too hard. *Honestly, I was more concerned that they might hurt themselves.*

Dean-*sensei* didn't need Sayuri to translate that for him. Good thing, because she had no idea *what* to say. "First of all," he replied, "I'm not American. I think I've said that I'm from Australia no fewer than five times."

His accent continued to make the kids laugh. Even Sayuri was mildly amused by it, since she rarely heard an Australian accent in real life. Still, she was mature enough to not giggle every time he said something, which was more than what any of her students could say.

"Anyone else have any questions?" Sayuri looked right over Shota's head.

The students gradually lost interest in teasing their new English teacher, but Shota was on a mission to ensure that Dean-*sensei* knew who was the dominant boy in the classroom.

As All Our Fires Burn

Why do you think you're in the front and center seat, Shota-kun... Every class had a "leader," and Sayuri was good at picking out who it would be within the first week of the year. *If only his mother wasn't proud when I told her the boy was making it to the front row...* Shota's antics were definitely encouraged at home, where he was the only child in a house obsessed with him. Deep down he was a good kid. In time, the world would knock some sense into him, but until then, it was Sayuri's job to keep him in line.

"They're very *genki* in your class, huh?" Dean-*sensei* stopped by Sayuri's desk in the teacher's room at the end of the day. "Everyone warned me that your third graders were rowdy."

"Kids being kids," Sayuri said with a sigh. "Thank you for understanding. They keep me on my toes." She didn't say what kept her toes curled, however. None of his business.

Thinking about that, however, reminded her of something she wanted to ask the only native English speaker she currently knew.

"Do you have any suggestions for drafting an apologetic letter in English?" She had been thinking about it ever since she blew the best thing that had happened to her two days before. *I spent the whole train ride home with my face buried in my bag, trying not to cry.* Was it grief from admitting to yet another person that her child was gone? Or was it anger that she couldn't keep Miwa's interest in her? *She kissed me. I kissed her. I don't know. But we were kissing each other, and she...* She what? Had wanted more? Was going for the kill before pulling away? Was clearly knowledgeable in all things lesbian lovemaking? "I have a friend who is trying to learn English for her job, and I need to apologize for something."

Dean cocked his head. "Why not say it in Japanese?"

"Apologizing in Japanese is very complicated, as I'm sure you've noticed. Picking a tone alone could make or break my apology. I could avoid it in English."

"Hate to break it to you, but English has a lot of the same problems."

Sayuri had been afraid of that. By the time she walked home, the sky rumbling once more, she decided that the apology she owed Miwa couldn't be best expressed over the phone. Nor did she have the supplies necessary to get her conflicting thoughts properly across.

She stopped at the only stationery store still open in the evening. When the proprietress asked what Sayuri specifically searched for, all she could say was, "I need to tell someone that I'm sorry and want to explain myself."

A dour gaze met hers. "*Kowai sou desu ne?*" the old woman said, empathy lacing her voice. "That's a serious predicament to be in. You can't pick whatever stationery meets your fancy of the moment."

"Indeed not."

"Here." Slowly, as if she trudged through the gravity of Sayuri's situation, the old woman shuffled to the back wall, where many of the mourning stationery was kept. Lest Sayuri assume the worst, the woman made sure to walk past the white envelopes and to a small corner that was kept impeccably clean, although it must not have received much traffic in the shop.

As All Our Fires Burn

"These are what you need. They don't mess around in saying that you're serious, but they're not grave." She handed Sayuri a small package of off-white cards bordered in a skinny gold film. Mature. Sophisticated. Yet feminine enough to keep someone like Miwa from trembling as she opened a card carefully written to convey her utmost thoughts and feelings.

It helped that they weren't terribly expensive, either.

Sayuri bought a new fountain pen to go with the cards. On the way home, she rehearsed what she wanted to write. Yet she had made it as far as making herself tea and heating up something instant for dinner and still didn't have a concrete plan.

She sat at her desk by the window overlooking her sleepy suburban neighborhood. Lights gradually went out as children were put to bed and husbands lay before the glow of their televisions. The only people up with Sayuri were housewives who still had too much to do.

Her new fountain pen tapped against the desk. The more she chewed the inside of her cheeks, the more she became convinced that she didn't have the right words to say.

"*Miwa*-san..." That was all she had written so far. In *hiragana* no less, because she still didn't know what proper Chinese characters Miwa used to write her name. *I bet the "Mi" is "beautiful."* It would be fitting, since Miwa was one of the most beautiful women Sayuri had ever seen, let alone kissed.

Then again, it could be the character for the number "three," in which case Sayuri could only say that Miwa had the beauty of three women contained within her small frame.

"*Please allow me to apologize for what happened Sunday afternoon.*" Every stroke of the pen was as careful as they could be, with Sayuri recalling her own lessons about penmanship to her students. "*I wasn't myself...*"

She reconsidered that. What she *meant* was that she didn't usually blab about her son *or* keep secrets from women she admired. Yet the way it was written made Sayuri sound like she meant to say she didn't usually kiss girls. When she did. Quite well, really.

Miwa had liked her kissing, right?

Sayuri slumped against her desk with a sigh. Useless. Everything, from trying to apologize to thinking about her love torn life, was *useless*. What was the point when Miwa would probably simply stay angry at her? Sayuri had a terrible habit of screwing up every good thing that came her way. Sometimes it took years for her to light the match that burned the grove of her accomplishments. Other times, it took mere weeks. That's how long she had known Miwa. *Weeks.*

Yet I've known her long enough to know that I like her. A lot. Sayuri had to come clean. She had to tell everything she had been hiding so she wouldn't look like a loon on the verge of breaking down on poor Miwa. She wouldn't dump any scary words like "love," but she would make her intentions clear in the most succinct manner possible.

She picked up her pen – and her pride.

Chapter 19

MIWA

"A flood could happen at any moment," the representative from the local disaster preparedness program said, as he led the station employees from one end of the platform to the other. Miwa held back a yawn that would betray how little sleep she had gotten since Sunday, when Sayuri rushed out of the apartment in a flurry of tears and shame. Every time Miwa lay down to sleep, she thought of two things: the feel of her body pressing against Sayuri's as they came deliriously close to having sex on the couch, and the sight of her running through that door.

No wonder Miwa couldn't sleep.

"Typhoons are perhaps the most realistic danger to create flooding in the tunnels." Like the trainer who had walked them through what to do in case of a tunnel fire, this man made sweeping gestures, pantomiming a wave of water coming down the tracks. "The rivers can overflow from anything and get all the way down here. Tsunamis, for one. Let's not forget what happened the last time a dam broke in this country!"

Unfortunately, he was the only one who remembered.

Overseer Endo asked him to focus on typhoon preparedness. The weather forecast had firmly announced that Sunday was D-Day, and while Miwa would not be working that day, she might have to deal with the fallout on Monday. Even if the worst of the storm was over, who knew what damage would be wrought? At least it wasn't a workday. If the trains came to a grinding halt for the safety of passengers, few businessmen would make it to their jobs.

Miwa did not look forward to biking through flooded streets. Hopefully, the worst of it would be over by Monday afternoon, when her shift began. Her current plan was to hold out the worst of the storm in her apartment playing video games. If the power went out, she had mobile games ready to go on charged devices. She was already stocked up on snacks and drinks. Worst she expected was being trapped inside for a day and losing power for more than a few minutes.

"Ban-*san*," Endo said. "You still with us?"

She snapped her attention back to the demonstration of what to do should the power go out while they were working the platform. "Yes, sir."

"Uh huh. Do try to look alive, would you?"

Miwa walked her bike part of the way home, because her mind was too full of thoughts to safely ride. She occasionally looked up at the starry sky, wondering if it knew that it was about to be the scene of a drastic storm already wreaking havoc in the Pacific. Like her own love life wreaked havoc in her heart.

She hadn't texted or called Sayuri since that shitty day. Nor had Sayuri initiated contact with her. It was over already, wasn't it?

So she thought.

One piece of mail stuck out above the rest when Miwa went to check her box. Bills fell to the bottom of the stack as she looked at the fine handwriting of the woman she both desperately wished to hear from... and dreaded ever speaking to again.

I can still feel her lips on mine... This was it. A formal letter telling Miwa's perverted gay-ass to stay far, far away from the well-to-do schoolteacher and mother of a dead child.

She needed a drink first.

A cold beer cracked open on her coffee table as Miwa withdrew the instant dinner she picked up from the convenience store down the street. Only when she enjoyed the first few refreshing sips and cleared an appropriate space on her table did she open the oddly-shaped envelope and read the inevitable.

"*Miwa*-san..."

At least Sayuri wasn't back to calling her Ban, as if they were two strangers still tentatively getting to know one another.

"*Please let me apologize for what happened Sunday afternoon in your home.*"

Miwa put down the letter before it could bite her. A few seconds later, when she had recollected her thoughts, she picked it up again.

"I was wrong to keep the whole truth about myself from you. When the wounds were opened, I grew scared and ran away. It was wrong of me. Please give me the opportunity to properly explain myself before we may decide to go our separate ways."

There was a request for them to meet sometime that weekend, preferably before the typhoon hit their area. Sayuri had Saturday off, and more words to explain herself than she could possibly write in one short letter.

Miwa stared at that exquisite handwriting before picking up her phone. It may be daybreak, but odds were high that Sayuri was getting up to prepare for work, anyway.

The call went straight to voicemail.

"Hi…" Miwa cleared her throat. "I got your letter. I'm sorry for calling you so late. Text me what time is good for you on Saturday. I'm sure we could meet in Ikebukuro again."

She hung up. Although she didn't hear from Sayuri before crawling into her bed and cursing the sun for already being up, Miwa pretended that butterflies didn't explode in her stomach and anxiety didn't cripple her ability to sleep. *It's all a façade of my mind…* She shouldn't have any expectations. Even if Sayuri told her everything she wanted to hear, Miwa knew better than to get her hopes up. Ever.

Still, they had kissed before. Miwa was the one who put a stop to it. Was it possible that they could have a moment like that again?

As All Our Fires Burn

No. Don't. Even so, Miwa finally fell asleep with thoughts of Sayuri's lips at the far edges of her subconscious. Her dreams were even more tantalizing.

***

"All company personnel please be advised of storm advancing to Kanto region." Miwa held her phone closer to her face, in case she wasn't reading the text from her employer correctly. *"Possible closures today and tomorrow. Please call in ahead of your scheduled shift to ensure whether or not your position continues for the day."*

Miwa cursed as she lowered her phone. Not because she had a shift anytime in the next twenty-four hours, but because the windows of the café were already rattling, and Sayuri was too far from home to turn around and go back. When they both left their apartments that morning, the sky was clear and blue. Now? That typhoon was moving at record speeds, and the weather report updated to warn citizens to stay indoors for the rest of the weekend. Too late for that.

Besides, Miwa was too curious about what Sayuri had to say. And, perhaps, she was invested in seeing her again.

It didn't help that Sayuri arrived in a pink knee-length skirt and a baggy white sweater that highlighted the femininity that transformed Miwa into a slobbering idiot. *I'm such a frump compared to her.* Miwa had dressed up in a pair of trousers and the kind of blouse that she would wear to company functions. Her hair was pulled back into a clean ponytail, and her makeup minimal enough to not call attention to itself – but if Sayuri had been paying attention, she would realize that this was the first time Miwa wore makeup in her presence. *I do it for pretty women and company functions.* The more Miwa's phone went off in her bag, the more she was reminded of the troubles plaguing her station. *"Please be aware that our station might be closing early today and opening late tomorrow – Overseer Endo."*

"I'm sorry I'm late." Sayuri was her own typhoon of nerves as she settled into the chair across from Miwa. "The train was delayed, and I couldn't figure out why."

"The typhoon is coming early." Miwa checked her phone one last time before shoving it into her bag. "The overland railways might be shutting down early today."

Panic renewed itself on Sayuri's face. "Here's hoping the subways will still be running."

Miwa didn't have anything to say to that. It was the perfect impetus to remind Sayuri of why she was there.

"*Ano...*" she glanced away before offering more. "Thank you for giving me the opportunity to apologize to you in person, Miwa-*san*. It means a lot to me."

Although she had been nervous – perhaps, even a bit excited – when she left her apartment early that afternoon, Miwa couldn't help but purse her lips now. While it would be impossible for them to pick up where they left off, Miwa had held onto a tinge of hope that things wouldn't be quite *this* formal. Clearly, however, Sayuri felt she had something serious to apologize for. Miwa simply hoped that it had nothing to do with kissing.

As All Our Fires Burn

Within two seconds, Miwa went from worrying that she came off too harsh, to wondering what Sayuri thought of the semi-formal attire.

"The fault is mine as well." Miwa waited for the waitress to bring Sayuri's drink before continuing. "I'm the one who made the situation difficult." There it was. She was willing to take the blame for the kissing. *I did it. I started it. I couldn't help myself. I'm an unrestrained wild woman.* Damnit. She couldn't even *think* that seriously. *I wish I were an unrestrained wild woman...* "*Hontou ni sumimasen deshita.*"

She said that with a straight back and her head bowing over the table. Sayuri sat against the back of her chair, as if she didn't know what to make of Miwa's apology. "I'm not sure why you're saying that, Miwa-*san*... I'm the one who held back important information from our relationship."

"I'm apologizing because..." Did she really have to say it?

Sayuri cut her off, anyway. "Please let me be the one to take responsibility for any ill-feelings between us." They both glanced at the window beside them as it rattled in a rush of strong winds. The skies were covered, now. A few tentative raindrops hit the glass, but at the moment, there was nothing to worry about. "I am willing to make things right. Let me know what I can do to put your faith back in me."

Such mighty words for what Miwa perceived to be *her* fault! *Seriously, how do I respond to this?* "I guess I only want the truth?" Nothing said a woman scorned like squeaking out requests.

Sayuri slumped her shoulders, her age showing the tiniest bit in her otherwise youthful face. It was the visage of a woman who had experienced enough pain and fright to put more wrinkles on her face, yet something about her – perhaps the sweetness with which she approached life – begged her to never let it show. If it was true that she had lost a child, then Miwa could certainly understand why that glower followed Sayuri like a dark cloud.

"All right. I owe you the whole truth." Sayuri bit her lip. "Before I begin, I simply want to say that the only reason I never mentioned these things was because I try to not let them affect my relationships with people."

"Perfectly reasonable," Miwa muttered.

"Anyway…" Sayuri stabbed her straw through the top of her drink and rubbed her forehead. "I've never been married. That much is true." More words were on the tip of her tongue, but whatever they were, each one disappeared down Sayuri's long and slender throat. *Great. Stare at her throat while she talks, you perv.* Miwa wondered if there was anything Sayuri could possibly say that would ruin things between them. Murderer? Drug runner? Eh. Miwa could be pretty desperate. Not that Sayuri needed to know that.

She did, however, need to know that Miwa was listening.

"I wasn't married, but I had a… partner." Sayuri cleared her throat. "We decided to have a child. So, we did. His name was Yuma."

The mood befalling their table was worse than the weather outside. Miwa glanced down at the pedestrians hurrying up and down the sidewalks of a busy street in Ikebukuro, one of the biggest shopping districts in all of Tokyo. It didn't look so busy now. The ants were scurrying to the station, hoping to get home before everything shut down for the storm. Plans were befouled. Relationships put on hold. Yet here Sayuri and Miwa were, acting like nothing else happened beyond them.

"He was three years old when he passed away." Sayuri sipped her drink. "I brought him into the city to go to Inokashira Park and to visit a friend of mine. It began to rain. I think it may have been one of the first typhoons of the season…" She shook her head. "It doesn't matter. It was late. I was careless in my car. We crashed."

That was all she said to begin with. *She doesn't need to say more.* An accident. A lost child. What else was there to know?

"I got out of it with hardly any scratches," Sayuri continued. "Yuma, though… he was alive when we got to the hospital, but I guess he never came out of unconsciousness. That was a year ago."

"I'm so sorry," Miwa said.

"Yes, well… I bear the responsibility for my son's death. My carelessness cost me everything."

"Everything but your life."

Sayuri sucked in her lips. "I think about that a lot. Why he died and I did not."

"What about your partner?"

"They weren't there. They were at work."

"No, I mean… what happened with them? Are you not together anymore?"

"No," Sayuri whispered. "Losing our son tore us apart. We couldn't come back from it."

"That's a terrible thing to have happen."

Sayuri sighed. "I didn't lose my job or my apartment. The administration was very kind and let me take personal leave to grieve for my son. It's been a long road since that night. I don't even drive anymore. I sold the car to help cover my expenses when I went on leave."

"You said that the night we met…"

Another sigh wracked Sayuri's body. "That was the first anniversary of my son's death. I came into the city to retrace my steps of that day. I don't know what I was thinking. I think I temporarily lost my mind."

"You really did not look well that night. I thought you might be sick."

"I was. Sick with heartbreak."

Miwa couldn't bring herself to say what must have been true. *You didn't care if you died, too.* Even in the weeks since she met Sayuri, there had been more training at work about what to do in case of jumpers. Other stations in Miwa's company had guardrails and gates that protected passengers from falling into the tracks. Not Amaya-jinja-guchi. It was a low priority station, due to the not enough traffic and it not exactly being a hotbed of suicidal activity. *You wanted to be with your son.* Instead, she met one of the most unlikely women in Tokyo.

Here they were. Having drinks in Ikebukuro while a typhoon picked up strength outside.

"That's really all there is to say." Sayuri nodded with finality. "I'm sorry I never mentioned that my son had passed away. I didn't even intend to mention that I ever had a son."

As All Our Fires Burn

"I'm sure." Miwa didn't know what to say. What *did* someone say to a grieving mother who tried her best to forget such a loss ever occurred? There were no words. None good enough to get the sentiment across while avoiding more pain for the woman always on the brink of tears. "Perhaps it is fate that we met, though. Something or someone is out there facilitating everything, depending on who you ask." Christians, mostly. Although some Buddhists in Miwa's life liked to make a big deal about hands of fate and accepting things that could not be changed. "I guess we were two lonely people, and something made our meeting happen."

Sayuri snorted. "Lonely… I suppose so."

"You said so yourself that you don't have many friends."

"No. Most of them disappeared when my partner left me. I'm on good terms with my coworkers and neighbors, but I would hardly call them friends. Guess you could say I haven't been actively hunting for any since the accident."

"I've never experienced anything like that," Miwa began, "but I can sympathize. I find it difficult to make friends. Let alone keep them."

Sayuri briefly placed her hands together, face downcast as she gave one last formal apology. "I sincerely hope that what happened last weekend won't affect our friendship."

"*What happened.*" "*Our friendship.*" Two phrases that might as well be the wooden stake in any romance that kindled between them. "I don't think it will," Miwa said. She wouldn't mention the *other* thing that happened. *The kissing. God, the kissing…* Miwa tried not to blush in front of her friend.

"The drinks here are pretty good, huh?" That was Sayuri's way of changing the topic. It even came with a fake little laugh that got Miwa right in the heart. *I wouldn't mind waking up to her laughter every day.* How could they make that happen. Could Sayuri call her every morning and give her a daily dose of that medicine? Or was there any hope that they might live together one day?

Now she was getting ahead of herself.

They fell back into their usual conversation. Work. Hobbies. What it was like living in their respective cities. Not once did they come close to discussing what happened before the truth came out the other day. Miwa didn't know if it was because of how public their conversation might be, or if because they silently, mutually agreed to overlook that moment. For now.

Didn't help that Sayuri continued to look like a glistening angel who had recently descended from Heaven to warn every one of the oncoming storm. The way she tilted her head whenever she had a poignant thing to say, was enough to drive Miwa crazy. She had to prevent herself from huffing like a belligerent child every time they dared to come close to remembering what it was like to make out on Miwa's couch. *I was there too, you know,* Miwa thought with a sigh. *I was on top of you for five whole seconds. I had my hand up your skirt and my tongue down your throat.* The one thing Miwa never failed to remember was how easily Sayuri had kissed her back. *I'm not the first girl you've kissed...* Sayuri continued to mention a "partner." Had it been a woman? Was that why they weren't married and had to go the IVF route to have a baby? Had to be. So why wasn't Sayuri confessing that as well?

"Miwa-*san?*"

She realized she had been totally checked out while Sayuri talked about an incident between the new ALT at her elementary school and one of her students. "*Gomen,*" Miwa apologized. "I was distracted."

Sayuri wanly smiled, as if she understood what might have caught Miwa off guard. *Like she could be thinking of me that way...*

Before either one of them could say something else, the waitress hurriedly approached and bowed multiple times before saying, "Excuse me, but we are having to close early. The typhoon is quickly coming."

Miwa looked out the window. Sure enough, the rains splattered against the glass and the winds knocked the SALE flags off the store beneath them. City workers in bright reflective gear hustled up and down the narrow streets, bidding people return home or find other shelter.

"Guess we should go home," Sayuri said with wide eyes. "Before the trains stop running."

There were a dozen messages on Miwa's phone when she pulled it out of her bag. They all said some variance of *Such-and-Such Line shutting down in ten minutes.*

Sayuri was on her phone as well, reading a news report that she soon relayed. "It says it's coming so hard and fast that they're expecting flash floods and power outages as soon as two hours from now." Her cheeks whitened as she then said, "I haven't shuttered up my apartment *at all.*"

"Come on." Miwa stood up, bill in hand. "If we pay right now, we might get to the station in time for the last trains."

They weren't the only ones with that idea. Miwa's ponytail whipped against her face, and Sayuri's skirt fluttered around her thighs as they pressed against the wind to get to Ikebukuro Station as quickly as possible. A herd of people came with them, the rabble that rode the winds insinuating everyone had read the same reports and heard the same messages on the warning system. In the distance, a high-wind siren sounded. The natural wind tunnels created between the towering buildings of northwest Tokyo almost prevented them from getting to the JR station in a timely manner.

Unfortunately, bad news abounded.

"There has already been flooding around Kawagoe," one girl was overheard saying. "All the trains have stopped running beyond there!"

"At least Fujimi is before Kawagoe, *ne?*" Miwa said to her friend, who was tall enough to look over the heads of most of the crowd. Railway officials stood behind the closed ticket gates, announcing who had priority to board the last of the trains taking off for Saitama Prefecture. "The elderly, the handicapped, and families with children under the age of sixteen," did not apply to Sayuri.

"What about you?" Sayuri turned to Miwa to ask. "Can you get home from here?"

"I have to transfer, but..." She glanced at the digital boards keeping everyone abreast of the news. Winds howled behind them. "I think my subway from here is canceled, anyway."

"We apologize for the inconvenience!" A senior official, whom Miwa recognized from company newsletters, announced through a bullhorn. "All rail heading north is canceled due to high winds and flooding! Once again, we apologize!" He bowed at the waist multiple times, much to the chagrin of frightened passengers attempting to get home in the middle of a sudden typhoon.

Sayuri gasped. "You can't shut down all the rail from the second busiest train station in the *world*..."

Can only imagine how Shinjuku is holding out right now. Hell, a riot was probably ready to erupt at Amaya-jinja-guchi, and Miwa was totally missing out. *Not missing out trying to ride my bike home in a typhoon, though...* "The whole city must be a mess right now." They usually had a lot more warning when it came to mother nature going haywire. When Miwa attempted to check her phone for messages from her company, she realized her signal was spotty at best. Had a tower gone down? She vaguely recalled a bunch of them being up in Saitama Prefecture.

They attempted to find an open subway line, in the hopes that Sayuri could still get a part of the way home and maybe find a taxi for the rest. However, the only lines still open went from east to west. That didn't even help Miwa.

"*Dou suru?*" a panicked Sayuri asked as they were turned away from Miwa's own company. She did not envy her coworkers for having to give countless passengers the bad news. "What are we going to do? Where are we going to go?"

Miwa overheard the same few key phrases uttered by the other wayward passengers around them. She couldn't believe she was about to repeat them, either. "We better find a hotel room before all the cheaper ones are booked."

She anticipated a hundred responses from Sayuri, but none of them included, "Would we be safe in one?"

"If you think about it, hotels are probably the safest places to be." Few of them had enough windows for that to be a primary concern. They were also earthquake proof, so high winds were no worries. The worst part would be sharing an awkward evening with Sayuri as they were slammed into a room together for God knew how long. *Maybe if we hadn't kissed before...* Yeah, maybe it wouldn't have been so awkward. "Honestly, if you can't go home, the second best place to be would be my apartment, because at least it's free." Miwa snorted. "But we can't go there, either! Unless you feel like riding this thing out in a manga café or karaoke booth, we need to get a cheap hotel room. Now."

"Cheap" and "Ikebukuro" did not go well together. This was a neighborhood of five-star hotels and a few cheap hostels, but those were definitely booked up for the next few days. Their best bet was a "rest" hotel, which was how Miwa chose to think of them instead of their alternative name.

Love hotel!

Sayuri was the lost tourist in Tokyo as Miwa took her hand and led her back into the city. Umbrellas that had opened only a few minutes before were now turned inside out and rattling against the pavement. Drenched by rainwater, Miwa ducked into the eaves of the nearest hourly-rate hotel with Sayuri's hand still in hers. There was a small line of couples and friends who had the same idea. While they counted their money and tried to make the best of the situation, Miwa politely asked Sayuri if she would be willing to split the cost of a room for a night.

"If you think it's best…" Sayuri held her hand against her chest. Raindrops slipped off their bodies and puddled around their feet. The poor receptionist on duty looked both scared witless for her own stranded hide and overwhelmed by the sudden influx of drowned rats for customers. At least they were out of the wind.

"Tell you what. As soon as we're settled in, I'll pop into the nearest convenience store and get our rations."

"Our what?"

A panel showcasing the romantic themes of available rooms gradually dimmed as one room after another was booked. *Damnit. There goes some of the cheaper ones.* Miwa wasn't looking forward to a tropical getaway theme or, worse, a "cowboy's paradise" complete with a giant inflatable bull to "ride." *Jesus. Where do they come up with this shit?* Miwa hadn't been to a love hotel since she hooked up with a girl from a gay bar. *That was years ago!* Had it really been since college? She was getting obnoxiously old.

"Rations," she then repeated to Sayuri. "We're gonna need food and drinks to get us through the storm. Won't be great stuff, but we won't go hungry."

"Might be nice to get out of these wet clothes, too." Sayuri instantly reddened after she said that. "I mean… it would be nice to get a shower. I *mean*…"

Too late. Miwa thought about her naked. In the shower. With water spray. On *her body.*

"Ah. It's our turn." Miwa cleared her throat and approached the desk. "Let's see what they have left."

She had her brilliant idea in the nick of time. There was exactly one cheaper room left, and thank the Lord, because it wasn't some terrible kitschy theme that would make them think about awful sex the whole time they were imprisoned in there against the typhoon. *Even if we were gonna do that... there's something to be said for taste.* Last time Miwa was in a love hotel, it was one of those two-hour wham, bam, thank all the ma'ams places with shared bathrooms and plastic for sheets. While people often used those places to take naps or give them a place to rest if they missed the last train of the night, they were definitely more suited for horny couples looking to blast off in a somewhat private place.

This was much better.

They were both 4,000 *yen* poorer in the end, but the peace of mind would be worth it. Well, almost. Sayuri continued to fret that her apartment wasn't properly shuttered to protect the windows from the high winds. She muttered about it on their way up the elevator, room keys in hand.

"Of all the days for a typhoon to be one day early," Sayuri said as they stepped into their room. "You'd think this was planned!"

In another life, Miwa probably had planned this. She didn't know whether to thank her alternate-universe self... or to kick her in the shins.

Chapter 20

SAYURI

"Ah, *yokatta!*" Sayuri sighed in relief to hear the good news on the other end of her phone. "I don't know how to thank you, Shimazaki-*san*," she said to her neighbor. "I'm completely caught unaware down here in Tokyo. I've got shelter with a friend, but I'm worried about my apartment."

"The winds aren't quite as bad up here yet," Mariko reassured her over the phone. "Should be fine for me to pop into your place and close the shutters for you. Now, where's the spare key again?"

Sayuri told her, this time while Mariko wrote down the instructions. She bade Sayuri to please stay safe in Tokyo, and Sayuri in turn asked her neighbor to look after everything in her stead. With any luck, Sayuri would be back in her apartment by Sunday afternoon, the worst of the storm over and the trains running again. She focused on that after hanging up and plugging her phone into the complimentary charger the room offered.

Five minutes later, Miwa returned from the convenience store across the street, her clothing drenched and her hair flat against her head. *Because it wasn't bad enough that she was dressed like this today...* Sayuri had almost been felled where she stood when she saw Miwa in the café. What did she think she was doing, wearing office clothing and a hint of makeup? *She also had to go and pull her hair back again...* Sayuri was a sucker for hair pulled away from a woman's face. Didn't matter if a girl chopped off all her hair like Emiko did, or if she wore the kind of smart ponytail Miwa had embraced earlier that day. Her hair may have been ruined now, but the effort was still there. Even if Ms. Office Lady had two bags of convenience store goods hanging from her hands.

"Wasn't sure what you'd want, so I got yakisoba and udon for hot food." Miwa placed the bags on the coffee table before the couch. "I like both, so it's up to you."

"Thank you." Sayuri also accepted a bottle of cold green tea. There was complimentary hot tea offered in the room, but her nerves had made her throat dry and her mouth parched. She didn't hesitate before popping open the cap and taking a swig of ice cold *o-cha*.

"I also got the usual assortment of snacks." Miwa freed herself of the bags – and the wet jacket clinging close to her frame. "Help yourself. I raided the 100 *yen* section. Me and half of Ikebukuro..." She wandered off toward the bathroom. A towel was soon in her hand, drying off her hair after she released it from its tangled mess.

Sayuri looked away before her eyes became glued to Miwa's ass. *I can't believe I'm in a love hotel.* Sayuri wished she could say that it had been forever since she last stepped foot in one of these places, but one of Emiko's last Hail Marys to save their relationship was to sweep her partner into a fancy love hotel room and "make love to her all night long." Yet Sayuri had spent most of the night complaining that Emiko had wasted the money. Instead of having sex, they bickered about everything *but* the things that bothered them: Sayuri was still in mourning, and Emiko was desperate to have a life again.

Too bad she had already moved on by then. Sayuri had sensed it. Which was probably why she now associated love hotels with relationships falling apart.

"I really appreciate everything you've done, Miwa-*san*," Sayuri called toward the bathroom. "I'm afraid I'm utterly useless in a crisis."

"I'm sort of trained for these situations."

So was Sayuri, wasn't she? Part of being a schoolteacher was knowing what to do with a classroom full of children should a disaster occur. Fires, earthquakes... *typhoons.* Had there been classes that day, surely she would have been the one to break the news to her students that they were going home early. Instead, they were probably sitting in their homes, cursing that their weekends were ruined by foul weather. *Mine too, kids...*

Was it ruined, though? Miwa had not only accepted her apology after hearing her spiel... but they were now hanging out together for the indefinite future. This was assuming that Miwa still actually liked Sayuri. She kept spacing off during their conversation in the café, hadn't she? Maybe she wasn't interested. The kiss in Miwa's apartment had ended because of *her,* after all. *She* ended it. *She* broke it off. Sayuri could no longer remember who started it, but Miwa definitely ended it.

Like a fight.

Sayuri opened the bag containing the hot yakisoba and tried not to think about how much her son loved it. She was halfway through eating it when Miwa walked over, wet hair down and clothes stripped down to her pants and sleeveless powder blue blouse. It was Sayuri's first time seeing how toned those arms were.

She was a sucker for toned arms...

"How's the food?" Miwa asked.

"I make better."

Miwa snorted. "Not what I asked."

"It's satisfying." Sayuri wasn't satisfied, though. While the convenience store food would keep her full, she would continue to feel empty inside. *How can I be full when I can't stop staring at her?* Every few seconds, Sayuri replayed those precious moments they had last weekend. How fair was it that they came so close to expressing something so wonderfully raw, only for it to end the way it did?

Now they were in a love hotel. How ironic.

"Maybe we should watch some TV." Sayuri picked up the remote from the coffee table. "The news might have something."

As All Our Fires Burn

Miwa barely breathed while Sayuri flipped on the television. Two seconds later, it had both of their attentions.

"Holy...!" Miwa slapped her hand over her mouth. Whoever watched the TV last had left it on an X-rated channel. Neither Sayuri nor Miwa were prepared for uncensored sexual intercourse between a man and a woman. "Wow!"

Sayuri hurried to change the channel, embarrassment on the verge of destroying her sanity. Unfortunately, the next three channels were also nothing but pornography. By the time they came upon a woman in a bunny suit hopping up and down, her breasts nearly hitting her in the face with every vigorous bounce, Miwa was sprawled across her seat, laughing.

"When does it end?" Sayuri almost dropped the remote. "All I want is the news!"

"Suuuure," Miwa mumbled.

Finally, Sayuri found a non-pornographic channel. A travel show. Some old woman was off to Niigata Prefecture, sampling food and exclaiming how beautiful it was. "Excuse me?"

"I didn't say anything."

Funny. Sayuri was pretty sure Miwa had implied that someone *liked* all the porn. *Even if I did like visual stimulation, Ms. Ban, I can assure you that I do not care for anything that includes firehoses.* She couldn't even bring herself to call it by the appropriate word. "Firehose" was what she called it with her son, so that's what it was in her head.

"Think I'm gonna take a shower." Miwa hopped up from her seat, fingers threading through her wet hair. "Get the typhoon off me."

Hildred Billings

Sayuri didn't doubt that was a good idea, but she wasn't about to suggest they go together. She'd have to wait for Miwa to finish. In the meantime, she was still on the hunt for the news.

Good thing Miwa was out of the room, though. Because Sayuri found more porn than proper TV shows. When she finally got a news report, it was nothing but doom for the next twelve hours. "The typhoon is expected to pass in the early morning, with the eye of the storm reaching Tokyo at about ten in the evening," the newscaster said. "We hope that everyone stays safely indoors."

Looks like we're here for the whole night. At least that meant the lines should be running in the morning so they could go home. Small favors that would be at this point.

"What's the damage?" Miwa appeared in one of the hotel's bathrobes, her wet hair a little more in control now. She stood before the coffee maker, back turned to Sayuri. So much for that cute butt she had been staring at earlier. "Is half of Japan blown apart?"

Sayuri glanced away. "Something like that."

"*Taihen desu ne.*" Miwa turned around, the coffee maker gurgling to life. Her robe was slightly open. Enough for Sayuri to catch a glimpse of skin along Miwa's thigh. *My heart is racing. My skin is hot.* This was bad. Sayuri was bound to make a fool of herself if she hadn't already. "Wish I were home playing video games right now."

She sat next to Sayuri, who was once again reminded of what happened the last time they sat on a couch together and talked about video games. "Miwa-*san*..." Sayuri said, her mouth still dry after drinking half of her cold tea. "Forgive me, but I think we should talk about..."

Miwa waited a few seconds before asking, "Hm?"

"About what happened last weekend."

A pause erupted once more. "Thought we already did talk about that."

"We talked about what happened *after* we... you know."

Miwa relaxed into the depths of the couch. Yet her body language was anything but inviting toward Sayuri, who remained on her side, one eye always on the TV. A commercial break meant there was no point expecting another weather report anytime soon. "I didn't think you wanted to talk about that."

"I thought *you* didn't want to talk about it."

"Look..." Miwa uncrossed her legs, but not her arms. She was still as off-putting as the nosiest teacher in the school lounge. "Maybe we should forget about it."

"Why?"

Miwa did a double-take toward Sayuri. "Because it was a weird thing that happened."

Sayuri's knitted brows created a crease down the center of her face. "I don't think it was weird. Felt pretty natural to me."

Miwa scoffed.

"You know that partner I keep talking about?" Sayuri couldn't believe she was admitting this. What if she had read the signals incorrectly? What if she had gotten this all wrong, and Miwa wasn't anything like her? Let alone *willingly?* "Well, it was a woman. Her name was Emiko, and she was the other mother of my child." Sayuri didn't assign words to her identity, let alone *touch* the word identity itself. She didn't want to open that can of worms. Nor did she want to scare Miwa off with terms that may have given her the wrong impression. "When I say I take responsibility for what happened last weekend, that's partially what I mean. I'm older, and I should have known better." Damnit. That wasn't exactly what she meant to say. *I'm already screwing this up.* "I mean, I'm the more experienced one." Damnit! "I mean..." *I mean I should be able to control myself.*

The power went out.

The TV. The lights. The damned coffee maker that had been close to beeping. Everything died. The only source of light in the room came from the tiny, narrow window that only allowed a modicum of light on a *clear* day, let alone one ravaged by a typhoon. Sayuri was on the verge of tears. What else could possibly go wrong?

"You've gotta be kidding," Miwa spat. "I was really looking forward to that coffee."

"I'm a lesbian."

The word echoed in the dark, quiet room. Sayuri instantly regretted it. What if that was the last thing she ever told Miwa? Did she really think the dark would protect her against possible prejudice? Just because they had already kissed once didn't mean Miwa felt anything like that for her. It didn't mean she was willing to board Sayuri's gay train and ride it all the way to the terminus station.

"*Gomen,*" Sayuri said. "I shouldn't have..."

As All Our Fires Burn

Her head hit the back of the couch. She hadn't seen Miwa coming for her, let alone with her lips at the ready and her hand searching for whatever part of Sayuri's body it could find.

Chapter 21

MIWA

Everything, from Sayuri calling herself a lesbian to them being alone in a dark, silent love hotel room, had to be a lie. Either a lie or the most fantastic dream Miwa ever had.

There's no way she's actually gay. Was she testing that by kissing those lips again? At least this time Miwa knew who started it first. *Me. I'm the one starting this, and I don't intend to stop it again.* That ball was now in Sayuri's court.

After a moment of surprised hesitation, Sayuri wrapped her arms around Miwa's shoulders and brought her down to where she belonged. Right on top of the woman she wanted more than she wanted to breathe.

Good thing, too. Because breathing would not be easy when Miwa was so determined to suck Sayuri's face off her head.

As All Our Fires Burn

Is this really happening? Maybe she had slipped into the same dream world that devoured her a week ago, when she went for that kiss she was sure would destroy her friendship with Sayuri. *Yet she thinks it's her fault?* Sayuri couldn't be farther from the truth. Maybe they had kissed each other, yes, but to imply it was all her and not Miwa was as false as implying Miwa didn't live for what happened right now. *Are we really kissing in the dark?* In a love hotel? Did she really have a typhoon to thank for this moment?

Miwa's thoughts brought her to hesitation. She wanted to know what would happen if she gingerly eased her lips off Sayuri's and gave her a chance to speak.

Too bad she couldn't see her. Were Sayuri's eyelids fluttering open to the darkness like Miwa's?

"Wow," Sayuri said.

Miwa's hand descended from that soft face to the wrinkled, damp blouse still covering Sayuri's skin. *Aren't you cold? You should take a shower...* Of course, there were other ways to rid a woman of her chills. That bed had looked mighty comfortable. "Wow?" Miwa repeated. "Good wow? Bad wow?"

"Just... wow."

This was not helping Miwa's sudden insecurities. Good thing Sayuri couldn't see her floundering façade and her drying lips that had pursed too hard at the first sign of resistance. "*Gomen.*" She apologized, yet she did not hurry to get off Sayuri, who was still trapped in the corner of the couch. *She's bigger than me, but maybe I'm stronger. Doesn't matter. She could throw me off her. Or she could give me a hearty "get the hell away from me" and*

I'd take it to heart. The more Miwa played these situations through her head, the more she was convinced they would happen.

Yet Sayuri said no such thing. "Why are you apologizing?"

"Because I..."

"Did the one thing I've been hoping you'd do since we met?"

Could that be true? Miwa's balance suffered as she lost her grip on the back of the couch. Weren't there better places for her to put her hands? "I had no idea."

"Most people don't."

What did that mean? "You're really okay with me having those kinds of feelings for you?"

Miwa wished she could see the nuances of Sayuri's demeanor, but in the darkness, all she could make out was the scrunch of two shoulders and the slight rise and fall of her chest. The storm picked up enough strength outside that, even within the confines of one of the most private hotel rooms in the city, the sounds of wind and rain echoed. *Damnit, this is probably how I was conceived.* Miwa's mother used to joke that someone was a "typhoon baby." Other kids were "snowstorm" babies or "rainy season" babies, and it took Miwa forever to figure out what the hell that meant because none of those people were *born* during those seasons. More like nine to ten months afterward.

They didn't have to worry about that here. Only a few other life-altering issues.

"I told you I was a lesbian, Miwa-*san*," Sayuri finally said.

"Doesn't mean you want *any* woman throwing herself at you like a deranged asshole."

Was Sayuri chuckling? When Miwa was falling over herself with insecurity? Yeah, that would help the situation, immensely. "You might be surprised."

I can't get a hold on what the hell she means. Sayuri didn't care what woman wanted her, as long as one did? She didn't care much about sex, only the connection? She didn't care how Miwa identified, as long as this happened? *She's gotta know that I'm a lesbian too by now… has she figured it out? When did it happen?*

"So… last week, when we…"

"I was ready," Sayuri said. "Didn't mean I thought it would actually happen, though."

I ruined it! Nausea rocked Miwa back and forth on top of Sayuri, who was still giggling like it was her first time at the dyke rodeo. It definitely wasn't. This woman had a long-term female partner. Serious enough to have a kid together. She was definitely worldly in the ways of lesbian love! *Meanwhile, I've had like two casual girlfriends and barely enough one-night stands to confidently say I know how to give a girl an orgasm.*

Just what Miwa needed! New insecurities!

"You want me? Like that?"

"Why are you asking me these things," Sayuri began, her testy tone reminding Miwa that she was with a schoolteacher, "*after* you've kissed me twice already?"

Miwa blushed. *Like having my own teacher scold me.* "I kiss first then ask questions later?" Great way to get in trouble. Sometimes, that happened.

"Rather you keep kissing instead of keep talking…"

Damn. Sayuri was getting sassy. Was this the true her that dwelled in the perfectly poised façade of a feminine schoolteacher? Miwa's fantasies only had room to imagine a lover who was careful, attentive, and gentle in the bedroom. The thought that Sayuri might be more of the power bottom type than an outright pillow-biter made Miwa explode in both sexual urgency *and* fear. Fear that she wasn't good enough. Fear that she really didn't know what she was doing. And fear that she couldn't give Sayuri what she wanted from a lover.

But those were mere excuses, weren't they?

"Ae you nervous?" Sayuri asked.

"Me?" Miwa hadn't meant to squeak that. "*Me* nervous? I should be asking you that."

"You think I'm some flower that needs a gentle touch?"

"I mean… not really, no. I saw you went right for Satin in that stupid game."

"That was an accident!" Sayuri's arm pumped into the air, almost hitting Miwa right in the face. She happened to dodge at the right moment. "I didn't know it was that kind of game until she tied me up and spanked me!"

The fervor with which she spoke made Miwa laugh. "You liked it, huh?"

"I had honestly never seen anything like it in my life."

Liar. Dirty, dirty liar. Miwa was glad that Sayuri couldn't see her grinning like it was her birthday, and *this* was the present she unwrapped. "I've never spanked someone before, but I used to tie pretty good knots in school."

The blathering that commenced made Miwa laugh even harder. "I don't… you shouldn't… oh, my goodness. Please, no spanking!"

"So you *are* a fragile flower, Sayuri-*san?*"

"I like to think that there is some middle ground!"

Fingers curled within Miwa's wet hair. Such a gentle touch came from a woman who claimed she didn't *need* gentle and fragile. Nor did she need to be rocked so hard that she lost all sense of herself. Miwa wasn't expected to be anything more than herself.

Slowly, she lowered her head and kissed those soft lips again.

Sayuri muffled her surprise by giggling against Miwa's mouth and folding both arms around her shoulders. There was no escape now. Not with Miwa holding her so tightly and kissing her so deeply that it was like being sucked into another world.

Miwa gave herself over to that world. What was the point of trying to stay in hers, when this one was so much better?

"Do you really want me?" she whispered directly into Sayuri's ear, while their bodies easily folded together on the couch. "Because I don't want to play games. I don't want to mess it up like I did last week."

"Yes." Sayuri's hand gently glided beneath Miwa's robe and found her clean yet slightly sweaty skin. "Please. *Daite.*"

Miwa hadn't heard such a sweet euphemism in a long time. To be held meant many things. Closeness. Fondness. A burning desire that could only be cured if they embraced as tightly as possible. A lot could be accomplished in a simple embrace. Kissing, for one. Sweet little whispered words of love and devotion. Fondling, scratching, and tempting nips of the lips that awakened the tingling in their skin. And sexual satisfaction, of course. Miwa was close to going for it. Yet her hand was pulled off the back of the couch and found its new home on top of Sayuri's breast. She had no idea who put it there. It could've been herself. It could've been Sayuri. Either way, it was there, and it made them both groan like it was the most scintillating sensation to ever touch their bodies.

I can't see you, Sayuri-san, but I know you're the most beautiful woman I've ever come this close to making love to. The blouse eased up Sayuri's torso. A pushup bra made of lace and underwire was soon in Miwa's hand, and she buried her face in the crook of Sayuri's neck to mute her groan of disbelief. The closer they came to fulfilling their prophecy, the more Miwa lost control of herself. *I'm not letting you leave this room until...* Until what? Until Miwa had kissed every inch of her body? Until Miwa had wrapped her tongue around each tender nipple, then the nub between Sayuri's warm thighs? Until all ten of her fingers were wet from giving this woman pleasure? Until she had heard Sayuri's voice sing to the heavens that she was coming, again and again?

Until Miwa knew what it was like to feel it in return?

Sayuri untied the front of Miwa's robe and snaked her arms between skin and cotton. Miwa's eyes rolled back as she breathed into the nape of Sayuri's neck, aware that all of her was now exposed to the darkness. Her nipples touched the scratchy lace of Sayuri's bra. Her stomach pressed against the bare skin beneath her. Their kisses, when they could be bothered to touch lips, became more and more desperate, until it was apparent that their lips simply wanted to touch something, anything.

"I'm gonna lose my mind," Miwa warned her lover. "I think we'd be stupid to not take advantage of the big bed in this room."

"Are you a mind reader? Because I was thinking the same thing."

"Yet that requires us getting up."

Sayuri pushed herself up. Miwa's robe fell down her shoulders and arms, and the only thing keeping her from blushing a new typhoon in her face was because the darkness of the room prevented Sayuri from getting a full view. Miwa closed the robe as she got up and followed Sayuri to the bed.

It soon fell open again when Sayuri took her by the wrist and pulled Miwa down.

This was it. This was what it meant to be head over heels for a girl.

The words were few between them. How could they speak when they were so preoccupied with other activities? Yet when they did share their thoughts and feelings, it was always much of the same. *"You're so soft." "You're so beautiful." "You smell so good."* Before Miwa could be self-conscious that she said something so meaningless, it was thrown right back at her, and she understood how nice it was to hear. *"Touch me here, please." "Don't be shy. You won't hurt me."* Those phrases had to be uttered by both, because although they were clearly experienced in the ways of pleasuring other women, there were still suppositions to combat and fears to assuage.

What Miwa really wanted to say, however, remained locked away in the back of her throat and swallowed deep into the pit of her stomach, like a key to the most damning room in the house. *"I love you, Sayuri."* How lovely that would be to say. Yet Miwa knew it was too soon. Too fast. They had only known each other for a few weeks, and this revelation that they wanted one another romantically was still brand-new. So maybe Miwa wouldn't say any of that, but she knew how to express it using her body and the way she encouraged Sayuri to love her back.

"You're still all wet," Sayuri chided when Miwa magically ended up between her legs.

"Excuse me?" How could she tell? Hell, Miwa hadn't even known the truth yet!

"From your shower. Your hair is damp."

Miwa pulled her hair aside, her whole body pulsing with the heat that came from being both aroused and embarrassed. She didn't dare say what she thought Sayuri meant. "You're wet from the rain still, you know." Miwa straddled one of Sayuri's legs. She could only assume it was the left one, but it was difficult to tell in such dark conditions. Not that Miwa was opposed to some delicious mystery. "Maybe you should take that shower." Boldly, she pulled Sayuri's blouse up over her head and cast it aside. Whether it landed on the bed or on the floor, she had no idea. She was beyond the ability to care now that the woman of her dreams was half naked and waiting for

Miwa to shower her with purposeful adoration. "I could help you take all of your clothes off."

"*Muri,*" Sayuri said with a warming laugh. "The power's out!"

"Oh, right. Darn." Miwa bit her bottom lip as she gently grinded against Sayuri's bare thigh. "Guess we'll have to warm you up the old fashioned way."

"How's that?" Bless her, Sayuri was attempting to sound anything but like she was in a fit of giggles as her breath caught in her chest. "Friction?"

"You said it, not me."

Sayuri tugged on the robe still wrapped around half of Miwa's body. A valiant attempt to toss it onto the ground, but it struggled to release Miwa's waist. Just as well. Having her damp hair fall on her breasts was enough to make her *cold.* Having that bit of coverage on her hips and thighs abated the fears Miwa courted.

She tucked her hands beneath Sayuri's body, searching for the snaps to her bra. Miwa half-expected her lover to say something about it. Instead, Sayuri said, "You're wet, Miwa-*san.*"

"We've established that."

"No. I mean you're *wet.*" Sayuri jerked her thigh between Miwa's legs. Point well made.

Miwa could barely contain the breaths falling from her lips with little abandon. "I bet you are too!"

"Why don't you find out?"

"Listen to you! When did you get so coy?"

"I've always been coy, Miwa-*san*." Sayuri pulled Miwa back down again. This time, her leg stayed firmly in place, and Miwa had no choice but to let out her pent-up cry as her slit met the brunt of her lover's leg. "You're the one making assumptions about me. Don't you want to find out what I'm really like?"

Miwa wasn't sure she'd survive it. Yet she would be a damned fool to turn down the opportunity.

"I'd like to find out what you're really like beneath your cool countenance," Sayuri continued. "Show me."

She was *definitely* a power bottom! One that Miwa was in no business to ignore.

The worry that the power might suddenly turn back on and ruin the ambiance they had come to appreciate niggled at the back of Miwa's mind. Yet the storm was strong enough to keep it knocked out while they explored one another's bodies in the darkness, either taking careful attention of every sensitive spot they found or brazenly going after the kind of hedonistic acts they both fancied. Miwa gradually lost the fear and shame that hounded her from the moment she first kissed Sayuri and worried that she had ruined their chances for friendship. It helped that Sayuri was no delicate dove who preferred to lie on her back and make the occasional sound. When her hands were not all over Miwa, guiding her in the darkness, they were grabbing the bedspread and the damp strands of hair shielding them from a world always threatening to bring back the light. Kisses were purposeful. Whispers devoid of regret. Every time Miwa planted her lips somewhere on Sayuri's body, the results were the same: little gasps and moans that colored the backs of

Miwa's eyelids. It didn't matter that the room was blackened. She still squeezed her eyes shut when she rolled her lover's nipples between her fingers, as if that would better commit the moment to memory.

"*Sawatte.*" The urgency in Sayuri's voice grew as she took Miwa's hand. It was soon placed between Sayuri's thighs, dangerously close to the one place she longed to know. "Before I die because I've gone crazy."

This isn't my first time touching a girl. Why am I so nervous? Miwa knew why. Sayuri was special. She felt "something" with her she never did with her previous girlfriends, let alone the one-night stands that were nothing more than grunting and panting for an hour. Miwa wanted this to be special, although she knew the best thing to do was to simply go for it.

So, she did.

Perhaps there were other people who wouldn't appreciate the wondrous sounds Sayuri made when she was touched. Those same people probably wouldn't appreciate the scent of her body, the feel of her little hairs on her mound, or the taste of her sweat as it danced upon Miwa's tongue. For Miwa wasn't a woman who could simply ease her fingers into a girl and leave it at that. She needed skin in her face and kisses on her throat. Sounds of lustful transgressions and the blazing fury that was her own body gearing up to explode in a bonfire of desires too scandalous to mention.

What she got was someone who couldn't stand to be idle.

Sayuri always straddled the line between climax and already being finished, but Miwa only gauged that because *someone* wouldn't stop trying to get on top of her, touch her, or take off clothes that were no longer there. The god of hedonism had decided to bless their private hotel room with realizations that this might be their first and only chance at making love. Miwa didn't want to believe it. Yet she too fell into the urgent spiral to touch everything at once and to bring as much pleasure to the woman on the other end of her hand.

She was so warm.

There was no warning that Sayuri was about to orgasm. No sudden sounds and movements that Miwa had anticipated. No clenching, no writhing, and no heat that hadn't been there before. One second she was on top of Sayuri, stimulating the softness between her legs, and the next?

She had never heard a woman scream like this before.

It wasn't pain, although there was certainly torture contained within that unbridled sound. What began as an ordinary moan had burst into a guttural groan that shook the foundation of the bed and almost deafened Miwa. Her fingers were in danger of being cut from her hand. Cries that she go harder, *faster,* were accompanied with shaking legs and a tight vise around Miwa's shoulders. *She might take me down with her. I can't complain. This is how I want to die.* Those trembling legs certainly felt nice between Miwa's. She didn't care if that was the only pleasure she experienced that evening. She could spend the rest of her life reliving this moment and thinking it one of the best of her life.

Yet what Miwa had not counted on was what happened to Sayuri when she was given such a blessing.

"Ah!" Miwa fell over, a crazed woman on top of her, pinning her down to the bed and covering her in the heavy kind of kisses that said she wasn't going anywhere. The fingers fumbling for Miwa's slit said much of the same thing.

She had been wrong. *This* was the moment she would treasure for the rest of her life. Even if they got married. Even if they had kids of their own. Even if all of Miwa's career dreams came true.

No moment was more precious than the one when Sayuri made Miwa feel like the most wanted girl in the world.

Chapter 22

SAYURI

The power came back on an hour later. Phones lit up with texts updating the owners about the track of the typhoon, and what it meant for transportation. Lamps brought the lovers out of the darkness. The TV clicked on, the same travel show from before now displaying a ticker warning everyone about the typhoon – in case they had never heard about it.

Miwa rolled over and grabbed the remote. "*Mou. Urusai.*" She turned down the volume and smacked her tangled hair against the pillow. "Nice while it lasted, I guess."

"You could turn everything off again." When did Sayuri's voice become so raspy?

"I could, but that requires effort." Miwa dropped the remote and turned back toward Sayuri. Her groggy eyes were squeezed shut, blocking out the light. Enough for Sayuri to take matters into her own hands and shut off the lamp beside her. "I'm totally out of energy. Used it all up on you."

"You should eat something."

Miwa snorted. Sayuri couldn't help but blush. They had been so absorbed in kissing each other for forty-five minutes that they forgot the other places that liked oral attention. Sayuri told herself that there would be a next time. She wanted to believe it, at least.

"I'm serious." Sayuri hated that the inner caretaker came out of her already, but how could she help herself when she was now so connected to the woman next to her? "You should eat. You bought that food earlier, but did you eat any of it? No."

"I was busy. In the shower."

Sayuri grinned. "What were you doing in the shower?"

Miwa picked up the remote again and flipped through the channels. "Washing my hair and getting the storm off me. What? You think I was in there thinking about you?"

"Why wouldn't you be?"

"*Mou.* You're ridiculous."

She settled on a channel that was nothing but a digital fireplace. The glow was a bit intense, but at least it was quiet and not, well, *porn.* Sayuri could only take so much of the kind of sex she had avoided most of her life. *When I wanted the kind of sex we just had.* She couldn't help it. She curled up next to Miwa and sighed.

"So… what happens now?" she asked.

Miwa folded her arms behind her head. "What do you mean?"

"Between us." Sayuri had intended to wait asking that question, but now it was out of her mouth like a bird taking off from the nest. Whatever happened next? It was meant to be. "I wasn't expecting this today."

"Yet here we are, naked in bed together." Miwa's yawn brought her hand to her mouth. She winced when she realized she still needed to wash up after having her fingers deep inside someone else's body. "What do you mean what happens between us? I'm assuming we're a couple now."

Sayuri's heart was suddenly lighter than the rest of her body. Did it dare to flutter up her chest and expose itself to the world? It would be foolish enough. "I wasn't sure what you really felt about this. Sometimes I find people who decide it's not for them after we… well, you know." That was the state of her dating life before meeting Emiko, who had been one of the first women Sayuri had ever met who was confident in her sexuality and unafraid to express it.

Miwa glanced at her with the intensity of a woman who couldn't believe what she was hearing. "Are you telling me that I couldn't convince you that I'm gay, too?"

Sayuri's eyes widened. "You are?"

"I didn't think I had to actually say the words 'I'm a lesbian,' like you did. Was hoping it could remain implied."

"You've been gay this whole time?"

"What, you mean you *weren't* attracted to my mighty lesbo energy? I'm somewhat offended, Sayuri-*san*."

Giggling, Sayuri cozied up to her lover, one hand pressed firmly between Miwa's breasts. "You don't have to be so formal with me anymore. Or, at least, I hope we don't have to be formal with each other."

Miwa wanly smiled. "I'd like that."

"Miwa…" Sayuri tried saying that name without any honorifics. It had a certain ring to it. "It's been a while since I had someone like you in my life."

"Since your ex, right?"

"Yes. Several months ago."

Miwa winced. "Try a few years for me…"

"I find that hard to believe."

"Why? It's true."

"Because you're so…" How could Sayuri explain it? Miwa was so much woman in such a small package that she was like a grenade ready to go off with the right stimulus. *All I have to do is pull her pin and… BOOM!* Sayuri would wistfully remember this day for a long while. Namely, how Miwa had unabashedly taken her to places she had forgotten existed. "Skilled."

Whatever Miwa had been anticipating Sayuri to say, that had *not* been it. Her laughter rang out like bells with the power to herald Sayuri's reawakened libido. "That's flattering, but I'm pretty sure that's not necessary for keeping girlfriends around."

Might work on me.

While the fake fire crackled on the TV and they lay in silence, Sayuri remembered when she first entered a relationship with Emiko, the woman who had asked her out after only ten minutes of knowing her. *All the jokes about lesbians moving quickly are true, I guess.* Or maybe Sayuri was such a romantic that she courted women the way she wanted to be. Fast. Hard. And with wedding bells always on the horizon, assuming it was possible for someone like her. *I knew I wanted to have children with her by the end of the first month.* Sayuri fell hard, and quickly. She never thought of it as a detriment before. Yet what if it was? What if she rushed into things too quickly?

Miwa must have sensed her faraway hesitations, for she said, "Maybe it's true that we were fated to meet. Could think of better ways for it to happen, but I guess you can't be picky when it comes to meeting your new girlfriend."

Girlfriend. She said it. The G word.

"It might be problematic that we work different hours. Not to mention, I'm a schoolteacher, so I have a lot going on…" Sayuri's schedule was packed whenever class was in session. She had recently volunteered to oversee the English club for the older elementary schoolers. Sports day and culture day were around the corner. She wouldn't have more than a Sunday off for God knew how long. Before Miwa, she had preferred life that way. It kept her busy, and her mind distracted from the things she had endured in the past year.

"We both have Sundays off," Miwa was quick to point out. "I think for the right person that it can be worth the wait until something works itself out."

Sayuri's chest swelled in pride. How wonderful was it to have someone who couldn't wait to see her? "We could spend every Sunday having coffee, playing video games, and, um…"

"And, *um?*"

As All Our Fires Burn

She had been confident when those words were nothing but space in her head. Now that they were out, however, Sayuri realized how embarrassed she was to think about Miwa so sexually. Even though they had just done it and now lay naked together! *In bed!* "I could spend every Sunday telling you to touch me."

"That wasn't all you said." Miwa propped herself up on her elbow, the grin on her small face ready to devour every inch of Sayuri's body. "*Irite, Miwa-saaaan.*"

Sayuri was hotter in the face than she had been earlier that day. "I did *not* sound like that!"

"How would you know? You were so far gone I thought you had transformed into a succubus."

"Would there be a problem with that?"

Miwa came down a few more inches, her nose barely touching Sayuri's. The heat from her breath as it came from her flaring nostrils was enough to lull Sayuri into a gleeful doze. "Not at all," Miwa muttered, before that sentiment was sealed with a kiss.

Perhaps it had meant to be a short, unassuming kiss. Naturally, it transformed into something more.

Sayuri once more took full responsibility. After all, she was the older one, and she should have shown more restraint when she pulled Miwa down on top of her and silently begged to make love again

"Oh. Is this what these look like?" Miwa's teeth massaged her bottom lip as she peeled back the covers and drank in Sayuri's naked body. Being so exposed in the light was exhilarating, although a tinge of embarrassment overcame the woman who couldn't be held back from more lovemaking. "I'd been wondering."

"You could've *asked* to see them!"

"I could have, but then I couldn't surprise you by doing this." Miwa lightly blew against one of Sayuri's nipples, and that was it for their mutual sanity.

Sayuri lay back against her pillow as Miwa maneuvered between two spreading legs. No thought went into it. None that was necessary, because they were both experienced women who relied on their sexual instincts.

Even so, Sayuri was not prepared for the tongue that lazily licked her slit. Nor did she expect to open her eyes and see such a fiercely feminine countenance looking back up at her.

Only two things went through her mind. The first was that this felt better than she ever imagined. The second? *I can't wait to do this to her.* She had her chance a few minutes later, when she all but clamped her thighs against Miwa's face and demanded that they indulge in a mutual exchange of oral delights. Their height difference only proved to be a minor problem. Luckily, they were both excellent problem solvers.

***

Miwa returned with more drinks from the vending machine in the hallway. She found Sayuri sprawled across the messy bed, albeit adorned in the other bathrobe after finally leaving her wet clothes out to dry. She had yet to take a shower. A part of her wanted to wait for Miwa to suggest they take one – or, better, a bath – together. Sayuri didn't have the courage to ask first. She was afraid Miwa might say, *"I've already taken a shower, silly."*

"Thanks." Sayuri accepted the fresh bottle of cold tea. The TV played a game show rerun interspersed with updates on the typhoon. The eye of the storm was fast approaching, and people were hopeful it would give them enough time to catch a train home. *They can't seriously keep the lines locked up for a whole twelve hours...* They could. They would, if it meant not being responsible for the potential deaths and injuries of hundreds. "I'm parched."

Miwa flopped onto the bed with a bottle of grape soda. "Me too. Used up a lot of fluids, you know." She waited for Sayuri's expected reaction. "So let me get this straight... you're far from shy when we're doing it, but as soon as some clothes are put back on, you're more retiring than a stereotypical schoolteacher.

"Maybe," Sayuri squeaked. "It's different when you're overcome with the realities of lust."

"You telling me you're not lusty right now?"

Sayuri almost snorted her soda. "I gotta take a break!"

Miwa's hair, now dry from the shower she took hours ago, created the perfect curtain between her coy demeanor and the woman she flirted with. "So that's what it's like being in your thirties, huh? You gotta take more breaks?"

"*Mou,* where did this side of you come from?" Sayuri batted her eyelashes. It took her a few moments to realize she used to do that with Emiko, whenever she became an inconsequential flirt with her partner. "Are you like this with every girl you go out with?"

"Why? Do you have a problem with it?" Miwa brought her face slightly closer. Sayuri didn't know why she turned away. Overwhelmed by the pretty complexion coming her way? Convinced that all of this was a dream? It had been so long since Sayuri felt like this around anyone. Even before the death of her son, she had struggled to feel such affection around her ex-partner. *Losing Yuma was but the catalyst that ended that relationship.* Sayuri tried not to think about the fact that Emiko had another girlfriend waiting in the wings when she broke up with the mother of her child. *She was cheating on me, wasn't she? For how long? How many other women?* Sayuri couldn't stand the thought, yet there she was, courting it while looking into Miwa's big eyes that glistened like glass.

"You were so polite with me only a few days ago. It's like the moment you kissed me, you turned into this crazy lady who can't stop making sexual come-ons."

"So... you like it?"

Sayuri sucked in her bottom lip and flopped onto her back. Her robe opened, and it wasn't on purpose.

Yet she wouldn't fix it.

"You've got another side to yourself, too." Miwa drew a gentle line down Sayuri's jaw, eliciting a light gasp that even Sayuri didn't know was inside of her. "I like that I'm the one who gets to see it."

"What kind of side do you think it is?"

"Uh, you spent fifteen minutes going at me like I had a chocolate fountain between my legs. I think we both know what kind of side it is."

"You were counting the minutes, huh?"

"You're commenting on that, and not me saying I had a chocolate fountain between my legs?"

I don't recall anything tasting like chocolate. Sayuri would definitely remember that. "I love how confident you are in your sexuality," she said. "Honestly, how did I not realize it before?"

"What? That I'm gay?"

"Yes."

Miwa rolled onto her side. "It's not like I advertise it. Like most, I keep a low profile."

"Would it be a problem for your job?"

"Hmmm." Miwa considered that by sucking in her cheeks. "They have to be pretty conservative with their image, obviously. They would be really unimpressed if they found out I'm gay. It's why I play along with their stupid games when they pick on me for being single."

"It's not like you have a relationship with the public. Not like me. I'd be in *big* trouble if all the parents suddenly knew I was a lesbian." She hated to admit it, but having her son was a good deterrent to rumors. The only people who knew she used IVF – let alone lied about having a boyfriend – were her family and doctor. Not even the administration knew, since she didn't use her insurance to procure to procedure. Only the aftermath, which was pregnancy and childbirth. *As far as anyone knew, I conceived the natural way.* Out of wedlock, though. She had pushed the boundaries by being an unwed mother. A good role model of a teacher would have married the father, right? Or made the pregnancy go away without anyone knowing about it. *How could I do that when I worked so hard to have him, though?*

"It's true that most of our regular passengers don't know me from the prime minister's wife, but the company wouldn't care. I don't want to risk it."

"Sounds like we both can't risk it."

"You had a partner who lived with you, right?"

"True. She also wasn't exactly the most feminine woman in the world." Emiko used to joke that her feminine name made her more determined to butch up. "We were very careful. It helps that a lot of people don't overthink two women living together, especially if one is unmarried with a baby."

"What about before that?"

"We didn't move in together until I got pregnant. It was more practical, and our son was a good cover. She was just a 'friend' helping me out because the deadbeat dad wouldn't have anything to do with me." That was the story she gave the administration when they admonished her for her "behavior."

Miwa stared into the depths of her grape soda before taking a sip and screwing the cap back on. "Sounds like you've known you're gay for a long time."

"Haven't you?"

"Like a lot of other things, I hadn't expected it with you."

Sayuri hadn't wanted to start this conversation so early in their so-called relationship, but there had never been a better time than that moment. "How long have you known?"

As All Our Fires Burn

A snort colored the otherwise sweet demeanor on Miwa's face. "Since puberty? Isn't that when most girls know?" She quickly amended that. "Sorry. I know it's not that simple for a lot of women, but it was for me. I remember the day I realized I would never like boys."

Sayuri waited for her to say more, but Miwa was silent. "What day was that?"

Sighs peppered the air. "I had a boyfriend in middle school. Really sweet guy. You know, for a middle schooler." Miwa matched the knowing grin on Sayuri's face. *No kidding. I've taught a few middle school boys.* They cared about video games, sports, the latest anime aimed at teenagers... and all the crazy sex stuff they were discovering for the first time. *Some of the conversations I've overheard... I need a shower for my brain.* "He was all about the kissing," Miwa continued. "I kept indulging him because I thought I would learn to like it. Then I realized I didn't like kissing him. So I thought maybe I was with the wrong person. When I told my mom, she said I would find better kissers as I got older. Then I was in the locker room after PE, and..."

"Oh, dear. The locker room." Sayuri remembered it well.

"Suddenly I was imagining what it would be like to kiss one of the girls changing her clothes. Things came over me, you know?" Miwa laughed. "I'm an adult now. I guess I can admit what those 'things' were."

Yes, yes, the urge to kiss and touch another girl. Like Miwa, Sayuri first realized her sexuality with the help of a teenaged libido that begged a girl to have more sleepovers with her friends.

Was this a good time to tell Miwa that the first time Sayuri kissed a girl was when she convinced her friend to "practice" kissing with her?

"I never dated a boy again. Although I didn't go out with any girls until college. I had a lot more freedom during those years, and I was finally old enough to sneak into some of the bars. Actually, think the first one I ever went to was here in Ikebukuro." Miwa paused. "It's closed, though."

"So you started dating girls from the bars?"

"Didn't you?"

"No…" Sayuri picked at the little hairs growing out of her chin. "Actually, I don't care for the bars very much. I don't like being around so much smoke and loud conversation. Plus the 'fun' is always so late, and I'm not much for staying up late."

Miwa smiled. "No wonder I've never seen you around there."

"You go a lot?"

"Not really. Especially not recently. Don't have the time or energy." Miwa gently took Sayuri's hand and pulled it away from her chin. Their fingers intertwined. The crazy thing? Sayuri wasn't entirely convinced it had been on purpose. "So how do *you* meet girls, then? Is there some dating app I don't know about?"

Sayuri didn't know if she was laughing because of their handholding, or because she suddenly remembered the way she met her ex. "You won't believe this, but I got completely lucky with Emiko."

"Emiko… is that your ex-girlfriend?"

As All Our Fires Burn

"*Un.*" Was that Sayuri's first time mentioning that name in front of Miwa? "She's a *very* headstrong woman. Also very out. She works for a rail company like you, but on the mechanical side, so there's less pressure for her to be in the closet since she's not a 'public' figure."

Miwa sagely nodded.

"Anyway, I met her a neighborhood party one of my friends put on. I could tell she was gay within thirty seconds of her entering the room. Naturally, I was intrigued, and I wanted to know if she was single. Luckily for me, Emiko is a very forward woman, and she asked me out ten minutes into our first conversation. I don't think she expected me to say yes."

"Wait, wait. Your *neighborhood* party? So your whole neighborhood knew you were gay?"

Sayuri shook her head. "Old neighborhood. Different city in Saitama. I transferred schools after I got serious with Emiko. I wanted to be closer to the metro, and we could afford the apartment with our combined incomes."

"Was this before or after you high-tailed it to the fertility clinic?"

"*Before,* obviously! What, how much do you think I rush things?"

Miwa giggled. That may have been the first time Sayuri ever heard such a sound coming out of her lover's body, and she couldn't say she hated it. *I love women, after all. I love the feminine sounds, the smells, the looks...* Even Emiko at her most masculine was still the pinnacle of femininity to Sayuri, although she never said it. "Not enough, honestly."

"What's that supposed to mean?"

"What do you think? I've been waiting for you to come on to me ever since we met!"

"*Mou,* why do I have to be the one to do most of the work? Is it because I wear plaid?"

"It's because you wear that uniform with the white gloves."

"Sometimes I wear a hat, too. Comes in really handy during the cold months."

"A hat? I don't suppose there's any way we could do it with your uniform on…"

Miwa rolled her eyes. "I don't get the uniform fetish some people have. The thing is hot and itchy."

"Definitely hot."

"Are you even listening to me?"

Sayuri had a witty reply locked and loaded, but both of their phones buzzed at the same time. Sayuri saw her message first.

"*Select lines opening at ten PM during the eye of the storm. For those traveling north, it is highly recommended to catch trains as early as possible, as it is not known when they may shut down again for the night.*"

"A whole lotta words to not say much," Miwa said, putting her phone down. "Guess that means we should go home. It's nine-thirty.'

Sayuri glanced up at her. "We've paid for the whole night."

"Yeah, but…"

"But what? Neither of us have work tomorrow. I don't have anywhere to be. If my place is damaged, it's already happened. Rushing home before midnight to beat the rest of the storm isn't going to solve anything."

"You make it sound like you don't want to go home now."

Sayuri placed her phone on the nightstand and wrapped her arms across the nearest pillow. "Maybe this means some places will be open until the usual closing time. We could get a proper drink and act like it's a real date. Then, you know, come back here..." She was getting ahead of herself. *I'm already imagining what we'll do.* Take a bath. Lie naked in bed. Rent a movie on the TV or cuddle up together to stream videos on their phones. It was the kind of sweetness Sayuri had sorely missed from her life. Shutting down her emotions so she could deal with the overbearing grief from the past year had done its part. Perhaps it was time to openly move on from her losses – both of them.

"You're saying you'd rather stay here? With me?"

Sayuri wrapped her hand around the naked leg poking out from Miwa's robe. "I don't care where we go, as long as it's with you."

She meant it, too. Although she was the first to admit that, with the second half of a strong, quick typhoon on its way, it was perhaps best to not travel anywhere. Except maybe to a bar that happened to be opened somewhere down the street. Ikebukuro was a huge place. Surely, there would be some hole-in-the-wall bars of patrons and owners who couldn't – or didn't want to – go home? Some saw a typhoon and hundreds of stranded people as the perfect opportunity to make some extra money. Sayuri and Miwa weren't rich, and God knew they dropped a large chunk of cash on this room, but they could both afford a drink and an hour of fun conversation in the corner of a bar.

Of course, that would require getting up, getting dressed, going out…

"I wouldn't mind staying here," Miwa said. "We've got food and drinks…"

"And good company."

Miwa picked up the remote and turned off the TV. The lights soon went out. "You say you don't like staying up late, huh? Guess we should get some sleep."

"I can stay up a little later…"

Sayuri knew that her girlfriend had been bluffing. Even so, she was still pleasantly surprised when Miwa rolled forward, lips prepared for another kiss. "Me too."

They didn't go out that night. Hell, they barely made check out the next morning, because they spent too much time being silly in bed and arguing over where to have lunch. The storm had largely passed, leaving behind a gloomy drizzle and streets that were finally beginning to lose the flood. The trains were working again, but they decided to stay in Ikebukuro until most of the weekend was gone and Sayuri had to go home to prepare for a week of work. Miwa wasn't too excited to part, either, but her hand lingered in Sayuri's at the train station, while they made plans for the next weekend.

Promises to text. To call.

Sayuri rode the train home with rain splattering against the windows and an accouncement every few stops that there was a mandatory wait as "precautions." Most of the other passengers were simply excited to finally get home. Sayuri, however, sat in her seat and remembered every stroke, every kiss, and every other sensation Miwa had given her in the past twenty-four hours.

Something was stoked in the pit of her abdomen. Hope. Desire. The crazy notion that there might be more to life again, and that it wasn't crazy for her to finally move on.

Yet for every shred of hope she held in her heart, another part of it warned her that she had felt this good before, and that what she had with Miwa was still young and volatile. Anything could happen. Anything at all.

They could drift apart. They could fight. They could forget what it was like to be in love with one another, if that's what it even was – and not simply infatuation.

They could get married and have a family. Sayuri could have another chance at the life she always craved.

The fire was more than stoked. It was blazing with impunity, ready to swallow everyone around it whole. Her ribs were the tinder letting the fire blaze. Her skin brought the heat to life and cast it out into the cold, cruel world. Her heart was the center of the beast, pumping the flames through her veins and keeping a permanent smile on her face. *So that's why lips are red…*

Sayuri had never felt so warm before. Not since she could remember.

Chapter 23

SAYURI

The school day ended early on Wednesday, and after Sayuri finished up her paperwork in the teacher's room, she texted Miwa to ask her how her day was going. She hoped to catch her attention before Miwa started her shift at the station. Sure enough, Sayuri was halfway to the supermarket, bookbag in hand, when she received a reply.

"It's better now that I'm talking to you."

A high school student on his bicycle almost mowed Sayuri over. That's what happened when a girl stood in the middle of the narrow sidewalk, gaping in delight at her phone screen.

"Sumimasen!" the student called. Luckily for Sayuri, she hadn't been grazed, let alone hit. *Close call.* She held her phone to her heaving chest, hoping the fright would subside soon.

As All Our Fires Burn

"*I hope you know I almost got hit by a kid on his bike when I read that.*"

"*One of your students?*"

Sayuri was safely beneath the awning of the supermarket. A constant flood of young mothers and aunties maneuvered in and out of the store, their cloth bags full of dinner and after school snacks. Sayuri rubbed her phone against her skirt as raindrops began to fall. There were rumors of another typhoon heading their way, although the meteorologists seemed convinced that it would pass Japan. "*Rainfall heading our way again! Potentially high winds, as well. Please be careful.*" Sayuri wouldn't complain. The last typhoon had blown in one of the luckiest moments of her life. She had also made it home Sunday evening to find that the neighbor had properly shuttered the apartment for her son's teacher. One of the first things Sayuri did when she rejoined reality was arrange for a gift basket to be delivered to the Shimazaki household. Mostly fresh fruits and bath products for Mariko, although she asked for a couple of toys for Shota as well. *That boy is spoiled enough, but I can't help it. I want to spoil kids.* She wanted the spoil lovers, too, and she had been formulating a plan for Miwa over the past few days.

"*I have to work on Saturday,*" Sayuri texted. "*How about you come to my house on Sunday and I'll cook you a late lunch?*"

She waited for a flood of people to come out of the cramped supermarket entrance before looking at her phone again. She didn't want to seem *too* desperate, even to herself.

"*You want me to come to your place already? I'm flattered.*"

That wasn't an answer! *"We've already kissed in your apartment. Seems only right that you come kiss me in mine."*

She hesitated before hitting send. The moment she did, Sayuri let out the smallest of squeals. What could she say? She wasn't often this flirtatious over text. Sayuri was the kind of woman to let down her guard and show her softer, more seductive side in person. For a schoolteacher, she often asserted that she wasn't great with words.

"You want to cook? I'm lucky. Everything is about my mouth."

"Do you want to stick everything in it?" Sayuri nearly died. To the point she accidentally knocked into the outdoor display of autumn apples, currently on sale because they were already bruised. Well, now they were bruised even more.

"I like sticking food in my mouth, yes," Miwa replied. *"Especially homecooked food. What are you making?"*

"What would you like?"

"For food, or afterword?"

"You're too much!!!"

"Is that a problem?"

Sayuri sighed. Her sweaty fingers struggled to type the words she wanted into her phone. *"No problem."*

"Good. Because I wouldn't mind having your pu..."

"Kawashima-*sensei!*"

Sayuri jerked up, her bookbag slipping off her shoulder and nearly landing on top of the banana display. Five feet away from her, Mariko Shimazaki apologized for startling Sayuri while on her way out of the supermarket. Sayuri, meanwhile, couldn't put her phone away quickly enough.

As All Our Fires Burn

"Shi... Shimazaki-*san*." The whole name came out in a flood of air that Sayuri almost swallowed. "Wh... what a surprise." Was she red enough to trigger suspicions that she was sexting outside of the supermarket? Because she sure as hell felt like it. "Did you hear about the rains coming?"

Mariko *tsked,* her motherly face the difference between a concerned friend and a nosy neighbor about to make Sayuri's life hell. "Thank you *so* much for the gift basket, Kawashima-*sensei.* I made sure not to tell Shota-*kun* that you're the giver of his new favorite bath toy."

The image of that rowdy boy winding up Anpanman toys to jet across his bathwater was definitely the thing to sober Sayuri's thoughts. "And I won't tell the other students in class that he still plays with toys in the bath."

"It's a miracle if I can get him out of there so I can use those lovely bath beads you gave me. Really, it's too much for simply breaking into your apartment to close the shutters."

"If you hadn't, I don't know what I would have come home to see."

"How *did* you weather the storm, so to speak, Kawashima-*sensei?* You said you were stuck in Ikebukuro, of all places!"

Good thing Sayuri already had a story, in case anyone asked. "I stayed with a friend. The train lines actually opened back up later that night, but I took the opportunity to catch up with someone I hadn't seen in a long time." She meant her heart, and the hope contained within. "Everything worked out, I guess." Not until she finished sighing a maiden's breath did she realize how big her grin was. *That's one way to give myself away.*

"A friend, huh, Kawashima-*sensei?*" Mariko could throw a sly look right back at her. "Good luck with your 'friend,' *sensei,* because it's probably been much too long since…"

The air soured. Mariko had almost mentioned the unspeakable, although she surely meant "*much too long since you got some, Teach.*" Yet they both knew that's not how it would come across. For Mariko, it carried the double-pain of reminding her that *she* could one day lose her son, like Sayuri had. *That's right. I'm the one everyone pities. I'm also the one all the other mothers treat like she's cursed.* What if her terrible luck rubbed off on them? Most of them weren't having more kids, let alone any other sons. While things weren't quite like they used to be, even during Sayuri's childhood, there were still some things pregnant mothers prayed for above all else. "*Let my baby be healthy. Let it be a son.*" Losing a son was considered the unluckiest curse to ever afflict a woman. Yet Sayuri was willing to bet that many of those same mothers assumed it was what the schoolteacher got for not marrying the father. Some malignant spirits really were that petty.

Mariko read the mood and slowly backed away. "Have a pleasant evening, Kawashima-*sensei*. Please let me know if you ever need my help again. I'm always happy to assist with another woman's household." She turned, her black bob swishing through the air before being splattered against the back of her neck thanks to the rain.

Sayuri hurried into the supermarket before she was too ill to shop for dinner. The knowledge that she couldn't escape the pain that continued to haunt her conscience, even when things were going well for her, made her breath hitch in her throat. She stared at packages, boxes, and containers, wondering what they contained and whether she should buy some to make at home. Did she like yams? Turnips? Radishes? How about this particular brand of curry? Did she need more rice? What prefecture did these fish come from? She vastly preferred one type of fish over the other, but which one was it?

She couldn't stop thinking about what her son might like to eat for dinner.

He was old enough for me to get to know his tastes. Yuma was going to be a spicy eater, his mother could tell. He was already pushing his luck with curries and noodles, the kind Emiko drenched in hot sauce and peppers because nothing was too hot for her. More than once either she or Sayuri turned around to discover their son stealing spicy food from his mother's plate. The doctor said it *probably* wouldn't hurt him, but all Sayuri could do was look forward to the day when it was safe enough to push Yuma's palate.

We ate curry udon before getting in the car to go home. Sayuri stared at the boxes of curry, entranced by the bright colors and illustrations depicting adults and children enjoying the various flavors and spices from around the world. She wobbled on her feet before remembering where she was, and that there were other customers trying to shop for *their* dinners.

Sayuri grabbed the first familiar box. She then recalled that she wanted to make curry the day Miwa came over.

Miwa… She had forgotten the text left hanging on her phone.

"Let me make curry for you." That wasn't the response Miwa had probably expected to see twenty-five minutes after saying what she wanted in her mouth. *"I make great curry. Besides, you seem like you could use a good homecooked meal."*

The subtext in her message was, hopefully, indiscernible to Miwa, who must be on her way to work. *Let me take care of you. Don't you get it? I need to take care of someone. I've lost all the people I take care of. You think it's enough to mother other people's children all day? It's not the same. I need someone I love in my home.* Sayuri hated to admit that it was her truth. Caretakers were pushovers, weren't they? They could be so weak. So helpless when the people they cared for didn't reciprocate the love. No, what hurt the most was knowing that sometimes it simply wasn't enough. She had taken care of her son every day since conceiving him, yet he still left her. Emiko had never wanted for food, baths, or affection, yet she still went after another woman as soon as she realized Sayuri would be grieving for God knew how long. *How is it fair she moved on so quickly?* No, that was wrong. Emiko hadn't truly moved on from their son's death. She simply found different ways to cope – and that included putting distance between herself and the woman who looked like her son. How unfair was it? All Sayuri wanted was a family.

She hustled home through the rain. By the time she reached her warm and dry apartment, she was as wet as a drowned rat caught in a storm. Yet she was finally alone, and allowed to be depressed in peace.

"I'd love a homecooked meal. Send me the directions to your place whenever is convenient, and I'll be there on Sunday. I can't wait."

As All Our Fires Burn

Miwa wasn't the kind of woman to litter her texts with emojis, but Sayuri was. When she saw such a message on her phone, she couldn't help but fire back a line of red hearts that throbbed when she pressed Send.

Yet she was still numb. Perhaps she wouldn't "feel" again until the greatest potential for a new life was back in her arms, assuming Miwa was the kind of woman to be relentless with her affection when they were alone.

I would like that... She would also like to continue surprising Miwa with how loving *she* could be. Because, in a perfect world, they were equal amounts subdued and candid.

Finally, Sayuri felt a little warmth again. She hoped the candle burning in her heart would keep her thawed until she saw Miwa again.

Chapter 24

MIWA

Miwa didn't know what she expected Sayuri's apartment to be like. All she knew was that she did not expect a proper *mansion,* like the ones she saw in TV dramas and advertised in the subway station where she worked.

The place was three times as big as Miwa's, and she couldn't simply attribute it to the suburbs vs. inner Tokyo, or a difference in salaries. *We probably make the same amount of money.* Yet Miwa could never see herself living in a place as nice as Sayuri's, with its sterile concierge, views of her neighborhood, and enough windows to make Miwa understand what her girlfriend had been so worried about during the typhoon. The kitchen was big enough to cook healthy, filling meals, unlike Miwa's half-kitchen that barely had a single hotplate and toaster oven. Hell, there was enough *room* for things to be rightfully put away and not cluttered half to death. A girl could breathe in Sayuri's apartment!

She stood in the middle of her girlfriend's living room, wondering how much the whole place cost. If it was the same as Miwa's apartment, she swore to God...

"Please, have a seat."

Miwa spun around. Sayuri stood behind the kitchen counter, chopping up onions and carrots for their late lunch. She wore an infuriatingly pretty outfit of a baggy white sweater, complete with swooping neckline, and a gray and lavender skirt that swished around her legs when she walked from one end of the kitchen to the other. Her hair was down on one side, carefully kept away from the food prep while also framing her wide face. Rings glistened on her fingers. Her makeup was spectacularly fresh. Miwa was an unkempt child compared to this homemaker.

"I've been standing for over an hour." That's how long it took to get to Fujimi, and that included the ride to Ikebukuro Station. Miwa wasn't lying when she said she wanted to stretch her legs for a bit. "Sorry if I'm making you nervous."

Sayuri shrugged as she turned around to rinse off her cutting board in the stainless steel sink. "I only want you to be comfortable."

"Mind if I use your bathroom?"

"*Douzo.*"

Miwa only asked because she didn't want to be presumptuous. It had been so long since she was in a girlfriend's apartment, that she almost forgot what it was like to have proper manners. Better to overdo it and look thoughtful, than to be a total asshole.

The sounds of stir-fry in the kitchen followed Miwa into the toilet on the other side of the living area. *God, there's even more room in here than in mine.* She beheld the mauve walls and the tasteful fake greens drooping down from the back of the toilet. *Maybe I should ask if her I can move in, so I can play video games on her big TV.* It wasn't *that* big, but still bigger than Miwa's. Not that it was hard to accomplish that when she had so little room in her dingy apartment. The things she did to live somewhat close to work... *I still have to ride my bike for almost half an hour. What am I doing?* Living as cheaply as possible without enduring an hour-long commute like some of her coworkers.

She stepped out of the water closet and washed her hands in the sink by the shower room. Everything, from the plastic along the mirror to the metal on the fixtures, was polished as if Sayuri scrubbed her apartment every weekend. Between that and the smells of a homecooked meal wafting in from the kitchen, Miwa was liable to believe that her new girlfriend was destined to become a world-class homemaker. *I never thought I'd be with someone like her.* Miwa dried her hands and turned around.

She was not expecting to come face-to-face with the picture of a little boy.

Although Miwa recognized Yuma's face – partly because he looked so much like his mother – she had never seen this photo of him on what must have been his *Shichi-Go-San* celebration. The boy was dressed in the traditional clothes all children wore to celebrate turning three years old and coming out of the most dangerous part of childhood. Yet most of the photos Miwa saw of these festivities, including her own baby picture in her mother's house, showed crying, confused children who were still not used to having their professional photograph taken. Yuma, however, was nothing but a big smile.

It would have been one thing if Miwa only saw this photo. Except it was enshrined in the small alcove reserved for the venerated ancestors most families took precious care of in the years following their deaths. Those who cared at all usually enshrined their parents or grandparents. In a home like Sayuri's, however, there was only one death in the immediate family that impacted her to the point of leaving fresh fruit in the alcove and old incense burning.

A well-worn cushion was neatly placed before the shrine. Sayuri's permanent knee-imprints showed that she regularly sat before her son's photograph.

Are those his... Miwa looked away. She didn't believe in ghosts, nor did cemeteries bother her, but knowing that a part of Yuma's ashes were probably in the golden urn beneath his photograph put a sour taste in her mouth. It was one thing to be told that this boy existed. Quite another to have him sitting before Miwa, smiling above his own ashes.

"Miwa?" Sayuri sang. "*Daijyoubu?*"

"*Un.*" It was the only response she could muster before tearing herself away from the alcove. She was lucky that Sayuri couldn't see her. "Admiring your décor!"

"Really? It's pretty basic, isn't it?" Sayuri stepped out from the kitchen and met her girlfriend in the living area. Steam from their lunch blasted behind Sayuri, but she was completely unfazed. "I'm always thinking that I should redecorate, but who has the time? Or the money, for that matter."

"At least you have space to decorate." Miwa shrugged. "Remember what my mess looks like?"

Sayuri was about to say something, but was cruelly interrupted by a small grease fire erupting behind her.

"*Abunai!*" Miwa cried. She searched for the fire extinguisher, currently nowhere in sight, while Sayuri spun around and expressed her ire with an inconvenienced groan.

"*Daijyoubu!*" she insisted, hand grabbing the top of the pan's metal lid and smothering the small fire. The way she took care of it implied that this was a normal occurrence in her house.

Maybe she wasn't that great of a cook, after all.

"Everything's fine." Sayuri waited a few moments before peeking beneath the lid. "What if I told you that was supposed to happen?"

"Is your secret curry ingredient charring the veggies?"

"Perhaps?"

Miwa slumped down at the table. "Unbelievable. I'm kinda worried about you." Not to mention her so-called homecooked meal.

Chuckles replaced the furor in the kitchen. "I'm well-acquainted with fires around here, I assure you."

"That's not reassuring at all."

As All Our Fires Burn

Sayuri set everything back to order in the kitchen before approaching the table where Miwa sat. "You're really pretty today, by the way," she said.

"You're gonna change the subject?" Poor Miwa's heart was still fluttering, and it wasn't only because of the way Sayuri's clothes moved with her body. "Thought we were gonna die. Whole place. Poof."

"Have you ever thought that you might worry too much?" Sayuri sat down across from her. "I thought I was the worrywart around here."

"*Mou...*" Miwa didn't find this half as funny as her girlfriend did. "When you said you were gonna redecorate, I didn't think you'd do a quick and dirty 'charred walls' look."

Sayuri's delicate fingers took Miwa's hand. The lump she didn't know she had in her throat went down in an instance. "Will you ignore the fact that I called you pretty?"

"...Maybe."

"Why?"

Miwa was still trapped between accepting the compliment and fearing that everything she loved about Sayuri was why they would never work as a romantic couple. *How can I be pretty compared to you? Look at you. You're the quintessential housewife in her thirties. Even your day job is perfectly appropriate for a nice woman like you.* "I'm not pretty at all today." Not that she hadn't *tried* to be pretty. Careful consideration had gone into Miwa's outfit before she left her apartment around noon. She wore her favorite pair of black leggings and a baggy forest green sweater cinched with a chocolate brown belt. Why, she was practically a bastion of femininity! She had even tied a green ribbon in her hair before putting on the only pair of fashion boots she owned. They were so unused that they maintained their shine even through the rain.

Sure, Miwa had thought herself positively dressed up when she left her house that day. Now? Looking upon Sayuri in her gorgeously thrown-together outfit while she sat in her elegant home that overlooked her half of the city? Miwa didn't know what to think anymore. She certainly didn't think she was in any way comparable to Sayuri's beauty.

"How can you call *me* pretty when you look like you belong on the magazine cover for *Gorgeous Lady Weekly?*"

Sayuri chuckled again before transforming that into uproarious laughter. "*Hontou?*" she asked. "You really think I'm so pretty that I outshine you or something?"

"Jeez! When you put it that way..."

"I think we're at an impasse," Sayuri said, one finger tucked beneath her chin. "We both think the other person is prettier than ourselves."

"How am I prettier than you?"

"I don't think you appreciate how cool you always look."

"I don't look cool!" Especially with her cheeks on fire. *I'm so far from cool that I'm on the surface of the sun.* "It's a miracle if I'm able to put on clothes that go together. The only reason I look so nice right now is because *everything* goes with black leggings. I'd have to wear a crop top or something to look pathetic."

Sayuri tilted her head. "Ooh. A crop top. I'd like to see that."

"Don't..." Miwa had to look away before she died of embarrassment. "*Mou,* don't you have some curry to make or something?"

"Don't worry about it. It's still charring."

"You can't be serious!"

Oh, but she was! Sayuri wasn't kidding around when she implied that her secret ingredient was slightly burning her food. Miwa had no idea what to expect when she was presented with chicken curry arranged on a large, white plate bordered with vines and flowers. *She definitely didn't get these from the dollar store.* Not like Miwa's kitchenware, which came from a healthy combination of Daiso and Seria. Colorful plastic in no way compared to the elegant dining she now enjoyed in Sayuri's brightly lit apartment.

She took a bite of the carrots stewed in the spicy curry, fully expecting to bear the brunt of burnt vegetables. Instead, she exclaimed, "*Umai!*" She had never tasted anything like it. Nothing was burnt, exactly, but there was that heavy taste of charcoal lingering in the back of every bite. The spice on top of it brought Miwa to a new understanding of experimenting in the kitchen. *How much can I bet she discovered this way of cooking her curry totally on accident?* "I'm hooked. You got anything else?"

Sayuri was halfway through a bite when that made her laugh again. "You're funny. I was half worried that you were going to hate it."

Miwa scooped a large spoonful of curry and poured it over the helping of rice on the other side of her plate. "This actually feels like a healthy meal. Where have you been all my life?"

"*Not* in the convenience stores and fast food restaurants you apparently get all your meals from."

Miwa wasn't used to people calling out her eating habits. Her coworkers weren't much better than her, especially Kohei, who was also unmarried and as likely as Miwa to grab something from a burger joint or the hot case at the local convenience store. *If we feel really fancy, we get something from the cold case.* That high dining they experienced in the love hotel was the extent of Miwa's food experiences. She hadn't been lying when she said it had been years since she enjoyed regular home cooking.

Sayuri looked on with a hint of pride etching across her cheeks and down her chin. When was the last time somebody complimented her cooking? *Too long ago, I'm guessing.* While Miwa didn't exactly wolf down the food, she didn't pick at it, either. She made sure Sayuri saw her eating every bite and savoring the flavors dancing upon her tongue. *I mean, I might as well enjoy it, right?*

"I don't get to cook for people very often." Sayuri tapped her spoon against her half-eaten meal. What was wrong with her? Didn't she like her own cooking? "Sometimes I'll make a meal for the neighbors if they're sick, but for the most part, I only cook for myself. It's nice to know that I'm not totally hopeless in the kitchen."

If she were totally hopeless, then I would be beyond burned. "Who taught you to cook? Your mom?"

Sayuri's face instantly fell. "Yes. She got me into cooking. We used to do it together all the time. Since… well, in the past few years, I've mostly taught myself through the internet, cookbooks, and experimentation."

"Ah. I see." Miwa was sorry she struck a sore nerve.

Although Sayuri didn't need to explain it, she did anyway. "My mom isn't exactly supportive of my 'lifestyle,' as she calls it. Probably not surprising, huh?"

"She knows?"

Sayuri hesitated before grabbing the salt and adding some to her curry. Miwa didn't think it was needed, but Sayuri was probably happy to have anything to distract her antsy hands. "I told her when Emiko and I... when I decided to have a baby." She gently put the salt shaker back down, her fingers lingering against the plastic before she gazed down at her food again. Such a despondent look didn't suit her. What could Miwa do, though? Besides listen. Sometimes, that was all she was good for. "I don't think she ever expected that I was anything but 'normal' in her eyes. It took her a long time to realize what I was saying. When she met Emiko... I knew my mother wouldn't be excited by how I turned out, but I didn't expect her to be so cruel, either."

I did. About Miwa's own mother, that was. *I knew she would be awful about my sexuality.* So Miwa hadn't tried to hide it. When her mother caught her kissing another girl, it was just another day in the Ban household. Yelling. Screaming. Threats to whoop a girl's ass or send her to Christian school. Miwa's mother often ran out of steam when her favorite shows came on in the evening, but when she remembered that Miwa might be a poor influence on her younger brothers, the screaming started up again. *I didn't mind it after a while. Better she scream at me than my little brothers.* Her father, on the other hand, never had any idea what was going on.

"She loved my son, though," Sayuri continued. "It was like she forgot I was gay whenever she was with us. We were like a regular mother and daughter going out shopping with a baby strapped to one of our chests." Her faraway look distracted her from finishing her lunch. "She even talked nicely to Emiko about the baby. She really cared about him. I thought she might be coming around when she saw how happy we were as a family..." Sighing, Sayuri wiped something from her cheek and scooped up more of her lunch. "After the accident, it was back to the usual for her. When my ex dumped me, she went right back to finding me men to date. She didn't get it. I guess she thought Emiko was pretending to be a man, and I fell for it or something. We haven't spoken in a while."

Miwa didn't know which was worse: a mother who wouldn't talk to her at all, or a mother who only spoke in screams and threats. At least one acknowledged her existence. "Sorry to hear that. My mother knows about me, too, and it's more or less ended our relationship."

"*Kowai sou.* I hate that it's the usual story."

"I think she'd tolerate me if I didn't have two little brothers she's convinced I influence."

"I didn't know you had siblings."

"Yeah. Two brothers. I don't know them very well. We have an age gap." Miwa had been in middle school when her first brother was born. The second was still a baby when she went off to college. She knew their names. She vaguely knew what they looked like now, but she had no idea if the presents she sent for their birthdays meant anything. "Sometimes I'm convinced my mom could tell I was all sorts of wrong, so she tried having more kids to replace me."

"I'm sure that's not the case."

"*Sou kashira...*" Miwa absentmindedly tugged at the ribbon in her hair. *She says her ex was butch enough that her mother thought she might be trying to be a man...* What would Sayuri's mother make of Miwa, then? A confused girl? Nobody ever mistook Miwa for a man. That was painfully evident at the subway station every time she came across a conservative passenger or an oblivious foreigner. Yet she was nowhere near as feminine as Sayuri. Miwa often wondered if it would be a consideration if she weren't gay. Straight women got to be less than ideally feminine all the time, and nobody asked questions. "She's a strange woman. Maybe she's where I get all my messed-up shit from."

Sayuri shook her head. "You're not messed up."

"Honestly, you don't really know me yet."

Miwa hadn't meant to say that. It was supposed to be a nice day with her new girlfriend. Yet it came out of her mouth, like a comet blasting through the atmosphere. *Fuck. I'm an idiot.* Here Miwa was, enjoying a nice meal her girlfriend made, and she goes to offend her. *Like a true idiot. It's like I want to ruin this for myself, or something.*

"I know enough about you to know that you're a good person," Sayuri said. "That's all I care about right now."

Miwa couldn't suppress the wan smile attempting to cross her face. "That's kind of you to say."

"I mean it."

Something was off about this meal. No, not the food. Was it the atmosphere? The company? Which was it? An environment that wasn't anything like Miwa's usual style? Or the woman who was clearly out of her league? Sayuri wasn't only older than Miwa. She was more self-assured. She obviously had her shit together, if she could afford a place like this *and* keep it clean. And she had already performed the song and dance of maintaining a long-term relationship on top of motherhood. *It feels like dating my older sister.* Miwa didn't have one, but she could guess what it might feel like.

"*Doushita,* Miwa?" Sayuri pushed aside her empty plate and folded her hands on the table. "Have I done or said something to offend you? Oh, it's the curry, isn't it? Maybe it's not agreeable with your stomach."

"It's fine." Miwa forced a smile. "Everything is more than fine."

"If there's anything I can do…"

Stop being so perfect. Miwa knew that her girlfriend couldn't help it. Sayuri was naturally the epitome of perfection, wasn't she? If she weren't gay, she would be the kind of Japanese woman society upheld as the gold standard. Perfect wife. Perfect mother. Perfect schoolteacher and member of her community. Miwa could never compare to someone like that, even if she wanted to. *What right do I have being in this house? What right do I have thinking about kissing her after I eat her fantastic food?*

As All Our Fires Burn

"I've told you that you're really pretty, right?"

Miwa cleared her throat when she heard that. "Are you sure I'm really your type? When we..." she cleared her throat again. "It was dark. You couldn't really see who you were with."

"Is that the problem? You think you're unattractive?" Sayuri was close, but Miwa didn't give her enough to go by, now did she? "*Mou*. I don't know how many times I can tell you you're pretty, Miwa. I guess if you don't believe me, then that's all there is to it."

"You sound like such a schoolteacher sometimes."

Sayuri giggled. "I have to. It's the only way to survive when you look after hundreds of kids every day." She glanced to her right, reveling in some faraway thought Miwa wasn't yet privy to knowing. "Sometimes you sound like such a customer service person. I think you know more *keigo* than I do."

"Probably." Miwa wouldn't deny it. How could she? Studying *keigo* was one of the peak requirements of accepting her job when she passed the first round of hiring in her group. Luckily for her, she had some part-time stints in retail. Not exactly the same kind of flowery, highly formal language she had to know on a train platform, but it gave her a good head start in her studies. She liked to think it helped her pass the second round with flying colors. "You know... I'm sorry. I've been really on edge since I got here because I'm realizing I don't know a whole lot about you. I mean, you've told me things, but actually seeing your apartment and your memories reminds me that I'm still convinced this is all a dream. Maybe I'm not good enough for you."

Sayuri scooted back in her chair. At first, Miwa thought she might be coming over for a hug, but her girlfriend stacked the dishes before carrying them to the kitchen. Her swishing skirt almost made Miwa forget what she was so concerned about.

"If you weren't good enough for me, Miwa," Sayuri sweetly said, the clattering of dishes in the sink almost drowning out her lovely voice, "you wouldn't be in my home."

That *totally* didn't add more pressure to this relationship!

Miwa attempted to assist with the dishwashing, but Sayuri told her to sit on the couch and pick them something to watch on TV. *At least I don't have to worry about every other channel being porn here…* She said that, yet her eyes kept going back to the stack of dating sim games neatly piled up beneath the TV. The used gaming console had a sticker from the original owner. Sayuri probably didn't know what it meant, but Miwa could tell that the first person to own that console was a huge Demon Death Squad fan like her.

"Anything good on TV?" Sayuri collapsed onto the couch next to her girlfriend. Mere inches separated them, yet Miwa had never felt so far away from her.

"Nope."

"*Taihen.* Maybe we should play some video games. Unlike you, I got two controllers with my system."

Miwa snorted at that unexpected comment. "You don't have any two-player games! They're all dating sims."

Sayuri bit her lip. How could a woman dressed and styled like her suddenly look so flirtatious? "You want to mess around with Ms. Satin?"

As All Our Fires Burn

So, this was the direction their date was going in, huh? Miwa had half a mind to scold her girlfriend for giving her whiplash. "Thought you'd never ask, Satin-*san*. I've been waiting for you to pick me up from a bar and tie me up in your bed all day."

The annoying thing? That stupid nickname stuck. From then on, Miwa called Sayuri that moniker whenever they were alone. It never failed to get a reaction.

Chapter 25

MIWA

One thing must be admitted: Sayuri's bed was *way* more comfortable than the one in the love hotel. It also smelled like her, which was the kind of bonus Miwa could get used to should this relationship continue.

Not that she had a lot of opportunities to smell the residue of Sayuri's shampoo when the source was *right there* for most of the night.

Miwa's worries were for naught. Her girlfriend wasn't so meticulous that she had to tell Miwa what to do or how to behave. She didn't mind if Miwa leaned over to whisper dirty jokes in her ear while they "played" a dating simulation that was too ridiculous to believe. Nor did she care if Miwa cuddled up next to her, determined to figure out *how* soft Sayuri's clothes really were. (Soft enough to make Miwa whistle.) The only time Sayuri protested was when Miwa reached beneath her girlfriend's blouse and walked her fingers up that curving spine. And she only protested because she had been caught completely off guard and wasn't prepared to giggle so much she acquired the hiccups.

She doesn't realize how she comes across, huh? Miwa realized what an honor it was to see this true side to Sayuri the beautiful schoolteacher. Easy enough to assume she was miss prim and proper or a little authoritarian. That was the image Miwa conjured when she thought of her prettiest teachers from her childhood. *I wonder how much of it was true, and how much of it was my projections.* There were kids in Sayuri's class today who would never know the real her. They'd spend the rest of their lives making assumptions about Kawashima-*sensei* that simply were not true. Like did they know that her favorite flavor was orange? Or that she had a stuffed Totoro on her bed? "*It was a gift from an old friend. No, not that kind,*" she had said when Miwa asked about it. "*She said every schoolteacher needed a popular character from their own childhoods, so they would always remember what it was like to be a child.*"

Miwa hadn't spent a lot of time thinking about that. She was more invested in covering her girlfriend's skin with kisses. The more, the better.

She hadn't expected Sayuri to suddenly become the shy lady once the door was closed and they realized what they were about to do. Against her baser instincts, Miwa insisted that all they had to do was talk in the privacy of Sayuri's bedroom.

They could turn down the lights to the lowest setting and bask in the glow of their intimacy. Not that Miwa expected things to stay pleasantly sweet for much longer. All Sayuri needed was a little nudging, and she unleashed the ravenous side of her that still begged Miwa to do as she pleased. As long as it felt good.

The best part of turning their attentions to the sexual side was forgetting everything else. Miwa didn't think about how far she traveled to be here, or that she had work the next evening. She didn't dwell on how uncomfortable she had been when faced with Sayuri's grief. There was only focusing on her, on each other, and what it meant to be in bed together.

It didn't matter that they were no longer strangers to intimate touches or the kinds of kisses that were illegal in some parts of the world. Every time they stopped long enough to remember what they were doing, Sayuri commented that she loved feeling this way, and Miwa concurred that nothing felt better than wrapping her arms around her lover... and touching her in ways she had longed to all week.

I love how soft you are. I love how tender you are. I love the sounds you make when I touch you here or when I kiss you so hard you can't breathe. Miwa thought she knew what it was like to be in the throes of passion until Sayuri climaxed for the first time that evening. Hands wrapped around the back of Miwa's neck as Sayuri dove into her pillow and emitted such an animalistic growl that Miwa almost forgot who she was with.

I love how quickly things get wild when we're in bed.

It was only their second time indulging in the physical sensations of love, but Miwa was convinced that it would always be a wondrous adventure. She hoped they could do this every weekend. She longed to know what it was like every night. Not that she was convinced that they would be moving in together anytime soon.

Okay. Maybe she thought about it when Sayuri threw herself on her girlfriend and mauled her with affection. *I love how all I have to do is make you come one time and you're suddenly tearing me apart, as if I'll never know how you feel right now.* Miwa didn't know what happened to their clothes. She didn't know who turned the light back on. All she knew was that she greatly appreciated the view of Sayuri's glistening body after she kicked back the covers and invited Miwa between her legs again.

Did they want to go on all night because this relationship was new? Because it had been a long time since either of them felt loved like this? Because there was something more to what they had?

Did Miwa care?

"You've got a mole right here." Miwa had a fine view of it, with Sayuri's arms wrapped around her and legs kicked back in the bed. She pressed a finger against the tiny brown mole on Sayuri's hip and enjoyed the purr it elicited. Whether she was a kitten or a tiger, Sayuri was the epitome of a kitty-cat who only wanted to play. "Did you know that?"

"I may have been acquainted with it before." Sayuri's hand slipped down the length of Miwa's naked body. "Where are yours? Will I find them before you tell me?"

Sometimes, Miwa wondered what the hell they were doing. Not *literally,* of course, since that would be painfully obvious to anyone peering through the window and having the best day of their year. But moments like those, when Sayuri was nothing but a flirtatious, sexual being who couldn't get enough of Miwa, seemed almost too unreal. Was Miwa still dreaming about a woman she wasn't supposed to have? Had she fallen asleep after receiving Sayuri's thanks, and became trapped in this world where she lived out her greatest fantasies? *Too good. There is no way she can actually be gay. Let alone into someone like me.* When she expressed those sentiments later that evening, when they lay entwined with one another, Sayuri told her that she had feared the same thing.

"Women like us don't simply find each other," Sayuri said, before launching into a large yawn. "We spend half our lives hunting for other women who might be into us. Then we beg our friends to set us up on blind dates with anyone who might be a little queer. It doesn't just *happen,* you know? Feels like a trap of some kind."

"Didn't you just 'happen' to meet your ex at a party?"

"Yes, but..." Sayuri scrunched her brows. A pretty feat that Miwa wanted to see more often. "This feels much more random. What are the odds?"

Miwa couldn't believe she was now the big believer. "We shouldn't question it. Otherwise, we might wake up from a dream."

Sayuri slowly brought her face forward and bestowed a kiss upon Miwa's awaiting lips. The slow and sweet lovemaking that commenced suggested that neither of them wanted to admit that this might be a dream.

As All Our Fires Burn

Miwa never asked if she could stay the night. It was implied when she fell asleep from exhaustion, Sayuri cuddling up behind her and whispering that she hoped they both woke up together in the morning.

Sure enough, Miwa awakened around five, her limbs sore and her body begging for a shower. She easily pulled herself away from Sayuri's grasp and helped herself into the shower room. Sayuri was still asleep when Miwa emerged, wrapped in a towel she had borrowed from her lover's cabinet.

"Satin-*chan*," Miwa cooed, her nose lightly grazing Sayuri's cheek. "I'm gonna head home so I can rest up before work." She'd have to shower again, but at least she could grab a nap first. Or she'd spend the first morning of her work week playing video games and thinking about her naked girlfriend. "Did you set your alarm for work?"

"*Un*," came a half-asleep reply.

Miwa kissed her girlfriend's forehead and ensured she was comfortably wrapped in her bedding. It was difficult to see her in the dark bedroom, but Miwa knew Sayuri looked like a princess sleeping in her castle.

"*Oyasumi*." Miwa smoothed down some of Sayuri's hair before showing herself out of the apartment.

She met the cool, brisk air of a September morning and allowed herself a deep inhale that stimulated her lungs and woke up her brain. She'd need that brain working if she wanted to get home in one piece. Knowing her luck, she'd take the train going in the wrong direction. *Ikebukuro, dumbass.* She had to transfer there. yet how difficult was it to make sure she *got* there?

Drunk on pussy? Whew. She was going to end up at the other end of the Tobu-Tojo Line, wasn't she? *Shinrin-koen, here I fucking come.* She wouldn't care. Miwa was already going to spend another week at work spacing off and almost forgetting to signal the trains coming into the stations. That's what happened when she couldn't stop thinking about sticking her mouth all over Sayuri's body. Head to toe. Mostly the middle.

God, she has great tits.

That was the thought that made her miss the woman coming out of her house with bags full of trash. Miwa bumped right into her, and the poor woman dropped one of her bags. Luckily, it didn't split open and spill trash all over the street.

"*Ara!*" Sayuri's neighbor exclaimed. "I'm so clumsy!"

Miwa snapped out of her daydream and leaped down to help the woman with her bag. "No, no, *I'm* so clumsy! Oh, my God, *gomen nasai!*"

"Please don't think anything of it. It's dark out here." The woman stood up with her bags, hair blowing back behind her face. Miwa likewise popped up and fixed her own hair. "Hey, aren't you Kawashima-*sensei's* friend?"

Miwa suddenly lost the ability to breathe. "Excuse me?"

"Oh, pardon me. She told me she was having a friend over this weekend, and I saw you two last night."

"Saw... us..." The first thing Miwa assumed was that they were *caught.* They hadn't closed the blinds before they started making out on the couch! Not that Miwa thought they would have to, so high up in the building, but what did she know? She wasn't used to neighbors so nosy! "You saw us…"

The neighbor nodded as if she hadn't said a single damning thing. "I saw you two very briefly through the living room window. Oh, I promise I wasn't prying! I have a great view of Kawashima-*sensei's* apartment from my bedroom balcony. It's why she likes me to keep an eye on it for her when she's away. Well, that and my son is one of her students…"

"Yes, I'm her friend," Miwa said. "Just a friend."

The neighbor slowly nodded. "*Sou desu. Jya,* it's great that Kawashima-*sensei* has friends visiting her. She always seems so lonely since… well, I'm sure you know."

Miwa pursed her lips to keep from biting them. "Yes, well, I don't get to visit from Tokyo very often."

"Oh, were you the friend she stayed with last weekend during the storm?"

No use denying it. "Yes."

"I see. My name is Mariko Shimazaki." She quickly bowed, hands still full of garbage. "Pleasure to meet you."

Miwa had no choice but to return the pleasantries. "*Douzo* yo*roshiku*. I'm Miwa Ban."

"From Tokyo, huh?"

"*Hai.* I'm heading to the station now. I have work in western Tokyo this afternoon."

"Oh, don't let me keep you from making your train. They don't get too frequent until around seven."

Oh, Miwa knew all about commuters and how they gummed up even the most frequent of lines. "Indeed. Sorry again for bumping into you, Shimazaki-*san*. I really must be going now."

They bowed to one another again before Miwa booked it to the train station. She was in such a hurry that she forgot her train pass didn't work on the local lines. For the first time in years, a station attendant came out to fuss at her. If only he knew who she was!

Miwa hurried onto the next train heading to Ikebukuro, sitting between a salaryman yawning his way to work and a student hurrying to catch up on his homework before getting to class. *Are we in trouble?* Miwa fished out her phone and opened her chat window she kept with Sayuri. As she was about to confess what happened with the neighbor, however, she realized there was no point in it. All it would do was put Sayuri on edge in her neighborhood. *She had been so peaceful when I left her sleeping.* Miwa's phone screen dimmed. She turned it back on again to resume her message.

"*You looked like an angel when I left you. I hope we can see each other again very soon.*"

She nodded off into a nap and didn't jerk awake again until the announcer informed her she would soon be arriving at Ikebukuro, the terminus of the line. Miwa risked checking her messages as she joined the rush of people filing out of the train and getting a jump on Ikebukuro's hectic pace.

"*I'm already thinking about next time. I wish you could kiss me before I head off to work.*"

Miwa tried not think about the neighbor seeing that. "*I did. You were asleep.*"

As All Our Fires Burn

She received a long list of *emojis* that were nothing but hearts and lips. If the neighbor saw *that*, she would lose her mind.

Here was hoping she hadn't seen what those lips and hearts could actually do.

Chapter 26

SAYURI

"Shota-*kun!*" Sayuri called across her classroom early Thursday morning. "That better not be what I think it is!"

He sheepishly put away his trading cards and pretended that he had spent the past five minutes staring at his English book. Dean-*sensei* made a valiant attempt to lead the class through a tape recording that taught them how to use "a" and "an," but the class was so rowdy from the happy pop tune blasting on the speakers that everything was utterly useless.

Perfect opportunity for little boys to be little shits.

He thinks he can get away with murder because I'm looking down at my paperwork. ALT time was the perfect excuse to get some lesson planning done during class. The other opportune time was during silent reading, not that her students were great at that, either. The boys had a habit of flagrantly playing with their trading cards when they were supposed to be silently studying or doing a project. The girls weren't much better sometimes. When they weren't slapping stickers on each other's things, they were doing hair and gossiping about their favorite TV shows.

It was a crazy microcosm of society, and it used to make Sayuri happy to witness. Now, however, her thoughts were always preoccupied by what she would rather be witnessing.

Like Miwa taking a shower. The most agonizing thing that week was when Miwa teased her every night by announcing, *"Taking off my clothes to shower now."* Emojis of water spray and rain droplets did not help Sayuri's overactive imagination. Sometimes she prematurely hopped in the bath so she could say, *"Me too."*

Damnit. There she went again. Daydreaming.

"That's how you grammar!" Dean-*sensei* was contractually obligated by his program to spread out his arms and smile at the end of the song. The poor man could actually get in trouble with his employer if the teachers didn't think him *"genki"* enough, even if it meant overcompensating by looking like he was a "crazy foreigner" stereotype. "Any questions, kids?"

They didn't understand what he said.

"Thank you, Dean-*sensei!*" Sayuri leaped up from her seat, clapping for the dancing monkey who came with his own music tapes. "Can everybody say, *'Thank you, Dean*-sensei'?"

Some semblance of that phrase echoed. Shota was the loudest of them all, bless his mispronouncing heart.

The ALT showed himself out of the classroom. Sayuri readied the classroom for the next lesson, Japanese.

The kids made the usual jokes about swapping from one language to another. They also found Japanese dreadfully boring, since it was nothing but rote memorization. So was English, but at least those came with funny-talking foreigners, songs, and games that were supposed to help them remember phrases like, *"I'm fine, thank you!"* Japanese was *kanji* times infinity because, as these children were learning throughout their school-age years, there was no end to the amount of Chinese characters used in their native language.

"Let's start today's lesson talking about our favorite *kanji* that we've learned so far." Sayuri always kept one eye on her students, mostly Shota, because this was their best chance to start a game she wasn't supposed to know about. "Mika-*chan*, can you tell me your favorite *kanji?*"

A little girl in the front row, wearing red barrettes and a Minnie Mouse T-shirt, groaned.

"C'mon, everyone has their favorite Chinese characters."

"*Nai!*" she cried.

The students laughed. Sayuri had half a mind to write a possible character for "nai" on the whiteboard, but the joke would go right over everyone's heads. "Pick a random one that you know, then."

She thought about it for two seconds before saying, "*Ame.*"

"Excellent." Sayuri spent eight strokes of her black marker writing the Chinese character for *rain*. "What's the easiest way to remember this *kanji,* class?"

As All Our Fires Burn

"Looks like rain beneath an umbrella!" someone answered.

"Strange, isn't it? You'd think the rain would be *over* the umbrella." Sayuri demonstrated what that might look like, and even she laughed at how absurd it looked.

It worked. The whole class, including Shota and Mika, were laughing.

"Looks like somebody peeing on a house!"

Ah, they were definitely laughing now, because Shota always had to get the last joke in.

"Uh huh," Sayuri said. They had to move on. Now. "So what's *your* favorite *kanji*, Shota-*kun*?" she asked. She might regret it.

"*Muri!*" he proclaimed. "I can't possibly tell you, *sensei*. It can only be expressed…" he slapped his hand on his chest. "By myself."

"Well… this is true." Sayuri often didn't know what the hell he was going on about, but she supposed that was half the fun of teaching Shota Shimazaki, the leader and class clown of her homeroom. "Fine. Why don't you come up and show the class?"

She approached his desk in the front row and handed him the marker. A chorus of *Ooooh!* hit the room, since the only times kids had access to the markers was when they were answering math problems or when Dean-*sensei* thought it would be fun to give the kids some "exploration time" with the English language. It usually ended with rainbows and pictures of smiling poops all over Sayuri's whiteboard. *Exploration, indeed.*

Shota snatched the marker from his teacher's hand and marched up to the board. The room fell silent in eager anticipation of what he might do. Honestly, Sayuri was curious as well. Here was hoping it wasn't more poop. That was *not* a proper Chinese character.

He slowly curled a line down the board. Sayuri squinted in concentration. This already didn't look like a real *kanji*.

"*Jya, dou ka...*" Shota muttered, as if he had suddenly forgotten what he wanted to write. He drew a few short lines around the big one and called it good.

One of the girls attempted to read it before Sayuri could parse what it said. "*Kokoro?*"

"Ah!" That had to be it. Except Shota had curved the line in the wrong direction, and one of the other lines was terribly misplaced. But from the other beginner *kanji* most third graders learned, what else could it be? "I can see it. Is that what you meant to write?" Either the boy was brave or he had some other joke in store. Because "kokoro" meant the feeling-filled heart everyone had inside of them. Far from what the average nine-year-old boy would say was his favorite Chinese character.

"*Chigau, yo!*" Shota spun around in utter disbelief. "Why the hell would I be writing *kokoro* on the stupid board! That's some girl's character!"

The class laughed. Sayuri leaped right into damage control.

"What did you mean to write, Shota-*kun?*"

"*Hi.*"

"Ahhh." Sayuri saw it now. Poor Shota had really fumbled one of the first and simplest of characters kids learned, but the botched up stroke made it totally incomprehensible. "Thank you, Shota. You may have a seat."

He slumped into his desk, embarrassment coloring his cheeks. Miswriting a common character hadn't been an intended joke. Sayuri needed to delicately correct it so her neighbor's son wouldn't feel afflicted and singled out in a class of pranksters.

"It's very easy to confuse 'kokoro' and 'hi' when you're starting to learn *kanji*," Sayuri wrote both words on the board. "When I was a little girl, I often got *kanji* confused. For the longest time, I thought that *kaiyoubi*," she said, referring to Tuesday, which included the character 'hi', "was actually pronounced "kokoroyoubi.""

Half the class repeated that silly notion. The days of the week were named after the natural elements of the world, with fire representing Tuesday. The thought that it might be "heart day" instead of "fire day" would be something Sayuri never lived down after confessing it to her class. Sometimes it was worth being the butt of an eternal joke.

"As you can see," she said, pointing out the differences between the characters, "they both contain four strokes and practically mirror each other. You'll get the hang of it if you practice more."

She left those characters up on the board while she continued with the main lesson of the day. While students copied down the *kanji* they were to study over the weekend, Sayuri stepped back and took a hard look at "heart" and "fire." *I really did mix them up as a kid, didn't I?* She had forgotten about it until Shota reminder her. *I also mixed up "blood" and "plate" all the time, but that's way more common of a mistake.* She tugged on the little hairs growing from her chin. *I wonder why I would make a mistake like that.*

It bugged her for the rest of the day. After school, when she sat at her desk in the teacher's room and stared at the stack of homework she had collected earlier that day, she picked up her phone to text Miwa.

"Did you ever mix up the characters for 'heart' and 'fire' when you were a kid?"

"Where did that come from?"

"One of my students did it today, and I realized I did the same thing as a child."

"I dunno. Maybe?"

"I used to think that kaiyoubi *was actually* kokoroyoubi…"

"Holy shit, that is freakin' adorable."

Sayuri snorted, garnering the attention of her coworkers on either side of her. As soon as they went back to their own homework checks and lesson plans, she continued to text.

"Makes me think about the heart being a tinder box, deshou?"

"Careful not to strike a match around it."

Sayuri had to contain every ounce of giggling within her when she typed, *"I think it might be too late for me."* She swallowed the cynical part of her that said she was foolish for sending that to Miwa. That's what it took for her to press send.

The fact it took more than ten minutes for her to receive a reply nearly killed her. *She's riding her bike to work right now. She can't look at her phone.* Sayuri inheld a deep breath while she told herself that. She pulled over a stack of workbooks, grabbed her favorite pink marker, and began the monotonous chore of checking her students' Japanese homework.

Shota sure didn't know his stroke orders, huh…

Sayuri's phone glowed with an incoming message. Against her better judgment, she closed Shota's workbook and grabbed her phone.

"Who lit the match?"

Sayuri considered that response for a few minutes. Much longer than anyone would have expected a woman to look at her messaging app. When she finally looked to one side, she realized that her coworkers were one-by-one staring her down. Nobody cared how long it took her to finish her work for the afternoon. They cared that she was acting strangely, particularly for her. Other teachers spent half their after school time texting with their families and friends or writing something down in their personal planners. Sayuri, however, preferred to get through her work and head home before it got too dark. It was a habit she picked up when she had a family awaiting her there. *I couldn't wait to get home and see them.* How long ago that felt now.

Maybe things really were changing in her life.

"I don't know. Maybe you do?" Was that coy enough for Miwa? Sayuri wasn't yet comfortable confessing that she was having love-oriented feelings about Miwa. Not out loud. Not via text, either. Now, if *Miwa* started the love…

"Jya, if I find out who has lit you on fire, I'll scold them for you."

Sayuri dropped her phone with a grunt. Totally not what she wanted to read! *Thought you were more romantic than that,*

Miwappo. She also didn't have the guts to call Miwa that to her face. Yet ever since she saw the handle on the PlayStation Network, Sayuri had taken to calling her that more and more. In her head, anyway.

"*Daijyoubu desu ka,* Kawashima-*sensei?*"

She almost threw up her fiery heart when she heard the principal's voice behind her. Sayuri quickly put her phone away and swerved in her seat, prepared to get the scolding of her life, although she had done nothing wrong.

"*Dai… daijyoubu,*" she insisted. "Forgive me. I lost track of the time."

"*Mou…* if you need to talk, you know where my office is."

How pathetic of her! She had been acting like such a numbskull that the principal emerged from his office and called attention to her behavior in the middle of the teachers' room. Although none of her coworkers looked directly at her, she could feel their curiosity and derision drilling a hole into the back of her skull. *If they think there's something suspicious about me…* Sayuri knew how to play the game of staying in the closet. Yet it was a difficult game to play when she completely lost herself.

She closed Shota's workbook and opened one of her blank notebooks she kept in her drawer. She wrote the *kanji* for "fire" with a bold, red marker, its hue reminding her of such a destructive element.

How could she ever mistake it for a different word? Let alone one like "heart?"

She leaned back in her seat, pulling the strands of her long hair apart as she prepared to put it up in a ponytail. *I'm so childish sometimes.* She was a woman who had given birth and fallen in love more than once. How could she act like such a little girl?

Sayuri hurried through her workbook corrections and grabbed her coat to leave. Somehow, even with all of her dithering, she managed to escape the school for the day before half the other teachers. Then again, she often suspected that some of those people were never in a hurry to get home.

The moment she walked through her door, she threw down her bags and pulled her phone out of her purse. Sayuri was barely on her couch when she furiously sent another text to Miwa the flirtatious wonder who drove her *nuts.*

"I was talking about you, by the way."

She sent that with finality. *Now, to make dinner and take a bath.* Maybe not in that order.

Yet before Sayuri could leap off her couch and get to work in the kitchen, her phone blew up with a new message from Miwa. Wasn't that a feat when she should be at work by now?

"I hope your heart isn't the only thing I set on fire. But if it is, I wouldn't be complaining."

It was a good thing Sayuri was at home. Because she sent what was probably the naughtiest text of her life.

"All of my insides are on fire when I'm with you."

No, she didn't directly refer to her private parts, but everyone damn well knew what she meant when she sent that.

*"You're not the only one getting all hot right now, Satin-*chan.*"*
"Save it for the next time we hook up."
"Did... you say, 'hook up?'"

"See? I'm a bad girl, sometimes."

Somewhere in the depths of Tokyo, one subway platform attendant was laughing so hard that her coworkers were as confused as Sayuri's. *Good.* Sayuri enjoyed having that effect on the woman who fired her up.

Chapter 27

MIWA

The Friday night rush carried with it the usual carnival of students staying out past curfew, drunken salarymen stumbling their way home, and stylish young women coming back from terrible dates that made them swear in ways Miwa hadn't heard since she last hit a bar in Shinjuku.

"Because it's dangerous otherwise, please stand behind the yellow line at all times." The automated announcement *said* that – over and over, and over and *over* – but few of the passengers heeded the warnings as they scrunched together on the platform and threatened to spill into the tracks like Sayuri had months ago. Along with Kohei, Miwa marched up and down the platform, kindly asking people to *step the hell back* until she received the notice that the next train was on its way. *Babysitting adults is a job*

in itself. The whiny young women made off-handed comments that jumping in front of the train was better than going on another hopeless date. The delinquent students, trying to look cool in their name-brand clothes while talking like old people, dared each other to step a toe into the tracks. Yet it was the drunk salarymen who were the real danger. They tended to step so far back from the yellow line that they crossed over the *other* yellow line.

"Look at this lady over here," one young woman muttered to the other, while Miwa debated whether to take their threats to jump in front of the train seriously. "You think she gets a lot of dates being a train employee?"

Great. They were talking about her. *Where's that train when you need it?*

"No way," the other girl said with a derisive snort. "She's not even cute. What guy is gonna want a woman who tells people what to do all day?"

"She'd have better luck as a stewardess."

"*Deshou?* Then you get to travel everywhere. Maybe date a captain!"

Miwa had to refrain from rolling her eyes. Luckily for those women, they were saved by the alert Miwa received in her earpiece. She took great pleasure in blowing her whistle and making those terrible young women jump out of their fuzzy jackets and pleated skirts.

A new group of passengers got off the train, but by then, it was Miwa's break, and Shinnosuke came down the stairs to relieve her so she could eat her dinner.

As All Our Fires Burn

"Ah, *yokatta*." She allowed herself that breath once she was enveloped by the blessed silence of the staff room in the back of the station. She removed her hat and gloves, placing them in her locker before pulling out her *bento*. The only sound came from the oscillating fan hanging in the corner of the room – and Overseer Endo clacking away at the computer near the gates. "Finally, some peace."

Yeah, right.

"Ban-*san*!" Endo leaped up from his seat and motioned to his office door. "Is it time for your break already? Come have a chat with me really quick. Promise it's worth your while."

Miwa had half a rice ball already in her mouth. "Huh?" She almost choked. Good thing she had yet to bite into the *umeboshi*. That was a surefire way to gag in front of her supervisor. "Who's watching the window?" she asked after swallowing.

He shook his head. "This won't take long."

What choice did Miwa have? Telling her overseer to fuck off so she could eat in peace wasn't exactly an option. She closed the lid on her bento, wiped her mouth with a napkin, and stepped into the tiny office Endo usually avoided during most of his work day. Probably because it was more cramped than a toilet stall – and because it kinda smelled like one.

"How's life, Ban-*san*?" She didn't like this. Not how friendly her overseer was, nor the fact she was called into the principal's office. *This reeks of me winning some award instead of being in trouble.* Yet Miwa had no idea what kind of accolades she could possibly receive. "You still live over by Shibuya, right?"

"Uh…" He was close, she guessed? "Yeah." Not really that close. She was closer to Shinjuku than Shibuya… but Endo didn't need to do that. "May I ask what this is about?"

"No need to be so formal right now. Sit, sit." He flopped into his rolling chair and shot halfway across his room. Unfortunately for him, that was a whole four meters. "I was recently telling my wife about your lack of proper dating prospects, and she thought she might have a resolution for you."

Miwa's face fell into her lap, not that she could let her boss see it. "My dating prospects?"

"Been thinking about that night we went out drinking and you mentioned you hadn't dated in a while. *Maa,* can't be easy working nights in a job like this *and* live the life of a nice young lady. Not that I can do much about it from my position, other than put a good word in for you." He chuckled. The man was interfering with her personal life, and he was *chuckling.*

Yet overstepping personal boundaries was basically in the job description of men like Endo. How many underlings had he arranged dates for? Some men – and yes, women – saw it as their eternal duties to properly look after their younger charges, ensuring that they ate, got enough sleep, and got married by thirty. *Hear that it used to be twenty-five. My, how times change.* Miwa wanted to gag on the rice ball no longer in her mouth. What had she done to deserve this?

"My wife has a few friends who have sons looking for a nice lady to date. Turns out, one of them has a similar schedule to yours, so he can meet you when you're off. Isn't that lucky?"

Miwa hardly knew what to say – that wouldn't offend her boss, anyway. "The luckiest."

"Now, I don't personally know this young man, but if my wife vouches for him, then I'm sure he's an upstanding kid who has a lot going for him. Know what I mean, Ban-*san?*"

"I…" This was it. This was Miwa's chance to put a stop to this before she ended up on a date with some strange man she had never met. All to placate her supervisor's wife, who probably saw matchmaking people she didn't know as a grand hobby. "Actually, sir, I'm seeing somebody right now. It also might be getting serious." She had to add that, so the Endos knew she was *not* in the business of shopping around.

Endo sat back with a small start. "You are? Serious in such a short amount of time? Well, I'll be. Turns out you didn't need my wife's help, after all."

They both smiled awkwardly at one another. "Yes, sir." Miwa stared down at the back of her hands, where veins throbbed slightly enough to remind her that, yes, her heart was still beating, although this was one of the most embarrassing moments of her life. "It's rather sudden, but it's possible I've met someone that I might spend a long time with." She wanted to believe it. For now, when facing her boss's meddling, she *had* to believe it. "I really appreciate you and your wife looking to help me, but things might be okay now. Sorry if I made you two worry."

Endo's brows went from staking claim at the top of his face, to slowly descending his nose and making him look as if he now realized how badly his office smelled. Yet instead of questioning Miwa about her own personal life, he said, "Congratulations, Ban-*san*. Now, I'll do you a favor of not telling the guys about your new boyfriend, huh?"

She wanly smiled, not because she thought he was hilarious, but because she was on the verge of throwing up at the mention of *your new boyfriend.* "Appreciated, sir. Thank you."

"Especially that Tanaka, huh?"

That caught her off guard. "What about him, sir?" Had Kohei been saying things about her? Whether inappropriate or not, she didn't appreciate her coworker talking about her behind her back. *Here I thought he liked me well enough...*

"Oh, you don't know? Tanaka-*san* is always asking us if we think you're seeing somebody. If you ask me, he has a crush on you."

Oh, no. Oh, no, no, *no.*

"Well... if he asks you again, I guess it's okay if you tell him that I'm seeing someone." Miwa said.

Endo nodded, as if he understood her newfound position. "Thought as much. We don't encourage our employees dating one another, anyway. Can cause issues on the platform. Like, what if you rejected him? Or you broke up? You can see the awkward position he's in."

Suddenly this was about Kohei and *his* feelings? Miwa furrowed her brows to match her boss's. "Tanaka-*san* and I have never dated, sir. We're simply coworkers."

"Oh, I hadn't thought you two ever dated. For one thing, you're way out of his league." That caused an uproarious laugh that made Miwa shake in her seat.

"*Sou ka...*" Miwa looked up at the clock hanging above Endo's head. "If I may, sir... my dinner..."

"Right, right. Go on. Get out of here. Thanks for entertaining an old man."

Endo was far from being "old," but Miwa didn't have the energy to refute it. She barely had enough to scurry back to the staff room and finish her dinner. All the while, she thought about Kohei possibly having a crush on her, and what that might mean for her professional relationship with him.

When she returned to her shift on the platform, she exchanged looks with Kohei, who slightly nodded in acknowledgement and immediately went back to glancing up and down the tracks. An instinct they both shared.

Nah. No way. Miwa bowed to Shinnosuke. He would be back in half an hour to allow Kohei to go on break. Until then, Miwa was alone with her coworker on the platform. They were too far between trains to have many passengers bothering them.

He never once looked back at her. Not until they received the signal that a train was about to pull into his side of the platform.

Back to work. No time to think about things out of Miwa's control.

※※※

"...Then he had the gall to climb up on his desk and thump his chest like a monkey!" Sayuri told an outrageous tale of how one student made her life hell that past Friday afternoon, yet she was nothing but laughter, each guffaw interrupting her story. "The worst part is that the English teacher absolutely encourages that kind of behavior. You should've seen how hard he was laughing! It was up to me to regain control of the whole class!"

Miwa snorted over her empty plate of pasta. Two ice-filled glasses – one that used to hold melon soda, and the other what the restaurant called "healthy tea" – was all she had to show for the size of her meal.

This wasn't her idea of "a grand dinner" when she asked Sayuri to meet her in Ikebukuro that Saturday. Yet when they agreed that getting a love hotel later would be best for their schedules, it was also agreed that they should go easy on dinner. A family restaurant it was.

At least they sprung for the one with a nice view of Nishi-Ikebukuro's busy streets. Amazingly, the restaurant wasn't that crowded for that time of night. Let alone on a Saturday. *Maybe people don't want to bother coming up here because they have to climb two flights of stairs.* Miwa almost couldn't blame them. She climbed so many stairs at her job, that doing it on the weekends was rude of the universe. *If I block my view of the drink bar and the old women in uniforms, maybe I can pretend there's a candlelight dinner going on in this booth.*

"Your class sounds really *genki*," Miwa said with a sigh. "I'm exhausted from hearing about it."

"I get exhausted hearing about *your* job." They leaned in closer, elbows propped up on the table while they conversed on the far side of their dirty dishes. "Especially what you said about those mean young women talking about you. How dare they?" Sayuri was so irate on Miwa's behalf, that one of them couldn't help but laugh.

It had been Miwa, who loved that look on her girlfriend's face. *I feel like she'll kick some serious ass on my behalf.* Whether that would actually happen was another story. Poor Sayuri probably wouldn't last long in a fist fight. *That's another thing I like about her, though.* Miwa didn't need her women highly feminine and delicate, but she did appreciate them not being big on fighting.

"I've heard worse on the platform," Miwa said with a smile on her face. "Usually from men and old aunties, though. *Mou,* they're the most judgmental groups." The men found her completely unfuckable, and the aunties bemoaned her lack of makeup and unladylike posture she had to adopt for the company. *Basically, they think I'm unfuckable too.* How tragic.

"They're so wrong, though." Sayuri touched the webbing between Miwa's fingers. "You're one of the prettiest people I've ever seen."

"Pfft. You're only saying that. Besides," Miwa sat up, before anyone saw Sayuri being so physically flirtatious at their *very public* table, "how can I possibly compare to you? You're like... the most beautiful woman in the Kanto region."

"Stop, you!" Sayuri was so red from embarrassment that she almost matched the pink sweater wrapped around her torso. "*Ara,* only Kanto? What about the rest of Japan? Why can't I be the most beautiful Japanese woman? *Mou,* step up your game."

"Hey!" Miwa almost knocked over the specials' menu that had been left at the edge of their booth. "Don't put me in that kind of spotlight! How am I supposed to know what you will or won't believe?"

They were only a nose touch away behind the menu. If they wanted, they could steal a kiss in a room full of people who never expected to see two women locking lips. (Not in person, anyway. That's what late night TV was for.)

"I can be a really humble woman," Sayuri insisted. "Until I'm in a relationship. Then I want – no, demand – to feel like the prettiest girl you know."

"First it's not good enough that you're the most beautiful woman in Kanto. Then you want to be the most beautiful Japanese woman. Now it's the whole world?"

"I didn't say that. I said the most beautiful one *you* know."

"All this started because you were trying to convince me that I'm pretty..."

"You *are* pretty." Sayuri took Miwa's hand and squeezed it as if it were a common sight. "So pretty that I thought about you all week."

Miwa glanced over the top of the menu. No one was watching them, right? Sayuri might feel brazen because they were far from her school district, but that didn't help them if someone made a stink about their behavior.

"All week, *ka na?*" Miwa allowed her most girlish grin yet to flash behind the menu. "No wonder you let little boys and girls create absolute ruckus in your classroom. You spent too much time thinking about adult things instead of your work."

As All Our Fires Burn

Sayuri slowly shook her head. "If only you knew."

I have a pretty good idea. Miwa grazed her teeth against her bottom lip, attempting to contain her excitement. "It's a miracle I didn't make trains crash this week because I couldn't stop thinking about that thing you do with your tongue."

Sayuri's eyes widened. "You're gonna talk about that here?" she whispered.

"If I can't stop thinking about it," Miwa began, eyes already glazing over, "I might as well talk about it. You know, get it out of my system."

"So naughty!"

"Come on. You saying all your thoughts about me are only about my ethereal beauty? You're lying."

"Well… there is the way you kiss."

"Just my kissing?"

Sayuri clicked her tongue. "I don't think you understand what thoughts of that quickly lead to. Especially when I'm in, say, the bathtub."

"Tell me more about this bathtub."

Their voices were low enough and their pride blown up to attempt stealing a kiss behind the menu. Miwa closed her eyes and leaned it for a quick peck on the lips. She could already smell Sayuri's sweet perfume.

"May I take your plates…"

Adrenaline shot through Miwa's body as she jerked back so quickly that she almost crashed one of her empty glasses to the floor. The waitress that had come to take their empty plates yelped at the sudden movements. Half the restaurant was now turned in their direction, attempting to see what the commotion was about.

Just a couple of lesbians being inappropriate in public, really.

Sayuri pretended to be fascinated with the dessert menu. She must have been so practiced in being cool and calm in public that she actually made Miwa look like the crazy one at their table.

"We should get a parfait to share," Sayuri said, as if they hadn't been caught kissing by some young college-aged waitress. "What do you think?"

"Share... a parfait..." The waitress scurried away with a stack of dirty dishes. Miwa almost envied her. "What are we? Cheap high school students?"

Sayuri nodded. "Today we are."

"*Moooooouuu.*"

Sayuri talked her into it, though. They picked the smallest chocolate and banana parfait on the menu and made a grand show of eating it as quickly as they possibly could. Not because they were in a hurry to leave – all right, maybe a little – but because there was a contest to see who could hold off brain freeze the longest. They had regressed from high school students to the kind of kids Sayuri saw on a daily basis.

By the time they left the restaurant, there was only one thing on their minds. If they were always on the brink of being found out, they might as well take it as private as possible.

Miwa had done her research ahead of time, now that they weren't pressured by a typhoon to get the closest room they could afford. It meant meandering down a windy and dark street that made Sayuri take her girlfriend's hand and mutter that the place gave her the creeps.

Yet the woman behind the main desk was friendly. She didn't look twice at two women checking into a room with no luggage or the threat of a typhoon nipping at their heels. She was paid to not judge who came in and out of the rooms.

They split the cost fifty-fifty as previously discussed. It was a miracle they kept their hands off each other until they were in the small elevator taking them up to the fourth floor.

"Know what we should do?" Miwa asked. "Find out how many people can fit into the bathtub."

"Are you trying to tell me that I stink?"

They kicked off their shoes and latched the door behind them. Miwa was already taking off her clothes on her way toward the bathroom. If she left a trail of clothing behind her, would Sayuri find it in time to meet her in the tub? "I'm trying to tell you that I want you naked and wet!"

"*Mou.*" Sayuri stopped in the bathroom doorway, her clothes still on. Miwa, meanwhile, was buck naked as she kicked on the faucet and propped herself on the edge of the two-person tub. "What kind of wet?"

Miwa rolled her eyes. "What kind do you think, huh? You're an educator." She splashed some of the hot water against the tiled wall. "I'm sure you can figure it out."

Honestly, it wasn't rocket science. Although Sayuri argued with her that there was a reason she never focused on becoming a science teacher.

Chapter 28

SAYURI

The world wasn't that cruel of a place to a woman falling in love.

Didn't matter that the days were increasingly shorter and the temperatures gradually dropping. Sayuri often left for work at the crack of dawn and returned home long after the sun had gone down. Yet as long as she had someone willing to text her, call her, or otherwise spend time with her when she wasn't teaching the bright minds of Japan's children, she could get through the loneliest time of the year.

She especially needed the distraction on her son's birthday.

It was a cold and rainy day when she wandered to the supermarket after leaving the school early on a Wednesday. She swore she was holding up well, considering that this time last year she was a sobbing mess who refused to leave Emiko's weary embrace. *I'm doing better this year. I've accepted the fact that my son is gone, my old relationship is over, and new things are happening.* She inhaled the crisp evening air as she stepped through the sliding doors and was instantly assaulted by the cheery music and recorded messages asking her to purchase this and that. She bypassed her son's favorite fruits in the produce section, barely acknowledged the snacks she used to buy him, and ignored the exasperated mothers chasing down their children while shopping for dinner.

What got her was the chubby baby in his stroller.

Sayuri had to double-take after catching a glimpse of the little boy who looked so much like her own. While Yuma had no longer been a baby when he passed, the one in the stroller next to his mother looked *so* much like him that Sayuri almost forgot how to breathe.

He could be my son reincarnated... How strange she did the math that quickly. Even stranger she immediately went to *my son, reincarnated.* Sayuri didn't believe in that kind of thing. So why would she consider it simply because she saw a chubby baby who looked like so many others?

Because it was what she wanted to see. Her conscious had spent the whole day trying to forget her son, that she now fought with her subconscious that refused to let go of his memory.

Sayuri hurried to buy her groceries and head home. She made it all the way to her street before finally breaking down crying.

At least the rain had finally let up. At least she had someone to call who wasn't her ex.

"Miwa-*chan*," she pitifully said into her girlfriend's voicemail, "today is a really bad day for me. It's Yuma-*kun's* birthday. He would have been five year's old today." She should be throwing him a birthday party with his friends from the neighborhood and daycare crawling all over her apartment. The fact that Emiko's presence had been replaced with Miwa's didn't affect Sayuri at the moment. "I'm sorry for calling you like this, but... *aitai, yo.*" She sniffed up more tears. "I really wish you were here with me right now. I could really use some of your kisses." Wasn't it miraculous that one kiss from the right person could put her heart at ease, if even for a second? "Anyway, I know you're at work right now. *Gomen.* I can't wait to see you this weekend."

Sayuri hung up and wiped the tears from her eyes. Only then did she realize that someone else was on the street with her.

"Kawashima-*sensei?*" Mariko carried a cloth shopping bag in one hand an umbrella in the other. "*Daijyoubu desu ka?*"

"*Sumimasen,*" Sayuri apologized. "It's my son's birthday. It's difficult."

Mariko instantly understood. "I'm so sorry. If there's anything I can do..."

"No. Thank you." Sayuri finished wiping her face and continued toward her apartment building. "You're kind to ask."

If only she knew how kind Mariko Shimazaki could be.

As All Our Fires Burn

***

"I'm not that great at this!" Miwa called from Sayuri's kitchen. "At least I can make tea."

Good, because Sayuri wasn't in the mood to get up and make tea for herself, or her girlfriend. Ever since she was caught crying in the rain earlier that week, she had been fighting off a flu.

She thought she was fine that Saturday morning. She woke up fine, although she later realized that was a byproduct of being excited about Miwa coming to visit. *I had all these plans to cook for her again.* Sayuri liked cooking for people. It made her *happy.* So why was she curled up on the couch, staring at her TV while rain fell outside? Was it only the flu? *Side effect of being a schoolteacher. I get all the worst germs.* She got her flu shot as soon as they were available. Maybe it was the wrong strain?

"You shouldn't be near me." Sayuri muttered that when Miwa came around the couch with a hot mug of tea in her hands. Miwa placed it on the coffee table, her beanie still pulled down her forehead, pressing her long hair against the back of her neck. *What I would give to have the strength to thread my fingers through her hair right now.* "You should honestly go home before I infect you. You work with the public."

"Which means I'm probably already infected with whatever's going around."

"Put on a mask." She meant the one Miwa had been wearing when she walked through the door. It was now in Miwa's bag, not doing much to protect her from Sayuri's mouth germs. *At least she hasn't kissed me. I really want a kiss, though.* Sayuri hadn't seen her girlfriend in a week. She was due a sweet – and not so sweet – kiss. She also wanted the comfort that came with Miwa's lips on her own. Instead, she bade her girlfriend to completely cover up her mouth with a mask.

"It won't do any good now." Miwa sat at the other end of the couch, tea in her hands as well. She softly blew the steam away. "I brewed the herbal tea you had, by the way. You should drink it. Good for you."

Sayuri stared at the steaming mug on her coffee table. "I'll wait for it to cool."

"*Maa.*" Miwa sank back against the couch. "You'll be here a while. I made it extra hot for your throat." She placed a soothing hand on Sayuri's side.

"Why are you doing this for me?"

"Hm? Why wouldn't I? Everyone needs somebody to baby them a little when they're sick."

"I'm not sick."

Miwa sighed. "You're shivering with a pile of blankets on top of you."

"Am not."

"Yes, you are." Miwa sipped her tea.

Sayuri buried her face in the cushion. "I'm sorry for making you still come here, even though I'm sick."

"What makes you think I wouldn't come here, anyway? Like I said, everyone needs some babying when they're sick."

"It costs time and money for you to come all the way out here."

As All Our Fires Burn

"It only costs me from Ikebukuro. Everything before that is covered by my company pass."

"Still, it's money."

"I came here to spend time with *you*. It doesn't matter what we do or don't do. The most important thing is that we're together in meat space."

Sayuri slowly lifted her head. Damn. Why was her face so heavy? "What did I do to deserve someone as kind as you?"

"*Kind?* I'm doing the bare minimum, honestly."

"It's not the bare minimum if it means so much to me."

Miwa rubbed the spot where her hand lay. "I'm here because I want to be. Don't feel like we have to make love every time I come over."

Was the heat in Sayuri's cheeks from blushing? Or from the flu slowly overtaking her body?

I know how I got sick. It took a lot to get her sick, even when she was a child or the type of person who didn't take as good of care of herself as she should. Yet when she was already down in the dumps, let alone staying out in the rain for hours on end... let alone because she didn't care about what happened to her? It was like asking for that virus she incubated from one of her students to mutate until it completely consumed her. What good was an immune system if it had no will to thrive? *I didn't care enough about staying well.* Sometimes, remembering to take care of herself wasn't a priority. *All right, a lot of the time.* Her career as a schoolteacher was the only thing that kept her somewhat on top of her health. Now that she had a girlfriend again? Damnit. She needed to treat herself better.

She was already a fairly healthy eater, but exercise, sleep, and staying out of the elements often eluded her when she was depressed.

"*Oi.*" Miwa patted Sayuri's side. "Do you need me to put you to bed? I could clean some stuff up and hang out for a while."

"I couldn't possibly ask you to do any of that."

"You don't need to ask me. I'm offering."

Is this because she doesn't want this to feel like a wasted trip? At this rate, Sayuri would pay for take-out. So much for her plans to make homemade udon to beat the chill coming through her window. *I'm a terrible hostess. I'm a terrible girlfriend.* She rubbed her forehead, aware that a little heat originated there. *I've wasted her Saturday, and now I'm probably gonna get her sick.* How dare she? What right did she have to do this to a woman who could be doing better things in her apartment? Like playing video games?

Sayuri pushed herself up and forced tea down her throat. It was hot enough to scourge the gunk in the back of her throat, but not enough to make her feel overall better. "I don't mind staying on the couch, if it's all right with you. If you want, you could play some of my video games…"

Miwa's smirk was almost enough to make Sayuri feel better. *She looks like she's figured it all out.* Meanwhile, Sayuri had no idea what was going on. She waffled between wanting to kiss Miwa and wanting to cry from embarrassment. Was she ever like this with Emiko? *No…* They had already been going steady for a few months when Sayuri got sick for the first time. And Emiko had been sick before her, allowing the motherly tendencies always lurking within Sayuri to thrive in their natural element. *If I hadn't become a teacher because I love kids, I would've been a nurse.* She was always most adept at being a housewife, though. Why not make money doing what she was best at?

I'm not supposed to be taken care of... it's all backward...

Miwa leaned forward, elbow digging into her knee. Her hair fell toward the floor, the beanie on her head highlighting the bridge of her nose and the way her thin brows moved whenever she considered her girlfriend. "You wanna watch me play the games you can't beat, is that it? You know, there are whole YouTube channels for that..."

Sayuri barely knew what she was talking about. What did YouTube have to do with video games? "I bought some more used games from different genres last time I went to the shop." Sayuri pointed to a blue plastic bag by the TV. She hadn't the time to go through her recent purchases yet. "Maybe there's something good in there? I don't mind spending time with you on the couch and staring at the TV screen." She forgot to add that said staring would be quite vapid. As long as the tea stayed hot, however, she would survive.

Miwa got up from the couch and rooted through the bag. Every so often, she shook her head or blew a large sigh from her inflating cheeks. Toward the bottom of the stack, though, she discovered something that made her laugh.

"You have a *train* simulator?" She held up the old game case that looked like it had been well-loved by its former owner. Either him or his dog. Sayuri couldn't tell. "Oh, man. This is some gold right here."

"I can't tell if you're being sarcastic or not."

"Me? Sarcastic? *Muri.*" Miwa turned around and popped the disc into the console. "I haven't played this in a long time. I think it's a port from an older version, but sometimes the old games are the *best.*"

"What is a train simulator?"

Miwa grinned over her shoulder. "You pretend to drive trains. That's the most basic premise." A loud and colorful logo, sponsored by one of the local train companies, appeared on the screen. "Some of the more advanced ones give you challenges to complete, like getting to places on time or memorizing routes. If you do well enough, you drive up ridership because you've won over customers... so that's a challenge too." She started a new save file before hopping back on the couch. "I think in this one you can upgrade the stations based on daily ridership levels. You can incorporate other lines, subway stations..."

"So it's a station simulator?"

"You can do both, but it's mostly about driving the trains."

Sayuri didn't really get it, but Miwa was the train nerd. She might as well play what she loved best – and Sayuri might as well watch the hypnotic train drive down the tracks, picking up and dropping off passengers while dodging hazards and completing challenges. *I'm gonna fall asleep...* Her eyelids became heavier with each challenge Miwa completed. Eventually, Sayuri fell into a light slumber.

Soft laughter fell from Miwa's lips every few seconds. The game created sounds of accomplishment and dismay, complete with the nostalgic sounds of trains all across Japan. Hot tea continued to steam from Sayuri's mug and remind her that she had something healthy to drink. The couch slowly swallowed her into its embrace. Her legs draped across Miwa's when she finally sat back in her seat, mumbling that the game was "so unrealistic, but great." Occasionally, she rested her arm on Sayuri's supine body and made herself right at home.

For the first time in years, Sayuri felt truly comfortable. In her skin. In her couch. In her home.

She didn't recall much of the rest of the weekend. All she knew was that she was pleasantly surprised to wake up Sunday morning and find Miwa in her bed, dressed in a nightgown she borrowed from her girlfriend and snoozing as if a whole day's worth of train simulations had totally wiped her out. Sayuri dragged herself out of bed to shower and make breakfast for them both, but she only made it as far as the toilet before realizing she really was too sick to function. Somehow, Miwa left the apartment later that day unscathed. And, somehow, Sayuri didn't feel as lonely although she was alone again. Knowing that they would see each other again soon was all she needed to feel a little better on such a gray day.

Chapter 29

SAYURI

Sayuri got herself up Wednesday morning with a little skip in her step. Not only was she mostly recovered from her flu, but it was only a half day at school, and she had a phone call planned with Miwa in the middle of the afternoon. *Gotta finish up my paperwork early so I can make the call at home!* She did herself up as if she were going on a casual date, since *really* doing herself up would be a bit much for school.

Her flats clacked against the asphalt of her narrow street. The moment she heaved her bookbag up her shoulder, she encountered one of her favorite neighbors at the corner. All signs pointed to Shota Shimazaki having already headed off to school. That left only his mother to look up from her plant watering and catch Sayuri's gaze.

As All Our Fires Burn

Usually, Mariko was nothing but pleasantries, even if she had a current beef with her son's teacher. Yet for some unholy reason, on that particular Wednesday morning, she jumped out of her skin and nearly dropped her skinny garden hose. Her evergreen plants received an extra dose of water that morning.

"S... *sensei!*" she stuttered. Sayuri stopped in her tracks. "How nice to see you again. It's been a few days."

"Ah, yeah. I'm afraid I had the flu." Sayuri took Monday off, but was back to teaching Tuesday. "I'm sure Shota-*kun* told you all about the substitute on Monday. I got a report saying he was... very *genki* with Yamada-*sensei*."

Mariko still looked as if she saw a ghost. "He may have mentioned it, but I did not know that was the reason you were gone."

"Did you think it was more serious?"

Mariko finally turned off her hose. "You could say that." She firmly turned her back on Sayuri. "Have a good day, *sensei*. Afraid I have too many chores to attend."

"Of course. Have a good day as well." Sayuri barely made note of this encounter as she proceeded toward the elementary school.

She sauntered into the teachers' room ten minutes early, and sat at her desk as if the world were the most amazing place she had ever encountered. Students rushed by, saying good morning. The sun was out for the first time in over a week. Even her coworkers were mostly smiles as they spoke of the upcoming events both in the school and around town. There were many plans to go into Tokyo for the last time that year, since soon the snows would come and cause complications with the trains. That was the only thing to slightly dampen Sayuri's mood for a while. *It will be harder to see Miwa, huh?* They would somehow survive.

"Kawashima-*sensei*," the principal barked from his office door. "A word, please?"

She perked up from her work, brain in overdrive trying to figure out what he could want, and so curtly. *Did I not fill out my sick day paperwork correctly?* She thought she made it clear that she was better now. Was it an insurance thing? Probably. The insurance they used through their school was notoriously finicky about how a woman filled out her paperwork. *One time I didn't use the exact name of the virus I had, according to my doctor, and I spent months trying to get reimbursed for my medications!* It was even worse when she had a baby.

"Yes, sir?" She stood in the doorway, unsure if she should shut the door or not. "Is there something I can do for you?"

"Not right now." He flopped down into his chair behind his desk. A newspaper was spread out before him, and he pretended to be more enamored with political headlines out of China and South Korea than whatever he wanted with Sayuri. "We can talk after classes are over today. Make sure you're here at one, sharp."

"All right, sir." *One?* Depending what he needed from her, Sayuri might be late for her call to Miwa. *I hope I don't totally miss it.* Miwa didn't get the occasional half day on Wednesday like Sayuri did. She had to be at work at four-thirty, and that's all there was to it.

As All Our Fires Burn

Somehow, she persevered with her good mood and carried her morning classes off without a hitch. Her students were lively, yet behaved. Dean-*sensei* managed a game that appeared to sink into the students' heads while not leaving them behind a ragtag team of energy and dysfunction. She got an extra break when they ran off to the science lab to learn about mass and momentum from the dedicated science teacher. It was the perfect opportunity to sit down in the teachers' room and collect her thoughts.

Too bad so many of her coworkers were caught up in whispers around her. A feat, considering there were only a few of them in there at that time of day. It didn't help that the principal's assistant was always looking in Sayuri's direction whenever she happened to glance up from her desk.

Something wasn't right. Instead of dwelling on what-ifs, however, Sayuri focused on the positive. Like her willing students who were excited to end their half day with art class.

"Look, *sensei!*" Mika held up her picture of a blue flower for her teacher to praise. Sayuri moved from another desk to check it out for herself, but by the time she reached Mika, the young girl was already moving on to her next picture. "You like it, *sensei?*"

Sayuri tilted her head, like she had seen Miwa do so many times. "What kind of flower is it?" A rose? Chrysanthemum? Why, she had no idea that her students were so patriotic!"

"*Yuri,*" Mika said, as if she were the principal of the school.

"This doesn't look like any lily I've ever seen."

"You should like it because it's your name, *sensei!*"

"Her name is Kawashima," a super-astute classmate said.

"Her *real name* is Sayuri, *duh!*" Mika snapped back. "Don't you know anything?"

Sayuri had to calm them down before they began fighting in her classroom. That was when she had a poignant yet casual discussion with her class about teachers and the fact that, yes, they also had "real" names like their students. Yet it wasn't polite to call teachers by their given names, so nobody should try it. (Somebody would definitely try it.)

The kids became antsier as lunch approached. Stomachs grumbled, although they wouldn't be filled at school that day. Instead, kids would erupt from the school gates, rushing home to have lunch with their families while Sayuri took a bento into the teacher's room and avoided getting sticky rice on her work. *If I eat it fast enough, I can get home in time to call Miwa in the privacy of my bedroom.* This was before she remembered she needed to meet the principal at one. Classes ended at 12:15. It could take fifteen minutes for the students she was responsible for to vacate the premises and give her ample chance to steal away into the teacher's room. Would it be enough time to eat?

Her chance to find out came within a few minutes. The music played over the speakers, announcing the end of the day. Children rushed to their cubbies and coat racks to grab their belongings before Sayuri had to croak at them to line up in boy-girl lines for the end of the school day headcount. Only then would they be led out of the classroom and to the front grounds, where *hopefully* their parents either awaited them or they joined their walking groups to go home.

As All Our Fires Burn

Sayuri didn't get to the teacher's room until 12:40. She wolfed down her lunch, checked for food in her teeth, and approached the principal's office. She had been so busy with the children and getting food in her stomach, that she missed the other adults marching into the principal's office with business on their dour demeanors.

She saw them now. Two people, one man and one woman, who represented the school administration and the teachers' union, respectively. Sayuri swallowed the sudden rush of bile shooting up her esophagus. If other teachers were coming in after her, she wouldn't be as worried. Perhaps it was a short dialogue with everyone in the district. Or maybe there was news to relay that couldn't be done through a simple missive.

No. She was the only one called into the office. Talking directly to the principal was bad enough. With two more important people looking at her as if she had massively fucked up? Her life was about to take a turn, wasn't it?

"Have a seat, Kawashima-*sensei*," the principal said. "Do shut the door behind you."

She looked between the people staring her down before following orders. Her head nodded in acknowledgement. Nobody moved.

Brief introductions began. Sayuri already knew the other two people in the room, yet only in passing. She had been to her share of public administration meetings. She also talked directly to many people from the union who collected opinions on such matters as, *"Is the insurance good enough?"* and *"Do you believe our history textbooks accurately portray Japan's involvement in the*

Second Great World War?" Being put on the spot was enough to make Sayuri's stomach turn on a good day. If she were the kind to have a political presence in her community or an online blog, she would be throwing up right now.

As it was, she had neither. She was a well-behaved woman who kept to herself and espoused traditional values, or at least as far as her neighbors were concerned. The last time she was called into a meeting like this? Everyone was "concerned" about her having a child out of wedlock, and how it might affect her ability to teach. Which translated to, *"You look like a giant, lawless slut and we're worried that it would look bad to such young and impressionable students."*

She had talked her way out of that one and managed to keep her job, although she forfeited a few raises in the process. This was a woman who always stood for the national anthem, regardless of her personal feelings, and spoke with high deference to those in charge. *I have too many skeletons in my closet for them to go poking around.* When her students asked her what the lyrics to "Kimi ga Yo" meant, she simply said, *"We wish the emperor a long and happy reign."* Didn't matter that she always mentally followed that with, *"Although the emperor doesn't mean anything anymore... aren't we a democratic society?"* Yet she had seen her fair share of fellow teachers reprimanded by the administration for not doing their supposed civic duty. They were usually quietly investigated, as well. After all, the administration had to find *some* reason to fire them that wasn't just, *"They wouldn't stand for the national anthem. They didn't face the Hinomaru. Sack 'em."*

As All Our Fires Burn

Ugh. Politics. Sayuri had a feeling she was about to get a dose of them now.

"Kawashima-*sensei*," the representative from the administration, a man named Mr. Satou, greeted. "I have a simple question to ask you on behalf of everyone here."

She slowly nodded, her face draining of all heat and color.

"Do you consider yourself an honest woman?"

A small breath hitched in her chest. She looked between the principal and the woman from the teachers' union, Mrs. Ichinose. *I voted for you.* Ugh. "Yes," Sayuri firmly said. "I tell my students that honesty is the marker of a person with excellent potential for greatness."

"Admirable," Mr. Satou muttered. "We do have records of your honesty. Four years ago you were quite honest with us when you informed us that you were expecting a child with no intention to marry the father."

"Yes, and I thought that had been hashed out. Besides, my son…"

"Yes, our condolences," Mr. Satou continued. "This isn't about that. We were merely establishing the precedence of your honesty when in the face of unpleasant topics."

"I see."

He stood before the desk. Mrs. Ichinose kept a wary eye on him while the principal completely checked out. "I'm afraid we must discuss unpleasant things again, Kawashima-*san*. It turns out that there are… accusations… against you."

She gasped "About what, exactly? I have been nothing but a model citizen and done my job to the best of my abilities."

"It's true that Kawashima-*sensei* is a popular teacher with the kids," the principal cut in.

The others ignored him. Mr. Satou had other things he wanted to say. "These accusations insinuate that you indulge in homosexual practices."

Sayuri was so gobsmacked that all she could do was gape at Mr. Satou and slowly tilt her head to the left.

Her goldfish impression was not lost on him. "What do you have to say about this, Kawashima-*sensei*?" he asked. "We appreciate your honesty."

What in the world *could* she say? It wasn't a matter of telling the truth or outright lying to save her own hide. She was simply too shocked to give them an immediate answer. She wanted to cry, "*It's none of your business!*" Telling them she was pregnant had been the extent of discussing her sex life with any of these people. Wasn't that bad enough? To basically announce, "I've had sex, and now it's resulted in a child?" That wasn't how it happened, of course, but that was the image she projected into the principal's mind when she sat down four years ago to discuss insurance and maternity leave. Sayuri was a woman who valued her privacy. She rarely gossiped with her coworkers or got drunk enough with her own best friends to talk about sex. Sharing the occasional dirty talk with her romantic partners was the extent of her verbal expressions. Miwa was one of the only people in the world to ever hear Sayuri talk about an orgasm.

Oh, my God, what would Miwa say right now?

"I honestly don't know what to say," Sayuri sputtered. "Who is making these accusations? What evidence would they even *have?*" Furthermore, what did it have to do with her job? *I know what it means.* Homosexuals weren't a protected class in their district. If the administration decided she was a liability with the parents and community at large, they had every so-called right to send her packing. The nicest thing they could do was keep the reason hushed. *They will ask me to resign. That's what they will do.* Make it look like she held all the cards in this decision. Well! First, they would have to prove that she was gay!

"A simple yes or no will suffice, Kawashima-*sensei*," Mrs. Ichinose said. "We appreciate your cooperation and honesty."

She really hated that word right now.

"You think I'm a lesbian?" she boldly said the word in front of them. Both the principal and Mrs. Ichinose sat slightly back in shock. "I would say that, either way, it's honestly not your business what I do or don't do in the privacy of my own home. Yet I also recognize that parents will not rest until rumors are quashed, or I am removed from this school." She still hadn't given them the yes or no answer they beseeched. "You want honesty? I will give you honesty." Here she went, playing with the fire they burned around her feet. "I am a supporter of the LGBT community, yes. I do not discuss these matters with anyone, however. I attempt to keep my political leanings away from work and the children, as I'm sure we all do."

She was met with a trio of grim faces.

"Perhaps someone has overheard me verbally giving my support to gay and lesbian people of this country. In which case, all I can say is that I am guilty as charged, and will do my best to keep it from interfering with my work."

"Kawashima-*sensei*," Mr. Satou said with a sigh, "that does not answer the question. Are you gay? Yes or no."

"I'm honestly too embarrassed to directly answer one way or another. What you're asking is basically about my sex life, and I do not take kindly to it." She made direct eye contact with all three of them. *I feel like I'm dealing with small children. Trying to get answers out of* them. "Whether I say yes or no, you will have an image of what I do in my bedroom, and *who* I do it with! Besides, I have given birth! Isn't that personal enough for you?" She banked on their ignorance about IVF and the existence of bisexuality. There were plenty of people, especially older ones like the principal, who would hear rumors about her lesbianism and counter them with, *"But she's given birth! How could that be possible if she doesn't like men?"*

"We apologize, Kawashima-*sensei*," Mrs. Ichinose said with a countenance that was hardly apologetic. "We assure you that this is an uncomfortable topic for us. However, as it affects the perceptions of this school and what it means for its students, we are under obligation to get to the bottom of it. Now, please. Do you, or do you not, engage in homosexual activity?"

They no longer cared about her identity. Perhaps they wouldn't give a shit if she was gay, as long as she stayed femme, motherly, and abstinent. *Better to be the pure Madonna who happens to look at other women than the lascivious Whore who eats pussy.* What a time to think about Miwa. Oh, hell! How could she not?

It was now or never. Did she condemn her career when she had nothing else? Or would she lie to save herself? A woman who built a part of her identity on how *honest* she was?

She was still an adult. Adults knew what must be done to save their own hides.

"I do not," Sayuri said, shoulders back, and chin high. "Now, are we finished with embarrassing me?"

"Thank you," the principal said with a chuckle. "You see?" he then continued to Mr. Satou and Mrs. Ichinose. "I told you this was all a big mis…"

"We have eyewitness accounts that say otherwise, Kawashima-*sensei*."

Her lips and mouth dried the moment Mr. Satou said that. *What in the world is he talking about?* Sayuri had always been careful, including recently! No kisses outside her home, unless she was in a big, faceless place like Tokyo. Not even handholding, the thing which wasn't unheard of among best female friends who wished to express affection or not lose one another in a large crowd. *I used to hold my friends' hands all the time when I was in school! It wasn't sexual!* She didn't even hold Miwa's hand in Fujimi!

"You do, huh?" Sayuri's brain was running a mile a minute as she attempted to figure out who the hell ratted her out, and how had they even known? "I'd love to know what kind of 'evidence' they have, and why this person is so assumedly trustworthy."

Mr. Satou removed his phone from his pocket. Whatever he pulled up, it must have contained an email or the notes he needed to remind him of what had been seen. "Naturally, we would not have come in here and asked you about these allegations unless we had more or less confirmed it for ourselves, Kawashima-*sensei*. The woman you are currently 'seeing' is an employee of one of Tokyo's many rail lines, is she not?"

If Sayuri had not exposed the truth on her face before, she did now. There was no denying the damning expression blossoming on her face. *Miwa! Don't tell me they know her name! Don't tell me they're about to rat her out to her company!*

"She has been seen coming and going from your place frequently. Not to mention, how many times you two have been seen together in public, both in our city and in Tokyo."

"I hardly see how having a close friend makes me…" This was absurd, no matter how she looked at it. Something else was afoot. Someone was out to get her, and it didn't matter if they knew the truth or not. "Yes, my best friend is a woman from Tokyo who works for one of the subway companies, but that doesn't mean we…"

"Kawashima-*sensei*," Mrs. Ichinose said softly, while the principal gaped at her as if he didn't know how to take Sayuri's biggest secret. "This is serious. Deny it as you might try, there is no coming back from this. Even if you are telling the truth and there is truly nothing between you and this woman, there is the fact that you once lived with…" she cleared her throat. "A known homosexual. Emiko Yoshida, yes?"

Sayuri gasped.

"It's in your records that you two shared a household before she moved out after your son's unfortunate death. We looked the other way as long as nobody complained and you did not flaunt your sexuality before the townspeople. However, we cannot overlook this when there are rumors floating about. It's best for you to come clean, so we can help you."

Help me? What exactly did they mean by that? Not like Sayuri trusted these people with her personal best interests.

"Yoshida-*san* helped me with my son when he was a baby. You already know his story. I would prefer to not rehash it."

"Understandable," Mr. Satou said. "But I'm afraid we cannot overlook the evidence. Even if it turns out that everything you say is true, Kawashima-*sensei,* public perception will not be in your favor. That's why we're here. To *help* you."

She pursed her lips. "While also saving the school's image, I'm sure." A lesbian teacher? With elementary schoolers? The nicest parents would silently judge her but be too lazy to say or do anything, as long as she didn't create a disturbance with the students. All it would take, however, was a few *juku* mothers convinced that the sky was falling because some perverted homosexual was in their children's midst. Didn't matter if she were male or female in this particular case. There were too many stereotypes about LGBT people and their relationship to children. The most foul-mouthed mothers (and a few fathers) would get riled up with their self-righteous indignation, convinced that she was out to groom their children for either the homosexual agenda or her own sick pleasures. Yet the school board knew what a good teacher she was. Could it be true that they actually wanted to help her keep her job?

"What exactly is happening here?" she asked. "Is this a proper interrogation? Is my job on the line because of what a few busy-bodies think is true?" Sayuri leaned forward, eyes narrowed on each face staring her down. "I want to know exactly what 'evidence' these so-called witnesses have against me. I don't want conjecture and overactive imaginations. I want to know *what* I've supposedly done."

Two people cleared their throats. The principal looked like he wanted to sink into his chair and disappear forever. Mrs. Ichinose shuffled the papers in her lap. Mr. Satou scrolled through his phone, forehead sweating.

"They are pieces of a larger puzzle, Kawashima-*sensei*." Mr. Satou handed her his phone. A bullet list appeared on the screen. "I don't see why you can't see them for yourself."

She squinted to read the tiny characters on his tinier phone. *"Woman seen picking up fast food take-out under Kawashima-sensei's name."* Sayuri scoffed. That must have been the previous weekend, when she was sick and called in a take-out order to the neighborhood KFC. Miwa had gone to pick it up. *Why would I think putting it under my name would be damning? It shouldn't be!* Besides, who the fuck was at the God damn KFC spying on people?

"Seen having a public phone conversation on the street with previous woman. Phrases included 'I want to see you,' and other terms of affection."

Red laced the room.

Mariko Shimazaki!

"Ara, *sensei*..." Mr. Satou gingerly took his phone back before Sayuri could crush it in her hand. She was so incensed that other people's property were of no concern to her. *Might as well make that another gay stereotype, asshole!* How could Mariko do this to her? Was Sayuri not a good neighbor and great teacher to her son? What else had Mariko seen? *Oh my God, she's been in my apartment, unsupervised!* Not that Sayuri decorated her apartment with artistic vulvas or other signs of lesbian sexuality. She wasn't even in a relationship with Miwa the night Mariko was last in her home!

The video games. She may have seen them, since Sayuri kept them in a plastic container by her TV. The ones on top were the ones she played the most, and the artwork included busty images of young women attempting to seduce the player. Relatively harmless on its own, but within the context of the rumors and other "evidence" against her...

Like Emiko. That was the closest Sayuri had ever come to outing herself. *I only wanted a family. I wanted to live with my beloved. I wanted my son to have both of his parents in his house. I wanted a family, for fuck's sake!*

Why was it too much to ask? Why did people have to pry, to stick their noses into places they did not belong? What was so bad about a woman creating a family like everyone else did? Just because her partner was a woman instead of a man... did that make her such a bad person? Did it mean she couldn't teach the children she always wanted to help?

Mariko's betrayal continued to sting. They had never been *best* friends, but Sayuri often stopped to talk to the housewife about things good neighbors often discussed. That included their sons, what to make for dinner, and how the weather affected their chores. If a new utility provider came to the neighborhood, they immediately went to each other to talk about the pros and cons of switching. It was the kind of neighborly acquaintanceship that sustained a woman who didn't have many other friends.

Had she been judging and sneering at Sayuri behind her back all this time?

"Seems I'm guilty regardless of the truth," she said. "So, what happens now?"

She attempted to swing back into professionalism. Getting angry and snapping at the people who claimed to want to "help" her was not going to, well, help. Sayuri must continue to prove that she was worth protecting. The principal's word about how great she wouldn't do a damn thing if she looked like an angry lunatic in front of the school board and the union.

Mrs. Ichinose rounded the desk and offered Sayuri the most sympathetic visage she could muster. "First, I want to assure you that while there may not be legal protections in place for your situation, the teachers' union is prepared to protect you as much as we feasibly can. It's in our best interests to keep our members' private lives from affecting their employment, as long as they can continue to teach well in good conscience. I assume you're invested in remaining a teacher at this school, Kawashima-*sensei?*"

She inhaled a deep breath, refocusing her energy on putting her best foot forward instead of lashing out like an emotional dipshit. "Of course. I love my job. Teaching children is my greatest passion and was my lifelong dream before it finally came true. Regardless of my sexual orientation… it doesn't have anything to do with my abilities as a teacher."

As All Our Fires Burn

Mr. Satou cut off Mrs. Ichinose before she could reply with more reassuring words. "Be that as it may, this is an image thing, first and foremost. We cannot condone the employment of a teacher whose private life distracts her students or has parents who take this to the media. If we don't do something, I'm afraid that the disgruntled parents may get the media involved."

Would that be so bad? Sure, everyone would know what a dirty pervert Sayuri was, but maybe it was time a big case hit the press and then the courts. *We should be a protected class...* Some things were slow to be covered in locations around Japan. There were a few specific cities that attempted to be more socially progressive when it came to the LGBT population, but hers was not one of them.

Ultimately, however, Sayuri did not want to be the face of that campaign. It would also drag Miwa into the fold, and what if she was fired as well? If not for her sexuality, then for being in the press! Talk about an image crisis...

"The administration would like to temporarily suspend Kawashima-*sensei* starting today," Mr. Satou flatly said. "Paid suspension," he added for the union's benefit.

"Now, hold on," the principal interrupted. "I don't know anything about her personal life, nor do I care to, but is it really so serious that we need to bring in a substitute for the indiscernible future?"

"I'm afraid so," Mr. Satou said.

Sayuri was sweating from her forehead to her palms. She gathered her skirt between her fingers, a pointless redirection when it only made her look more worried. "Suspended. For the first time ever. And this is why? I can't believe it."

"We're sorry, Kawashima-*sensei,* but we hope that it will only be temporary while we figure out what to do. Perhaps it will blow over. We can help you come up with a reason for your 'leave.' Nobody has to know the reason you've been suspended."

"Suspended! This is going on my record, isn't it?"

Mr. Satou was hardly taken aback by her outburst. "Honestly, there were a few things already on your record. Like your child out of wedlock, and the fact that you lived with a known homosexual."

Damnit, Emiko! All well and good for her to be mostly out to the world when it didn't affect her image as much as it did Sayuri's. How long had Sayuri been under suspicion? From the moment she told the administration she was going on maternity leave? Or only after Emiko moved in with her and was added to her list of contacts at her apartment?

Had her doctor ever reported her?

How about the other neighbors?

Or the mailman, who once delivered a package with a Lambda symbol obnoxiously stamped on the front?

Paranoia had never been Sayuri's strong suit. The only time she felt such intense paranoia as now was when she was convinced every germ on Earth wanted her son's body for its own. That was easily brushed off as New Mom Syndrome. This, however…

She had a reason to be paranoid.

As All Our Fires Burn

"I think a paid suspension would be agreeable, considering the assumptions," Mrs. Ichinose said. "The union expects a thorough investigation, though. If the administration decides to fire Kawashima-*sensei* to save their image, we want a generous severance package and referrals to another district."

"Trust me, we don't want this getting out if we can help it." Mr. Satou sighed. "Our continued apologies, Kawashima-*sensei*. We know how this difficult this must be for you."

"Do you?"

All three faces turned toward her at the same time.

"I've already lost my son and most of my other relationships," Sayuri muttered. "This job is one of my only reasons for living. Take it away, and…" She would do a lot worse than wander through the busy intersections of Roppongi and stumble into the subway tracks. Even with Miwa to support her…

Ah. Miwa.

"We want to prevent that," Mr. Satou assured her. "Here. These are our suggestions for you during the course of our investigation. Trust us when we say that we will be calling upon you again for more interviews. We will do our best to make it as speedy as possible."

He handed her a card and a piece of paper. She couldn't bear to look at them.

Chapter 30

MIWA

Miwa stared at her girlfriend from her side of the table in a nondescript café in Ikebukuro. The Sunday buzzed around them. Friends, families, students studying and employees making their money. They were the kind of people who filtered in and out of Miwa's station, going about their lives while she focused on hers. Since when did the energy feel so good, though? While Miwa was used to the crowds and found them less claustrophobic than many others did, she didn't usually feast on the energy like she did right now. Maybe it was the good mood she was in. Maybe it was her desire to show her beautiful girlfriend off to the masses.

Sayuri's hair was down, blending into the fuzzy black sweater she wore over a white blouse and black-and-white skirt.

Black winter leggings hugged her long legs. Even her crossbody bag matched her perfectly paired ensemble. Miwa leaned her elbow against the table and continued to stare at Sayuri as if she were God's greatest gift to Earth.

I think I love her. Miwa wasn't scared of the prospect. True, they were moving quickly, considering how their relationship originated, but she didn't mind it. There were many stereotypes about lesbians moving quickly in relationships. *Desperation, they say.* Miwa had another theory. *Women are more open with their hearts and their needs. It's easy to know what page we're on with each other.* A wistful sigh blew through Miwa's nostrils. She wondered if Sayuri was ever going to drink her coffee.

Damn. Why did she look so dour?

"*Doushita?*" Miwa touched the sensitive spot between her girlfriend's fingers. "Everything okay?"

Sayuri glanced at their intimate scene and pulled her hand away. Miwa was only mildly offended, and quickly forgot as soon as she saw the rosy hue to her girlfriend's cheeks.

"I'm fine," Sayuri said. "Some stuff going on at work, that's all."

"Oh? Are the kids okay?"

"My students are fine."

"Good." Miwa drank her water and pushed the cake they shared around the plate. She attempted to feed her girlfriend a small piece. Sayuri shook her head, drumming her fingers against the table. *Did I do something?* Sayuri had missed their phone conversation on Wednesday afternoon. Not that Miwa had a ton of time to indulge when she had woken up late and still needed to shower and eat before going to work. Yet the text she received from her girlfriend that said, *"I can't make the call today. Stuck at work,"* worried her for most of the day. Sayuri was usually more forthcoming with information.

It was depression, wasn't it?

That was fine. Well, it wasn't *fine,* but Miwa was willing to understand what terrible emotional onus her girlfriend was under since losing her family in such a horrific way. It had only been a year ago. How could she be expected to heal so quickly? A miracle she was even entertaining Miwa now. *She's so strong. If I were her, I don't know what I would do.* Cry. Die. Perhaps in that order?

Should I confess that I'm falling in love with her? Too soon. Miwa burned with the desire to swear her allegiance to Sayuri's life, but it was waaaay too soon. She should wait until Christmas. A solid few weeks away.

"We should plan something romantic for Christmas," Miwa said. "I have to work, though. Do you?"

Sayuri shrugged. "Don't know," she murmured.

"I haven't done anything nice for Christmas in a really long time. Not since I was a kid, I think." Her mother used to make a decent deal about the Western holiday. They always had the best fried chicken in the neighborhood. To the point her mother's friends asked for the recipe so they could replicate it in their own kitchens. The secret? *She bought it from a family restaurant in the next town over.* Miwa would get a small stack of presents while Christmas cartoons played on the living room TV. Her father often had to work, and usually there was school… but from the evening on, the Bans were a whole family, and Miwa often felt like it was her birthday.

She wondered if her mother still bought that fried chicken for her newer, better children.

"I used to make my own Christmas cake," Sayuri said. "My son actually liked it. So did Emiko. Never cared much for it myself."

"What? Eating it? Or being compared to it?"

Sayuri snorted. "Both, honestly."

They were silent while eating their (not Christmas) cake and sipping their hot coffees. A light drizzle blanketed the sidewalk outside. Umbrellas bumped against the building, and since the café didn't have an umbrella stand or offer plastic wrap for those coming in, the café floor was covered in stagnant raindrops. Coats constantly went on and off. Stacks of wet bags piled up on empty chairs. The air was rich with the aromas of hot coffee and teas, but nothing was stronger than the perfume of the woman sitting at the table next to them. She *bathed* in it.

"Are you sure everything's okay?" Miwa asked her girlfriend.

She slowly nodded. "Could be better, but I think I will be okay."

That brought a modicum of relief to Miwa. "You wanna get out of here?"

It was still a bit early to check into a love hotel, or at least if they wanted to spend the night. *She can't, though. She has work in the morning.* Better to go now and make love for the rest of the rainy afternoon. They could grab dinner afterward. Maybe a couple of drinks. Take their time going home to their lonely apartments. Miwa had a new video game to play, but she would rather spend time with her girlfriend any day of the week.

Sayuri took her time nodding. When she finally did, it was with her bag in one hand and the tray in the other. She hadn't drunk most of her coffee. Maybe it was too acidic for her sensitive stomach.

They went to one of their old stand-bys a few minutes away. Once they were in the elevator, Miwa wrapped her arm around her girlfriend's midsection and said, "I can't wait to get out of these wet clothes. How about you?"

Nothing about Sayuri's demeanor was excited to be heading into a private hotel room for the sole purpose of spending some much-needed private time together. *Is she on her period?* Miwa didn't have that thought until they were in the room, removing their jackets and putting their bags on the floor. Shoes were left by the door. Sayuri went straight to the bed and sat down. She didn't turn on the TV or offer to make tea like she sometimes did.

Maybe she hadn't heard Miwa's question.

"Hey..." she sat next to Sayuri, one hand searching for hers. "I know I keep asking, but do you feel okay? I'm starting to worry. You're not acting like yourself." Was it true that she was bothered by something happening at school? Oh, no. Maybe she was in trouble for something she said or did in front of her class. Miwa didn't read the papers often, but that sounded like the #1 reason teachers got into trouble with their schools. Yet wasn't Sayuri one of the model teachers? *I would've died if she were my teacher when I was a kid.* Then again, maybe Miwa would have figured out her sexuality a lot sooner.

Sayuri sat up, yet continued to stare straight ahead. "I'm fine. Really. It's simply been a long week and I'm a little tired."

"Oh." Did that mean she didn't want to do anything too… strenuous? Maybe they should've saved money and gone back to Miwa's place to play video games. Love hotels gave them more wiggle room, but the main appeal was making love without regard for the neighbors. "If you'd rather not do anything, say so."

Sayuri wasn't a woman of many words that day, however. She was more inclined to pull Miwa down onto the bed with her and communicate with nothing but kisses and the soft moans she made when she was deeply involved with what they did.

So happened Miwa spoke a similar language.

Nothing surprised Miwa as they began to make love. Not how long it took for the clothes to come off, nor the way Sayuri covered her girlfriend with light touches and heavy kisses – and sometimes the other way around. *It's like she's committing me to memory.* Miwa didn't have a problem with it. She loved to be adored as much as she loved to adore the woman she was with. She didn't really care why they paid such careful attention to one another. Honestly, to Miwa's love-stricken brain, it was a simple side-effect of being enamored with a woman. Wasn't it easy to kiss Sayuri all over? To call her beautiful things? To give her the pleasure she deserved? Wasn't she one of the most deserving women in the world? *If I could give her this world, I would.* One of those Christmas movies she always watched as a child was from Old Hollywood. Something about lassoing the moon for the prettiest girl in town. *I would do that and more.* If she could. Miwa was but a humble woman, with few skills, talents, or dreams. Everything was simple, from her career aspirations to the kind of family she wanted. *A house, a wife, maybe a kid or two.* She didn't need a lot of money. She didn't need a lot of space. All she needed was a companion who made her breathe as if she had completely forgotten how.

Sayuri was on top for most of that blissful afternoon. Not uncommon for Miwa to lie on her back and look up into the glistening eyes of the woman she loved. For so long, however? Sayuri was like a love sprite, relentless, untiring, needy… they may not have exchanged many words that day, but maybe it wasn't necessary. Words were overrated. Miwa came from a career that was all whistles and hand gestures. There were other ways to communicate.

I could blow her *whistle!* If Sayuri would fall onto her back for a few minutes…

Not happening.

Miwa hoped for at least an hour's worth of cuddling, but she wasn't terribly surprised when Sayuri hopped out of bed and searched for her clothing so soon after they finished. She probably wasn't feeling well after all.

"You want to go somewhere else?" Miwa propped herself up in bed. "Or are you heading home?"

Sayuri tucked her hair behind her ear. "I should head home. Before it starts raining harder."

As All Our Fires Burn

They were past typhoon season, and Miwa knew better than most how much it took for overland trains to give up the ghost during a rainy day. *Way more than to make her legitimately concerned.* "*Nee*, Satin-*chan*," she said in the softest voice she possessed. "What's really going on?" A woman didn't make love like that and bail as quickly as possible. Not so far into a relationship. "You're not acting like yourself."

Sayuri stared into the depths of her skirt before sniffing something up her nose. *Is she crying?* Miwa dropped her strong façade and extended a hand to her girlfriend. Sayuri took it and allowed herself to be drawn into her girlfriend's naked embrace.

"Someone outed me to the school board," Sayuri said. "I've been suspended so they can 'investigate' the claims and decide what to do."

Miwa almost dropped her girlfriend's hand. "*Nani?*"

Sayuri continued to nod. Her inability to make eye contact did not inspire Miwa to believe that everything would be fine. "I think it was my neighbor. She's the parent of one of my students, although I didn't think she had a problem with me…" Sayuri sniffed again. "I managed to not come out to them. Although they *really* drilled me. I think… I think they're going to fire me in a few weeks."

Miwa squeezed Sayuri's hand. "You can't be serious!" Who was this neighbor? Was it the lady who talked to Miwa and made her feel more than a little uncomfortable? *She seemed the type!* Miwa had no evidence, of course. At any rate, she was too fearful for her girlfriend's future as a teacher to properly think of who might have ratted her out to the local school board.

"I'm so sorry. Is there anything I can do?" No wonder Sayuri had been acting so strange and distant all week! It was amazing she could be *this* put together!

Yet when Miwa asked her again if there was anything she could do to help the situation, Sayuri merely shook her head with a sigh. "I think I need to lie low for a while. Don't give them any reasons to be suspicious. My ability to contain myself is under scrutiny right now and, well..." She gave Miwa a sympathetic look. "I don't think this is helping."

Miwa jerked upright. "You think there are cameras in here, or something? Who the hell is going to know what we're doing in private?"

"I didn't think people could know with how careful we already were. Guess we weren't careful enough."

"Only way we could be more careful is if we don't do anything at all, even in private!"

Sayuri looked away.

"Come on. You can't be seriously thinking that."

"You don't know what I could be seriously thinking." Sayuri shrugged Miwa off and hurried to put on her bra. "You have no idea what I'm dealing with right now."

"To hell I don't. You think I've never worried about my boss finding out I'm some stupid queer?" Miwa reached for Sayuri, but she was too far away. Made even more obvious when Sayuri stepped two large paces away from the bed so she could shimmy into her skirt. "Please. Please don't do this."

Although Sayuri had said nothing to the effect, her demeanor blared everything Miwa needed to hear. *She's breaking up with me. Now! After we just did it!* Had that been her plan all along? Or was she originally going to do it at the café, but couldn't help her gayness one last time? *That's why it seemed like she was committing everything we did this afternoon to memory.* Because it was the last time. Perhaps the last time for a long while for Sayuri, who was going so far back into the closet that she would never have the pleasure of finding someone to love.

"I don't have a choice," Sayuri said, disgust bubbling in he throat. "Besides, I don't want to risk them outing you to *your* company. They know who you are."

Miwa's own face was paler than the sheets beneath her.

"It's not that I don't care about you, Miwa." Sayuri still wouldn't look at her. "Or that I'm ashamed of what we've done. I simply can't risk it anymore. I can't lose my job. *I can't.* It's the only thing I have left!"

Miwa had almost followed her until then. "Aren't I something you have left?"

Sayuri picked up her things with a huff and raced toward the door. Miwa attempted to follow, but she was still naked, and even the hallways of a love hotel frowned on guests running around in the nude.

The door closed. Miwa sank back into the bed, shocked that everything happened so suddenly. *She's gone...* Maybe Sayuri could still be reasoned with. It would be a while, though, wouldn't it? Not until the investigation was over. Not until she could think clearly again. Not until she prioritized what was most important in her life.

God knew how long that would be.

Chapter 31

SAYURI

Sayuri knew she had done the right thing. It might have hurt like hell to lose the one person she had come to love over the past year, but she couldn't risk it.

What, exactly? *Oh, so many things.* She couldn't risk her job, of course. Teaching was her passion, the one thing she was actually *good* at, and she would be damned if she was fired because Miwa hung around a little too closely for the administration's tastes. Yet that made Sayuri sound like a selfish git who didn't give a single shit about how it affected Miwa. *That couldn't be further from the truth.* The other thing she couldn't risk? Miwa losing her job in the aftermath of Sayuri's firing. Who knew how far it would go? Perhaps the odds weren't great that someone would quietly inform the powers that be in

As All Our Fires Burn

Miwa's company that she was poor for their image. All it took was one spiteful person to ruin someone else's life. The sooner Sayuri and Miwa cut ties, the more likely they were to both keep their jobs.

I did it to protect us. So why did Sayuri spend most of her days curled up on her couch, staring at the TV and wishing the investigation would be over with already?

Because she was heartbroken.

The look on Miwa's face when Sayuri left the love hotel would be burned into her memory for the rest of her life. Love. Betrayal. The dawning realization that everything they had was over as quickly as it had begun. Sayuri had run out of there while Miwa was still naked in bed. They weren't supposed to make love that day. The plan had been to breakup with her at the coffee shop.

Yet I was weak. Sayuri couldn't look away from those lips, which Miwa kept meticulously moist in the driest months of the year. She was ready to kiss. All day, if they could spare the time. Her eyes had been full of love for Sayuri, something that hadn't been witnessed since the day she told Emiko that she was finally pregnant.

What had Sayuri done? Stomped on that love. While she hadn't anticipated Miwa falling in love with her so quickly… well, if it could go the other way, why not toward Sayuri as well? *I thought I was simply foolish for being in love with her already. Because I'm always so desperate for a family.* Sayuri turned onto her back, staring up into the void that was her darkened living room. A blanket draped across her, but she was still cold. She had always wanted a place decent enough for a family-sized *kotatsu*. That was one of the long-term goals she and Emiko held as their son grew up. Goals that fizzled away when Sayuri took a wrong turn in Tokyo.

Her phone blinked on the nearby table. It was probably a push notification from the local newspaper or the neighborhood association, but she was too afraid that it was Miwa – or her own mother – to answer. What if it was from the school board? The union? Sayuri was too depressed to check her phone. She preferred to roll over on her couch and stare at the back of her eyelids.

She slowly slipped into sleep.

While she knew little about the meanings of dreams or how they came to be, she was not surprised to soon find herself standing in a hospital, watching the emergency responders and nurses fly up and down the hallways with people who had survived a train crash somewhere on the other side of the city.

Dreams had a funny way of imparting information as if it was fact. Melting faces, broken limbs, and collapsed lungs rushed by her while people screamed that fifty more were coming. A TV hanging on the hallway wall was turned to a news report that showed a helicopter hovering over the wreckage of two overland trains that had collided on the same track. Fires erupted, both on the trains and in the nearby buildings that hugged dangerously close to the tracks. Anything that could've been described as "the worst possible outcome" was featured in the news ticker. Children on outings with their parents and their schools. Old men and women on their way to a festival to celebrate the elderly. The first time that particular line had allowed the local seeing-eye dog school to bring their trainees onboard to practice maneuvering in public. Everyone was dead, of course, although the dedicated search and rescue squads continued to call for survivors. In the strangest twist Sayuri had ever seen in a news report, the local newsroom didn't bother to cut away whenever a dead body was transported in front of the cameras. It was like they wanted her to witness the carnage.

A few seconds later, she realized that a car had been caught up in the wreckage.

That's my car... And that was her in the driver's seat, mangled and unidentifiable. The only reason Sayuri knew it was her was because she recognized the car... and because a ghost always knew to which body it belonged.

"Mama?"

A sharp jolt traveled down her spine. Sayuri slowly turned around to find her little boy sitting on an abandoned gurney, his hands outstretched to her. The first thing she did was run to him and attempt to hold his little body close to hers. Yet she went right through him. Ghosts weren't allowed to touch the living.

It was the exact opposite of what happened in real life. While no trains had been involved in Sayuri's accident, she had walked away relatively unscathed while her son fought for his life for the rest of the night. A battle he was doomed to lose.

Was this the universe righting its wrongs? Had it come to claim Sayuri so her son could live?

"Mama!"

Tears welled in her eyes. Tears of happiness and relief that he was still alive. Tears of unbearable sadness that she could no longer touch him.

"We've got more coming through!" a nurse called down the hallway. She was right next to Sayuri, ignoring the hardly-injured little boy on his gurney and completely oblivious to the ghost in her way. "Somebody find us some more stretchers! We need more blood!"

They were the sound bites Sayuri often heard in TV shows and written into the books she sometimes brought home from the library. *"Give me 50 CCs of this and that!" "Damnit, nurse, what do I look like, a miracle worker?" "I did everything I could to save him!" "Why, God, why?"* Sayuri was momentarily distracted from her crying son to behold everything going on around her. More victims of the train crash rolled through on stretchers and in wheelchairs. Some of them bled from untended wounds. Others moaned that they could see the ghosts in the hall. Others were completely passed out, yet sitting upright in wheelchairs. As more came down the hall, the victims transformed from normal people with grievous wounds to zombies moaning about the Apocalypse. Sayuri was still relatively unperturbed.

Until she saw the last woman rolled in on a stretcher.

"Miwa?" What had she been doing on a train? It wasn't even her company! All the way out in Saitama? Why?

"Sayuri?" One eye slowly opened. "What are you doing here? Are you dead?"

As All Our Fires Burn

"What are *you* doing here? Why were you on that train?"

"I was coming to see you."

"But why?"

"Because it was a nice day to come say hello."

Sayuri awakened with a jerk. The light in the kitchen was still on, but night had unceremoniously fallen outside. Groaning, she sat up and rubbed the sleep out of her eyes with one arm slung over the back of her couch. The blanket fell away. While it was colder in her apartment now, the heat from the blanket had trapped her in a sheen of warmth that now made her yearn for the chill outside.

Wasn't it trash day?

Sayuri attempted to forget her dream as she dragged herself to the kitchen and gathered the bag of burnable trash. She was still yawning when she popped out of her building and headed toward the corner of her narrow street, where every household in the neighborhood gathered to put their garbage bags beneath tight nets for the collectors to grab at dawn.

She wasn't the only one out there.

Sayuri never guessed she would bump into Mariko around midnight. She was such a perfect asshole that she did the "correct" thing and take her trash out no sooner than two hours before the scheduled pickup. *Fuck that. A woman needs to sleep.* In what imaginary world did housewives wake up at five in the morning, get dressed, eat breakfast, and still have time to drag the garbage across the street so they could wave at the municipal workers driving down the narrow lane? Not in Sayuri's world, dreamlike or otherwise.

Maybe somebody wasn't so perfect, after all!

"Ah! Kawashima-*sensei*..." Mariko laughed, nerves plaguing her body, as she turned around and unexpectedly met Sayuri's gaze. While Mariko had deposited her family's garbage, Sayuri still held hers between her fingers. "I didn't expect to see you there. Is everything okay? Nobody's seen you for a few days. Shota-*kun* says they've had a substitute for most of the week..."

How amazingly bold of her! It was a damn good thing that Mariko couldn't see her neighbor's furrowing brows or the fangs coming out over her bottom lip. *You. I know you were the one who turned me in to the school board.* There could not have been anyone else. What right did this woman have to act like they were the best of friends after what she had done?

"I've been taking an indefinite leave from work," Sayuri said. "There's a lot going on in my life. I want to make sure I'm in top physical and mental condition to serve the children to the best of my ability." Her robotic tone did nothing to inspire confidence, both in herself and the woman before her. Mariko cocked her head as if she had no idea what to make of Sayuri's assertion.

"I do hope that you're feeling better, then, Kawashima-*sensei*. If there's anything I can do, please do not hesitate to let me know. I plan on doing a lot of cooking this week, and could bring you over..."

"I think you've helped me enough."

Sayuri had thought it, but never intended to actually say it. Yet there it was, sent into the universe for Mariko to hear and take personally. A little yelp of disbelief echoed in the cold street. Sayuri's heart beat a kilometer a minute. She didn't care if she embarrassed herself in front of her accuser. Of course, there was a tiny part of her that considered she might be wrong about Mariko. Maybe someone else had figured it out. Another neighbor. Another parent.

Then again, what did it matter? Sayuri was on the brink of losing everything, anyway.

"I don't know what you mean," Mariko began.

Sayuri didn't have time for her games. "You know exactly what I mean, Shimazaki-*san*. I know you're the one who reported me to the school board. There's no one else it could possibly be, so cut the shit."

Before, Sayuri would faint that the thought of speaking to a *neighbor* this way, let alone the parent of one of her students. Beyond that, Mariko had pull. She was a member of numerous organizations, including the PTA and the local neighborhood ethics board. Yeah. She had serious reasons to dig into Sayuri's personal life if she thought she smelled something unclean. A perfect housewife like her, who blew up her own ego with lofty roles in various organizations? This would be another winning trophy on her mantle. She could proudly tell her housewife friends, "*I got rid of that dyke at the school for you. Next stop? Ridding our neighborhood of her perverted heart.*"

Mariko's big eyes were the only things Sayuri could see in the darkness. Damnit. Maybe she *had* made a mistake.

"Why, Kawashima-*sensei*." Did she have to sound like a berated student? Because Sayuri encountered her share of those every damn day. "I was hoping that you might use your leave of absence to get some help. I know that losing your son was hard on you, and I *do* empathize with how horrible you must feel because of it, but turning to such unnatural things isn't the answer. Besides, it's terrible to expose the children to your…"

"You. *Bitch*."

"Kawashima-*sensei!*"

"How… how dare… how could…" Sayuri was ready to spit fire. Yet when she tried to heave the first of the hot flames rising through her esophagus, she was met with nothing but obstructions. Her conscious still bade her to tone down the aggressive tendencies and act like a mature adult.

Too bad being a mature adult might have gotten her into this mess to begin with!

Sayuri backed away. There was no use arguing with a woman who was so biased she might as well be tacking up fliers about the horrors of homosexuality around her neighborhood. *Even more convinced now that I did the right thing in dumping Miwa.* Miwa had to be kept as far away as possible from Mariko. God only knew what she might do if she really wanted to teach a schoolteacher a lesson.

"I've been doing some research!" Mariko called after her. "There are places you can go! Really nice ones out in the countryside! Get some sun and fresh air! I don't normally condone psychiatry, but they can help you get back on track!"

Sayuri shut her out by the time she reached her building.

"They can help you get that family you always wanted! A *real* family, with a husband who can…"

As All Our Fires Burn

The fiery smoke fuming from Sayuri's nostrils was enough to silence the nosy neighbor. Sayuri sent her one last look of pure contempt and fled up to her apartment. The insults that one woman had hurled at her were enough to send tears down Sayuri's cheeks again the moment she stepped into her dark apartment. It wasn't until she was back on her couch, dabbing her eyes with a tissue, that she realized she still had her garbage in her other hand. She should have thrown it at Mariko, instead.

Chapter 32

MIWA

That autumn was particularly dull in color and energy.

The rains came, off an on through the weeks of earlier sunsets and chillier temperatures. The humidity refused to leave Tokyo's grip, yet Miwa was applying lip balm to her dried-out mouth every time she could sneak it on the train platform. The only reason she bothered was because cracked lips would get her yelled at by her superiors. She was down in the dumps enough to avoid that.

People switched from their colorful warm-weather clothes to their bleak black coats and clear umbrellas that created a sea of unperceived mediocrity. From the moment she stepped out of her apartment, bundled in a warm hat and heavy coat from the most recent UNIQLO sale (although she passed up on the

As All Our Fires Burn

nicest cashmere-lined ones... not even her paycheck could take that hit) she was a cog in the depressing system. She looked like everyone else. She was as robotically polite as everyone else. She even bought the same food at the convenience stores as everyone else — to the point she often got there too late at the end of her shift and faced an empty wall in the frozen section.

Somehow, she didn't care.

Miwa had never faced concepts like depression before she met her ex-girlfriend. *Are we all depressed?* She thought that while staring at the faces of passengers trying to make their way home. For the first time since high school, she realized that many of her peers often had the most downturn gazes and body language that implied they would rather be anywhere than where they were right now. It wasn't mere *I'm tired of work and want to go on vacation,* but the deep-in-the-bones kind of fatigue that led to other rail companies investing in platform barriers.

Do we all hate our lives?

She was projecting. She must be. People like Overseer Endo seemed perfectly content with his life. He was always laughing, talking about his family as if they were part of some grand circus act, and smiling at the passengers that came up to his booth with their inane questions. The station master — whom Miwa rarely saw outside of meetings, thanks to her late shift — often praised the employees for their hard work and diligence. Although that extended to Miwa as well, she found it difficult to take the compliment as an excuse to keep working hard. She barely had the energy to keep an eye on the platform and blow her whistle.

She missed Sayuri.

There was no one to talk to. No one to tell her woes. She tried going to a gay bar one Saturday night, not to find a hookup, but to take up the atmosphere of women who loved other women and were willing to talk about it. Although a few people, including the friendly bartenders, approached her conversation, Miwa discovered that her words were not forthcoming and she couldn't say anything beyond, "My girlfriend dumped me." That earned her a few pats on the back and words of empathy, but who wanted to talk to a woman carrying around that kind of bad energy? Not like she wanted to talk to them either, after she got her alcohol and numbed some of the pain.

Would it have been worse if Sayuri dumped her earlier on in their relationship? Yes. No. Regardless of how many times Miwa mulled it over, she couldn't decide if having Sayuri as her honest-to-God girlfriend for a few weeks hurt more than never knowing her love at all. Perhaps ignorance was bliss. Perhaps it wasn't. Did it matter? What happened was what happened. So why couldn't she move on, already?

I know, I know... it hasn't been that long. Of course it hurt to be dumped by the woman she was falling in love with so quickly, but that wasn't the whole source of her pain and depression, was it?

She finally had someone she cared about in her life again. For the first time in so long, Miwa had a real friend. A confidant. Someone who was excited to see her every time they met.

As All Our Fires Burn

She hadn't realized how lonely she had been until Sayuri broke up with her. Miwa had always been content with her loner lifestyle. She occasionally met up with school friends, and she went out with her coworkers whenever they invited her, so she wasn't *totally* starved for socialization… but could she say that any of those people were her close friends? That they knew things about her that she never told anyone else? Miwa had spent so many years going to work, going home, and playing video games or building model train sets that she forgot what it was like to have a real social life. Romance and sex didn't have to play into it, but it did, this time.

The hole Sayuri left behind was what really gnawed at Miwa's consciousness. She often walked to the edge of the platform between trains, looking down into the metal tracks and glancing back and forth into the gaping maws of darkness. Working in a subway station protected her from the harsher elements outside. Snow and biting cold. Blazing hot sunshine and humidity that choked a woman. Yet it didn't expose her to a lot of sunlight. Even when working the night shift, Miwa missed out on most of the day's sunshine. How could she avoid that? She slept through most mornings! She already had the schedule of someone too depressed to function. The fact she made it to work on time every day was becoming more of a miracle.

I get it now. She thought that while staring into the metallic world of the dimly lit train tracks. Her boots touched the edge of the platform. A light flickered above her – someone should really file a maintenance request. Kohei answered an old man's questions on the other side of the platform. Her earpiece was silent. Occasionally, heavy footsteps came down the stairs as passengers awaited the next train going in either direction. The only person to talk to Miwa for five minutes wanted to know where the elevator was. She was so lost in her own head that she originally pointed the young lady in the wrong direction. *I get why she wanted to jump.*

Miwa didn't have her own suicide ideation. She had never sunk so far into that kind of toxic headspace that she considered ending her own life, let alone fantasizing about it while she sat in a café and pretended to be enamored with a light novel. But she understood. For the first time in her life, she got what drove some people to such extremes that ending their lives on the front end of a moving train sounded like the best way to go about their day.

It wasn't something Miwa liked contemplating. Not when part of her job was keeping people out of the tracks. Not when she was often writing out and stamping official documentation for people late to work because the train lines stopped due to jumpers. Not when she was dating a woman she met because someone was so far gone in her own grief and misery that she didn't care if she died.

Jumping in front of a train was clean and quick. Almost nobody survived it. That's why so many intent on ending their lives did it. It was why so many rail companies were investing in barriers and gates along the platform. While they advertised the costs as "accident prevention," the truth was, the odds were higher that someone ended up in the tracks on purpose as opposed to accident. Murders were sometimes committed, yes... but in the end, the companies were protecting themselves from legal liabilities and "inconveniencing" their passengers every time a train was held up due to someone's death. It happened all the time when Miwa was a kid. It happened all the time now.

If I really wanted a fast death... Miwa took a step back from the edge. It didn't alleviate her anxiety or depressed state. It did, however, keep her from jumping out of her uniform when the automatic message came through her earpiece, alerting her that the next train was thirty seconds away. She placed her whistle in her mouth and stood in the marked spot that would put her as safely close to the train as possible. Passengers automatically filed into lines one second before the voice on the speakers announced the upcoming train – and kindly asked everyone to stay behind the yellow line for their own safety.

As her shift progressed, she was able to set aside the ill feelings inside of her and get her job done. It helped that it was a busy night for her small station. It was the time of year when more people headed inside to get out of the cold, rainy weather, so they were more likely to take the train than walk. At one point, Miwa witnessed a sight she had never beheld before: five minutes before midnight, and both sides of the platform were stuffed with people. There wasn't a festival in the area. No concerts. No event at Amaya-jinja. Just a ton of people heading home when the restaurants started closing for the night.

They were all dressed in their uniform black coats and carrying their clear, convenience store umbrellas. Miwa snapped out of her stupor when she heard the train coming. Her whistle warned everyone to stay back. Only one person kept the tip of their umbrella over the yellow line. The train blew by, coming to a gradual stop a few feet away from Miwa. She politely waved to the driver, who nodded before marking something down on a tablet.

Thirty seconds later, she blew her whistle again and signaled for the engineer to leave the station.

"Ban-*san*," Kohei said when he approached her after the last train of the night left the station. In some curious miracle, not a single passenger was mysteriously left behind, as often happened when there were more people than usual during the night shift. "Is everything okay?" He gestured his gloved hand toward her sour demeanor. "You haven't been looking well lately."

The warning that he might have a crush on her continued to blare in the back of her head. Not that Kohei had ever said or done anything unsavory toward her, before or after that revelation was bestowed to Miwa's addled brain.

"I'm sorry if I'm making it difficult for everyone else to work." Miwa didn't think twice about taking responsibility for how she looked. If Kohei noticed something, then doubtlessly the passengers were not impressed with her countenance. *I'm probably going to get a talking to from management.* Miwa was under more pressure than most to always maintain a pleasant demeanor, both on the job and off. Nobody cared if Kohei looked like a stoic, serious man in his company uniform. Miwa wasn't afforded those same privileges.

As All Our Fires Burn

Then again... maybe the reason he noticed had more to do with his feelings toward her than how she actually looked.

"That's not what's bothering me," Kohei said. He motioned for them to amble up the stairs and finish their shifts in the staff room. "I'm more concerned about you being in a bad mood. Is everything okay?"

She looked askance at him, one hand on the railing as they slowly made their way up the large flight of stairs. "I'm sorry. It's personal stuff. I shouldn't be letting it affect our work."

"I know that's what we're told... but..." Kohei adjusted the hat on his head. "We're coworkers. You think we've drunk together enough times for you to feel comfortable telling me what's up?"

She chuckled. *You really drink a lot of Kool-Aid, huh, Tanaka?* "I'm sorry." She wouldn't stop apologizing. "I was seeing someone for a few weeks. They recently broke it off. I guess I took it more personally than necessary."

"Oh." He looked away as they reached the top of the steps. "*Oh.*"

"Yeah. Like that."

"Damn. I'd be a mess, too. Actually, you're taking it better than I would."

She somewhat didn't doubt that. "I'll be fine. Takes some time to move on, you know?" Miwa truly hoped that was the case. The thought of feeling like this for weeks, months, *years* made her want to throw herself down the stairs.

"Yeah. Still sorry to hear about that. If you need anyone to talk to... well, I'm a master at dealing with rejection. You might say it's a hobby of mine." Kohei's nervous chuckle only made Miwa feel a little better as they slowly approached the staff room. Overseer Endo was still talking to a few passengers on the far side of the ticket gate. The way he moved his arms implied he was giving some really lost people directions to where they needed to go. "You wanna go grab a drink from that bar on the corner? My treat. To help you feel better about getting dumped."

Miwa removed her gloves before entering the staff room. "It's kind of you to offer, Tanaka-*san,* but I'm not sure that's a great idea. We've got work tomorrow."

"One drink. We can be out of there in an hour, and you can ride your bike home. Hey, maybe the beer will warm your blood for that cold ride, huh?" He laughed again. "You don't get tipsy easily, do you? Because that might prevent you from riding the bike."

"I *did* have to walk my bike home the last time we all went out drinking."

"You drank like four beers that night. Maybe more?"

"How would you know? You were drunker than me!"

Endo sent them a look before starting his end-of-shift paperwork. The lost passengers were gone, and some of the lights in the station were shut off. The only brightly lit areas were the exits and the far back corner of the staff room, where Kohei and Miwa rummaged through their lockers for their street clothes. On a busy night, they would rock-paper-scissors to see who got to use the employee bathroom to change first. Miwa had a feeling Kohei would let her go in without any issue.

As All Our Fires Burn

"All right. One drink, if you're buying." She grabbed her bag first and bypassed her coworker on her way to the bathroom. *I might regret this. What if he thinks this is a date?* Miwa *had* told him that she was recently dumped. Did he think she was looking for a rebound? The man didn't know she was gay. He might think this was his big chance to score a date – or more – with Miwa. *Why did Endo have to put that in my head?* "Let me change first."

She had to wait for Kohei to change after her, which meant she loitered in the staff room long past she normally would – in her street clothes, anyway. If there was paperwork or something onerous to report, she would do so in her company uniform. For Endo to walk in and see her yawning at the four-person table in the middle of the staff room meant she waited for something.

"Need help, Ban-*san?*" Unlike the staff who walked or rode their bikes home, Endo had the privilege of driving his car to his house a few blocks away. He only removed his hat, gloves and jacket before throwing a jacket over the shirts his wife ironed for him. His stiff pants were always the sight sprouting from his heavy jacket. "I'm getting ready to lock up."

"I'm waiting for Tanaka-*san* in the restroom. We're going to get a drink at the bar down the street."

Endo cocked his head with a soft chuckle. "Thought you were seeing someone, Ban-*san?*"

How could she politely say "none of your business" to her boss? *I can't. Not possible.* All she could do was skirt the question. "It's a friendly thing. You know, we work on the platform together all night and it's important to build up that camaraderie."

She regretted saying it the moment it came out of her mouth. Endo immediately took the bait. "Yes, 'camaraderie' is very important in this job. I know how important your career is to you, Ban-*san*." He pulled his hood up over his head. "It's important to make the proper connections."

"It certainly is, sir."

Kohei stepped out of the restroom with a nod to the supervisor. Endo gave him a knowing look as he escorted the pair out of the station so he could lock up the office and ensure that nobody was in the bathrooms or hanging out in the stairwells. Every once in a while, they got a poor passenger who was either too drunk to find the exit or an elderly woman who ended up stuck in the bathroom for twenty minutes. Everyone went home late on those nights.

"Don't drink too much," he warned them as they stepped out into the chilly late November night. "You've got another shift tomorrow."

"I told Tanaka-*san* we're only having one." Miwa turned to her coworker. "*And* he's buying."

"Whoa! If I had known that, I would've invited myself along!" Endo waved at them before getting into his car at the far end of the small lot by the station. Miwa bypassed her bike, safely locked up behind a dumpster. Not that bike thefts were big in that corner of the city. As long as she grabbed it before the trash collectors came by and felt generous in their job descriptions... "Have fun, you two. *Otsukaresama desu.*"

As All Our Fires Burn

They said their farewells before Kohei and Miwa headed down the street. The light from the local dive bar shimmered above the alley in which it humbly stood, and luckily for them, that late at night the place was only half full with locals. The power of the uniform meant that even the usual passengers at Amaya-jinja-guchi Station didn't recognize the street-clothes-wearing employees sitting at a small table in the corner of the room. Western music played over the speakers. The Who and The Ramones. Maybe. Miwa wasn't great at old American music. *Or are they British? I honestly don't know.* It hurt her head to think about. Maybe she needed a stronger beer than she normally got.

"What are you having?" Kohei had yet to sit down. He searched his pockets for his wallet before facing the bar. "I usually get an Asahi Super Dry."

"Sapporo, please."

"Two beers coming right up!" He scurried to the bar. Miwa pulled out her phone, anticipating a message from someone. It wasn't until she saw her blank screen that she realized Sayuri didn't message her anymore.

Something fell into the pit of her stomach.

Kohei hurried back with the beers. His was in a bottle, but Miwa's came straight from the tap. She didn't know how fancy he might have gone for her. He was paying, after all. What if it turned out her beer was so much more expensive than his? He might think that this was a date, or that she still owed him something... *God, why do gender politics have to be a thing? I simply wanna have a drink with my coworker.* She didn't have these thoughts around Kohei until Endo let slip the man might have a crush on her.

"Thanks." The one thing she *really* thanked him for, however, was getting single-servings instead of a pitcher of beer. *Speaking of gender politics...* It was one thing when she was expected to pour the beers at a group outing. There were supervisors there. Traditional ones, who looked at the youngest employee being a woman and felt comfortable in who he told to serve, because he was always in the right. Kohei was only a little older than Miwa, however. Yet maybe if he expected her to pour, she would know this was more business than pleasure. Damnit. She couldn't win! "It's kind of you to treat me."

"You've been a bit down for a while, and when you told me it's because you had a breakup... sorry. I shouldn't refer to it."

"It's fine." Miwa might regret saying that. "These things happen. I shouldn't let it affect my work." She took a sip of her beer. It was a bit maltier than usual. *Damnit. He sprung for a costlier one.*

"I know a lot about breakups..." Kohei had yet to touch his beer. Instead, he removed his jacket and draped it across the top of his high-backed stool. "Been in a few of them myself. I guess that's what it means to be younger."

"We're not *that* young." Wasn't he about to turn thirty?

"Yeah, but most of the guys in my family didn't settle down and marry until their late thirties. Sometimes I thought I might want to be different, you know? My mom and dad always said I was the romantic of the family. I'm the youngest of four boys, by the way."

Miwa's eyes widened. She knew Kohei had brothers, but not that he was the youngest. Or that there were *four* boys altogether. "That means you were either beat up all the time, or you were babied to high-heaven."

"Depends on who you ask. My dad thinks I was babied. My mom thinks I was bullied."

"What do you think?"

Kohei shrugged. "I turned out fine either way."

What a non-answer. "I've got brothers, too. Little ones. Way younger than me."

"I remember you saying something about that."

"I don't really know them. The youngest one is still in elementary school. By the time they were old enough to have personalities, I was gone."

"I don't really know my oldest brother. He ran off to Osaka to become a musician, and sometimes I read his online blog."

"Did he make it big?"

"Big?" Kohei chuckled. "No. I don't know. Depends on your definition of hitting it big. Is he a household name in Japan? No way. But I hear he gets steady work with his bands around Kansai. He also does session work for the labels down there. Works at some live houses. Has a wife and a kid… that's all I really know."

They were silent. Kohei drank his beer while Miwa stared at the logos adorning the walls. Domestic beers. Foreign beers. They were arranged by main ingredient, with the rice-based beers on one side and the barley beers on the other. Sometimes she forgot what went into alcohol. Just like most people forgot what went into running a train station. *Fewer people know what goes into being a teacher.* There she went, thinking about Sayuri again.

"You seeing anyone right now?" It was an innocent, friendly question that two male employees would ask each other at any outing like this, but Miwa knew she played with fire. Kohei may have been a sweet guy, but it was possible he'd take things the wrong way, and she didn't want to hurt his feelings – or hurt their coworking relationship. "

"No," he said. "I casually date here and there. Blind dates, group dates… stuff like that. They don't usually go anywhere. Used to get really excited about them, you know?" He snorted. "Then I realized that they don't really work. At the rate I'm going, I'll need to find a matchmaker."

"I'm sure it's not that dire."

"Eh, ask my mother. She likes to think of me as her baby, but it drives her bonkers that I don't have a steady girlfriend. She keeps telling me, 'Kohei-*kun,* what you need is a cute little lady with a round face and curls! One who knows how to cook, because you're hopeless in the kitchen.'"

"Did she ever teach you how to cook?"

"Of course not. She was too busy stuffing my face." He gestured to his perfectly average physique. "Can't you tell?"

Miwa had no idea how to respond.

"Anyway… you don't want to hear that. What do you think about the position that's opening at the next station over? You gonna go for it?"

Miwa perked up. "Position?"

"Day shift junior overseer. Busier station, too. I'm sure a ton of people are applying, but I figure it can't hurt to go for it, too. I like our station... and our coworkers," he made sure to get in, "but we're not going to advance through the company very quickly there."

"At least we'll get priority consideration."

"True, but how long do we want to wait for Endo to retire or Shinnosuke to get transferred elsewhere? I might actually be married by then."

Miwa kept her arms folded on the table. "Honestly, I don't expect a lot of advancement in the company."

"Why not? You're a great employee. Because you're a woman?"

Miwa shrugged.

"I won't pretend to know a lot about that. I don't see why you shouldn't advance, though."

"Maybe everyone else is seeing how depressed I am lately."

"*Ano*, if I may ask..." Kohei cleared his throat. "What happened? You must've really liked that person if you're so down about it still."

"Yeah. It was getting pretty serious."

"What happened?"

"Our relationship was compromising their job."

"Ouch." Genuine sympathy crowned his visage. "Really sucks to hear that."

"Thanks." Miwa didn't want to dwell on it. As much as she had loved Sayuri, it was a huge message from the universe that she needed to move on. *It will be hard, but it's what I must do.* If only she had more going for her than work and video games. Perhaps the real reason she came out with Kohei was because she was starved for someone to talk to.

"You know..." He rubbed the back of his neck and completely avoided eye contact. *Oh, no.* "Sometimes it's easiest to find someone to date close to where you live and work. This person wasn't in the company, right?"

Miwa narrowed her eyes.

"Right. Ahem." He downed more of his beer. Probably not for the courage, but Miwa could never be too sure. She sure as hell wasn't drinking much now. "If you're interested, maybe we could..."

No. She had to nip this in the ass, right now.

"I don't think that's a good idea," Miwa said. She slipped off her stool. So he didn't totally waste his money, she took another drink of her beer. "It's nothing personal, Tanaka-*san*. You're not the type of person I look to date."

His face was so pale that he might as well be the moon shining through the gray clouds outside. "*Sou desu...* I know I'm not much. Don't have many prospects, aren't that good looking, and I'm not super smart. But I like you, Ban-*san*. You've got a good head on your shoulders. You're so nice to the passengers when other attendants lose their patience. You're also..." The color returned to his cheeks. He was probably about to tell her that she was pretty.

"Tanaka-*san*. It's not happening." Miwa inhaled a deep breath for courage. "I'm sorry. Like I said, it's not personal, but I'd prefer if it's not brought up again."

As All Our Fires Burn

"Damnit. I've driven you off now."

"We can still be friends. I like you as a coworker." Miwa had her jacket on. "But it's not possible for personal reasons."

He glanced at the rim of his glass before saying, "I knew you would reject me, and that's okay. I had to ask. Would've bothered me forever if I never asked, but I know you're not into people like me."

"It has nothing to do with your appearance, Tanaka-*san*. Or your job, or…"

"You're gay, Ban-*san*. It's okay. I know. I simply kinda hoped I was wrong."

This time she was the one so white that she almost passed out. "Excuse me?"

"If you deny it, I will believe you. But you don't have to. I won't tell anyone."

"How did you…"

He shrugged again. "I'm observant. It's the one thing I've got going for me. Figure it's what makes me a good platform attendant, because I've gotta observe people's behavior all day *and* pay attention to the trains coming and going." When Kohei looked at her again, it was with a wan smile. "Don't ask me how I know. I just do. You didn't do anything to out yourself. Just, you know, when you work with someone for so long, you figure things out about them. Like you being…" He lowered his voice. "Never mind. You don't have to respond to it. I'm sorry, Ban-*san*."

She gritted her teeth and showed herself out of the bar. The last thing she heard was the heavy sigh on Kohei's lips.

Chapter 33

SAYURI

The days grew shorter, rainier, and colder. Christmas decorations and music had already permeated the urban landscape, but after the final month of the year commenced, Sayuri became convinced that it was the most verboten Christmas season. *Worse than last year's.* That said a lot. The plans to take time off work to take her son to grandma's house for a few Christmas celebrations and then full-blown New Year's rituals out in the countryside were waylaid by tragedy. This year was quieter, yes, but the impending sense of doom in Sayuri's heart meant she still spent most of her days holed up in her apartment, awaiting the inevitable.

The so-called investigation into her personal life was still ongoing. Occasionally, Sayuri received an update from the union asking for more information and assuring her that, "As long as you don't have anything too damning to hide, we can help you." That didn't make her feel better. While she hadn't exactly said she was gay she didn't like that Mrs. Ichinose assumed she was a mild-mannered teacher who would never partake in perversions, and that this was simply a misunderstanding with a few hot-headed parents.

Sayuri also heard from the principal when an update in the curriculum was needed. *I can't believe I'm still drawing up the lesson plans for my sub.* Didn't help that they had switched subs twice already. The first one couldn't handle the dynamics of the classroom for more than a few days, and the second had a family emergency that pulled her away from Fujimi City. The third sub was a man who politely requested Sayuri to draw him up some lesson plans for the rest of the year. While it gave Sayuri something to do in her lonely apartment, the bitterness that resulted from her not teaching these lessons herself made her grit her teeth.

She did not expect Dean-*sensei* to come by after the first half-day of the month.

"I heard you weren't feeling well, Kawashima-*sensei*." He wore a mask, whether to prevent her from catching his germs or vice-versa, Sayuri had no idea. "My wife suggested I bring you over some old-fashioned Australian remedies."

"You're really too kind. Would you like some tea?" It was the least she could do for the man who came all the way over with a small basket of goodies. Nobody else from the school had done that. Then again, Dean probably didn't understand the nuances that went into her situation. Most of her coworkers didn't want to "get involved."

Dean took her up on the offer. At least he understood *that* nuance.

It was the first time in weeks that Sayuri had a reason to heat up some decent tea for a guest. *Last person I had here was Miwa...* She had to pause before her stove and block out those memories before going through the motions of serving tea.

"The kids really miss you," Dean said as they had their tea in the otherwise silent living room. The man was polite enough to not let his eyes linger on the shrine dedicated to the little boy he must have heard about Kawashima-*sensei* once having. Instead, he was entirely focused on his porcelain cup. "Especially Shota-*kun*. Every time I go in there, he asks me where you are."

Bristles claimed Sayuri's already trembling body. *Maybe I really am catching a cold.* "He's such an energetic boy. Quite the handful, too." She smiled. "But he's also really loyal, if you ask me. If he likes you, he'll stick by you."

"That's what makes him a good classroom leader, huh?"

"He gets it from his mother." Sayuri sipped her tea. "I don't know if you've ever met her, but she's a very headstrong and opinionated woman. Although she's more passive-aggressive about sharing her views than her son. She would tell you it's because she's a proper woman."

Dean's face fell at Sayuri's candidness. It was easy to be more open with a foreigner. They came from a different cultural background, where openness was permissible, sometimes asked for, which was crazy to Sayuri's limited experiences. *I come from a place where everything is bottled up inside.* She didn't simply mean her Japanese identity. Her family was particularly introverted with their needs and desires. *We're all a product of our parents to some extent.* She often wondered how Yuma would have mimicked her as he grew older.

"You're refreshing, Kawashima-*sensei.*"

"It's nice talking to someone from the other side for me, too." Sayuri never had quite this kind of relationship with the other foreign English teachers her school employed. Yet it helped that Dean was fluent in Japanese and quite adept at navigating the culture. Both he and his wife were familiar with the differences between Australian and Japanese cultures, whereas previous teachers were so green that they were more pet amusements than bona fide coworkers. "There is a lot of drama that goes on for the average schoolteacher."

Dean hesitated before asking her anything. "You're not sick, are you, Kawashima-*sensei?* That's what we were told."

"I'm sure. The truth rarely comes out in these situations, especially if you are an outsider."

"Thanks for the reminder," he said with a laugh.

"That's why we call you *gaikokujin.*" The official term for "foreigner" was a loaded word. The word literally meant "outside country person," because there was nothing more important than denoting who was Japanese and who wasn't. Even people whose families had been in the country for generations were still called outsiders because they weren't Japanese to their cores. Sometimes, Sayuri wished she could know what that was like. Could she go somewhere else and leave this behind her? "You are on the outside looking in."

"What's really going on? If I may ask."

She considered her words carefully. "I am on paid leave. It was not my choice."

"Oh. I see."

"You are not supposed to know it, I guess, but I am being investigated for something by the school board." When Dean looked like she had admitted to having an affair with a student, she explained, "It has nothing to do with my job, but you must understand that what I do in private reflects upon me as a teacher. The school board is first deciding the validity of certain accusations against me. Then, depending on what they decide is truth, I will either return to work or be fired."

"I had no idea."

"I did not tell you this, of course."

"Of course." Yet there was no doubt that Dean would run home to tell his Australian wife all about this. They would probably whisper about how tough the Japanese system was. *"Back home, that would mean she was a child abuser or something." "Yes, but here it could mean anything. Maybe she has a gambling problem, or they found out she's really Chinese. Who knows? It could be so small we're in shock that it's a problem at all."*

Dean offered her his sympathies before leaving. Sayuri stressed that he should not repeat anything she said. *You seem to, but does it mean anything?* Sayuri almost didn't care anymore. Maybe it would hurry up the investigation so she could be let go and start her life over again elsewhere.

As All Our Fires Burn

She'd almost prefer that to being told she was clear to go back to work. Everything was too tainted now.

***

An unexpected knock came to her door.

The knock actually wasn't what was so unexpected. Only who Sayuri saw standing on the other side of her door.

"Shota-*kun!*" Was she seeing things? The little boy gracing her *genkan* was none other than the leader of her classroom, the little boy who always gave her something to laugh about… and the son of the woman who had put Sayuri into her current spot. "What are you doing here?"

There was nothing to laugh about now. Shota looked like his puppy recently passed away, or maybe he heard that his parents were divorcing. *That would be the scandal of the neighborhood.* Sayuri would have been one of the first to hear, even if she only went to the supermarket every other day. The sole reason Shota looked up at her was because she was a person he respected – as much as that meant on any given day. His sweatshirt was sprayed with the mist of the rain, and his baseball cap was turned backward on his head so Sayuri had a grand view of that serious face.

"*Sensei,*" he said with such ferocity that Sayuri took a step back. "You need to come back. These substitutes are NG."

"I'm… sure they're perfectly acceptable." He really shouldn't be saying that any adult was no good. Everyone at the school did their best to work with students like him.

"No way, *sensei*. I thought the one who couldn't talk louder than a mouse was bad enough, but the current guy we got doesn't know his ass from his elbow." Shota said it with such conviction that Sayuri momentarily mistook him for an irate uncle complaining about the new butcher on the corner. "You're the only one who can teach that class."

"I'm sorry, Shota, but right now I'm…"

"I know my mom did something." He put his hands on his hips and looked up at her, right in the eye. *My goodness. I didn't know he had this side of him in there.* "She's always sticking her nose in stuff that doesn't need her help. You know how many times I've told her that she needs to butt out of my friendships? She's always yammering about good role models and people of decent morals. Whatever that means!"

Sayuri's face softened. "It's because she loves you. She wants you to be a good person."

Shota snorted. "You think I'm not a good person, *sensei*? You see me more than she does most days."

"I didn't say that, Shota-*kun*," Sayuri softly said. "Your mother is a fighter for what she thinks is right. I think you've picked up a lot of that from her." He could take things too far, but when it came to defending his friends, Shota didn't hesitate. Whenever his behavior toward other students crossed the line from having fun to bullying, he would always take those few moments of contemplation to say he was sorry – and at least *try* to not do it again. Sayuri was confident that things would calm down as he grew older. Most nine-year-old boys she taught were prone to a little wildness. "Nothing wrong with it."

"I don't wanna be like her." He paused. "She ruins things."

"What do you mean?"

"For one, she's the reason you're not teaching right now, right?"

"Why in the world do you think that's the case?"

"She doesn't like you, *sensei*. I know she's nice to you a lot, but then she comes home and says such mean things about you. She's been talking forever about making me switch classes so you're not my teacher anymore."

Sayuri swallowed. "I see. Thank you for telling me."

"When your son died," Shota continued, "she said the meanest thing I ever heard." He didn't even wait for Sayuri to tell him she didn't need to know. "She said that she was happy your son wouldn't grow up to see the things you did. I asked her what that meant, and she told me I was too young to understand. So I asked her why the hell she said it in front of me." Shota stomped his foot. "She acted so coy, *sensei!* Like she had forgotten I was there! She thinks I'm so stupid. She doesn't get that I hear what she says and know what it means." His head pointed downward again. "So… what did she mean?"

He removed his hat to scratch his head. The hat flopped back on top of his scalp a moment later.

"Shota-*kun*…" Sayuri knelt down to his level. "Your mother believes in a lot of things that are important to her. I don't want to tell you that I think she's misguided or mean. I only think she doesn't understand things that are new to her. Where we disagree is because I lived a different lifestyle from her. It's one she doesn't think is compatible with being around children, when in reality, people like me can be perfectly fine parents and teachers. It hurts me to know she said that about my son, but I will not hold it against her. Maybe one day you will be the one to show your mother that being different isn't so bad, and that there are different ways people can live while still contributing the same things to their neighborhoods."

"Man, *sensei*," Shota said with another huff, "that sounded like a whole lotta nothin'."

"You're gonna hate me for saying this," Sayuri said, "but you'll understand when you're older."

"Ha! You know, there have been times in class where I wished *you* were my mother, *sensei*. You're really nice, even though I can be a bit of a butthead. I think your kid was a lucky one. Kinda jealous he got to have you for a mom."

That's... the nicest thing he's ever said to me. Maybe the nicest thing most people had ever said to Sayuri. How could she prevent a tear from falling down her cheek? "I wish my son could have known you, Shota-*kun*. He was a gentle soul. Could've really used a big brother type in the neighborhood."

"I always wanted to be a big brother! Little brother, little sister... I don't care. I'd look after them, you know? But Mom says I can't have a little brother or sister. I don't think she and my dad really like each other." He scratched his cheek. "Probably shouldn't tell you that. She doesn't even know I figured out where babies come from."

"You have, huh?" This would be good.

"They come from the hospital, duh." Shota shrugged.

"They sure do, Shota-*kun*."

As All Our Fires Burn

"See? Bet you got your baby from the hospital."

"Technically, that is where I had him."

"And he didn't have a daddy! I told my mom she doesn't even need Dad to have a baby. She can be like you."

Sayuri almost choked on her spit. Things were starting to make a lot more sense. "I think you should head home. I don't want your mother getting angry at us for talking."

"Okay. But... please come back to school, *sensei*. We miss you a lot." He pulled a folded piece of paper out of his back pocket. When he opened it, he revealed the drawings and writings of the students who contributed to a *We Miss You, Teacher* card. Sayuri sniffed up her appreciation when she accepted it with a bow.

"That's not up to me to decide."

"I'm gonna talk to my mom about it," Shota said. "Wait for me, *sensei*. You're gonna be back by New Year's!"

"I'd like that." She held her paper to her chest before standing back up. "Thank you."

Before the boy was too embarrassed to speak, he grabbed his bearings and took off with another goodbye. Sayuri remained in her doorway. When she looked down at the paper her class had put together, she realized that there were names from the other classes as well.

There was also a note. "*We support you, Kawashima*-sensei."

For the first time in many weeks, Sayuri felt a glimmer of hope in her heart. Maybe things wouldn't be as good as they used to be, but like she had done before, she would rebuild her life from the ashes left behind after the worst fires of her life.

Chapter 34

MIWA

The surrealist day of Miwa's life commenced when she arrived for her shift. The men coming off theirs and spilling over to the start of hers were murmuring in the staff room. Usually, they did not spare her a glance when she grabbed her uniform to change in the bathroom, and today was no different. Yet there was no frivolity or forced propriety in their speech and mannerisms. They weren't ignoring her out of politeness. They were ignoring her because they were absorbed in hushed whispers she could barely understand.

"What's going on?" she asked Kohei, who had come in a few minutes behind her. He was still in his street clothes while Miwa put the finishing touches on her uniform. "What's got everyone so distracted? Did we have a jumper?"

As All Our Fires Burn

He glanced at the group gathered at the table before turning toward her. "No jumpers today. There's been a report... you didn't hear?"

Her throat dried. "No? I didn't get a text, if that's what you mean." Report about what? The company? Some scandal? Or was there another accident? Some other line? Some other rail company? *The fuck was going on?*

"Gas leaks at Renji-shima Station." Kohei shrugged. "They've shut it down but are still routing trains through. They only found out about the leak because some lady passed out. Everyone else wasn't feeling great, either, so they evacuated and tested the place. Turns out people were about to *die*."

"*Shinjirarenai...*" Miwa wasn't sure what she disbelieved the most. The fact there were gas leaks in a moderately sized station? *Two lines go through Renji-shima... including the line that stops here.* The station was two stops away, a common commuter hub for those starting their journey at Amaya-jinja-guchi. Or was she more shocked that the company was still running trains through the tunnels? The leak must have been up in the actual station, not down on the platform. She hoped, anyway.

Still... that could not be safe. How desperate was the company to make some money that day? *One of those days I wish I worked for Toei or Tokyo Metro.* JR didn't feel like such a pipe dream anymore.

"By the way," she continued. "We good?"

It had been a couple of days since Kohei asked her out and she subsequently rejected him. He looked fine now, but that could have been his professionalism trumping everything else.

"Yeah," he said. "We're good, Ban. No worries."

He stole away to change into his uniform. Miwa bowed to the coworkers surrounding the table, then reported to Overseer Endo to receive the same orders she got every day. When she braved asking about the closure of Renji-shima Station, he merely said, "Yes, the station is closed. Please inform all passengers if they ask. Those who need to change lines are being routed to Shinjuku."

That'll add to some commute times. "Is our station okay?"

"I wouldn't worry too much about it. We had some gas guys in here at the start of my shift taking readings of our gas levels, and they said everything was good here. We're simply grateful that they discovered the leak at Renji-shima before anyone was really hurt."

That was his official stance, and Miwa had to accept it. She bowed out of the office and began her shift as soon as Kohei was there to walk down the steps to the platform with her.

Murmurs permeated the platform for the first half of her shift. She always worked through the nighttime rush hour, and that night was a particular barrel of fun as she informed many passengers that, yes, their transfer station was currently shut down until further notice. Trains would be stopping to stay on schedule, but the doors would not open. No, there was nothing she could do about it. A special recorded message played over the speakers all evening. The glimpses she got of the monitors on the trains showed that they were dedicated to relaying the same information. Many of the passengers getting off at Amaya-jinja-guchi were in a bigger hurry than usual.

As All Our Fires Burn

Had there been birds in the station, they would have flown away long ago.

That was what niggled at the back of Miwa's mind for the first half of her shift. *Something's wrong.* It was possible that she merely fed off the awkward energy dissipating through the station with every wave of passengers that came and went. Or she felt damned around Kohei, who remained professional on the platform but didn't chat with her like he usually did. *Because we're so busy and things are so strange right now.* That's what Miwa told herself. It's what she *had* to tell herself.

She rarely had time to contemplate her platonic relationship with her coworker, however. There were too many passengers to reassure and trains constantly coming in and out of the station.

Kohei had returned from his dinner break when shudders *really* started going down Miwa's spine.

"Something's wrong," she told him between trains. "Do you feel that in the air? Something bad is gonna happen."

He looked as if he couldn't believe she was talking to him. "Things are kinda crazy today, huh? I wonder if the station is really gonna be all right."

He didn't specify which one he meant. There wasn't any time, for a flood of OLs and their business associates stumbled down the steps, tipsy and complaining about having to go all the way to Shinjuku Station to transfer to their usual lines. *"Maybe some gas would be good for us!"* more than one of them cried as they stood close to the platform's edge. Miwa studied them with the keen eye of a woman waiting for trouble. She stood at the far end of the platform, gloved hands twiddling together behind her back. She sucked in her cheeks and continued to sniff the air for something unsettling.

We would be able to smell leaking gas, right? They put that stuff in it that smells. She had suffered gas leaks before, both at home and in her own high school as little as ten years before. The first sign, aside from some dizziness, was the awful, sulfur-like smell that came with it. She didn't smell it now.

No, she wasn't worried about gas, now was she?

It's hot in here. She peered up and down the tunnels. No flickering lights. No horns blasting. Just the usual sounds of a small subway station on the outskirts of Tokyo's wards.

Something still wasn't right.

"Ban-*san*."

She leaped five feet into the air at the sound of Kohei's voice. He grabbed her by the arm to steady her before she fell into the tracks. Luckily, there were few people on the platform to see the strange moment occur. When Miwa finally regained her bearings, she clasped her hand over her heart and willed her body to calm the hell down.

"Sorry!" Kohei released her. "What's got you so jumpy?"

She chose not to dwell on that. "What do you need?"

He shrugged. "Was wondering if you had heard anything about the station opening up before last train."

"No!"

Kohei took a step back. "Okay, okay." He retreated as if she were being an unreasonable girl instead of an anxious platform attendant. "Going back to my position now."

As All Our Fires Burn

Miwa barely had the wherewithal to blow her whistle and signal the next train coming into the station. The drunk OLs hopped on and were on their way within minutes. While Kohei and Miwa weren't the *only* ones left behind, she was convinced that there were too many people remaining. It didn't help that she now smelled something... burning.

She was on her headset and looking up the tunnel the moment the alarms went off.

Red, flashing lights illuminated the platform. An automated message was triggered, asking passengers and personnel to please make an *orderly* exit up the nearest stairs – please avoid the elevator. Tired, half-drunk people gaped at the flashing lights. Kohei turned around in sharp circles. Miwa was the only one who immediately knew what had happened.

"*Abunai!*" she screamed, both into her headset and to the few people remaining on the platform. "Fire!"

She felt the heat before she saw the rolling flames traveling at incredible speeds down the tunnel. Miwa had exactly two seconds to save her own hide from being burned alive, yet her impeccable training kicked in before her own survival skills.

"Out! Get out!" She leaped away from the edge, arms motioning for everyone – including Kohei – to get the hell up the stairs. "There's a fire coming!" The first cries of fear and distress were emitted by passengers hustling up the stairs, now that the adrenaline was kicking in. Sprinklers exploded. The alarms continued going off. Endo was in Miwa's earpiece, yelling at everyone to evacuate to the streets, *now*. Kohei brought up the rear. By the time Miwa saw him again, he was illuminated in a hazy red glow. It was only then that Miwa realized the fire was right behind her.

Was it the adrenaline that prevented her from feeling the flames licking at her boots? From letting the smoke get to her? From acknowledging the heat that made her sweat in her uniform? *I could be on fire.* She was the closest to the inferno from the beginning. She *still* was, because she'd be damned if she left a single person behind before saving herself.

"Get out of here!" Kohei, drenched in both the spray of the sprinkler system and the smoke blasting down the tunnel, tried to push Miwa up the stairs. One businessman, stumbling in an attempt to grab the briefcase he left, was about to be abandoned. Miwa lunged toward him. One of the lights crashed from the ceiling and landed in the middle of the tracks. The fire immediately consumed it, creating a cacophony of the sparks and screams of one phenomenon meeting another. *"Go!"*

Kohei ran back to grab the man, crying over his briefcase now being licked by the flames. The smoke was so thick that they were both obscured to Miwa's panicking eyes. Her *stinging* eyes. She couldn't see or feel anything. There were voices in her headset, but none of them said a comprehensible thing.

All she knew was that she had to get to Kohei and the other man. Now.

"You idiot!" Kohei cursed. The businessman's dead weight wrapping around Kohei's shoulders. Miwa took up the other side. "Get the fuck out of here! I've got this!"

"Do you both wanna die?" It was so hot on the platform that Miwa no longer knew what it meant to breathe. Or maybe that was the smoke filling her lungs and building a terrible weight in the pit of her stomach. "You're too slow!"

"Stop talking and keep walking before we burn alive!"

Never before had the flight of stairs leading to the ticket gates been so steep. Miwa traversed them multiple times a day, yet she knew that this would be the last. *I might die.* She could drop the body on her back and use her last chance to flee, but that would mean leaving Kohei and an innocent passenger behind. She couldn't do that. Not when she took an oath to protect her passengers and her coworkers both here at Amaya-jinja-guchi, and beyond.

"Ban-*san!* Tanaka-*san!*" That was Endo's voice, a lone figure at the top of the smoky stairs. "What are you idiots doing? Get the hell up here!" When he saw they had a passenger trapped between them, Endo braved meeting them halfway down the stairs. He shoved Miwa out of the way and took her place as the strong left shoulder. There was no time to deliberate the meaning of that action. Not when he was yelling at her to get up the stairs.

Finally, Miwa hurled up the last of the stairs and encountered the barren station, where more sprinklers, more alarms, and more warnings continued to go off. There was less smoke for now, however, and Miwa used the opportunity to take a deep breath.

She barely could.

I'm not... I'm not okay... Like the businessman minutes before he collapsed, Miwa stumbled toward the opened ticket gates and braced herself against the wall. More cries of her coworkers came behind her, but she was already slipping down against the door to the staff area. *This isn't where I want to be. I need to head toward the emergency exit.* What was she doing all the way over there? Losing her damned mind?

I'm hot. I can't breathe. Her eyelids fluttered. Whoever said that fires were purifying was right. The last thought Miwa harbored in her smoke-filled brain was that her life hadn't been so bad, after all. If she died now? She wouldn't complain.

Only later would she realize how damnably dramatic that was. But she wouldn't disagree with herself.

Chapter 35

SAYURI

Sayuri was glued to her TV from the moment she first saw the news.

"*Gas leak leads to fire in Tokyo subway.*" On a good day, that would be a five-minute overview before moving to sports and weather. Fires happened all the time, right? Usually, it was put out in time, people were safely evacuated – inconvenienced, really – and the news cycle moved on.

It was a bad day.

The only thing on the local Tokyo metropolitan news was the subway fire. It dethroned everything else, from American politics to the latest scandal to wrack a pop idol. That meant billions of *yen* in damages. That meant whole train lines coming to a stop for the foreseeable future. That meant *deaths*.

"Two confirmed dead, dozens injured." It could have been a lot worse, but the media was hush about the identities of the two dead. If Sayuri's anxiety wasn't bad enough, she was soon subjected to the words "Amaya-jinja-guchi Station," which was declared the epicenter of the blast.

"We currently believe that this was a prefect storm of things going wrong," a so-called expert, with gray hair and wide-rimmed glasses, said on the morning news report. "The gas leak at Renji-shima Station was what started it. That was caught early on, of course, and most of us know that the station was shut down for the rest of the day as crews worked to fix the leak. Unfortunately, some of that gas managed to get far into the tunnels and the alarms did not go off. The fire could have happened at any time. We believe that what lit the match, so to speak, was a train sparking as it came into Amaya-jinja-guchi Station."

Oversights were accounted for. Apologies were made. Executives, and those who made decisions to keep trains running past a station known for its gas leak, made public pleas for forgiveness before a few resigned from their positions. Talking heads debated if this could have truly been prevented. "They followed all protocol on the books," an executive from another company said. "This was a freak accident. One that should have been foreseen, but what were the odds that enough gas got into the tunnels? The gas was taken care of the moment it reached semi-dangerous levels."

Tell me who died! Sayuri wished she hadn't deleted Miwa from her contact list. *I did it for my own good... so I wouldn't be tempted to text her.* Now she hated herself for it! The disaster happened during her shift. *She would've been down there. She would've faced that blast.* Miwa must have been injured, at least. Where was she? What hospital? Was there a funeral? Would Sayuri be attending yet another funeral of someone she loved?

She called the only person who might know something.

"Of course they're not going to say who died yet," Emiko said with a scoff. "I honestly don't know who it was. Not my company, you know? Sure, everyone's talking about it, but it's all rumor and hearsay. I know as much as you do right now. Look, I'll keep an ear open. What was her name, again? Ban? Yeah, I'll remember that one if I hear it. Take care, Sayuri."

That call did nothing to assuage Sayuri's worries. She paced in her apartment, biting her nails and wishing something, *anything* would happen. She was still waiting to hear about her investigation. Now she had to wait to find out if Miwa had been killed in such a tragic way? *What if she burned to death? What if her final moments were so terrifying that it's better that I not know?* The more Sayuri thought about it, the more she was inclined to huddle on her couch, head wrapped in her arms as she tried not to cry.

What if she spent her final moments thinking she was unloved?

Two days of the news gradually moving away from the reports later, Sayuri received an unexpected phone call.

It was Emiko, and she had done her ex a favor.

"You won't believe this, but I got someone down at the trainyard to talk." She soon cut Sayuri off again. "Your girl is alive. Or at least I'm pretty sure we were talking about her."

Sayuri's heart leaped at this little sliver of joy she was offered. Yet she couldn't let herself celebrate. Not yet. She felt like there was a huge *but* coming her way. "And?"

"I may have a lead as to which hospital she's in. That's all the info I can give you. She's alive and in a particular hospital. You'll have to call them to see if they can give you more info. I only know about it because a bunch of us are signing a card for those people in the hospital."

"I'll take whatever you've got!"

Sayuri's hand shook as she wrote down the name of the hospital. Emiko didn't have a phone number, but that was easy enough to look up. She also asked Emiko to text her the name of the hospital in case she screwed it up in her crazy haze. *I can't mess this up. I need to know that Miwa is alive. I need to know if there's something I can do.* Sayuri had already felt terrible for how things ended between them. Living in this purgatory with her job for the past month had taught her there were more important things than her image. Than her career.

Than almost... anything.

"Thank you so much, Emi." Sayuri let out her pent-up breath. "You know how I get in a tragedy. I've been sitting here thinking that..."

"I know, I know." Typical Emiko. She didn't want to be reminded of anything sad or depressing. "Let me know how it goes, huh? Can't say I'm not curious."

Sayuri hung up and immediately researched the number for the hospital. She received a busy signal and a prerecorded message that implored her to "try again later."

As All Our Fires Burn

She went to the shrine in the corner of her apartment and knelt before her son's photo. She had prayed before it multiple times over the past few days, but now it was with renewed, hopeful energy.

Sayuri prayed to her son, to whatever spirit that might be listening, to help heal Miwa and to let her know that someone was thinking about her. *I'm going to her.* Sayuri had made up her mind about that when she received the name of the hospital. *She came to me when I needed someone. Now I'm going to her.*

She lit a candle for her son and for Miwa. When she attempted to call the hospital again, she was met with the no-nonsense voice of a living human being who could hopefully answer her questions.

The altar was left behind as Sayuri sprang into action.

Hildred Billings

Chapter 36

MIWA

Another baseball game. Another. Freakin'. Baseball. Game.

Miwa had nothing against Japan's favorite sport, but would it kill the hospital to have anything else – literally *anything* else – on TV? She had been there for three days and struggled to find anything that wasn't baseball during the day. *I've never heard of some of these teams.* She sat up in her bed, hitting that button in the hopes of finding a travel show, a cooking show, a morning drama, news… hell, she would take undubbed Western flicks over another round of baseball. Meanwhile, the woman one bed over was on the verge of slamming two blow-up bats together every time her favorite team appeared on her screen.

They finally gave Miwa her phone, but the charge was always running out and the closest plug-in was too far away for her to use herself. When her phone wasn't charging, she was growing increasingly bored with her apps. Sure, she could read the news, particularly the news surrounding the subway fire, but it reached the point where her eyes crossed and she needed to take another nap. *"Get some rest!" everyone keeps saying. What am I, a baby?*

Every time Miwa thought that, she fell into a coughing fit that summoned the nearest nurse. Pillows were fluffed, bed heights readjusted, water swallowed and endless questions asked. Miwa only wanted to go home and play some video games while lying down on her futon couch. The food here wasn't anything better than what she could get in a convenience store. She might as well have some freedom back.

Yet her doctor recommended she spend a minimum of three days in the hospital to keep her under observation. She didn't remember much between the fire and arriving at the hospital. She had no idea what happened to her uniform, nor did she care. The only information she was given outside of her own health was that her coworkers were fine. Endo and Kohei had been discharged from another hospital the day before, but Miwa was the only one of the three who lost consciousness due to smoke inhalation. She never heard what happened to the businessman she helped save. *Probably in the same situation as me, if he lived.* There was a death toll in the news, but she couldn't account for anyone she knew. She was too worried about her job and getting home when she was finally discharged.

There were a few people she could call, most of them through work. The station master and some of the more higher-ups in her company came by the day before to offer their apologies and to commend her bravery – if she could dare call it that... she was just doing her job. They assured her they would pay all of her medical bills and work with her to relocate her to another station when she was prepared to come back to work after her paid medical leave. The only thing that caught her attention, however, was the offer of assistance in any related matter. When she asked if someone could escort her home when she was discharged, the station master volunteered. They asked no questions beyond, *"Could you let us know when and where that is?"* If they cared about whether she had close friends and family in the area… they never inquired.

So while she wasn't completely without her resources, she was ironically in the same situation Sayuri had been months ago. No friends. No family. Even if Miwa's mother would bother to inquire about her daughter's health, she wasn't about to come down from her rural house to actually *do* something. Outside of people from work and a few media reps, nobody visited Miwa, and she was fine with it.

Still, did it have to suck so much?

"Ban-*san?*" the nurse asked while Miwa continued to flip past one baseball game after another. "There's someone here to see you. She says she's an old friend."

Miwa stopped pressing buttons and slowly turned her greasy head toward the nurse. "Can't think of a single one who could come by today. What's her name?"

Someone had snuck past the nurse's station and now peered through the opened door. Miwa almost shot up like a rocket when she recognized Sayuri's big eyes and the fall of her dark hair.

She swore she smelled the perfume, too, but Miwa theoretically couldn't smell anything well for another few days.

"Yeah, sure," Miwa said with a squeak. "I'll talk to her."

The nurse gently chastised Sayuri for sneaking back there before informing her that she could visit Miwa for half an hour. A part of Miwa wished the nurse wouldn't leave yet. *Don't leave me alone with her.* Miwa didn't know what to say. What *did* a woman say to the person who dumped her? This fate was almost crueler than ending up in the hospital because her place of work caught on fire.

"Miwa..." Sayuri kept a healthy distance. Miwa attempted to keep a straight, platonic expression on her face, but every time Sayuri slightly moved and reminded her of what they had not so long ago... ugh. Miwa needed divine intervention to keep her from acting like an utter fool. "You probably don't want to see me right now, but I had to make sure you were okay. I saw the news."

Miwa looked way. Her neighbor the major baseball fan shouted something at her TV before slapping her hand over her mouth, a sheepish grin touching her ears. Miwa couldn't hold anything against her. Any distraction was a great one right now. "I'm alive, as you can see." She swallowed. Her first day in the hospital, she could barely swallow at all. Not without hacking up one of her lungs. She was finally off the oxygen machine, but they could put her back on it at any time. "I don't know anybody who died."

As All Our Fires Burn

"They said more than a few died... I was so worried about you until someone in the industry told me they heard you were here and you were okay."

Miwa had no idea who that could have been. "You could have called or texted instead of coming all the way into the city, you know." She swallowed again.

"I... erased your number after the last time we met up. Besides, you know me." Sayuri uneasily laughed. "I wouldn't be content until I saw you for myself."

"Here I am." Miwa shrugged. "You can go now."

Sayuri's sorry eyes widened. "Go where?"

"Go home. You've seen that I'm okay, so, you can go. Curiosity sated."

"I know that things are awkward between us now, Miwa-*san,* but I wouldn't feel right simply leaving you here. You didn't leave me behind in a hospital."

Damnit, she was drawing that parallel! "Things aren't only a little awkward. You..." Miwa checked on her roommate, who was so engrossed in the baseball game that not even an earthquake would interrupt her concentration. With a lowered voice, Miwa continued, "You dumped me. At a love hotel. Because you didn't like the attention you were getting at work. If you think that's only a *little* awkward, then I don't know what to tell you. Because I'm rather humiliated, thank you."

Sayuri didn't do it on purpose – probably not, anyway – but when her face fell like that, Miwa was weaker than her lungs that first day at the hospital. *If she were the manipulative type, I would really be in trouble.*

Miwa didn't expect her ex-girlfriend to mimic the executives of the rail company by taking a step back and bowing deeply at her waist. Anyone passing by would probably think she was related to Miwa's current stay in the hospital. *Might as well be. Can you be hospitalized for a broken heart?* Miwa didn't think she had taken it that badly, but now she wondered if part of the reason her survival instincts departed the other day was because she realized she didn't have much to live for. More than once she wondered about the businessman she helped save with Kohei and Endo. Did he have a family? A wife and kids? Parents who were counting on him to make sure they were taken care of in their advanced age? A job that relied on him? Employees that respected him? Neighbors that would miss him? It wasn't entirely impossible that his life was worth more than hers. Besides, she was doing her job.

Just doing my job…

"Please forgive me for the pain I caused you due to my selfishness." When Sayuri stood up again, it was with tears on her face. Not a lot. Not enough to make Miwa think her ex-girlfriend was playing it up. Enough to make her feel a pang in her chest, however. This time, the pang didn't come from the smoke she inhaled. "I thought I was doing the right thing for us. For me, mostly." She looked away again. "Although, honestly, my administration knew who you were. I didn't know how vindictive people could be. For all I knew, they would have thrown you to the wolves of your own company. I thought that by breaking up, I could be protecting you." Sayuri sighed. "But mostly, I was protecting myself. I admit it."

Miwa stared at her dirty fingernails. "I don't blame you. It still sucks, though."

There were a million words written upon Sayuri's face, most of them Miwa couldn't read. *Never said I had the greatest emotional intelligence in the world.* Yet she knew what at least one word etched upon that countenance said.

"*I'm sorry.*"

Miwa hadn't been expecting this. Not Sayuri's presence. Not the sensations of remorse and lingering love still inside of her. Not the fear of being alone after one of the worst moments of her professional life. Certainly not the hope that she might have the person she wanted most back in her heart.

"Things aren't so simple," Miwa said. "I can't simply forgive you and act like nothing happened. I'm grateful that you came by to see me, but I'm not sure we can pick up where we left off."

"No, I didn't suspect so." Sayuri sighed, the few freckles on her face calling attention to the forlorn cinch of her brows. "Things are never that simple. Yet I want to make things right. I want to be here for you, like you were there for me. Please… let me take care of you."

She said it so earnestly, yet Miwa couldn't throw her hope into those words. "You'll have to do better than that. I'm not completely without my resources. I don't *need* you to pull me out of here and dote on me like my mother."

Miwa hadn't intended to hurt Sayuri's feelings, yet she could tell that was exactly what happened when the room grew cold and the color drained from one woman's face. Sayuri looked like she was about to turn around and run out of the room. *I don't want that…* Miwa sucked up her pride and turned her attention to the woman reformulating her thoughts.

"I mean…"

Sayuri interrupted her with the force of a woman who didn't want to take no for an answer. Or, at least, Miwa would have a damn good reason for saying no if that's what she really wanted! "I'm not going to 'mother' you. What kind of weirdo do you think I am? The only people I mother are under the age of ten! Are you ten, Miwa-*san?* Because I thought you were a grown woman who sometimes needed a helping hand! That's not mothering! That's being helpful!" She cleared her throat. "Besides, what's so bad about taking care of people? It's okay to let go and be taken care of! It doesn't make you a bad or weak person! And it doesn't make me a weak person if I like doting on others and making them smile! *Mou!*"

The silly huff she uttered at the end of her spiel was what made Miwa smile. Such an indignant child. She wanted to talk about being a grown woman, and not a weak one at that? Well! She was quite the sight with her red, puffing cheeks and the slight stomp of her foot. So much for being the consummate housewife in her fuzzy blue sweater and the long, thick brown skirt wrapped around her legs. Her flats were on the floor, and that was all that mattered to Miwa, who found everything about Sayuri suddenly too charming to bear. *This is how you fall for a woman like her, idiot.* She warned herself that, but what did it matter? Maybe it wasn't so bad for one idiot to fall in love with another.

As All Our Fires Burn

"What are you laughing at?" Sayuri asked.

"You look so much like my mother on a good day right now."

"*Mou…*"

Miwa stifled her laughter. She needed to, before they turned into another coughing fit. "Sorry. I don't mean to offend you. I only wish you could see what I do right now."

"What do you see?"

Miwa had to think about that for a second. "Someone who is really sorry."

That softened the edges to Sayuri's demeanor. "Yes," she began. "I *am* sorry. I'm sorry for breaking up with you, when it's the last thing I truly wanted. I'm sorry for showing up like this and surely shocking you. I'm sorry for blowing up at you." She shook her head, her lovely black curls grazing her chest. "I don't think you really understand, Miwa-*san*." Sayuri was still calling her that? Before their breakup, Miwa gained increasingly cuter names. *Miwappo* had uttered from Sayuri's lips after she realized it was her girlfriend's PlayStation handle. Yet she was back to being Miwa-*san,* and she wasn't sure what to think about that. "*Suki yo.*"

Miwa gripped the thin blankets in her hand. *She loves me…* Miwa could hardly believe it. Sayuri. In love… with her? While it wasn't completely beyond her realm of comprehension, she didn't expect to hear it that day. Not ever. The ship had left port when Sayuri told Miwa they could no longer be together. Now, it was like the ship turned around and crashed back into the docks. *Maybe I'm still dreaming. Trapped in a dreamworld where these situations come true.* Miwa was about to wake up at any moment. A single tear would inhabit her eye, reminding her of how much she cherished her time with Sayuri, but she would know it was never meant to be. That's why Sayuri had dumped her. That kind of love and kindness never lasted for long in Miwa's life.

"You mean that?" she asked the apparition beside her. "You like me?"

"When I saw the news on TV, I thought a piece of my heart had been ripped out again." Sayuri mimicked the sentiment with her hand balled against her chest. "I hadn't felt like that since…" She swallowed, hard. "Not since I lost someone else really precious to me. I couldn't close my eyes. They were glued to the television as I awaited to hear the inevitable about who died and who was injured beyond help." A choke entered her airways. Sayuri cleared her throat again and licked her bottom lip. "Once I found out what happened to you, I knew nothing else mattered. I needed to come to you. I needed to *be* with you. The universe sent me your way when I was hurting the most. Now I needed to find you again. I didn't care what it meant for the investigation. They could see me kissing you for all I care!"

Miwa couldn't help but chuckle. "You could start right now, you know."

Sayuri immediately looked to the woman watching baseball, face so red that she looked like an apple.

"I'm kidding." Miwa held her hand to her head, as if that would settle the nerves now fooling her into thinking that everything was a lie. "I don't know what to say. On one hand, I want to tell you that I love you, too, but it's not that simple, is it?"

"No," Sayuri agreed. "It's not."

They were at an impasse. While Miwa held all the power in whatever decision she made, she couldn't commit one way or another. *I know which way I want to go, though.* She wanted her girlfriend back. She wanted those sweet moments. The hot moments. The hope that they might stay together for the rest of their lives, loving one another and building a home together. The first home Miwa ever really had that was wholly her own.

Except she couldn't forget how much it hurt when Sayuri cut her out of her life. To do so was a disservice to everything she swore she would do better next time.

If there was a next shot at love. What if this was Miwa's big chance? What if she regretted turning Sayuri away for the rest of her life?

"I love you, too," Miwa said, yet she couldn't look Sayuri in the eye when she uttered that declaration. "I was in love with you for a long time."

They were silent for a few moments, Sayuri's breathing rapidly increasing as she awaited Miwa to say more. When she could no longer bear the quiet – outside of the raucous baseball game playing on TV – she said, "But?"

"I need to know that you won't do that again. It wasn't only the way you did it." Miwa shuddered when she remembered being left alone and naked in that bed, mere moments after making love for what she now perceived to be the last time.

"The fact you did broke my heart. How could I come back to you when I fear it might happen again?"

"It won't happen again," Sayuri swore. "I know I made a mistake. That's why I want to make it up to you. While I understand it if you don't want to get back together again… please, let me do this one thing for you. I'll bring you back to my place while you recuperate. It can be platonic."

Miwa laughed. "I don't think we're capable of that if we're in the same room."

"What do you call this, then?"

The demure smile Miwa offered her was the only thing she could muster. "Me watching you grovel."

Sayuri mulled over her words until the nurse returned to check on them. Before the short woman in scrubs could say a single thing, Sayuri turned to her and said, "I'll be the one taking Ban-*san* home tomorrow. I've already left my contact information with the front desk. I'll be here at ten in the morning, and if she gives you any gruff, feel free to remind her that I'll be back as long as the trains are running on time." She gave Miwa one last smile before heading out the door. "I must be going. I hear that I have some more groveling to do, and I can't do it until I prepare my apartment for a brave invalid."

"I'm not brave!" Miwa called after her. "I was doing my job! That's all!"

"Now I'm doing mine!"

That was the last thing Miwa heard from her that day. She leaned back in her bed while the nurse went about making her comfortable again. *I don't need a nurse. I need my girlfriend.* Miwa couldn't help but smile as she sank beneath her covers. For the first time in many weeks – and certainly since the accident – Miwa had something to look forward to. She had no idea what would come out of it, or if she would regret it. Yet for now, she would cling to the fantasy that she was doing the right thing for herself. And her future.

Chapter 37

SAYURI

Sayuri looked around her apartment one last time before departing for the train station. *I must make sure that everything is ready for Miwa.* She never received a call that she was not required to pick up her ex-girlfriend, so with the will of the wind at her back, she would traipse through the December day and bring home the one person she was willing to give up everything for.

Everything.

She knelt before the shrine in the corner of her living room, praying to the spirits that deigned to hear her cries for help and wishes for good fortune. The sweet scent of incense wafted past her face. Candles burned brightly. The sight of her son's face looking back at her always put a smile on hers – and a stitch in her chest. Yet today, with his genial smile reflecting in the frame, Sayuri knew that good things would come.

Thank you for looking over us today. She clapped twice and blew out the candles. Smoke intermingled with the incense, obscuring the old photograph of a boy no longer on that earth.

Sayuri firmly turned her back on it. Not because she didn't care, but because she had things to do and a life to live.

She had bought most of Miwa's favorite foods and prepared both the couch and her bedroom for someone who might want to sleep on either. The video games were carefully organized and ready for someone to play. The carpet was vacuumed and the surfaces dusted. More than Sayuri had managed over the past few weeks living nowhere but in her own head.

The plan was to pick up Miwa, swing by her place to pack a few things and check her mail, and ride up to Fujimi where she would spend however long she wanted recuperating on Sayuri's couch and eating her meals. A part of her couldn't wait to have someone to fuss over again. Another part of her was so anxious that she almost threw up when she finally left her apartment.

She shouldn't have been so nervous.

Miwa awaited her in the hospital lobby, wearing a simple tunic and leggings she probably purchased from the gift shop since nobody had access to her apartment to bring her clothes. *I should have brought something for her to borrow!* Hindsight was 20/20. Besides, what was she supposed to focus on when she saw the woman she loved wheeled to her by a smart-looking nurse.

Start groveling, dumbass.

Sayuri bowed again. She bowed to the nurse for doing such a fine job. She bowed to Miwa in apology for what she had done before and to thank her for putting so much faith into another human being again. She bowed to every doctor walking by and giving her a strange look. Then again, how strange was it to see people bowing in a hospital, of all places?

"Oh, stop." Miwa leaned her elbow against the arm of her wheelchair and hid her face. "Just get me out of this place! Come on, you know what it's like in here."

Sayuri accepted the handles of Miwa's wheelchair and pushed her outside, where the warm sunlight broke through gray clouds and welcomed them to the sidewalk. Miwa helped herself out of the chair and shivered at the first touch of the cold. Sayuri had brought an extra sweater to wrap around Miwa's shoulders. It would be better, however, to get them both to the train station.

Three transfers were necessary to officially make their way to her apartment out in the suburbs. Miwa was silent for most of the trip, and Sayuri attributed that to what the discharge papers had said about her lungs and taking it easy. Unfortunately, there was some walking involved at a few stations. A subway line was the most convenient at one point, and when Miwa took that first step onto the escalator deep into its depths, she froze against the railing and refused to speak until they were above ground again.

This was going to be tougher than Sayuri anticipated. Luckily, she was good with such challenges.

As All Our Fires Burn

"Here, you take the seat." The train out of Ikebukuro was packed for the first few stations, and Sayuri had to stare down some teenager in one of the priority seats to secure it for Miwa. She would be damned if Miwa was forced to stand for the entire journey. Sayuri even went as far as grabbing the handle above Miwa's seat and standing in front of her. While people weren't in danger of falling into Miwa's lap, Sayuri would be damned if any of them disturbed her rest as the train moved away from Tokyo. After a few stops, however, the seat next to Miwa's opened and Sayuri took her opportunity to rest with her.

"Thank you for doing this." Miwa clutched her overnight bag she packed in the ten minutes she lingered in her apartment. "You really didn't have to."

"Yes, I did." Sayuri placed a reassuring hand on her ex-girlfriend's knee. "I love you too much to leave you to fend for yourself right now."

Miwa blushed. Her hair was pulled back into a loose ponytail that showed off her tender cheekbones and the little bags beneath her eyes. Sayuri was convinced that she had never been so in love with someone before.

They still had yet to exchange many words before pulling into their station. Sayuri didn't think twice about taking Miwa's hand and leading her off the train and through the ticket gates that dumped them onto a familiar street. The smell of smoke hung in the air, but Sayuri didn't think anything of it. That time of year, it was common to smell wood and incense burning to fit the season. Few people had proper fireplaces, but that didn't stop the perfume companies from cooking it into their fragrances.

"Do you remember the way?" Sayuri steadied Miwa's steps as they made their gradual way down the street. "Do you want me to let you go?"

Miwa gave her a coy look. "Do you *want* to let me go?"

There were layers to that question. The first one was on the surface. *"Am I bothering you? Would it be easier to take your hand off me?"* Sayuri never wanted to let go. Not if it meant possibly leaving Miwa in the dust.

Yet the other question lurking within Miwa's words was more important. *"Do you want to make sure nobody in your neighborhood sees us holding hands?"*

Sayuri had not lied when she said she no longer cared. She'd march Miwa right past the Shimazakis' door and essentially give the largest middle finger of her life. *I'll do anything for the people I love.* It had taken her too long to realize that wasn't a character flaw.

"I'm not letting you go unless you say otherwise." Sayuri squeezed Miwa's hand with a smile. That was enough.

For five minutes, Sayuri was allowed to live in a world where everything would be okay. Even if the world came crashing down around her, she had Miwa, and she could rebuild from whatever ashes were given to her if she had her beloved by her side.

Of course, such sentiments were born from the theory that they wouldn't be tested the moment they were released from the subconscious. Sayuri turned the corner of her street, Miwa's hand still in hers, unafraid of what – or who – she might encounter. Still, nothing prepared her for the scene unfolding on her quiet residential street.

A crowd amassed outside of their homes, assuming people were not content to peer from their windows. A firetruck was parked outside Sayuri's apartment building. Evacuated residents shrieked to one another as smoke billowed from one of the units.

It took Sayuri three seconds to realize that it was *her* unit.

There were few times in her life when everything came to a terrifying standstill. Two of those times occurred a little over a year from one another: when she crashed her car and killed her son, and when she brought Miwa home to find out her apartment was on fire.

Her cries of disbelief and horror did not go unheard within the crowd. Her neighbors certainly recognized her, and those who were brave enough to approach her with pity in their eyes gave her their pithy reassurances that *"surely, it's not as bad as it looks."* The fire chief in charge of the scene approached her as more of his men emerged with nods of *job well done*.

"Are you Kawashima-*san?*" the middle-aged, muscular man asked with a gruff voice.

It took Sayuri a few seconds to realize what he had asked. Her focus remained on the smoke billowing out of her living room windows. "H... *hai*. What happened?"

The fire chief shook his head. "We don't know for sure yet, but we believe an unattended candle on your shrine may have started the fire. The smoke makes it look worse than it is, honestly. Most of the fire burned itself out before it could spread too far, but there is extensive smoke damage to most of your belongings and some of your neighbors'."

This was, of course, said in front of the whole neighborhood. The neighbors in question scowled in Sayuri's direction. People from nearby houses, most of whom were only mildly disturbed by this, shook their heads in disbelief. Miwa was the only one too out of it to realize what exactly had happened. All she could muster was, "Does this mean we should go back to my place, then?"

Sayuri didn't respond to that. Her eyes searched the crowd until she met Mariko's gaze over the heads of three aunties whispering among themselves. Mariko turned deathly white and looked away.

No, Sayuri didn't suspect foul play. *I only have myself to blame.* An unattended candle. On her altar. Her son's portrait was probably nothing more than ash now. Like his little body shortly after the last time she held him.

Sayuri had lost everything. Again.

Not everything. In her stunned haze, she reached for Miwa's hand and held it before everyone else. Miwa's eyes were glazed over as she ignored the smoke filling the air, but her hand was warm, and nothing stopped Sayuri from realizing how lucky she still was. *If I hadn't gone to fetch her, this wouldn't have happened today.* Sayuri could replace her things, however. She couldn't replace the people who mattered most to her.

She pulled Miwa into her embrace. She didn't care who saw them. She didn't care what it did to her career. None of that mattered. Not when Miwa hugged her back and said everything would be all right.

Of course it would be. They were alive, weren't they?

EPILOGUE

MIWA

There had been warmer summers in recent years, but Miwa wasn't concerned about that. She welcomed the cool evening breeze touching her cheeks as she rode her scooter home from the city's main train station three kilometers away. The company that poached her from the subway line, citing her "outstanding bravery" and "dedication to the oaths we take," asked her to wear her uniform to and from work. Always fun when she got home in time for her trousers to be a dusty mess.

Ten years had passed since that day in the subway station. More than nine had passed since Miwa joined a new company, complete with an uptick in pay and slightly better benefits. She needed them, too, since her lungs were a little weaker and affording a therapist to help her with the PTSD she took home that day helped her move on with her life. Although everything had happened so fast back then, now that Miwa was quickly approaching forty, she was of the opinion that things had been nice and easy for a long time.

Moving out to the far edges of the Tokyo suburbs had helped. Out there, they were practically in the countryside, complete with active rice paddies, smaller schools, and the kind of friendly townsfolk who saw themselves as an active unit always on the path to better their town. Miwa and Sayuri had received a few strange looks when they first moved into the house they bought thanks to the generous promotion Miwa had received in her company, but the townsfolk were too polite to say anything as long as the new neighbors contributed.

Oh, we have. Miwa was one of the most familiar faces in her neighborhood, since she was now a prominent figure at the main train station that went into Tokyo. There wasn't a neighbor she didn't know by both first and last name. They knew hers quite well, too. Hers and Sayuri's, the woman who was often seen tutoring small children and helping the elderly with their chores and errands. Assuming she had time after her own, of course.

Miwa couldn't believe it had been so long. As she approached her neighborhood and eased up on the gas, she wondered if she would see her partner fussing with the plants in their humble front yard. Or maybe she would be chatting with the old aunties across the street – the ones who always patted Sayuri's stomach and arms, telling her she still had one more baby in her. (Naturally, they all knew a man about her age in dire need of a baby.) Or maybe Miwa would bump into her on Sayuri's way home from the market. She would squeeze onto the scooter and slowly ride with Miwa to their house.

It had happened more than once over the years.

Life had been good to them. It may not have always been easy, like when Sayuri had to walk away from being a schoolteacher after the investigation turned out to *not* be in her favor and the union declared there wasn't much they could do for her. *That seems so long ago now.* Sayuri had taken it better than Miwa anticipated. Yes, it had been hard dealing with both the loss of her job *and* her apartment, but they got by. Sayuri was as resourceful as any experienced housewife and found ways to contribute while she stayed in Miwa's tiny apartment. Eventually, they moved into a bigger one together. *We moved to a ward that supports same-sex relationships.* Miwa had come out to her company when she requested her ward to recognize Sayuri as a member of the Ban household and qualify for the rail company's insurance. *We've moved a lot, but it's always been good.*

They had been living in their current home for a few years, and Miwa had no reason to believe they'd be staying anywhere else for the rest of their lives. The neighbors were accepting of their unconventional relationship, even if they said some strange things sometimes. (Like offering their grandsons to impregnate Sayuri. That would *never not* be weird to Miwa, who politely opted out of those conversations every time they cropped up.)

This town was home. The city hub was Miwa's professional stomping ground. She commanded respect there, both as the day shift overseer and as a hard worker who was always there for her subordinates and a reliable source of help for her superiors. They treated her well... as she had found out that day.

"*Tadaima!*" she greeted two aunties at the edge of the neighborhood. Waves followed Miwa's slow scoot toward her house overlooking a vast rice paddy on the edge of a forest. Kids were always underfoot, whether they lived there or belonged to one of the aunties looking over the kids while parents were at work. Miwa kept her eye out for a certain pair of twins who were always happy to see her, but it wasn't until she pulled up to her house in the middle of the block that she heard the raucous chorus of two six-year-olds.

"*Okaeri!*" Peals of excitement hit the air as the front door opened and a pair of tank tops bolted for the gate. The littlest one pulled it open while the biggest waited for Miwa to park her scooter. Only then did they descend upon her as if she were the coolest woman in a uniform they would ever know. *Here's hoping I'm not. There's a big world out there!*

Sayuri bounded out of the house, draped in a wrinkled sundress and a stained apron. Her sweaty hair was pulled back into a loose ponytail that showed off her emerging crow's feet and the fine wrinkles crawling across her neck. *She only gets more beautiful with age.* Many of the neighbors couldn't believe that Kawashima-*sensei* was in her forties. Somehow, though, they found it perfectly acceptable that Miwa was about to turn forty herself! *It's the uniform.* That's what she reminded herself every time. *It makes me look more mature.*

"*Mou!*" Sayuri rounded up the twins so Miwa could dismount her scooter and lean against the nameplates that declared this house theirs. Neighbors gradually filled the streets, most of them eavesdropping, but a few approaching with curiosity in their eyes. Nobody said a thing. Except for Sayuri. "Well? Did you get it?" Her expectant face was almost too distracting for Miwa to remember what she was about to say. "You're killing us!"

Neighbors nodded. Little girls clung to Sayuri's skirt. Miwa had no choice but to make her announcement now, in front of God and township.

"You're looking at the new station master."

Sayuri had never looked so relieved in her life. The neighbors were the ones cheering, and Miwa had no doubt that their personal recommendations helped play a part in her achieving the greatest moment of her career. *I can finally get excited about it!* A smile emerged on her face, and it was one of the most exhilarating smiles of her life.

"*Yokatta!*" Sayuri embraced her partner in their small yard. The girls were excited, although they didn't understand that Miwa was now the most important person at the biggest train station in town. Well, as soon as the current station master's retirement was official. Miwa wasn't the youngest station master that place had yet seen, but it would be a miracle if she could outlast the current man's thirty years as station master. "I'm so proud of you! Get in here so we can have dinner!"

"Yes, ma'am." Miwa thanked the neighbors for sharing in her joy and promised to meet them later for some pre-summer festival fun. More than a few people walked up and down the street in their summer *yukata* and *geta*. Miwa couldn't wait until it was her turn to get out of her sweaty uniform and into something more comfortable for the warm evening air.

Not that she was given two minutes of peace.

"Can we get cotton candy later?"

"Did you bring me home candy from the station?"

The incessant questions from two curious little girls followed Miwa into the master bedroom, where she dressed down to her tank top and a pair of shorts that would finally let her body breathe. The fans lazily spun, but all they were good for was moving the hot air around. The AC was on in the living room, and that was where Miwa was determined to go, two girls nipping her heels. She would never remember what she told them that day. All she knew was that she had never been so proud of herself – both for achieving her career dreams, and for raising two healthy little girls.

It had been a no-brainer that Miwa and Sayuri wanted kids, although Sayuri was hesitant to go through it again. Yet the look on her face when she found out she was carrying twins had proven that nothing had ever been a better decision. Yuka and Mari were rambunctious children who often exhausted Miwa at the end of a long work day, but she wouldn't have her daughters be any other way. It helped that Sayuri stayed home most of the day, taking care of half the neighborhood on top of her own children.

"Did you see this rock I got?" Yuka asked Miwa on their way into the kitchen.

"Can we go to Tokyo soon?" Mari threw herself against the breakfast table.

"Did you know that all our cartoons are 'reruns' right now? I need a rerun on my summer."

"Mama was talking to Auntie Eguchi earlier and was like *pera pera pera* I thought I would die from boredom."

"Will you come to our kindergarten for parents' day? Mama said you should come."

"Are we gonna have to move because you got a new job?"

"One day I'm gonna have a scooter, too. You're gonna buy it for me."

"Hey! What do you think of this one?"

Mari bent over and unleashed a fart as loud as the pots that had been clanging in the kitchen when Miwa walked in. Yuka howled in laughter while Miwa rubbed her temples and bade her children to go play video games. She promised she would join them in a minute. After all, her children could not be trusted to play games *properly* without the master's supervision.

Where is your mother? Sayuri had departed the room as soon as Miwa and the children walked in. Then again, there was only one place she could have gone. The tatami room across the hallway.

Sure enough, Sayuri knelt before the altar that housed the images of everyone she had lost in her life. A reprinted photo of her son had the spot of honor, while her mother calmly looked after him in Heaven. The woman had lived long enough to see her granddaughters and rekindle some form of a relationship with Sayuri before succumbing to kidney cancer.

As All Our Fires Burn

Although Sayuri had been saddened by her mother's loss, she said she was relieved her son was no longer alone.

Miwa waited for Sayuri to finish her prayers. She stood with a smile on her face. Someone had been thanking the spirits for Miwa's success at work.

"Guess what!" Sayuri clapped her hands together as soon as she stood upright. "I got sparklers for tonight. The shopkeeper gave me a bunch of free ones for the girls."

Miwa leaned against the doorway. Sounds of Mario erupted around them, but they only had attention for one another. "They're going to love that."

Sayuri's softened smile followed her out of the room and back into the kitchen. "Let's go out as soon as we eat dinner. It's almost ready."

Miwa was about to follow her until she realized her partner had forgotten to blow out the candles on the altar. Again.

There was no time to experience the sheer excitement bubbling within her as she congratulated herself on a job well done. Not when there were children to mind, dinners to eat, and wives to praise at the table. Miwa had nearly forgotten her good news since she was swept up in the fervor of putting on cotton robes and heading out with their neighbors to enjoy the summer night by the river. Mosquitoes buzzed above their heads until the sparklers lit up and drove them away.

Mari and Yuka were absorbed into a large crowd of children running up and down the riverbank, bright sparklers in their hands. Sayuri and Miwa sat on a bench. Every so often, someone came up to say hello and to congratulate Miwa on her promotion. But, as usual, people were more concerned about the pair of girls screaming louder than any other child.

"I always think about how my son would have loved nights like these," Sayuri wistfully said. "It doesn't make me sad anymore. I only wish he were here, playing with those kids."

Miwa took her hand. "He is here, Satin."

Sayuri rested her head against her partner's shoulder. "I know."

The sky soon exploded in a few fireworks. A taste of the bigger celebrations to come that month, as the summer reached its peak and the spirits of the other side drifted in and out of the mortal realm. But that night, like most nights, were about the living. The kind that loved to stare at the bright, ominous lights that were hotter than the sun and more destructive than the emotions that often bubbled in people's hearts.

Miwa didn't fear them. She knew Sayuri didn't, either. That was all that mattered as they welcomed one another's storms into their lives.

As All Our Fires Burn

Hildred Billings is a Japanese and Religious Studies graduate who has spent her entire life knowing she would write for a living someday. She has lived in Japan a total of three times in three different locations, from the heights of the Japanese alps to the hectic Tokyo suburbs, with a life in Shikoku somewhere in there too. When she's not writing, however, she spends most of her time talking about Asian pop music, cats, and bad 80's fantasy movies with anyone who will listen…or not.

Her writing centers around themes of redemption, sexuality, and death, sometimes all at once. Although she enjoys writing in the genre of fantasy the most, she strives to show as much reality as possible through her characters and situations, since she's a furious realist herself.

Currently, Hildred lives in Oregon with her girlfriend, with dreams of maybe having a cat around someday.

Connect with Hildred on any of the following:

Website: http://www.hildred-billings.com
Twitter: http://twitter.com/hildred
Facebook: http://facebook.com/authorhildredbillings
Tumblr: http://tumblr.com/hildred

Made in the USA
Columbia, SC
26 July 2023